Copyright © 2013 by J.L. Spelbring

Sale of the paperback edition of this book without its cover is unauthorized.

Spencer Hill Press

This book is a work of fiction. Names, characters, places, and incidents are products of the author's imagination or are used fictitiously. Any resemblance to actual events, locales, or persons, living or dead, is entirely coincidental.

All rights reserved, including the right to reproduce this book or portions thereof in any form whatsoever.

Contact: Spencer Hill Press, PO Box 247, Contoocook, NH 03229, USA

Please visit our website at www.spencerhillpress.com

First Edition: May 2013.

J.L. Spelbring
Perfection : a novel / by J.L. Spelbring – 1st ed.
p. cm.
Summary:
A genetically engineered teenaged super-soldier in a dystopian Nazi future realizes that everything she has been taught is a lie and embarks on a journey to discover the truth.

The author acknowledges the copyrighted or trademarked status and trademark owners of the following wordmarks mentioned in this fiction:
P229, Remington SPC, S&W / Smith & Wesson, SG 550, Styrofoam, Taser, Taurus PT145, Volkswagen Beetle

Cover design by K. Kaynak

Interior layout and chapter artwork by Marie Romero

ISBN 978-1-937053-34-5 (paperback)
ISBN 978-1-937053-35-2 (e-book)

Printed in the United States of America

PERFECTION

J.L. Spelbring

To my mom, who taught me the meaning of perseverance.

1

Ellyssa, a.k.a. Subject 62, sprinted through the dark alley with a black messenger bag slapping against her thigh. The sirens that had pierced the night an hour earlier had finally faded, but she still wasn't safe.

Her mind raced as it flipped through the map she'd memorized. Turn right here, left there. She had to reach the train that would take her away from Chicago. There she might find safety…or her death.

She slipped behind a metal dumpster and backed up against the brick wall, blending into the shadows, breaths coming in gasps. Panic edged her nerves, and she released the reins.

For a few blissful moments, Ellyssa allowed herself to bathe in the physiological effects of panic. She felt her heart slam against her ribs and blood rush through her veins. But not for long. Panic brought less desirable traits—uncertainty and paranoia. She understood why her *father* would find the emotion useless, hindering the goals of a soldier and, therefore, had worked to eradicate it.

Regardless, it was an emotion, and she relished the feeling before she closed her eyes and slowed her breathing and heart rate, reining in the panic and tucking it away. Ellyssa opened her eyes, her face now a blank slate, completely unreadable.

She looked out from behind her cover and peered into the alley. Dark shadows wavered, but nothing solid moved. She reached with her mind, searching for any presence. Silence greeted her.

Pulling into the shadows, Ellyssa settled back against the wall and looked at the lightening sky. Soon morning would bring the shift change.

She unbuttoned the white lab coat, the uniform she'd been required to wear at The Center of Genetic Research and Eugenics, revealing a white blouse and tan skirt she'd stolen from the laundry. A couple of dark marks soiled the hem of the skirt, but the stains were small and unnoticeable. She shoved the hated lab coat into the dumpster, along with her old life. Kansas City was her new destination. She didn't know why, but that was what the dark-haired prisoner had put into her head.

Pinks and purples crept across the night sky, extinguishing the stars. Afterward, the muffled steps of the workers reached her ears from the street. With her bag tucked under her arm, she pulled her shoulders back and strolled into the sea of blond-haired, blue-eyed people on N. Michigan Avenue.

Hitler's vision of purity realized.

Everyone was dressed according to their jobs: tan bottoms and white shirts of the business industry; light blue coveralls of the city workers; the yellow smocks of the service industries; the dark blue and black authoritative colors of *Schutzpolizei* and the *Gestapo*, Swastika bands wrapped around their biceps.

The regular citizens all carried similar genetic makeups. Their hair was a variation of blond, shades of blue dominated the eyes, and both men and women had thin gymnast physiques. Even with all their similar attributes, not one ordinary citizen shared the ensemble of characteristics Ellyssa and her siblings possessed, including their intelligence…or their genetically-enhanced abilities.

The workers walked with their backs straight and heads held high as they maneuvered through the crowded streets, each to their assigned destinations. Much to Ellyssa's dismay, several dark blue uniforms and black coats walked amongst the pedestrians or stood to the side watching as the shift change occurred. She had to keep a low profile.

A female dressed in business attire, with a sharp nose and thin lips, stopped and stared at Ellyssa. Although her boyishly-styled hair was platinum like Ellyssa's and her siblings', her beady eyes were not the pure azure color, but more teal.

Ellyssa slipped a smile on her face with ease. *Although happiness is pointless and weakens you,* her father would say, *a smile deceives the ones beneath you and can be used to your advantage.* "Sorry, I dropped a paper and it blew into the alley," she said as a light breeze lifted her pale hair.

The woman raised an eyebrow, causing Ellyssa's smooth calm to falter. The woman looked familiar, and Ellyssa didn't like the way she was staring. She wondered if the female questioned her Germanic accent, even though it was slight. She knew most citizens spoke English, just as the Americans' had before The War. Certainly, though, accents were not a thing of the past.

Glancing at the nearest male in a black coat, she dug into her front pocket and pulled out a yellowed sheet. "Important notes." Nerves fluttered in her chest and a bead of perspiration formed on her forehead. *Lingering anxiety.* She pulled the reins on her feelings.

The businesswoman scrutinized her for a moment longer, then nodded and allowed Ellyssa in front of her with a customary pleasant smile.

"Thank you," Ellyssa said politely, as all citizens spoke. She took the offered space and, when facing away from the stranger, quietly exhaled pent-up air before falling into cadence alongside the others.

As Ellyssa walked, she kept her expression void while awe worked wonders on her brain. Besides field-training exercises far away from civilization, she'd never been outside of The Center's walls and, although approved learning books had provided illustrations, seeing the actual architecture was fascinating. Workers melted into the brown and redbrick factories and warehouses built along the street.

A bit further, other workers departed to enter different types of service stores with huge glass fronts displaying generic store names like "groceries" or "computers."

Ellyssa would've liked walking inside one of the stores to browse, but her newfound freedom wouldn't allow for such trivial pursuits. If she didn't make it to the train, she'd be eradicated as easily as the prohibited emotions she felt.

By the time she reached the bridge crossing the Chicago River, most of the crowd had dwindled down. Family homes nestled in neighborhoods popped up along the street. The windows were dark, and Ellyssa knew for the most part the houses lay empty, kids in school and parents performing assigned tasks.

PERFECTION

She wondered what it'd be like to return home from work and watch a movie on a television set or listen to music or even to lounge on a couch. Things she had encountered in her approved readings but never experienced within the confines of the sterile white walls of The Center. Of course, she had been bred to be superior to ordinary citizens, and her father held views of such inconsequential clutter restricting the mind.

"When cattle are happily grazing, they never raise their heads to know their surroundings," her father had preached.

Now, being on the run, she doubted she would ever experience such things.

Ellyssa forced her eyes back toward the road. According to her calculations, Himmler was less than sixteen hundred meters away. At Himmler, she would turn right and walk another eight hundred meters to South Canal Street, where she would make a left toward Union Station. Once there, she'd show her forged papers and board the train to Kansas City, the place the dark-haired Renegade had told her to go a few days ago.

Ellyssa had just stepped out of a training room as the guards dragged the Renegade toward interrogation. Although the Renegade's arms and legs were bound and tape held his mouth shut, he'd struggled against the muscular men. Mussed black hair had been clotted with dirt, and his cheek was green from an old bruise. As if the prisoner knew she was watching, his head craned over his shoulder and his chestnut brown eyes, wide and scared, locked on hers.

She'd started to open her mind to his thoughts, but she hadn't needed to. The Renegade had forced himself in. *Kansas City* screamed into her mind. Ellyssa had reeled at the strength of his words. No one had ever done that. She snagged people's words and feelings. Startled, she'd thrown up her psychic wall, like a stone barricade, to stop his voice before her siblings and father saw the stress on her face.

The door to interrogation had closed, and she never saw him again. But later that evening when she had been sitting in her room, his voice had called again.

"Don't forget. Kansas City," he had said inside her head.

Covering her ears, she'd tried to block his intrusion. His frantic words were too much for her barrier, repeating over and over again, beating against her skull. On the verge of losing control of the façade she'd carefully constructed since she'd been a child, the incursion stopped, like a switch had been flipped.

Carefully concealed fear had kept the encounter secret, but curiosity had made her obsessed with him and his special ability. It'd beckoned her, like a flower to a bee.

On her quest to find answers, she'd stumbled across information her eyes were not meant to see—a plan that would lead to her and her siblings' demise. Twenty-four hours after her discovery, she was walking down N. Michigan Ave.

Lost in thought, her barricade weak, Ellyssa didn't detect the mumbled words as they entered her head at first. They floated in under the daydream of the unknown male. Blinking, she snapped from her self-induced hypnosis.

The female with the thin lips still walked behind her. Ellyssa could feel the mind she struggled to keep quiet. There was a leak, though. Hatred and jealousy floated in the undercurrents. Ellyssa waited for the floodgates to open.

Should I stop her now? No, I'll wait to see if she turns toward the station, the female thought.

The female was a *Kripolizei*, one of the undercover detectives from her father's center. Panic shot up Ellyssa's and her gait faltered. She couldn't afford to alert the detective. Forcing herself to relax, she resumed what she hoped was a casual pace.

Her father must have discovered the lies she concocted. Using her fingerprints and eye scan, Ellyssa had created a false identity and bank account to buy a train ticket. She had then programmed the computer to completely erase her old identity from the mainframe when she swiped the new card. Ellyssa had become nonexistent, and Vada Owen, the secretary, had been born.

Before she reached Himmler, Ellyssa made a hard left at the legal crosswalk, crossed N. Michigan Ave., turned right, and walked along the sidewalk of Hitler Park. The park would be empty. Caregivers wouldn't bring young children for morning play until nine. Hoping the detour would throw the detective off her original plans, she entered the park via an obscured path. The trees closed around them.

Confusion emanated from the detective as she followed. "Excuse me, but the park is closed," she said in impeccable German. She placed her hand on Ellyssa's shoulder. "I believe you should come with me. Your name's Ellyssa, is it not?"

At the detective's touch, Ellyssa bristled. Reining in the response to break the detective's hand, she stopped and faced her.

"My name is Detective Petersen. Dr. Hirch is worried about you." She smiled a smile that didn't come close to reaching her eyes and flashed a badge. "I think it's best if I escort you back to home."

"Please, I would like to finish my walk first," Ellyssa responded in English.

The detective frowned. "I'm sorry, but you'll need to come with me. Now." She grasped Ellyssa by the upper arm.

Anger surged forth, wiping away any trepidation, but Ellyssa expressed nothing. She would not be returning to The Center.

She transferred her bag to the left hand and proceeded with the detective, but before they reached the edge of the pathway, she twisted, lifting her hand. Detective Petersen failed to respond as the messenger bag connected with her face. Grunting in pain, the detective covered her nose with her hands as she stumbled over an exposed root and fell.

Ellyssa watched as the side of the detective's head smacked into the thick trunk of an elm. The *Kripo* dropped to her side and rolled over, groaning. Then she went quiet.

Kneeling down, Ellyssa pressed her fingers against the detective's carotid artery. The pulse was a little erratic, but strong. She moved the detective's head to the side and assessed the injury. Blood oozed from a small gash.

Ellyssa stood and stepped over the detective, moving away from the path. Hidden within the trees, she set her bag down and removed blue coveralls and blunt-end scissors. She pulled the coveralls over her clothes and proceeded to snip off her long mane above the elastic band. Her hair fell loose. Running her fingers through the soft locks, she arranged it the best she could without the aid of a mirror. She picked up her bag and backtracked to the path. The detective was still out cold. Ellyssa dragged her behind a bush.

With caution, she left the park and proceeded to Himmler. The street lay empty before her. She kept her mind open, though, just in case. Nothing invoked suspicion as she neared Union Station. The hum of people's thoughts loudly rang in her head. Ellyssa slid her mental wall into place, cutting off the continuous stream. She'd have to rely on her instincts.

Ellyssa faltered on the steps of the train station. The pictures she'd seen didn't compare to the actual beauty. So much she had missed in her prison-style home.

Union Station had been completed in May 1925, way before The War. The Beaux-Arts style of architecture shouted the neoclassical movement of the era. The exterior constructed from Indian limestone and featured Tuscan columns and arches.

Wishing she had time to appreciate the fine details on her first visit to the city, she remained stone-face and continued moving before she attracted unwanted attention. She walked past the grand columns and entered the building.

The interior was even more beautiful than the outside. Ellyssa descended the steps into the Grand Hall. Pink Tennessee marble lined the floors, Corinthian columns reached the ceiling, and pilasters decorated the terracotta walls. Lifting her chin, she gazed at the vaulted skylight that rose over a thirty meters above her head.

"It's beautiful, isn't it?" said a male wearing a yellow smock. His dirty-blond bangs were gelled, exposing a broad forehead.

She stepped back. Her hand tensed around the strap of her bag as she quickly swept his mind before the barrage of images from the station patrons attacked her. The stranger was harmless.

He smiled. "Sorry, didn't mean to startle you. Can I help you?"

Ellyssa returned his gesture of friendliness. "Yes, this is my first day," she lied. "Can you point me in the direction of the janitorial closet?"

The male turned and pointed toward a set of signs. "If you turn right there and head down the stairs, directly to your left there will be a sign that says, 'Employees Only'."

"Thank you." She began to walk away.

"Wait."

Ellyssa's shoulders clenched. Anger bubbled at her response. She had spent her life training, keeping emotions in check, her physical response unreadable, and now she was going to let some ordinary citizen get the best of her? She forced herself to relax while plastering another smile across her lips and facing him. "Yes."

"Did you check in with the shift supervisor?"

"No, not yet."

"I can walk with you and show you the office."

The tension reached her jaw-line. "That would be fine," she managed without clenching her teeth, "but do you think I can visit the facilities first, please?"

"They are on the way." He extended a hand to the opposite set of stairs. "First day jitters?" he asked as she passed him.

A tentative grin pulled the corners of her mouth. "It shows?"

"Not too bad. You'll do fine." He turned and walked next to her. "Where were you assigned?"

Ellyssa wished he would just shut up, or that an opportunity would arise where she could make him. She knew he wouldn't be any match for her. Her expertise in the martial arts along with her extensive weapons training put regular citizens at a great disadvantage against her. She shrugged and offered him another smile. He seemed pleased.

"I understand. Don't want to talk about it. Well, I promise you will love working here. The people you meet passing through are very interesting."

"I'm not sure if my present position will offer such pleasantries."

He glanced at her coveralls and didn't say anything else. They continued the rest of the way in silence.

When they reached the restroom, he said, "I have to get back to work. Follow this hall to the end and the office is on the right. You can't miss it." He stood there.

"Oh, yes. Thank you. It was very nice to meet you."

He beamed. "It was nice to meet you, too." He held out his hand. "My name is Peter."

She grasped his hand with false enthusiasm.

"Maybe we will run into each other soon?"

"Maybe." She turned and escaped through the door marked, *FEMALES*.

Disinfectant hovered in the air of the immaculate restroom. Shining white tile gleamed under the fluorescent lights. Eggshell sinks hung on the right, and beige stalls stood to the left.

Ellyssa moved to the last stall and locked the door behind her. She placed her shoulder bag on the floor and shrugged out of the coveralls. She withdrew a plastic bag with hair accessories and makeup.

The door opened with the soft whisper of the hydraulics. She froze. Shoes clicked on the tile as the person went into the first stall. Picking her bag off the floor, Ellyssa sat on the porcelain seat and waited. After a few minutes, the toilet flushed, and the stranger exited after washing her hands.

She peeked out the door to make sure the bathroom was empty, then went to the mirror to straighten her crumpled white blouse the best she could. Wrinkles still gathered at the bottom, but the collar looked fine.

She twisted her bangs into small braids and pinned them back with two grey barrettes, then applied a soft, rose-colored lipstick and added some length to her eyelashes.

Satisfied with her appearance, she threw everything back into her bag and went to the door. She paused and listened with her ears. Mumblings from hundreds of people whispered. She swung open the bathroom door and made her way to the ticket counter.

A man with black-peppered hair stood behind the glass barrier. Like all workers within the travel industry, he wore a crisp white short-sleeved shirt with a blue cap.

She glanced around. Nobody stood directly next to her, but several patrons sat on benches or milled around nearby. Too many actually, but she chanced it anyway. She lowered her shield just enough to take a quick peek inside the director's head and saw the notes of some old tune. From what she could tell, he hadn't been alerted. If she was lucky, maybe none of the normal citizens had been warned. Her father, Dr. Hirch, must have been confident that she would be captured.

Shoulders back, she walked to the counter and handed him the forged papers. He glanced at the credentials, took her false credits, and handed her a ticket with a polite smile.

"Thank you," she said.

He nodded.

She sat on a wooden bench in the Great Hall with all the other passengers, most wearing the same clothes as she, and waited for the eight o'clock train. It was seven-forty, now. Except for the run-in with the detective, the morning had gone relatively smooth. Everyone would board in another ten minutes, and she'd be on her way.

Unfortunately, her ability didn't include precognition.

2

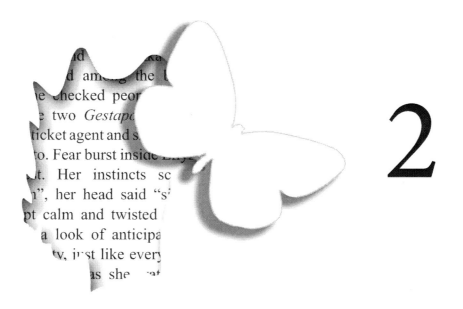

Men wearing black trench coats and Swastika bands zigzagged among the benches. Some checked people's papers, while two *Gestapo* approached the ticket agent and showed him a photo. Fear burst inside Ellyssa's chest. Her instincts screamed "run", her head said "sit". She kept calm and twisted her face into a look of anticipation and curiosity, just like everyone else was doing, as she watched the secret police.

The man behind the counter looked at the picture, then scanned the waiting room. His gaze passed over her more than once before his eyes locked on her. He pointed in her direction. The two men separated and walked on both sides of the benches toward her.

Heart thrumming, muscles bunched to run, it took all of her self-discipline not to burst off the bench like a scared rabbit from the brush. Ellyssa touched her bag in preparation to either escape or to show the faux papers, but the *Gestapo* passed her section and walked six rows behind her. Relief swept through her as she turned in her seat.

The two *Gestapo* approached a female in a white lab coat who wore her pale yellow hair in a long finger wave like Ellyssa had before she'd cut it in the park. The wrongly identified female's eyes widened in shock as the men stood on each side of her. They spoke to her in German, their voices authoritative and harsh. She shook her head, clearly unable to understand them. The shorter one on the left reverted to English. She reached into her attaché case and withdrew blue papers.

The taller of the two snatched the papers out of her hand and shook them in her face. She flinched while her lips moved rapidly. Her voice was high, stressed with frantic tones. As she talked, the shorter one placed his hand under her arm. Given little choice, the woman stood and went with the police as they escorted her down the row. The other secret police met them in the center aisle, and they left with the innocent female.

Ellyssa faced forward and melted into the wooden bench. She couldn't believe the trained eyes of the *Gestapo* couldn't tell the difference in hair color, much less the color of the poor lady's eyes.

A deep, throaty voice emitted from the PA system. "All aboard for St. Louis connecting to Kansas City. Please have your papers and tickets ready."

Ellyssa jumped up with her bag draped over her shoulder and went to the platform where the conductor stood. She handed him her papers.

Smiling, he punched a hole in the ticket and handed both documents back. "Enjoy your trip."

Relieved the conductor spoke with a pronounced German inflection, Ellyssa answered, "Thank you. I will." She glanced over her shoulder, halfway expecting the *Gestapo* to come storming back in, their mistake discovered.

"You look a little nervous."

She felt like kicking herself. Since childhood, she'd perfected a mask to display, emotionless and deadpan. But with all the sensations roiling inside her at once—anxiety, fear, excitement—she was wearing them on her sleeve. Of course, she'd never thought she'd be using her skills to flee. She pulled at the hem of her blouse and concentrated on smoothing her demeanor.

"Don't be," the conductor continued. "Trains are a wonderful way to travel." He reached behind her to take papers from another passenger.

"Thank you." She stepped onto the platform.

The few people who had boarded before her milled down the narrow hall, searching for their compartments. Ellyssa quickly moved to her designated slot before more boarding passengers could crowd the cramped walkway and went inside.

Compared to her sterile room at The Center, the compartment seemed almost homey. The mahogany paneled room held two berths, dressed in ivory satin comforters that matched the lace curtain covering the small window. A thin, silver table, decorated with a menu holder and a small vase of yellow daisies, sat directly under it. Mounted on the wall to the left, a flat-screen television and a radio with two sets of headphones offered entertainment she had never been allowed before.

Ellyssa pulled back the curtain and peered outside, wondering if anyone had found the hidden file. All seemed normal, people wearing business attire and none wearing armbands of red signifying authority. Apparently, the *Gestapo* hadn't discovered their mistake, yet. For the first time since she'd fled, her mind felt at ease.

Loud thrumming vibrated under Ellyssa's feet, and the train started to rock gently from side to side as it slowly pulled away from the station. Ellyssa left her compartment and walked five cars down. Using her gift, she peeked into each space until she found one that was empty. She glanced down the aisle before slipping inside the vacant room.

Settling onto the berth, Ellyssa drifted into a restless sleep.

3

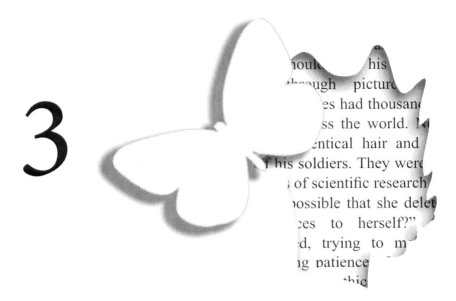

Dr. George Hirch watched over Leland's shoulder as his assistant scrolled through pictures. The Center's data files had thousands of employees across the world. None shared the identical hair and eye color of his soldiers. They were the purebloods of scientific research.

"Is it possible that she deleted all references to herself?" the doctor asked, trying to maintain his dwindling patience. He ran his fingers through his thick, silver hair.

Leland dropped his hand away from the mouse and turned to stare at George. "I've already explained to you that yes, it is possible," he said irritably. "I'm trying to locate anything she might've forgotten. I realize you're anxious, but breathing down my neck is not helping."

George's brow furrowed as he looked at Leland with contempt. Leland, a child of The Center, but a genetic foul-up with wavy golden hair and pale powder-blue eyes, had the nerve to talk to him with disdain. If not for Leland's somewhat above average intelligence, he would've been socialized into the general population, taking some insignificant job.

Leland was not like George, who had been one of the first purebreds, seventy years ago. Platinum hair, eyes the color of the sky on a clear day, pale flawless skin, handsome, the doctor had been the poster child of Hitler's vision.

At the age of five, George had had the fortunate opportunity of meeting the aging visionary when the *Führer* had visited The Center. Hitler had explained to George and the other subjects the meaning of his visions. It had been the most exhilarating moment of the young doctor's life, only surpassed when he'd discovered and learned to manipulate the genetic coding of perception. From there, his soldiers were born.

His mind wandered back to the inferior Leland, and anger burned through him. "Just find her," he snarled.

Leland shrugged and spun around in the computer chair. His fingers clicked across the keys. "This process of scanning pictures one at a time is going to take awhile. You might as well sit down." The younger man leaned his head toward the computer as people's faces flipped across the monitor.

Frustrated, George glanced at the screen. The familiar face of a female who worked on the second floor flashed, quickly replaced with some other woman who worked in the London facility.

Throwing his hands in the air, he returned to his executive-style desk and began analyzing Ellyssa's psychological profile, yet again, to compare her to her siblings. Her personality tests had all returned without any wavers within the boundaries. Her physical and emotional tests exceeded the scope of established parameters. She even surpassed her siblings in martial arts and weapons training.

Where did things go wrong?

"What have you found?"

Concentrating on Ellyssa's tests and profiles, the doctor started at the unexpected voice. Detective Angela Petersen, head of The Center's *Kripo* unit, stood at the front of his desk, peering at him with questioning eyes. A twig stuck out of her disheveled hair, and dried blood was smeared along her cheek. As if nothing was wrong, she smoothed her rumpled skirt and shirt before sitting in the guest chair directly across from him.

Angela was living proof that, after the initial tweaking of man, nature would've eventually weeded out undesirable traits. Besides being beautiful, with angular cheeks, bright eyes—although a little too small and the wrong color—and unlined skin, the detective was highly intelligent, physically toned, mentally stable, and proud of her abilities. Close to having the required qualities without modification but, unfortunately, still lacking.

"Ah, Detective. Your German is improving," George responded in his visionary's native tongue. "What happened to you?"

"Your precious daughter is what happened," she snapped.

He straightened in his chair, his lids widened minutely. "She attacked you?"

"Yes. It seems she is not as docile to authority as you thought."

After grabbing antiseptic from the top drawer, he walked around the desk and examined the gash on the detective's head. It was a small laceration, but deep. He soaked a cotton ball with the yellowish liquid. "This may sting a little," he said as he blotted the wound. "Tell me what happened."

"As we thought, she was heading toward the station, but at the last minute she crossed the street and went into Hitler Park."

"The park?"

"Yes, she said she was going on a walk."

The doctor chuckled while he dabbed the ointment on Angela's head.

"What?"

"She knew who you were."

"I was careful to keep my mind clear."

"An impossible task. But to be on the fair side, Ellyssa's powers are astoundingly developed, even beyond my expectations."

"Maybe I'd have been better prepared if I had known of her ability before she'd escaped," she hissed, jerking away when he applied pressure to the wound. "What are we going to do about her?"

"Well, Detective, *you* are going to capture her and bring her back home."

"She is more dangerous than originally anticipated." She pulled away from the doctoring hand and stood facing him. "You, yourself, said she would come willingly. That she would pose no problems. *You were wrong.*"

"What do you propose?"

The detective looked at him coolly. "Termination."

Apparently listening more attentively than George realized, Leland swiveled around in his chair and stood. "The children are not rats to dispose of when one bites you."

Angela ignored the tech and addressed the doctor. "They are bred for scientific research, born from genetically modified eggs and sperm in test tubes. She has proven herself a threat and is thereby dangerous."

"There has not been a termination for over thirty years, and that was only under extreme circumstances. Ellyssa is the first of her type. It would prove detrimental to my work if she were to be terminated."

"Have you thought of what could happen with her being free in the population?"

"I assure you she will not hurt any citizens."

"You don't know where her capacity for violence stops. You failed to recognize her ability to attack me."

"Self-preservation." He shrugged. "She must have seen you as a threat."

"Nonsense. I offered to escort her home."

"That is what you said verbally. Maybe you had other plans. Things she saw as threatening?"

"No," she answered, stiffly.

The doctor studied the young detective. Her chin jutted out slightly, and her hands rested on her hips. Although Angela's attributes would supersede those of many living outside The Center's walls, her imperfections, especially the emotions, were all too noticeable to him.

"It is too bad your genetic deficiencies have rendered the training The Center has to offer pointless. That is something I will need to rectify," Dr. Hirch pondered, his eyes settling to a point above Angela's head. After a moment, he focused back on the detective. "Petty emotions like pride would not interfere with your judgment."

Angela flinched as if he had slapped her. "Pride?" she said, through clenched teeth. "This has nothing to do with pride."

"She challenged your authority. You are not accustomed to that."

"Because of your reassurance, I was not expecting the attack. No fault of my own."

"Detective Petersen," he said, "you are exceptionally skilled at your job, but you have to realize that Ellyssa is a special situation. Besides her brilliant skill, her intelligence surpasses even mine, and her prowess is beyond the Renegades your job usually entails. A challenge for you. I will release her profile to you. Study it."

"You're making a mistake," she said.

George moved closer to Leland. "Regardless of your opinion, Ellyssa will be brought home safely. She is...needed," he said, while staring at a recognizable face hovering on the monitor.

The hair was different. Instead of long and flowing, like colorless ribbon, it was shorter, feathered along the sides of her pale skin, and slightly offset to the side. Her eyes were off, murky sea-colored rather than pure azure. Peering closer, he noticed the alterations she'd made to the photo. She must have been in a hurry, because the lines didn't quite match. Good enough to pass inspection by ordinary citizens, though.

Even with the short hair, he would recognize the face of his daughter anywhere. Large eyes, which seemed defiant as if taunting him, framed with long, dark lashes, shelved over a straight nose and angular cheekbones, stared back at him. Next to the picture, written in black, read the name, Vada Owen.

"Besides, there she is."

4

"Very nice, Ellyssa. Now, can you tell me what is on this card?"

As soon as Ellyssa closed her eyes, she reached into the head of the research assistant, Mrs. Tucker, plucking from it an image of the mountains with white, icy caps stretching across the limited borders of the rectangular card. She opened her lids and gazed at the assistant. Mrs. Tucker's face looked excited, and expectation wavered within the depths of her imperfect blue eyes.

"The Rocky Mountains," she answered.

Mrs. Tucker nodded, looking pleased, and Ellyssa smiled.

Then, Ellyssa's father, Dr. Hirch, stepped up and slapped her. The unexpected impact whipped her head to the side, and she brought her chubby hand up, covering the place where he had hit her. The coolness of her palm did nothing to stop the growing heat, and the taste of blood flooded her mouth. She blinked back the tears that threatened to spill over, and hardened her face into expressionless stone.

"Remember, Ellyssa, certain emotions only bring pain and, possibly, death. They cloud the judgment and will render you useless when you need your wits about you," he said. His expression was passive, but anger flickered in his eyes.

She nodded while he towered over her three-year-old body.

"We are done for the day. Go to your room."

She obeyed.

Ellyssa heard people walking, their steps short and hurried, long before she opened her eyes. She heard snippets of conversations in her half-awake dreams; people with unknown faces flickered in and out of her mind, saying strange things like "dangerous female" and "security breach".

It took a moment, but the meaning sank in and the haziness of disjointed images evaporated. Fully awake, Ellyssa jolted off the berth, her feet landing with a light thud.

She grabbed her bag and went to the door, pressing her ear against the thin paneling. Another person rushed down the corridor. Opening her mind, an image of her floated within a male's thoughts. He was looking at a picture. The image was of poor quality, the colors blended together, but the words printed below gave an accurate description of her. She closed the link as the murmuring thoughts of all the passengers barged in and swept away the image she'd just held.

Her father had taken the next step—one that he must be infuriated about. He'd contacted outsiders to help detain her.

Uncertain of the time, she crossed the compartment and looked out the window. The sun was out of her range of sight but, judging from the brightness, she determined late afternoon. A rolling landscape and a forest of densely packed trees zipped by. So unlike the flatness of Central Illinois.

Missouri.

Her eyes lingered on the lavish greenery before her—ash, oak, hickory, and pine. Intertwining branches reached toward the heavens. Directly next to the tracks were blackened rocks. She regarded the dangerous streaks of black skeptically. When she jumped, she'd have to make sure to clear the patch.

She calculated the possibilities and settled on a crouched roll at impact.

At the door again, she waited with her hand on the lever and listened for any other urgent activity. Not including the muffled musings of people in the adjoining compartments, the car remained quiet. She slid the door open and stepped into the hall. A worn red carpet spread the length of the car from one doorway to the next. Both ways remained empty.

She searched for the male who had been holding her picture. Through the windows of the adjoining cars, she saw him talking to another attendant. She moved to her right, and then froze at the sound of hydraulics moving, the fine hairs on her neck twitching.

Without turning around, Ellyssa let her barrier drop briefly and grazed the thoughts of an older male who was thinking of a pretty female…his daughter holding a baby. Air whooshing from her lungs, she turned and looked as an older man with thinning hair stepped into the car. He gave Ellyssa a quick grin before he entered his compartment.

Alone again, she continued toward the end of the car, where metal steps led down into the baggage compartment. She glanced over her shoulder. The attendant still stood there talking, oblivious to her being one car over. She closed her eyes and focused, weeding away the cacophony of thoughts and feelings from the other passengers, picking his brainwaves from all the ramblings—a near-impossible task.

Through the constant static, she saw her picture as the man showed another attendant with a nice face and curly hair. They were whispering in hushed tones. The man holding her picture was filling Curly-Hair in on the details. Police were to pick her up at the next stop, thirty minutes from now.

Apparently, they had not been warned about her psychic ability.

A musical voice danced through the cacophony of whispered thoughts and erased her hold on the male's thoughts. A female was thinking about a male she'd met at a party. Violins and a piano played as they spun around on the floor. He held her tight in his arms, and the female remembered the thrill as if he held her now.

A strange sensation stirred in Ellyssa, one that made her stomach roll and flutter at the same time. She cut the connection off in mid-thought, just as the tinny ringing of footfalls on the metal steps echoed around her.

Ellyssa glanced at the steps. A blue cap, covering darkish-blond hair, followed by the rest of the woman, bobbed into sight from the lower deck.

The attendant held a smile on her face that stretched from ear to ear. When she saw Ellyssa, it amazingly stretched even further, exposing white teeth. Apparently not all of the attendants had been informed of the dangerous female on the train.

Stepping onto the platform, she said, "Is there something I can help you with?" Her tone held a happy, high note to it, mimicking the musical quality Ellyssa had heard in her thoughts.

Ellyssa peeked behind her. The adjoining car stood empty, both male attendants gone, hopefully to the compartment she'd purchased. Relieved, she slipped a false smile on her face. "Is this the direction to the observation car?" she asked, directing her attention back to the attendant.

"Yes, two cars down. I was heading there myself." The lady beamed as if she'd found a new friend.

"Thank you."

The woman turned and hit the button on the side of the door. It slid back on its tracks with a snick.

"Oh," Ellyssa said while patting her pockets. "I left my camera in the room."

The woman's face fell, shrinking her smile to its original state of ear to ear. "I can wait, if you'd like."

"Please, do not bother. I am two cars back," Ellyssa said, wishing the lady would just go away. "I will retrieve it. Then maybe you can show me the best place to take pictures."

The thought seemed to please her. "I have the perfect place." She hurried through the door, pausing only a second while the door to the adjoining car slid open.

Ellyssa waited while the attendant strolled away. As soon as the woman's head bobbed out of sight, Ellyssa descended into the baggage compartment.

Except for the light that crept in from the platform above, pooling below Ellyssa's feet, the car was shadowed and cramped. Metal gates held a mound of luggage in place. A thin walkway led from the steps between the rows of towering bags; in the middle of the car, slivers of day peeked between the doors where the baggage was maneuvered in and out.

Ellyssa grabbed the top rail of the gate and made her way to the sliding doors. She grasped the lever and pulled, but the door didn't budge. It was evidently locked in place while the train was in motion. She'd have to disconnect the wiring.

With the aid of the limited light, she ran her hands down the smooth metal, over rivets, to the edge of the door, then down the wall until she touched the plastic-coated wires. Using the cable as a guide, she moved her hand back up until it stopped at a little box. She gripped the wire and yanked. Friction burned her palms as the cable slipped beneath her fingers.

Ellyssa reestablished her grip, wrapping the cable around her wrist and hand, and placed one foot firmly on the wall. Taking a deep breath, she kicked back with all her force. The cable easily snapped, catching her off-guard. Backpedaling, she stopped when her spine smacked against the gate.

The pain was instant and sharp, but quickly cooled to a soft throb. The flesh was tender to the touch, but besides the bruise destined to discolor her pale skin, no real harm done.

She returned to the door and wrenched back on the lever. The door slid with a groan, revealing a grassy landscape past the blackened rocks that whipped by at a staggering speed.

Holding tightly onto a handle bolted into the frame of the door, Ellyssa poked her head out into the wind. Her breath hitched in her chest as the sudden blast of air hit her. Her hair flapped wildly. She pulled back inside.

The original plan of hitting the ground and ducking into a crouched roll dissolved into bouncing and tumbling wildly along the long, green blades of grass. Jumping at the current speed was possible, but if she landed at a wrong angle…she shook her head. Whatever she was looking for certainly wasn't intended to end in massive injury or death.

Think. Think.

But what other avenues were there? Attendants stood outside the door of the compartment she'd purchased. Ellyssa knew police would be waiting for her at the next stop. She'd have to take the chance.

She moved into the shadows behind the luggage and slipped the jumpsuit over her skirt. Draping the bag over her left shoulder, she readied herself, calculating the distance to the grass past the jagged rocks. She grabbed the handle again and tensed on her haunches, but instead of jumping, she swayed to the right as a thin squeal of rubbing metal emanated from beneath her, then she rocked back as the train slowed.

Ellyssa leaned out again. Ahead, the ground gave way to a slope. Anything beyond was lost in greenery.

Another squeaking protest, and she swayed again. Were the police stopping the train before it reached town? Her father wouldn't be stupid enough to give her a warning. He'd want the element of surprise.

Ellyssa wasn't going to stick around to find out.

As the brakes were applied again, she ducked inside and tightened the strap on her bag. Peeping around the edge one more time, the drop-off quickly approaching, she counted to three then flung herself out into the air. For a moment, time slowed to a crawl. The black rocks, the landscape, and the grass sharpened into fine detail as she flew over them, then gravity snatched at her legs and everything blurred. At the sudden jolt of impact, she wrapped her arms around her head and let her knees buckle beneath her to absorb the shock. She tumbled through bracken and bramble.

Every stick, bit of unleveled ground, dirt clot, sticker, rock, and clump of grass struck Ellyssa's body with a vengeance. Pain exploded through her body, keeping her alert and aware of Mother Nature's retribution.

After a few more painful thumps, Ellyssa came to a stop on her stomach, her arms still wrapped around her head. She stayed motionless and listened as the rumblings of the train sped along the track.

As the roar faded into a soft rumble, she looked up and immediately regretted the movement. Tortured muscles screamed in agony. She watched the caboose disappear around the bend.

She wanted to run, but her body wasn't ready. Breathing in short, shallow gasps, Ellyssa wiggled her toes and fingers and flexed her legs and arms. Her muscles moaned, and the joint of her elbow popped, but nothing seemed broken.

Gingerly, she pushed herself onto her knees. Then, with even more care, she rose to her feet. Angry muscles shook under her weight as she looked down the tracks.

The shiny cars had disappeared around the bend and behind a wooded area. Just beyond the curved tracks, less than seven kilometers away, grey and black roofs, like the grains of pepper, peeked through clusters of trees and rolling hills.

The police would be there, waiting at the depot, stupidly thinking she'd soon disembark, completely unaware. But only if no one had seen her jump from the train. If that had happened, then they would be alerted already, possibly with close coordinates to where she lingered now.

She had to move.

Urgency signaled Ellyssa's taut muscles, and pain shot through her leg into her hipbone. Unexpectedly, she staggered before regaining her footing. She had to take control. This wasn't the first time she'd been pummeled. Defense and martial arts classes had left her bleeding and bruised, limping away the few times she'd been defeated. None of her peers held back, nor did she. Weakness was not tolerated.

Using her years of training, Ellyssa inhaled and, like her emotions, shoved the pain into a small box, then let adrenaline flow along with the release of endorphins. She sprinted across the grassy length onto a recently sown field, leaving evidence of her flight within the newly overturned soil.

Time was something Ellyssa couldn't afford to waste on erasing her steps. She had to hide, and was unsure of what lay on the other side of the tree line. For all she knew, the trees served as a divider between unseen farms to help with soil erosion, or maybe a vast forest stretched beyond the field. In either case, she was determined to put as much distance between her and the town as she could.

Her breaths even and deep, she picked up her pace. Puffs of dust kicked from beneath her hammering feet. Beads of perspiration formed on her forehead and trickled into her eyes. Warmth clung to the edges of her sinewy muscles, reminding her that pain from her tumble was sure to visit later.

Leaping over a low fence and slipping between rails, she left the train tracks about four kilometers behind. Gradually, the vegetation started to take more distinct shapes. Instead of a blur of greens, the darks separated from the yellows. Browns and tans peeked between the sheltering leaves.

Adrenaline surged, and a metallic taste flooded Ellyssa's mouth. She embraced the extra boost and plowed forward, bursting through the tree line and into an area thick with bushes, ferns, and tall trunks of various shades from greys to browns to rusted colors.

Safely hidden within nature's cover, she kept her strides long and quick. She angled left and ran parallel to the tree line. For a moment, she wondered why she chose that direction, but her speculations eased as an intense stitch in her side caused her sprint to dwindle to a light jog and finally into a fast-paced walk.

Huffing, Ellyssa stopped and stooped, hands on knees. The stitch was bad, but the threat of her overly taxed muscles seizing up was worse. She let her hands fall between her feet and stretched before she made her way back to the edge of the farmland.

From between two hickory trees, with limbs stretching over into a latticework of twigs and leaves, she peered out across the rolling field. The town was completely hidden, lying behind a canopy, except for one building with a steeple shooting free from the greenery.

She wished her gift could extend to the train station to snatch the thoughts of her pursuers. Had they searched the train? Did they know she had jumped? Were they organizing a search party?

Even though she couldn't predict their exact plans, she knew they'd eventually resort to using dogs. She turned and disappeared into the foliage, looking for trees to help hide her scent.

Depleted of the adrenaline rush and the sweet numb of endorphins, Ellyssa's muscles and bruised flesh moaned under her sweat-sodden clothes. Her thigh sang a song of pain beneath the crimson-colored rip running along the seam of the jumpsuit. She gingerly poked the threadbare fabric and hissed.

Ellyssa sat on a fallen log and extended her leg in front of her. The jagged tear ran from mid-thigh to her knee. Raw pink meat showed between the edges of the frayed material. She tried to pull the fabric free from the wound, but blood stuck the material to the tender flesh. She gave up and retrieved scissors from her bag, along with one of her two bottles of water.

She'd broken two of the most important rules of her training. The first was, always come prepared for anything. But she hadn't had the time after all the secrets she'd found. Her priority had been erasing her identity from the mainframe then disappearing.

The second rule was never underestimate the intelligence of the enemy.

The thought surprised her. Is that how she thought of her father now? Ellyssa shook her head. Just over twenty-four hours ago, she'd been an unknowing participant in her father's plan, doing as he instructed, trying to please him, although, she could never show that. Now, she was running from him.

Her heart ached, and Ellyssa let the feeling consume her while fishing out a tube of antiseptic, her only preparation for injury. Now was not the best time to entertain the feeling; she knew that. But she'd missed out on so much being locked away at The Center, away from all the inferior citizens. Being allowed to show of emotions was just the tip.

Ellyssa's father had spent years structuring a program to rid his experiments of feelings. She was his unknown failure. Since the age of three, she'd bottled up everything she'd felt and worn an impassive mask. Although she didn't realize it at the time, her ability to deceive had saved her.

After the run-in with the dark-haired man, she'd accessed her father's files and discovered what happened to subjects who'd failed to assimilate, along with finding her father's secret agenda. The most basic instinct, the first lesson drilled into her, was the instinct to survive. After reading her father's files, hers went into overdrive.

The betterment of mankind. Ellyssa scoffed.

Her father *was* the very enemy he'd warned her and her siblings about.

A foreign smile slipped across her face as she snipped away the leg of her coveralls above the knee. Breathing in, she yanked the fabric free. Fresh blood pooled in the gash before flowing over and trickling down the sides of her thigh. She poured water over the wound and cleared away as much of the dirt and pebbles as she could. The cut was ugly, and more pebbles were embedded in the flesh, but the wound wasn't disabling. She picked out the remaining debris, then swabbed on the pasty antiseptic cream. Using the pants leg as a makeshift bandage, she bound the wound.

After wetting her mouth, she gathered her items and shoved everything back into the bag. With great care, she stood, focusing most of her weight on her left leg before testing her right. Her thigh throbbed, but it was nothing that could hinder her.

Slightly limping, Ellyssa continued the search for a suitable tree to climb. She found the perfect launching spot thirty meters deeper into the forest. An old oak with a broad trunk and thick limbs stood next to a giant walnut, the limbs crossing over each other in a desperate attempt to hog the sunlight.

She pulled out leather gloves and slipped them over her fingers. Securing the bag to her side, she walked around the tree until she found a low-hanging branch. She squatted, hissed, and jumped; her fingers brushed the underside of the limb. A tidal wave of pain shot up her leg when she landed. She cried out and hobbled around in a circle, massaging the side of her leg until the worst of the throbbing settled into a soft pulsing.

She readjusted herself under the branch. Forcing the pain into the back of her mind, she hunkered down, swinging her arms in a wide pendulum motion, and leapt. She grasped the branch and, in one smooth motion, swung her left leg over and pulled herself up. There, she rested, short pants bursting from between her lips.

Moving from tree to tree would delay her pursuers, but not for long. Her tricks would be easily spotted. The more distance she put between herself and her would-be captors, the better her chances.

She forced herself up on the thick branch. Dangerously teetering, she grabbed low-hanging limbs to aid her balance. Like a squirrel, she moved from one tree to the next, keeping a rather twisted, southeast course until a break in the towering lumber forced her back to the ground, where she took up a slow-paced jog.

As the afternoon waned and the shadows grew longer, Ellyssa's jog changed to a trudge. Weariness pulled on every fiber of her being as she limped and stumbled and emptied one of her water bottles faster than she would have liked.

As darkness fell and blanketed the woods, Ellyssa paused with thoughts of stopping teasing the threads of her exhausted mind until the sound of gurgling and buzzing insects floating on the air captured her attention.

Water.

Although, she knew she couldn't drink the flowing water without the proper sanitization pill—a bit of information stored in her brain from field training exercises—her mouth still watered like Pavlov's dog. The water could be used for other things.

Ellyssa crunched over greenery and broke into a small clearing. Early twilight filtered through sparse clouds, tall grass shifted silently in a soft breeze, and silver moonlight reflected off a shallow stream that babbled over moss-covered rocks.

She tottered to the stream and dropped to her knees. She scooped up the cool liquid and splashed it on her face, washing away the dried sweat and dirt. It felt cool and refreshing on her bruised skin.

Temptation to pull the cool liquid between her lips overwhelmed her. The untreated water stopped her. She splashed more on her face, then rose on her aching feet.

Sloshing through the water, Ellyssa took to the middle of the stream, her legs feeling like weights were tied to her ankles. *The more distance the better*, played through her thoughts, keeping her going. Sleep would be a sweet blessing better enjoyed at a later time.

5

Though the hour was late and he was tired, Dr. Hirch looked up with a forced smile on his face when Detective Petersen strolled through his office door. By her expression, he doubted the news was good. He kept up the formalities, anyway.

"Ah, Detective Petersen. How is the search going?"

Before answering, Angela took a seat in the guest chair on the opposite side of his mahogany desk. Her eyes and cheeks sagged with weariness and, with the dark jacket she wore, the contrast made her look gaunt. She laid Ellyssa's file on his desk. "I made some copies."

"Of what, precisely?"

"Only things relevant to finding her. Her likes and dislikes. What she excelled in, which is everything."

Pleased, he smiled genuinely. "Of course. We only provide the best training."

"There is something I've been meaning to ask you," she said, meeting his eyes. "Are the other subjects like Ellyssa? Do they have special…abilities?"

"That, Detective Petersen, is none of your concern."

"For security purposes, I think it *is* my concern," she said, raising her eyebrows. "If I'd known before she'd escaped instead of afterwards…"

Dr. Hirch leaned forward in his chair. "It is *none* of your concern. Now," he said, dismissing the subject, "what news do you have?"

Angela opened her mouth as if to argue, then apparently thought better of it. "She escaped from the train," she answered, crossing her arms over her chest.

"How?"

"We aren't one hundred percent sure."

Dr. Hirch leaned back in his chair, rocking slightly as he stared at the ceiling. "First time out of The Center. Able to adapt quickly, blend... very astute," he mused, with a smile.

The detective's face puckered into a scowl. "This isn't a research project. She wasn't anywhere on the train. When the police interviewed the passengers, one said he thought he saw someone jump, but he wasn't sure."

George's eyebrows rose, wrinkling his forehead. "Do you think she jumped?"

"You know her better than I do."

Folding his hands together, he thought for a moment then nodded. "Yes, if she felt threatened and jumping was the only option, she would take that course of action."

"Do you think she feels threatened?"

"For unknown reasons, she left. She knew to do so was prohibited. I sent you after her. Yes, it stands to reason that she feels threatened."

"Then she could be dangerous."

Trying to remain calm, Dr. Hirch met the detective's gaze. "All the children could be dangerous," he said. "Your job is to bring her back safely. Do you understand, Detective?"

"Perfectly," Angela said, through tight lips. She rose to her feet. "One more thing."

"Yes."

"What about emotions?"

"She has been trained not to feel useless reactions that could jeopardize themselves."

"But she can still feel them?"

Narrowing his eyes, George leaned forward in his chair. "Yes, I suppose feeling is possible. Regardless of how she was conceived, she is human. But I, myself, structured her program. And Ellyssa's ability to fool me for eighteen years would be unlikely." He leaned back. "Why all the questions, Detective?"

"Have you ever thought that maybe something went wrong?"

"Never. Not since she was young has Ellyssa shown any inappropriate emotions. She is quite efficient. Why do you ask?"

"Because, when she stepped in front of me on her way to the train, she seemed nervous."

The doctor's eyebrows stitched together. "Nervous? What do you mean?"

"Exactly what I said. She was fidgety, and she over-explained her situation, like she couldn't stop talking."

"Interesting," he said, tapping his finger to his chin. After a moment, his eyes shifted back to Angela. "She needs to be brought home."

"Yes, I know," said Angela, her tone abrupt. "I think we should take the dogs."

"Dogs?" The idea of his creation being treated like a common Renegade, instead of the secret to a better humankind, sickened him.

"According to the train personnel, all exits were covered. If she was on the train, she jumped, and if that is the case and if she didn't sustain serious injury, she's on the run. The dogs will pick up her scent."

"And what if the whole thing was a ruse?"

"I have my best men searching for any sign for her in Chicago."

Dr. Hirch rubbed his forehead. The whole thing was getting out of control. It was bad enough he had had the detective involve more of The Center's secret police, but, also, the local authorities in Warrensburg. Secrecy was of top priority and becoming impossible to maintain.

"Fine. Take the dogs." He leaned forward, resting his elbows on the desk. "You have to understand the dilemma we are in. Ellyssa must be found, but by divulging as little information as possible."

"I understand."

He paused for a moment while he removed a ticket and the proper traveling papers from his desk drawer. He slid the credentials over to her. "Unfortunately, due to our circumstances, you will have to travel by train. It will leave in two hours."

She leveled her eyes on the doctor. "I will find her."

"Very good," Doctor Hirch said, dismissing her.

With a curt nod, Detective Petersen departed. As soon as the door closed, George reached into his bottom left-hand drawer and pulled out another file on his missing beloved creation. The file contained his lifelong work, each of the children's powers well documented and studied. When Ellyssa returned home, Hitler's future goals—his future goals—would soon come together.

Detective Petersen strolled through the long corridor of the sterile center on her way to her apartment. From her coat pocket, she removed a copy of Ellyssa's picture and unfolded it. The creases were beginning to warp part of Ellyssa's face, but the photo only served the purpose of keeping her quarry next to her, not for a reminder of her appearances.

The platinum hair, the bright azure eyes, and smooth, pale skin were embedded in Angela's mind. She served as a constant reminder that the detective had failed.

But Angela wouldn't fail again. Ellyssa would pay for the embarrassment and disgrace she had caused.

When she was a child and had been brought to The Center for training, she'd competed with the children born there, both types—the ones like Leland *and* the ones considered pure, whom no one ever saw. The visions of perfection were sectioned off in a secure part of the building, where only a few were allowed to go.

Angela had worked hard, studied hard, and excelled in physical fitness. She was just as intelligent, cunning, and beautiful—determined by the unwanted attention she received from male suitors. But even with working her ass off, her excellent record, and obtaining the position of Chief of the *Kripo* Unit, she still fell short. At least according to Dr. Hirch and The Center's prerequisites. But the detective knew without a doubt, if given the same type of training the pictures of perfection had, she would've excelled beyond them. Even with their *special* abilities.

Angela released the tension in her hands, where the edges of the photo crinkled under her grip. Fighting an urge to rip it apart and stomp on it, she placed it against her stomach and smoothed out the wrinkles.

After glancing at the photo one more time, Angela slipped it back into her pocket. She rounded the corner and stopped at the first door, extracting her card to swipe through the lock.

Because of the position as head of the *Kripo* unit held, her set of rooms was larger than the ones who worked beneath her. The apartment opened to a decent-sized living room, decorated in soft earth tones, and a black and white, walk-in kitchen. Immediately to the right of the kitchen, a small hall led to the bathroom and ended at the bedroom.

Angela went straight to the bathroom, shrugging off her jacket and clothes along the way, and turned on the shower. Steam rose in the air and coated the mirror with a sheen of condensation. She stepped into the hot water and quickly washed away her grogginess. There would be time for a nap on the train.

Her head wrapped in a towel, the detective hurried to her bedroom, where she changed into off-duty flared-leg jeans and a gold blouse. Then, she went to her closet where a military-green duffle bag hid on the top shelf behind blankets and other knickknacks. She yanked it out. The bag fell like it held bricks, and thumped against her thigh on its way down. She shuffled over to her bed and dumped the contents onto the cover.

A metallic clatter came from the growing pile, and the scent of old gunpowder and cleaning oil filled the air. Her green bedspread was covered in pistols and rifles. Unlike the authorized .40 S&W, the only weapon allowed when hunting Renegades, these firearms had been illegally obtained from the Renegades she'd captured over the years. None of them could be traced back to her.

Angela picked up an SG 550 assault rifle, liking the weight of it in her hands, and brought it firmly against her shoulder. She'd had the opportunity to sight it only twice, but the feeling of her finger on the trigger, the forced impact against her shoulder, and the odor of the powder as it filled her nostrils were all ingrained in her memory. Unfortunately, the rifle wouldn't accompany her on the trip.

She set it down and picked up the Taurus PT145. Perfect. A smaller handgun, designed for concealed carry. She removed the double-stacked magazine and loaded ten rounds of .45 cartridges. Sliding the magazine back into place and chambering a round, she held the gun. Her fingers felt at home around the contours of the polymer grip.

Placing the gun on the bedside table, Angela grabbed three more magazines and stuffed ten .45 rounds into each one. She couldn't imagine needing more. Then again, after what had happened at the park, who knew? She had no way of knowing whether Dr. Hirch kept other secrets, and she wasn't going to be unprepared again. The embarrassing episode of waking behind the bush back at the park had been enough. Even now, the humiliation burned through her with a vengeance of its own when she thought about it.

If she could only get the perfect bitch alone...

Renegades would be blamed, and Angela would have her revenge and walk away unscathed.

She set the box with the remaining cartridges off to the side along with the ankle holster and magazine pouches and grabbed another box just for good measure. She replaced the rest of the firearms in the bag and hauled her illegal possessions back to the closet to store away from prying eyes.

With the holster tied to her ankle, the gun nestled inside, the leather hugging the metal contours, she stood and looked in the full-length mirror attached to the closet door. Her damp hair, like spun silvery thread, draped over her shoulders. And her eyes, although tired and tinged with red, remained alert. Her body was toned and lean. She was just as deadly as The Center's children, and even more so with the stainless-steel weapon hidden by the flare of her jeans.

Pleased, Angela attached the ammo pouches to the inside of her waistband. In each pouch, she placed a magazine. They felt hard against her back, but not uncomfortable. She hid the extra rounds with a lightweight blue jacket that fell loosely around her waist.

Angela checked her watch. An hour left. She grabbed another suitcase and shoved in three pairs of off-duty pants and shirts, a set of camos, and other necessities. She wrapped both ammunition boxes in a pair of pajamas, placed them within her essentials, and zipped the suitcase closed.

After one last glance around the room to make sure everything was in order, Angela shut off the lights.

6

Ellyssa woke with her cheek against the cool moss-covered ground. Fine grass tickled her skin, and the sun warmed her hair. Soft gurgles of water rushed over rocks and intermingled with the hum of insects. For a brief second, she felt peaceful, before a dull throbbing echoed from her legs, up her spinal cord, and ended at her temple, informing her that she was not well.

She swallowed. Her throat felt swollen and scratchy, like she'd eaten a wad of sandpaper. Her tongue darted between her dry, cracked lips and pulled back the metallic taste of blood.

Tauntingly, just a meter away, the water bottle lay next to her bag. With the way she felt, it might as well have been a kilometer.

She wanted to close her eyes again, to let sleep take her away, but she couldn't. She had to keep moving.

Slowly, she pulled her hands under her chest and pushed. Her body screamed in protest. Her sore muscles felt tight, like her tendons were tied into knots. Especially her leg, which was heavy and unresponsive. Gritting her teeth, she stood and stumbled forward before crumpling next to the bottle. The three or four swallows left in the bottle sloshed tantalizingly and reflected the morning sun like glittering diamonds.

Ellyssa flicked her gaze toward the stream. Cool, thirst-quenching water ran over river rocks, shimmering with browns and greys. So was the possibility of bacteria. She turned away from the rushing stream and unscrewed the cap, then took one last small, unsatisfying sip.

Standing with care, Ellyssa slowly distributed her weight. Sharp teeth of pain clamped onto her wound. She yelped as her right leg buckled, sending her back to the ground. The already tender leg banged against jagged rocks and more skin scraped off. A slow burn mingled with the rest of the aches and pains.

Thoughts of the beating she'd endured while training were diminished to trivial nuisances. Nothing compared to the way she felt now.

Eyes watering, Ellyssa held her leg, refusing to let the agony get the best of her. *She is superior. Weakness is intolerable. Absolute control over all situations.* Her father's words repeated in her head, over and over, until she managed to push the pain aside and gain control.

Calmly, she regarded her right thigh. An angry redness spread from under the makeshift bandage. She gingerly poked it with her finger. An unhealthy yellow depression bloomed before the red reestablished its presence. After untying the bandage, she carefully pulled it away. Stringy pus, tinged green with red dots, stretched from the fabric to the wound.

Disgusting.

Ellyssa glanced at what little liquid was left in the bottle, her only source of clean water, and then the stream. Given little choice, she rose and limped to the babbling water, grabbing her bag along the way.

After retrieving the scissors and the antiseptic cream, she took off the coveralls. Blood stiffened the material of her tan skirt. She took it off, too. She cut off the remaining leg of her coveralls, then cut the clean part of the skirt into strips.

Using part of the skirt, Ellyssa scrubbed the wound while biting the inside of her cheek to hold back the screams. The pain was beyond belief, clouding her vision and rolling waves of nausea through her stomach. When she was done, she let the blood flow to clean the wound before re-bandaging her leg and shrugging back into the coveralls.

She gathered her items and stepped into the stream. Water lapped at her calves. She cautiously measured every step to ensure she wouldn't fall. She couldn't afford any more injuries. Her pace was already considerably slower than yesterday.

Ellyssa hoped the police were going upstream and the dogs, as they had undoubtedly been brought in by now, hadn't found her scent. Wishing she could walk on the bank, but knowing such carelessness would prove to be a fatal mistake, she picked up speed, pushing her already overly-taxed body. She kept her eyes downcast as she navigated the rocks. Her arms swinging in stiff arcs, she pressed on, forcing her legs to move faster. She'd regret it tomorrow, she knew, but nevertheless, she didn't slow.

Under the heat of the afternoon sun, perspiration gathered on Ellyssa's forehead and dripped down her face, stinging the sores on her lips. She took another sip of her dwindling water supply. Soon she'd be forced to drink the water she was sloshing through. She shoved the thought out of her mind to worry about later.

Right now another pressing sensation gnawed in the pit of her stomach, protesting the emptiness. Hunger echoed in the hollow depths of her gut. With the expenditure of her energy, water couldn't be her only source of sustenance. She'd have to find food. The forest in late summer provided all the nourishment she'd need in the forms of fruits and roots. If worst came to worst, the little minnows struggling to hold their positions against the current could be a delicacy.

She left the safety of the water and moved into the grass bordering the rocky edges. As predicted, just a few meters away from the stream, blackberry vines burst with ripened fruit. She hobbled over to them, her mouth watering and stomach rumbling in anticipation.

Ellyssa placed the dark purple fruit on her tongue and squeezed it against the roof of her mouth. The sweet juice soothed her burning throat. Sitting down, she picked another, and another, following the same procedure, until her stomach began to swell.

Making camp next to the food supply would be ideal, at least until she could decide on her next course of action, but that was a luxury she couldn't afford. She started to take turns with the berries, one in her mouth and one in an empty water bottle, filling the container with the fruit.

Squeezing her eyes tight, she pulled her feet under her and stood. Her body uttered a scream of defiance that, thankfully, calmed to a mumbled complaint. She wallowed back to the stream, submerged her feet in the icy water, and continued downstream.

She stumbled in the water until twilight consumed the east and the sun fell to the horizon in the west. Against the bluish-black sky, the first stars winked into view.

Shivering and completely exhausted, Ellyssa stopped her march and stepped onto dry land, where she dropped to her knees on a patch of grass. She took off her shoes and socks and dried her prune-like feet with a strip of cloth. No longer mobile, she felt the coolness of the night sap away the warmth in her body. Huddling into a tight ball, she lay on the ground and, almost immediately, sleep reached up and laid claim to her.

"Detective Petersen, they picked up the trail of the Renegade," said the Captain of the Warrensburg Department, Dyllon Jones. She still found his manner of speech strange, as if every vowel had to be drawn out, so unlike the way citizens spoke in the city.

Angela aimed the flashlight into his face.

Flinching, the captain brought the hand holding the radio up to shield his eyes. "Hey!" It sounded more like, *ha-a-ay*.

"Sorry," Angela said. She moved the beam down so it pooled on his chest. "Where?"

"About one hundred sixty-one meters away. She left footprints in the soil," he replied.

Angela gazed at the sky; stars glittered brightly against the black velvet. "Have them mark the area and call everyone in, but I want them back at five in the morning."

She studied the man again. Like the rest of the unit, he wore a dark green uniform, signifying area police. His face was beaded with perspiration, and his hair, which she knew was cream in color, clung to his head in a darkened mess. He wasn't a bad-looking man. Tall, lean muscles, defined cheekbones, strong jaw, perfect mouth; and when his lips broke into a smile, which happened a lot, his whole face lit up.

Regardless, Captain Jones fell short by the detective's standards. His hair leaned more toward a yellow than white, and his skin was darker than the alabaster of perfection. She did like his eyes, though.

They weren't the clear azure color of the perfect being, but they were interesting, a warm bluish-green color of the deep ocean.

As she scrutinized him, he pulled out the radio and relayed her orders. Static sounded, followed by someone answering, *yes, sir*.

The captain whipped out a bandana and sopped his forehead. "It sure is hot," he remarked, looking at her.

Hot was an understatement. Angela found Missouri not only to be hot, but very humid. She'd spent the better half of a day swatting at the persistent gnats circling her head. She flipped her head up in acknowledgement, which apparently gave him the go-ahead for more small talk.

"You're staying in Warrensburg, right?"

"Yes," she answered curtly and returned her attention to the map. From the corner of her eye, Angela watched Captain Jones' shadow as his weight shifted from one foot to the other as if waiting for a more elaborate explanation. Irritated, she rolled up the map and shoved it under her arm. "I need the dogs returned to the kennel."

"I'll take care of it for you."

"Thank you," she replied, as she walked toward her car parked on the side of the access road.

"See you tomorrow."

Angela lifted her hand in a halfhearted wave, then opened the door of the green Volkswagen Beetle and slid inside. She peered at Dyllon, who was standing next to the cardboard table she'd just left. The captain's arm flapped up and down as he gave orders into the handheld radio.

She hoped he wasn't going to pose a problem. The discipline in the smaller communities seemed to be lacking. Something she'd discuss with her superiors when she returned successful. Starting the car, Angela eased onto the blacktop and drove into town.

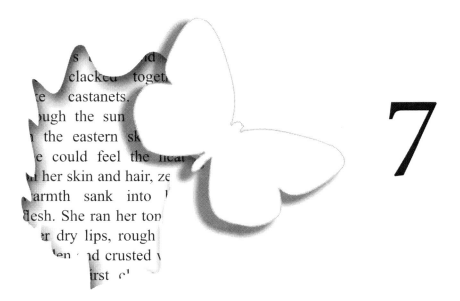

7

Tremors rocked Ellyssa's body and her teeth clacked together like castanets. Even though the sun hovered in the eastern sky, and she could feel the heat on her skin and hair, zero warmth sank into her flesh. She ran her tongue over her dry lips, rough and swollen and crusted with blood. Thirst clawed at her throat.

Was she sick?

In all her life, Ellyssa had never experienced illness. Diseases were eradicated in the general population, but this was a different type of sickness caused from the injuries.

She'd never felt so vulnerable. So weak.

She grabbed the empty bottle nestled under her arm and turned to face the bubbling stream. Refreshing water lapped over the rocks, splaying droplets glittering seductively under the sun. Her tongue flicked out, like a snake's, as if she could pull the moisture from the air.

Ellyssa shifted onto her elbows. Her muscles seized. Pain licked through her body, and a cramp bunched her calf muscle. Pressing her face into the grass, she stretched her toes outward. The cramp lessened to an irritating pull.

The water babbled, mockingly.

How far was it? Five meters?

Reaching her arms out in front, Ellyssa dug her fingers into the soil and pulled. Her body scooted along the grass. She wrapped her fingers around some shoots and a rock embedded in the ground before heaving her body closer to the edge of the stony shore. Exhausted, she lowered her head and rested on a flat river stone.

Displeased, Angela stood at the bank of the stream where the dogs had lost the scent of the escapee. She couldn't believe it. The trail had been so easy to follow from the field to the woods, before disappearing at a tree. It'd taken the dogs the better half of the day to pick up her scent again. Now, another obstacle. She sneered at the running water.

Every minute that ticked by led Ellyssa farther and farther away.

Her hands clenched into tight fists, the detective looked back and forth between the German Shepherds as they circled around with their noses to the ground and their tails wagging. Occasionally, one of the dogs broke through the water to the other side where it would continue its search.

Four members of the search team, two assigned to each dog, stayed close to the canines. Another group of three trailed behind. All of them had Electroshock weapons hanging from the sides of their utility belts. The vision of perfection was to be brought back alive. *Although, sometimes, unfortunate accidents do happen.* Angela wiggled her foot and felt the pressure of the holster against her leg. The doctor might refuse to see the danger, but she wasn't going to be caught by surprise again.

"There is no telling which way she went," Dyllon said, breaking her out of her reverie.

Slack-jawed, Angela glared at him. As if she needed him to inform her of the obvious. "I'm well aware of the situation," she muttered.

"I was just saying." Captain Jones waved his arm in an arc in front of him, like he was showing her the scenery. The remaining part of the sentence died on his lips when her expression twisted into a scowl. Shoving his hands into his pockets, the captain turned away and looked off into the forest. "How would you like to precede, Detective?"

"Search around the trees closest to the water within a fifty-meter radius. If your men have to leave the stream, make sure they understand to go back to the exact point where they left."

"Yes, ma'am."

Her mouth curved down. "She's not your average Renegade. She is smarter, faster, trained, and can be quite deadly."

Dyllon turned back toward her with a quizzical expression.

"Make sure your men understand the situation."

"Maybe, if I was better informed, you would find the whole unit more useful."

Raising her brows, she responded, "I have told you everything that will be useful in the investigation. You make sure your team understands."

She left Dyllon in charge and went back to the base camp, which was pitched close to the point where Ellyssa had first entered the wooded area. A few other people milled around the site. Two men were checking supplies, while a man and a woman were gridding a map into two-and-a-half centimeter squares.

She went to the table where her map lay already gridded. It was an older map from the 1940s, but it showed all the small townships that'd existed during the time; the modern charts lacked the details of towns that had been abandoned.

A few years after The War, people had been instructed to move to the bigger cities where they could work or in the outskirts to farm. Having all citizens in close proximity led to better control. All the smaller communities were now rotting away.

She used a compass to measure the equivalency of fifteen kilometers on the apex and drew a circle around the area where Ellyssa's scent had disappeared into the stream. While studying the chart, she listed all the small towns on a piece of paper.

When she was done, she reluctantly pulled out her cell phone to call the doctor. He wouldn't be pleased with the lack of progress.

Flipping the phone shut, Dr. Hirch opened the door to the lab. He controlled his outward appearance, but deep down, he was worried about the whole situation. Ellyssa had gotten farther than he'd expected.

"Report your progress," he said to the assistant. He managed to keep his voice smooth and steady.

"Almost done," Leland answered while he finished applying the adhesive to Aalexis' temple, where he would connect the next electrode.

Dr. Hirch's youngest daughter sat unmoving, waiting. Her blond hair was slicked back and pulled into a ponytail. Rows of platinum curls cascaded down her back where the hair escaped the confines of the elastic band. Except for the ringlets, thinner lips, and the defined chin, she looked almost identical to Ellyssa when she was thirteen.

When the doctor entered, Aalexis regarded the doctor for a brief second, expressing no real interest in him and appearing docile. He knew better, though. The young girl was extremely intelligent...and dangerous if the situation called for it. She soaked in her surroundings, mentally preparing for all scenarios. Plus, his daughter's growing ability to control her power was moving remarkably ahead of schedule.

Holding onto the thin black cables of the electrodes, Leland turned toward the doctor. "Any news?"

"Yes. They picked up her trail, but lost it," George replied, while checking the green spikes moving across the monitor's screen in rhythmic patterns. No rise, no sputter, just sixty BPM, as always. The only time there was ever a slightly elevated increase was during periods of extreme physical exertion.

Leland cocked an eyebrow. "Oh."

Dr. Hirch penciled the number down on the chart marked Subject 74. "Ellyssa made it to water. Angela has the dogs working on it now."

"Your detective will fail," said Aalexis, her tone matching her expressionless face.

George turned toward his daughter, but the young girl said nothing else. She stared at the doctor with cold eyes.

He ignored her statement. "How are you feeling today?"

"Fine. Thank you," she answered, without inflection.

"Good," he said, checking the connections before returning his attention to Leland. The younger man was situated at his desk, positioning his computer monitor. "Are you ready?"

"Almost. I've finished the new programming. We should have a better read on the electrical output."

"Good." He smiled at Aalexis. "And, are you ready?"

"Of course."

He walked over to the set of square steel weights and pointed at the five kilogram. "Move it," he instructed.

Aalexis' smooth forehead bunched, then relaxed as the monitor beeped at the slight increase in her pulse before returning to normal. The weight lifted off the ground and danced in the air.

"Place it on top of the other one," George said, pointing across the room.

Following the weight with her eyes as if guiding it with her sight, Aalexis moved the weight without effort and stacked it on top of the other, aligning the sides perfectly.

George never ceased to be amazed, no matter how many times he'd seen her perform the feat. Concealing his emotions, he glanced at Leland. His assistant stared at Aalexis with his jaw hanging open.

"Leland."

The younger man nodded and checked the monitor. "Same as before. Most of the activity is in the frontal and parietal lobe, and there is activity in the occipital lobe as she moves the object from place to place."

George directed his attention back at his subject. "Now try the twenty-five."

The heavier weight moved just as effortlessly to the side of the room, as if feather-light. Aalexis stacked it on top of the others.

"Any changes?"

"No. Same brain waves. Same activity. Of course, the neurological firing is off the charts for a normal human. Not for her of course."

"Very intriguing."

"Why so, *der Vater*?"

George broke his gaze off the recently placed weight and onto his daughter. Frowning, he said, "Your skill is growing beyond what was expected."

Aalexis held the doctor's gaze. "You let the physics of your known world cloud your judgment. Once you understand the atoms, how they move, how they hum in sequence, what charges them, you would understand."

Without so much as a flinch of her porcelain-smooth face, the twenty-five kilogram weight lifted off the ground, followed by the five kilogram. A stapler from his desk and his notebook joined in the eerie dance. They floated weightlessly in the air, hovering in space. "There is no weight or gravity to hold down the influences of your mind."

George stood transfixed; his composure melted, unable to stop gawking until a gasp from Leland grabbed his attention. He glanced at his young assistant, who was standing next to the floating chair he'd recently occupied.

Shaken and dumbfounded, he turned toward the little girl. Aalexis sat there, expressionless, her eyes turned toward him. She had never displayed her abilities like this before. He looked away from her and closed his eyes to reestablish his self-control. "Aalexis, enough."

"As you wish, *der Vater*." The hovering items sank silently back to their previous positions.

With a forced calm, he went to the girl and removed the attachments, gathering them within his hands. "Your talent is most awe-inspiring," he said, his voice holding steady.

"Are you pleased, *der Vater*?" Aalexis asked, with a snide undertone.

Stunned she'd asked such a question, and with the intonation she held in her voice, his gaze flicked to her face. Her eyes still held indifference.

"I am," he said, a bit hesitantly. "It seems you have been practicing outside of the lab."

Aalexis' expression didn't change.

"We are done for the day. Return to your room."

Without a word, Aalexis stood and left, the door closing behind her.

George faced Leland, who stared at the door, his lips moving.

"Leland!" the doctor snapped, breaking him from his trance.

The assistant tore his gaze from the door, amazement filling his features. "Did you see that?"

"Of course," the doctor said as he pointed to the desk where paper draped over the side. "What does the printout say?"

Leland ripped the long sheet from its feed and sat in the previously floating chair. He quickly scanned the readout, marking it at certain segments. After a couple of minutes, he said, "There are no changes in physiological data for the most part. Minor fluxes during the initial movement." He looked back at the doctor.

George nodded. "As I suspected."

"As you suspected?"

"Yes, Leland. Don't you see? No, I suppose you don't," he said, with a slight shake of his head. "She has transcended the scope of the physical."

With a feeling of sudden danger, Ellyssa's eyes fluttered open to a world washed with blinding white light. She lifted her head off the rock and looked into the sky. The sun had drifted well past the noon position.

Despite the afternoon heat, Ellyssa's body shuddered, as if submerged in ice water. Like before, the warmth grazed her skin, but didn't penetrate. All she wanted to do was curl into a tight little ball. If not for the sound of the water, she would've done so. A fire ignited in her throat, demanding to be quenched.

Ellyssa dragged her knees underneath her and pushed herself up onto her hands. Dizziness swam through her head. She paused and waited until her vision cleared, then persuaded her legs and arms to crawl forward. Plagued with vertigo, she swayed unsteadily on all fours as she inched toward the rushing stream.

The distance seemed to increase before Ellyssa. *Must be the fever.* She wanted to give up and lay down. *Weakness is unacceptable.* Ellyssa picked up her hand, and the ground lurched toward her, smacking into her chest, stealing her breath away.

Coughing weakly, trying to reclaim the air she'd lost, Ellyssa lowered her head and was surprised when her forehead dipped into the cool water. Using her toes, she pushed herself the last few centimeters then lapped like a dog, greedily swallowing the cool liquid until the blaze in her throat extinguished.

When nausea threatened to expel all she'd taken in, Ellyssa stopped. She moved away from the stream and rolled over onto her back to give her stomach time to settle. The sun beat down, shining on Ellyssa's face, but the warmth still stayed at bay. She shivered.

Time to move.

Ellyssa slowly lifted to her feet, pausing for a moment until the swimming in her head stopped and the waves of nausea settled to a gentle roll. She went back to the patch of grass and slipped on her dry socks and shoes. After doctoring her wound again, she returned to the stream, filled the bottle with the iffy water, and placed it inside her bag.

Thinking about nothing more than placing one foot in front of the other, Ellyssa stepped into the cold water that flooded her shoes and pricked her skin like thousands of ice picks. A feeling of misery engulfed her and, for the first time ever, she actually felt like crying.

Unacceptable.

Ellyssa straightened her shoulders and pulled her lips tight; then, like she had pressed a delete button, all emotion fell away. She'd be damned if the first time she cried would be over feeling sorry for herself.

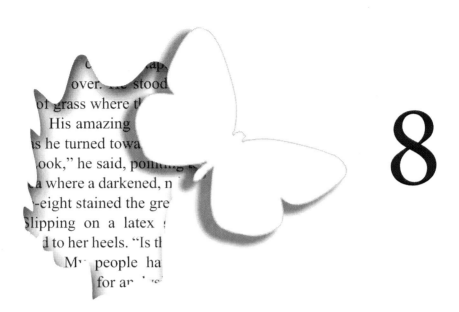

8

The first purples and dark blues streaked across the sky when Angela finally rolled up the map and sank into the chair. She was tired and irritated, her backside hurt, and her eyes were dry and itchy. The detective rubbed them with the palms of her hands.

Angela had spent half the day researching the ghost towns. A lot of the old towns had been born from mining operations, which meant abandoned mines would need to be added to the search. Complication after complication.

She glanced at Captain Jones. Dyllon sat facing away from her, purposefully turned toward the trees, waiting for the last search team to report. Ever since she'd snapped at him, he'd kept his distance, only talking when circumstances demanded it. For efficacy reasons, she'd have to fix the problem. She depended on the additional man-hours, unable to do the initial tracking all by herself. The world outside of The Center required her to show a certain level of civility.

Angela gathered up the items and stowed them away in her car. Maybe after dinner and a shower, she'd take another look at the map to make sure she hadn't missed anything. Then again, maybe she'd just go to bed and give her eyes a break.

"Captain Jones," she called, while returning to the camp.

At the mention of his name, Dyllon leaned back in the chair. His head turned in her general direction with robotic rigidity. He raised his eyes, but instead of meeting her gaze, she was fairly certain he was staring over her head. "Yes, Detective," he replied coolly.

"You and your unit have proven to be very useful. The Center… appreciates your help."

The corner of his mouth twitched as his brow arched. "And what about you?"

Angela sighed. "I appreciate the help too, Captain."

A grin twitched Dyllon's cheeks. "We are a little less formal in my district. But, as I am sure you know, our track record is infallible. We are efficient."

Angela thought *less formal* was an understatement; the lax attitude was unnerving. Their record was impressive, though; they'd delivered many members of the resistance to the camps. "I give credit where credit is due, Captain Jones," she agreed.

Dyllon's lips pulled into a smile that spread across his face. "You can call me Dyllon."

First name? The thought made her uncomfortable. But, if such informality was the way they did things here, she'd play along… somewhat. "Dyllon," she acknowledged, "you may call me Detective Petersen."

At first, Dyllon's smile faltered, but then he started laughing. "Fair enough," he said. "Nice to meet you, Detective Petersen."

The captain held out his hand in greeting, and Angela accepted. His palm was a little rough, and warm in a pleasant way. She shook once and let go.

Standing there, feeling awkward, Angela stumbled around in her head trying to find the instructions she had for the team for tomorrow.

"Follow me, Cap—I mean Dyllon," she said, walking to her car. "I want everyone back here at five in the morning. We will pick up where we left off."

"Five o'clock it is," he replied, still smiling.

She held his gaze for a moment before sliding into the car and slamming the door. As she turned the key in the ignition, the engine hummed to life. She turned to wave goodbye, but he was no longer paying attention to her, his body angled toward the tree line. The radio was in his hand, his thumb holding the side button as he spoke into the transmitter.

The detective frowned. She hadn't heard anything—not the crack of static or the squeal of feedback. Looking down, her hand fell to her waist where the radio sat in its holder. She turned the knob just in time to hear Dyllon say something about securing a perimeter.

Had they found her?

Excitement curling in the pit of her stomach, and the taste of revenge on her tongue, Angela turned with her hand on the door handle and silenced a scream before it erupted. Dyllon was peering at her through her window. His face twisted in amusement. While her heart found the beat it'd missed, she opened the door, pushing him back.

"What the hell?"

"Sorry, I didn't mean to startle you," the captain said but, judging by the slight lopsided grin he held, Angela doubted he meant it. "The search team found her scent. I told them to secure the area and issued instructions for two of the men to stay put. Their partners are on the way back with the dogs to retrieve sleeping bags. I hope that will suffice for the evening."

The detective's heart accelerated. "I should go there."

"Don't be silly," Dyllon said. "There isn't anything you can do tonight. It's not like in the city. We're deep in the woods. By the time we set up the necessary equipment and the spotlights, it'll be morning anyway."

Angela hesitated for a moment, one foot planted outside the car.

"I'll make the appropriate arrangements. Don't worry about anything." Dyllon flashed his stunning smile.

Angela's gaze slid between the wooded area and the car, the prospect of a good night's sleep tempting her. "Fine," she said, her mind made up. "First thing in the morning."

"First thing," Dyllon promised.

9

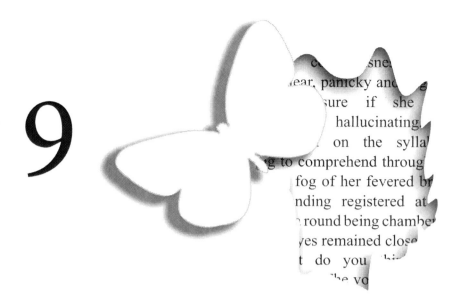

As soon as Angela ducked under the yellow caution tape, Dyllon waved her over, a smile lighting his face. He stood next to a patch of grass where the rocky shore ended.

"Look," he said, pointing toward an area where a darkened, misshapen figure-eight stained the green.

Slipping on a latex glove, the detective lowered to her heels. "Is that blood?"

"Yes. My people have already taken a sample for analysis."

Angela ran her hand over the fine grass to where the blades stuck together in the dried crimson, plucking free a blue piece of material. "She's hurt," she said, bringing the material to her nose. Faint traces of copper mingled with the forest scent.

"Considering the amount of blood, I would say she is badly wounded."

"If you look at the indentation mark," Angela said, indicating where the greenery lay crushed, "it's thicker here. I think it's her leg."

"Which should slow her down considerably."

The news worked wonders on the detective's mood. For the first time since Ellyssa had escaped, things might actually get easier. Angela stood, her lips spreading into a chilling grin.

Ellyssa hobbled to the edge of the truss bridge. Sun-bleached planks were missing from the deck and beams hung precariously from the long rafters. Wooziness rotated in her midsection as she looked over the side of the cliff. Turbulent water leapt over the jagged rocks, reflecting the sun in dappled shards. Stomach lurching, Ellyssa leaned against the branch she'd been using as a makeshift crutch and sank to the ground, closing her lids and hoping the nausea would pass.

When the dizziness steadied, Ellyssa turned and looked down the old paved road, wondering if she'd made the right choice to move back to land. Roots and vegetation jutted between the cracks of the blackened asphalt, nature on a quest to take back what had once been hers. The terrain was rugged, but no more than the slippery rocks she'd already navigated. At least her feet were no longer numb, and the tremors that had shaken her body had settled to mild shivers.

There was no going back or second guessing herself, now. Only one way—forward.

Ellyssa pulled out the water bottle and took a small sip, then poured some in her hand and wiped her face. It wasn't as cool as the stream, but it was still refreshing.

Using the crutch, she pulled herself up and limped over to the edge where broken asphalt met wood, her leg singing a tune of pain.

Ellyssa slipped the crutch lengthways through the flap of her bag and grabbed one of the few remaining beams crossing the triangulated latticework. She placed her left foot on the first plank of the bridge, testing it. It mumbled, but held. She pulled her right foot next to her left.

The next plank made a loud popping noise when Ellyssa tested it. Bypassing that board, she skimmed over to the next and stilled.

Nothing.

Pent-up breath whooshed from her lungs. She continued, moving slowly, skipping over the boards that groaned too loudly or dipped under the pressure of her weight.

Three-fourths of the way across, the muscles in Ellyssa's arms and legs quivered from the exertion and careful precision of moving. Her heart slammed against her ribs, keeping time with the pounding in her head. Her chest heaved short gasps of air. Vertigo accompanied her rolling stomach.

Sweat dripping into Ellyssa's eyes, she evaluated the remaining distance. Two, maybe three meters. Hard to tell with tunnel vision. She took another step. The rotted wood creaked and popped under her weight, like it was infuriated that she might make it to the other side. Ellyssa skipped to the next and continued.

Safety mocking her a little over a meter away, dizziness spun in Ellyssa's head again. She stumbled forward, landing roughly on the board. It snapped, shooting her leg through like a piston. Time slowed as she fell; everything was detailed in lines and vivid colors.

Fire burst in Ellyssa's lower extremities as her shin scraped along the wood and her knee smacked into the edge. The next thing she knew, her chest hit the plank in front of her, stopping her descent. Pain reverberated in her bones as she clutched desperately to the weathered plank that bowed with added stress.

Heart hammering, muscles twitching, Ellyssa pulled herself up and planted both feet as close to the girder as possible. She inhaled deeply, calming herself, as she calculated the remaining distance and hunkered down. Every part of her body screamed as she uncoiled and sprang.

Short of the intended goal, wood splintered and broke away as soon as she landed, replaying the mess she'd just escaped. Gravity reached up and claimed its prize. Arms flailing, her fingers stretched, desperate to find purchase, but they only clutched air. Splinters raked through her clothing and tender skin. She lurched forward, her chest catching onto the very last plank, forcing air from her lungs, and her fingers laid claim to the edge of the crumbling asphalt.

Her legs dangling, Ellyssa stilled, afraid to even breathe. A low moan grated across the rusted bolts holding the plank that served as her anchor. It popped and slipped. She kicked her feet, lunging forward up and over the weakening board and grabbing onto a tree root. With the last of her energy, she pulled herself onto the blacktop, and rolled over where the bridge remained ominously in her view.

Ellyssa's brain slammed against the inside of her skull; her muscles seized into screaming knots as the dizziness spiraled through her once again. She dragged in breaths of air as she rested on her side; her eyes locked on the wooden demon.

Ellyssa wished she had a torch.

As the sun fell, Ellyssa looked into the sky. Pinpoints of light filtered through the midnight blue of twilight while impending clouds rolled across the other portion of the heavens. A subtle hint of ozone thickened the air.

Peaceful. Tranquil. Unlike the war raging inside her body.

You are superior. You are the future. You are perfection.

Her father's words echoed in Ellyssa's head. She wondered what he'd think of her now: sick, broken, imperfect…disposable.

Needing to find refuge before it rained, Ellyssa adjusted the bag over her shoulder and crutched/lurched down what was becoming the never-ending road. It stretched in front of her and curved into darkness.

Resignation whispered to her fevered brain, to give up and sit down and wait for sweet death to take her last breath.

Ellyssa ignored the luring mumbles and continued.

She went around the bend and halted. Buildings of varying shapes and sizes stood eerily silhouetted against the light of the full moon, whitewashed like ghosts. Relief siphoned away the misery. She knew the town lay empty; the people moved long ago. No comforts of civilization, just shelter.

On the outskirts, barely visible, a silvery reflection caught Ellyssa's attention. She pushed away the overgrown vines. A faded sign claimed the town's name in white paint—WELCOME TO DEEPWATER - POP 956.

Welcome?

Ellyssa's mouth twitched upward into a partial smile. So surreal. The fever. She felt delusional.

Stepping within the town limits, Ellyssa followed the crumbling street past dilapidated houses and buildings sporting faded storefront signs and broken windows. Vines snaked along the bricks and wood, tearing at the decaying structures. Doors either hung loosely on rusted hinges or were gone. Subtle sounds of creaking glossed through the air, and the ticking of claws as the town's only occupants scurried.

Beyond exhausted, Ellyssa's feet dragged her forward. She sent her fatigued mind out, but beside the unreadable patterns of animals, there was nothing. No one was there.

Clouds quickly tumbled, stifling the night's light. A raindrop pelted Ellyssa's head. More fell around her. The suddenly cool air sent chills spinning down her spine. She watched the churning clouds. They had swept over the night canvas, blotting out the stars and blanketing the moon.

A flash of blinding light was followed by a loud crack, and what started as a few drops increased in number, wetting her hair and clothing. The chills turned to shivers.

Ellyssa moved as quickly as her body permitted up a wobbly step onto a brick sidewalk in front of an old storefront. The picture-glass window was filthy. She wiped away the dirt and pressed her face against the window. Darkness smothered the store in black.

Stepping back, she turned around. From what she could tell, all the buildings were the same: dark, empty, and falling apart. The store was as good a place as any. She shuffled to the entrance, her footsteps echoing eerily in the night, and went inside.

Complete darkness enveloped Ellyssa like a cocoon. She stopped and listened. Other than the deadened pattering of rain on the roof, and drips plopping on weathered wood, there was silence.

She swept her crutch in front of her. The wood slapped against something soft. She prodded and it gave way, gripping the stick. Stifling a scream, she yanked hard and stumbled back a step. Mold and the odor of rot resonated within the scent of ozone.

Fevered mind envisioning decomposing flesh, ragged muscles and tendons sloughing off bone, Ellyssa's breath seized and bile rose. On the verge of terror, a harmful emotion, she swallowed hard and leaned against the wall.

I'm hallucinating, she reasoned.

Rumbling resonated from the sky, and electricity sliced through the heavens, lighting the store in brilliance. She glanced at the pile.

For a split second, her hallucination was realized before darkness swallowed the image. Flash. A pile of rotten rags. She blinked. Another burst of light. Rags and old tarps.

Worn-out, Ellyssa slid down the wall and curled into a ball.

10

Mumbled voices with strange accents danced on the edge of Ellyssa's consciousness, fuzzy and unclear, panicky and angry…distant. Unsure if she was dreaming or hallucinating, she concentrated on the syllables, trying to comprehend through the swirling fog of her fevered brain. Understanding registered at the sound of a round being chambered.

Her eyes remained closed.

"What do you think she's doing here?" The voice was deep, hard. Definitely male.

"I don't know." Irritated. A male, too.

"Look at her hair. I bet she's part of a patrol," a musical voice hissed. Female.

"Really? Do you see what she's wearing?" Another male, but his tone was tinny, nasally, as if he had a cold. Very unpleasant.

"No. She's hurt. Look at her," said the male with the deep voice. "They wouldn't let her continue in that condition."

Ellyssa's mind wandered into the crowd. The readings she received felt surreal, dreamlike. She registered four people. Confused, worried, and angry. Especially the female. All of them surrounded her. Images of pump-action shotguns pointing at her crumpled body filtered through.

Her head throbbed. She pulled out.

"Whatever. She got lost." The female again. "Others will come." Footsteps faded toward the door. "I say we dispose of her."

"No," said the deep voice.

"I think she's right, Rein." The tinny sound grated along Ellyssa's spine.

"No," said the male with the deep voice…Rein? "The discussion is closed."

"Exactly when did we discuss this?" said the male who sounded irritated before.

"Shut up, Woody."

"I'm serious. This could be very dangerous. What if someone's looking for her?"

"Wake her up." The woman's footfalls echoed back to the others. "We'll ask her."

"I think she's already awake," said Rein. He tapped the tip of her shoe.

Ellyssa stayed still and kept her eyes closed, her breath even. She projected outward, ignoring the thumping and the haziness. She had to concentrate. She ventured from head to head. Her body remained the target of the barrels of shotguns—12 gauges. She waited.

"You do the honors, Jason."

"Cover me," said Jason, nasally. "Hey." Cold steel, like the feel of ice cubes, poked her wrist. Goosebumps rose and trailed up her bicep, finding her spinal cord. She fought against the shiver. "Wake up."

The sound of a boot scraping against the floor, as if the owner was preparing to kick, alerted her to danger. Before he had a chance, Ellyssa leapt to her feet.

"Stop her," someone yelled. She thought it was the one called Woody.

With one lithe movement, her foot connected with Jason's hand and the shotgun clattered to the floor. She whirled around and performed a back kick into the female's stomach. Hissy Voice backpedaled and fell against some shelves. Wood snapped on impact.

Ellyssa stumbled as darkness rolled on the edge of her vision. She struggled against it. She spun, feebly attempting to take out the one they called Woody. A shot fired and echoed around her, disorienting her. She fell.

"I told you this was dangerous." The voice sounded far away, like someone was speaking from the other end of a tunnel.

"Shut up and help me."
Blackness laid a cold hand on Ellyssa.

11

    A feeling of floating, and images of reds, browns, yellows, and white wavered in and out of Ellyssa's awareness. Colorful hues and shades blurred around the edges. Bright lights burned her eyes and scorched her flesh, especially her leg. Something was burning it. At one time, she thought she'd screamed. If not, she'd wanted to.

    Alternating feelings of hot and cold. Sweating and shivering. Angry voices. Intrigued voices. All filtered through. She wasn't sure whether any of it was real or if it was all a dream. She didn't care. She welcomed the darkness when it had sucked her away from the confusion. Welcomed the calmness and the blankness.

    Ellyssa would have welcome it now, but she was awake. The burning sensation had been extinguished. The pain had not. A thin blanket covered her, and she was lying on something softer than the ground, her head resting on a pillow. Musty air smelled like fresh dirt, as if someone had turned the soil recently. And even though the area seemed open and lit, from what light filtered through her eyelids, it felt dark and enclosed, too.

    She listened intently. Everything was silent. Before opening her eyes, she waited for another few seconds to make sure. In the distance, barely noticeable, she heard the shuffling of soft footsteps. Not the clicking of soles against tile, like back at The Center, but muffled and dulled. The owner of the footsteps entered the room and approached her bed. Cool, rough fingers, those of a male, gently grasped her wrist. She fought an impulse to yank away.

Whoever was taking her pulse let go and scratched something down on paper.

Ellyssa searched his mind. No ill-will tainted his thoughts. Mostly concern, and clear images of how she was posing as something once human. A ghastly face, greyish skin, sunken cheeks and eyes, cracked lips, and her hair stuck to her head in thick, tangled clumps. It would've been more befitting if a tag hung from her big toe.

Her head began to pound. She broke the link.

The male walked away, but didn't leave. She felt his presence lingering.

More footsteps, this owner stealthier, entered the room. She heard water sloshing in a glass.

"How is she, Doc?" whispered a deep voice she recognized.

The male who'd just spoken was from the store. What was his name? Rein?

"The fever is gone, and her pulse is steady and strong," Doc replied, his voice gentle and caring.

Ellyssa wasn't sure where she was, but she was far from The Center. The way they spoke was different than what she'd come across before. Their cadence was soft and slow.

It hit her. The sounds of the footsteps. The enclosed feeling. The scent of soil. She wasn't within the custody of anyone from society. She was underground.

Renegades.

She was a prisoner. Her heart skipped a beat. Barely breathing, she lay perfectly still.

Papers shuffled. "I was about to check her wounds. I could use your help."

After a brief hesitation, Rein answered, "Fine, but it will have to be quick. I have other things to do." His deep voice no longer soft, but sharp and irritated.

Both men neared her bed, and Ellyssa's muscles tensed. Pain flared, but not like she had already suffered. Not bad at all. She breathed normally.

"What do you need me to do?"

"It'll only take a few minutes. Don't get all in a huff."

Hands felt down her arms and poked the side of her waist. Fingers glided to the roundness of her hips and pressed against the hipbones, as if trying to flatten them. He moved down to her thigh, pressing against the edges of her wound. Pain flowed. She bit her lip and the hands touching her withdrew.

"Are you awake?"

Ellyssa didn't answer.

"I know you're awake, but if you want to pretend, that's fine," Doc said.

He slid his fingers under the edge of the bandage and gently pulled away the tape. "Word of warning—this is going to hurt."

Hurt? She'd felt pain before. Motionless, her chest barely rising and falling, she readied herself.

She wasn't prepared for what followed. Her eyes popped open, and she jolted upright as her torturer jabbed a fired wrought-iron poker into her wound. Two vises clamped over her biceps. She struggled, but in her weakened state, she didn't put up much of a fight. The vises pushed her back against the pillow.

"Sorry, but I warned you."

Her eyes wildly flicked to an older male, about fifty, his hair, the color of an oil slick with flecks of grey, cropped close to his head. He smiled at her. She glanced at his hands. They held nothing more than a soft-bristled brush.

"I know it hurts, but you still have an infection in the wound. It has to be cleaned," he apologized.

Ellyssa stopped struggling. Movement only intensified the pain. Lips pressed together, she watched the brush moving back and forth over her raw flesh, each stroke igniting another blaze, pushing a scream she refused to voice. He wiped away the red streams that trickled down her thigh with a blood-soaked gauze before they could drip onto the blanket.

Pain and blood were not to be a source of weakness, but watching the doctor work on her own flesh, along with her throbbing head and rolling stomach, was more than she could take. She lay back against the pillow and focused on Rein, separating herself from the pain.

Rein let her go and crossed his arms over a muscular chest that pulled tight the thin cotton of his black T-shirt. Deep lines creased between two of the most spectacular eyes she'd ever seen as they glared at her. They were a deep, dark green, like jades, set into a tan face. Chestnut hair stuck up all over the top of his head, like he'd just run his fingers through it and called it groomed. So unlike the neat, trimmed hair of the people at The Center.

Watching him made her chest feel all funny, fluttery-like.

When their gazes met, his face twisted further in anger, or maybe it was uncertainty, emphasizing the planes of his cheeks and chin. She glowered back at him, matching his fury, ignoring the stinging that had replaced the inferno while the doctor cleaned off the brush.

"Rein, that's enough. You're going to scare her." Doc patted her hand. She pulled away. "Just ignore him," he continued, without missing a beat. "No one's going to hurt you. You're perfectly safe."

"You have to watch her, Doc. I told you what happened at the storage."

Shrugging and cocking an eyebrow, the doctor said, "Are we going to have problems from you?"

She shook her head once. She wasn't in any condition to do anything. Yet.

He beamed, and small lines formed at the corners of his eyes and mouth. "There. You see? She isn't going to pose a problem."

The tendons in Rein's neck throbbed as he clenched his jaw. "Fine. Have it your way." He turned and stormed out. "I'll tell Jordan she's awake."

Still smiling, the older man peered at her. His eyes were a light brown, the color of sand, and gentle, with a touch of humor. Except for the color, his eyes reminded her of the way Leland had looked at her when her father wasn't around.

"I have to finish cleaning your wound."

She nodded once and gritted her teeth. It still didn't prepare her for the burn as the doctor mildly scrubbed the infected area. Without Rein to focus her attention on, tears squeezed from her closed lids and trailed down the side of her face, wetting her hair. After a few seconds though, sweet endorphins were released, and the pain dulled. He spoke to her while he worked.

"Most of the infection is gone. But it was bad. The pus was yellowish-green, and your fever was high. I don't have the proper instruments to measure it, but I would say it bordered around forty degrees Celsius. Luckily, we still had aspirin left. That, coupled with cold water, brought it right down."

He took a fresh bandage and taped it securely to her leg. "It amazes me, though." He stopped what he was doing and looked at her. "That you made it so far in your condition. The closest town is over eighty kilometers away."

She didn't say anything. Her face remained expressionless. Apparently unsatisfied with the lack of response, the corner of his mouth pulled back. She'd seen that expression on her father's and Leland's faces when the results weren't what they'd expected.

"What's your name?"

She swallowed. It was a difficult feat. Her mouth was dry.

"Not going to answer?"

She blinked and met the doctor's gaze.

"Suit yourself." He returned his attention to her leg and finished applying tape to the bandage. When he was done, he faced her again. "I bet you're thirsty. And hungry. You've been asleep for almost three days."

Three days?

Until the doctor mentioned food, she hadn't noticed the empty hole in her midsection. Her stomach rumbled. She nodded once.

The doctor smiled again. "That's a good sign." He grabbed the glass he'd filled earlier. "Can you hold this?" he asked.

Clear water sparkled under the lights. She nodded and struggled to prop herself into a slack sitting position. As she reached for the glass, something pinched her left hand. She looked down and noticed the needle sticking into the back of her hand, intravenously feeding her a solution.

She really was out of it.

"You were very dehydrated."

Ellyssa nodded again, and grasped the glass with her free hand. Water sloshed into her mouth as she chugged away.

"Don't drink too fast."

She peered at the doctor over the rim and took another long gulp.

The doctor shrugged. "I suggest you take it easy, or you'll make yourself sick."

She defiantly took another drink before bringing the glass down. While her caregiver checked the feed of her IV, she studied her new environment.

She was in a cave, but one that was well set up, as if the occupants had lived there for awhile. It was large and well lit. Long, fluorescent tubes hung from the ceiling. Wires snaked from them, out through the opening. A metal desk was shoved into the far corner, and three more cots lined the wall next to her. Opposite from the cots, more IV holders stood next to metal cabinets. The doors of the cabinets were closed, but she assumed they held other medical supplies. Thick beams crossed the ceiling.

"It isn't much, but it's home," the doctor said. "A long, long time ago, it was a coal mine. Who would've imagined making a home from a mine? Now, how about some food?"

Ellyssa nodded enthusiastically. Food. Besides the berries she'd found, she hadn't eaten anything filling since the night before she'd fled. Lemon-pepper chicken and broccoli with cheese casserole. For dessert, she had had chocolate cake with a raspberry sauce. Her mouth watered.

"Good." Doc sounded pleased. "If you can keep the food and water down, I'll remove that," he said, indicating the IV.

The doctor started for the opening, but stopped when another set of footsteps echoed down the hall. Whoever it was wasn't worried about being heard. The steps were loud and thumped with attitude. Ellyssa tilted her head to see around the doctor, but no one appeared. Instead, the visitor stopped just out of sight.

"Rein said the girl was awake."

The voice she definitely recognized, the intonation clinging to her spine. The male who'd tried to wake her in the store. Jason.

"So?"

"He sent me here to guard her."

"She is weak. I don't think you need that."

Ellyssa closed her eyes and used her gift to enter the mind of the doctor, while trying to ignore Jason's. Jason had stringy, dark hair hanging limply around his face. He stood in the shadows of the tunnel and carried a shotgun in the crook of his arm.

"That's your opinion," he said to the doctor.

Ellyssa pushed past Doc and entered Jason's head. His mind appeared simple, more barbaric. He didn't seem well-educated, but she assumed most people here didn't have the schooling she and her siblings had received. Images of her kicking him filled his thoughts. He wasn't happy about it, either. Through his eyes, she saw the doctor. The older man's forehead was pocked in anger. Clearly, the doctor didn't care for Jason.

"And this is my domain. You stay outside of this door." Doc jabbed his finger in the air. "Understand?"

"Fine."

Before the doctor stepped through the opening, he glanced back at Ellyssa. "I'll be back in a moment," he said, emphasizing *moment*, to make his point clear, before disappearing.

Ellyssa stayed with Jason for a moment longer to see if he was planning anything. He seemed content to stay where he was. She heard him shuffle, and then a sound like him sliding down the dirt wall.

Her head pulsed. Taking the hint, Ellyssa withdrew. She was in no condition to push her ability, and she needed to conserve her energy. Regardless of how nice the doctor seemed, these people were Renegades. Dangerous people she had been engineered to kill.

Ellyssa's eyes wandered around the rocky enclosure. Only one way in and one way out. She could hear Jason as he shifted positions.

She inhaled deeply and relaxed against her pillow. Her current circumstances proposed a problem she hadn't anticipated. The priority had been reaching Kansas City. Now, she was uncertain what to do. Maybe the dark-haired man had just sent random thoughts that she'd intercepted. But they'd seemed directed at her, as if he knew her capabilities. Of course, if it hadn't been for the stranger, she never would have stumbled across her father's lies.

From her earliest memories, Ellyssa had been taught that everything for the greater good was a necessity. She and her siblings had been trained to dispose of inferior beings. They were the solution, not part of the problem.

According to her father's files, though, they would be just as disposable when the time came. Her father's research was on its way to its apex; she was the foundation.

Thoughts racing around, Ellyssa's head started to thrum as if someone was trying to split her skull open with a jackhammer. She placed her glass on the little table next to her cot. Thinking hurt too much.

The next thing Ellyssa knew, the doctor was hovering over her with a smile. Surprised, she jumped. Her whole body, especially her leg, wrenched in pain. She stifled a cry.

"Nice nap?"

She jerked her head.

"I brought you something to eat. Here, let me help you." He started to reach for her, and she flinched. He paused. "I'm not going to hurt you. I promise."

Ellyssa popped into his mind and back out, before the jackhammering started again. The doctor was sincere in his intentions.

Relaxing, she let him help. Doc propped several pillows and rolled up blankets behind her back for added support, then grabbed the tray from the table and placed it on her lap. Chunks of potatoes and carrots swam in a brown broth. Next to the chipped bowl was a slice of bread.

"I want to see how you hold this down."

She reached for the spoon and scooped up a potato. She eyed it apprehensively.

"I promise it's good."

Stomach rumbling like thunder, she put the spoon in her mouth. The soup was warm and seasoned with salt and pepper, and the vegetables were cooked perfectly. Surprised, she drank the soup until there was nothing left but a little liquid at the bottom of the bowl. She sopped it up with the bread.

"How does that feel on your stomach?" the doctor asked, taking the tray.

She stared at him.

"Still not talking?"

Ellyssa offered him a small smile. That bit of communication pleased him. Doc's grin widened, and his eyes lit. He offered her a glass of water, which she accepted.

"Well, the least we can do is clean you up some. You don't smell like a flower garden."

He smiled as he said it, but she imagined he wasn't lying. The last shower she had had been the night she'd run away.

Doc went and poured some water in a basin and grabbed a washcloth. He set it on the table next to her, then uncovered her. Surprise registered when Ellyssa noticed her clothing had been replaced with a white gown. She had been seriously out of it.

After wringing out the cloth, he began wiping her arms and legs down. When he was done, he stuck the cloth back into the water, wrung it out, and handed it to her. "Why don't you clean…um…other parts?"

Turning around, the doctor went and stood between her cot and the entrance. Keeping her eyes on the male, she pulled the gown up and cleaned her lower regions. The effort exhausted her more than she'd like to admit. Done with the task, she tossed the cloth back into the basin and cleared her throat.

"Finished?"

She cleared her throat again.

Doc glanced over his shoulder before turning completely around. He grabbed a basin and filled it with water. "We'll get your hair later. Right now, you need to get some sleep."

Her gaze darted to the entrance.

The doctor leaned closer. "Don't worry about anything," he whispered. "I'll be sitting right over there." He pointed at the desk. "When you wake up, I'll bring you something with a bit more substance."

He removed the extra pillows and blankets, and Ellyssa settled onto her back. Her eyes followed him to the desk. From the top drawer, he took out a worn hardcover book. Wondering what he was reading, she drifted into sleep.

Rein navigated the long tunnels, his thoughts lingering on the girl they'd saved. Deep down, he knew it'd been dangerous for him to bring her back here; the others had protested, especially after she'd attacked them, but he couldn't leave her there to die. Her greyish skin, her eye sockets, dark and sunken, her knotted hair tangled into dirty clumps—he just couldn't do it.

He knew, as soon as he'd seen her, there was something about her. Especially when her eyes popped open, the blue reminded him of parting clouds exposing the sky after a rain. Then, even in her condition, the ferocity of her attack. She was definitely special.

He paused just outside the main hall. Jordan was speaking with the others, delivering orders. The frail frame of the elder stood in the center of room. He beckoned with a thin finger to Terri, a young girl with pretty features. She helped him shuffle to the wooden bench. Grunting, the elder sat and watched as the community worked together, picking up the remaining supply boxes stacked against the wall and moving them into the kitchen and storage areas.

Rein joined him, and the old man's full lips curled, deepening his wrinkles and exposing missing front teeth. Sweat beaded at the hair-line where his grey dreadlocks hung in clumps around his head, and his dark skin glowed under the fluorescent lights. He lifted a wrinkled hand and put it on Rein's shoulder.

"How is our guest?" he mumbled, as if speech further tired him.

"She's awake."

"I'm glad to hear it."

"I'm not so sure I am."

"Why?"

"I think I made a mistake. Her being here can expose us all."

Jordan cackled. "You did right, bringing her here."

"She's not talking."

"Great, not only is she using our limited resources, but she is refusing to give us information. That's the reason you brought her here, wasn't it, Rein?"

Rein swiveled around on the bench at the sound of Woody's voice.

Woody toted a small wooden crate, filled with ammo, over to Jordan. His ash-blond hair was darkened by the sweat running from his hairline down the side of his face.

He stared pointedly at Rein before setting the crate down in front of their leader. "This is the last."

Jordan pulled out a small box containing Remington SPC rounds. "Put the rest next to my pallet. I'll distribute it later." His black eyes rested on Rein as he handed him the ammo. "Tell our contact."

"We're scheduled to meet in a few days."

"Good." Jordan started to stand. Rein jumped up and helped the old man to his feet. "And don't worry about the girl. I trust your judgment."

Rein smiled, though he didn't feel he deserved the compliment. If he was wrong, he had risked everyone's life for nothing. The settlement founded after the Nazis had invaded would fall after all these years. He had known the chances, the possible danger, and he'd ignored the safety of the others because of a gut instinct. And, judging by the way Woody looked at him, his friend believed the same. His grey eyes flashed accusations every time he looked at Rein, like now.

"Would you stop it?" Rein asked, as he watched the old man walk away.

"Stop what?" Woody blinked innocently.

"You know what."

Sighing, he held his hands up as if in surrender. "Look, Rein, we've been best friends since we were kids. I'm telling you she is dangerous."

"I know. You keep reminding me."

Rein left the hall, doubt tugging at every fiber of his being. Only this doubt came with fair skin framed with white hair and sky-blue eyes that bore holes into him.

12

Dr. George Hirch entered the experiment room with Leland at his side. Light reflected off the glass cubicles that divided the room, and bounced off the white-tiled floor. Several assistants were busy within the cubicles, where they sat at tables across from his creations.

Sensing his approach, platinum blond heads turned, and four sets of intelligent, azure eyes settled on the doctor as the door closed behind him with a snick. His children were beautiful, like angels—lean, muscular, flawless complexions, hair the color of purity.

George waved, indicating for them to continue with their lessons. All at once, as if connected by a string, they focused their attention back on the assistants.

"Come, Leland." He paused at the first door, marked *Subject 64,* and watched Micah. The nineteen-year-old held out his hands and took a silver box. The doctor pushed the red button of the speaker located next to the door.

"What do you see, Micah?" asked the soft voice of the assistant. Dressed in the mandatory lab coat, the assistant leaned toward the young man. Long yellow locks flowed down her back.

Micah's eyes were closed while he ran his fingers along the box. He turned it over in his hands and felt along the other side. "A female in a black dress. She is crying. Tears are falling down her face. She's holding a picture of a male—her husband. She places the picture in this box with a wedding ring." He handed it back to the assistant.

"Good, Micah. Now, what about this one?" She handed him a torn piece of material. Blood spotted the cloth.

"Is that—"

"Shh." George held his hand up to Leland's face.

Again, Micah closed his eyes and rubbed his thumb over the material. When he opened them, his expressionless gaze rested on George. "It belongs to Ellyssa," he said, his voice monotone. "There is green—tall trees, plants, shrubbery. They are streaking by in a blur. She is cold. So very cold. And, she is hurt." The boy's face briefly twitched as if he could feel her pain.

"She is searching for something. Kansas City." Micah's gaze flicked back to George. "And she is muttering something about you."

The boy's strong jaw clenched and unclenched as his stare bore into the doctor. The tiny hairs on the back of George's neck stood erect. He handed the material back to the woman. "Why is that, *der Vater*?"

George looked around the room. All eyes, including those of the assistants, were on him. He faced Micah. "I do not know."

"Why would she run in the first place?" Micah asked.

"Until we find her, Micah, I am unable to perform the necessary tests for diagnosis." Doctor Hirch opened the door and went next to Micah. "Can you tell me why she has chosen Kansas City?"

"Kansas City is not her destination any longer. She seems to be lost."

"Where is she going?"

"*Der Vater*, you know I cannot see any farther than when the item was last with the owner."

George placed his hand on Micah's shoulder. "Thank you."

"You are most welcome."

"Continue with your lessons." He closed the door behind him.

"What now?" Leland mumbled.

"We wait."

Doctor Hirch went to the next cubicle marked *Subject 71*. Xaver stood at the back of the cubicle as a walnut-sized metal ball was launched at him. His rounded face was relaxed, nonchalant, as if bored. The ball stopped midair, as if it had hit an invisible barrier, and fell to the ground. Red digital numbers displayed 500 over smaller letters that read, "meters per second."

"Truly remarkable," whispered Leland.

"Yes," said the doctor. "The next test will be with bullets."

Leland shook his head. "He's only fourteen."

"Age is irrelevant."

"But...what about his safety? The experiment as a whole?"

The doctor's steely gaze settled on his assistant. "You are questioning me?"

"No, it's just..." Leland stepped back.

"May I remind you, my authority is not to be challenged by the likes of you."

"I understand," Leland responded, dropping the doctor's stare.

George watched him for a moment longer, then stepped past him, ignoring the empty cubicle marked *Subject 62* and stopping at *Subject 67*. Ahron stood with his back toward the wall. His thin, boyish frame was filling out nicely—baby fat had turned into chiseled features and a barrel chest. He was bigger and broader than Micah, even though he was three years younger.

His cubicle was set-up like Xaver's. Instead of balls, disks with sharpened edges were projected at the boy at regular intervals. George glanced at Leland, who watched, transfixed, as the boy flickered, then solidified. A disk quivered, embedded halfway into the wall behind him.

"Bullets next for him, too?" He did a poor job hiding his contempt.

"I think it would be appropriate."

Leland lifted a shoulder. "It just seems dangerous."

"Any weaknesses must be dealt with now, not at a critical time. It is why I created them."

He went to the very last cubicle. Aalexis—George's pride and joy—sat at the table across from her trainer. Blocks of various shapes and sizes had been placed in a straight line. The young girl's face displayed no emotion, but danger flashed in her eyes.

"Aalexis, just finish the training and then you may return to your room."

"I said no."

"Why won't you cooperate?" The nervous woman turned toward the doctor and shrugged.

Aalexis crossed her arms over her chest. "I told you, I am bored."

"Stack the blocks and you may leave."

"No," she said, her voice flat. Her forehead bunched, and the trainer's chair flew backward.

The woman toppled to the ground. Her scream cut short as her head bounced off the tile. The trainer didn't move.

"Aalexis!" George's stern tone hid the surprise. "You will stop."

The young girl stood and faced her creator. "As you wish, *der Vater*."

The doctor slid the door back. "Call the infirmary," he said to Leland as he entered. His assistant closed his mouth and nodded.

"What are you doing?" he asked, before he realized his inappropriate reaction. Straightening his jacket, he buried the shock he felt and composed himself, bringing to the forefront a calm demeanor for them to witness. He cleared his throat. "What are you doing?" he repeated.

"What I was trained to do," the young girl said. Her voice held no fluctuation. Her arms remained defiantly locked across her chest.

"You were never trained to attack people without orders."

"We were trained to respond to anger. I will not be subjected to any more tests."

"Go to your room."

"As you wish." The thirteen-year-old passed two interns as she walked away without glancing back.

George knelt next to the unconscious woman and lifted an eyelid. Then he ran his fingers through her hair until he found the lump forming on the side of her head. "She has a minor head injury. Watch her for signs of a concussion."

"Yes, sir," the intern responded.

The interns placed the trainer on the gurney and wheeled her away.

After they left, George addressed his assistant. "I want a full personality profile done on Aalexis. Do not have her practice for the next few days."

"What's happening?" Leland asked.

"I am not sure."

George scanned the other cubicles, but the rest of the children acted as if no altercation had happened just few feet away. Their young faces showed no sign of interest, as other children would have.

As expected, nothing fazed them.

13

"Hey. Are you awake?"

Doc's whispery voice grabbed hold of Ellyssa and yanked her from sleep. The older man hovered directly above her. Next to him stood Rein. His green eyes narrowed as he leered at her.

Feeling trapped, she tried to jump up but, like before, vises held her into place. Not as easily, though. Rein's face twisted in effort.

"Stop it, Rein."

"She just tried to attack us."

"No, we startled her."

Rein released her and stepped back.

A reassuring smile graced the doctor's lips. "It's okay. I brought you something to drink." Doc grabbed a glass from the tray. It was filled with watery orange liquid. "It's your lucky day. Orange juice." He helped prop her up and handed her the cool glass.

Ellyssa sipped while Doc removed the bandages. His eyes widened as his fingers ran over her wound. Only a small amount of discomfort accompanied the pressure.

"Hmm? It's healing faster than I would've expected. The gash is already closing up without the aid of stitches. I don't even think it's going to scar." Confusion crossed Doc's face. "Does this hurt?" He applied more pressure.

Ellyssa brought the glass down. The pain was still there but not too bad. She shook her head.

"Can you feel it?"

She nodded.

"Is it at all uncomfortable?"

Shrugging one shoulder, the corner of her mouth twitched.

He pressed again. "A little bit?"

She nodded once.

"It'd be a lot easier if you would talk."

She polished off her juice and held the glass out to him.

"Are you hungry?"

Her eyes widened, and she nodded with more enthusiasm.

"I'll get you something." He hesitated, looking at Rein.

"As long as she stays in the bed, I won't touch her."

Doc raised an eyebrow.

"I promise. Okay?"

The doctor walked toward the opening. Before he stepped out, he glanced back.

Frustrated, Rein waved his hands. "Just go."

"I'm trusting you," he said, and disappeared into the corridor.

Ellyssa listened to the fading steps, her gaze turning toward Rein. He watched her with the same amount of intensity and distrust. His eyes raked over her, scrutinizing her, and his jaw clenched so tightly the tendons in his neck jerked. Tensing, Ellyssa scooted against her pillow.

She grasped for his mind and saw herself through his confusion, wondering who she was and why she was there. Although still frail-looking, and her hair comparable to a bird's nest, her complexion was creamy again. Her strength was returning, and if needed, she could defend herself. His mind kept flashing to the night in the old store.

Never taking his eyes off her, Rein grabbed a chair and rolled it to the end of her cot, then took a seat. His arms, once again, crossed over his chest showing his tenseness, his distrust. He was much younger than she'd originally thought. Twenty, maybe twenty-one. Tanned, angular cheekbones, a straight nose, strong jawline, and hair that was a mess. Completely different than the males at The Center, Ellyssa found his dark features fascinating, attractive in a barbaric sort of way.

Her heart pattered.

"Who are you?" he asked.

She didn't answer.

He blew out air and rubbed his temple. "Why are you here?" he tried again.

When she didn't respond, he ran his fingers through his brown hair. "You're rather irritating."

Ellyssa's brow rose slightly.

"You've been here for almost a week. We've fed you, Doc healed you."

She stared at him.

"Look, are others coming?" Rein asked. "None of us want to hurt you, but we will if it comes to that." When she didn't answer, he rose to his feet and hovered threateningly over the end of the bed.

In less than a heartbeat, Ellyssa's training came to the forefront. No emotion, only self-preservation. Her muscles tightened, waiting to respond at a moment's notice. If Rein attacked, she would kill him.

Unmoving, they glared at each other. Then Rein threw his arms in the air and plopped back down in the chair. The wheels squeaked under his weight.

The threat removed, Ellyssa eased back. Warily watching him, she reached into his mind. Although Rein's face read anger, his insides felt worry, fear, and uncertainty for his friends and family. He couldn't bear the thought of something happening to them. He cared for them.

She'd never cared for anybody, nor had the emotion been reciprocated. Not by her siblings. Especially not by her father. To him, she was nothing more than a disposable weapon.

"Yes," she whispered.

He wheeled his chair over to the side of her bed. "Did you say something?"

"Yes, they will send others to find me," she answered, a bit more loudly.

He frowned. "Are you from Germany?"

Ellyssa thought that to be a strange question. "No. Why?"

"Your accent."

She shrugged.

"Hmm," he said, leaning forward. "Are you part of a search team?"

"No, I escaped."

He leaned closer. "You escaped?"

The closeness of Rein was unexpected. She could feel heat radiating off him. Strangely, her heartbeat quickened. She nodded.

"From where?"

"From The Center."

Disbelief slackened his jaw, and he scratched the side of his head as if perplexed by an unanswerable question. "The Center? In Chicago? Are you kidding me?"

Ellyssa shook her head.

The next instant, fury contorted Rein's features as he rose to his feet. He reached for her, but she was already on her feet on the opposite side of the cot. Blinking in surprise, he turned and stalked to the doorway.

"Do you know what you've done?" Rein asked. "What I've done?"

Waves of dizziness sloshed in Ellyssa's head from the sudden movement. Her muscles, not expecting the rush of adrenaline, trembled. Her vision swam, and her stomach uncomfortably tossed. She staggered back.

Closing his eyes, Rein ran his hand down his face. "I'm not going to do anything. Get back into bed before you hurt yourself and get me in trouble with Doc."

Ellyssa edged closer until her knee touched the cot. She wanted to see his true intentions, but the jackhammer had returned and ricocheted inside her skull.

"Please, lie down."

She hesitated for a second before doing what he asked. The scratchy canvas was welcoming, but the bed seemed to rock.

Rein stayed on the other side of the room, occasionally looking at her, mostly pacing. Ellyssa watched his blurry figure through slitted lids until she heard the doctor's footfalls.

Doc entered the room and stopped, his gaze jerking back and forth between them. "What's going on?" he asked.

"Your patient found her voice."

The older man's mouth puckered. "Oh, really."

"She's from The Center. They'll come for her."

Doc sat in the chair Rein had abandoned and leaned over with his hands clasped in front of him. "Are you part of a search team?"

Skeptical, Ellyssa didn't answer.

The doctor patted her hand. This time she didn't withdraw. "Hon, no one is going to hurt you. We have to know."

Rein paced behind the chair where the doctor sat, glowering at her as if she were a dangerous animal, worthy to be locked away in a cage. They had no clue how dangerous she could be. "She says she isn't," he interrupted.

Doc flashed the familiar smile she found herself growing used to. "Good. Why are you here?"

"She says she escaped."

Doc tossed Rein a look over his shoulder. "Would you let her speak?"

Rein's mouth popped open. Fighting back some remark dangling on the edge of his tongue, he pressed his lips together and folded his arms over his chest.

Ellyssa's eyes moved from the towering male to the soft face of the one who took care of her. "I escaped," she confirmed.

"Escaped? What do you mean? Were you in trouble?"

Her head felt cloudy, and the rush of words wanting to escape jumbled in her mind. She shook her head. "Not exactly," she uttered.

Doc took her hand and, even surprising herself, she let him. He didn't pose a threat, and his touch was warm, gentle…pleasing.

"It's okay. Take your time."

Ellyssa nodded.

"Why did you come here?"

"I was called," she mumbled.

"By who?"

Her eyelids felt so heavy. Her mind whirled. "A man with dark hair."

"What was his name?"

She felt herself drifting. "I do not know. He was special." Her eyes opened to the doctor.

"Special?" The voice sounded far away.

"Please."

"One more question. What's your name?"

"Ellyssa."

His grin broadened. "Nice to meet you, Ellyssa. My name is Mathew. Everyone calls me Doc." He gave her hand a gentle squeeze before letting go. "Get some sleep."

She heard the soft scraping of the wheels as the doctor stood. "Come with me," he whispered to Rein. Light steps stopped at the doorway. Whispering voices reached her ears.

"We can't keep her here. It's too dangerous," Rein said.

"She's still not ready to move. Besides, she might have information we need."

There was a long pause, and she started to sink into darkness. Rein's deep whisper stirred her.

"Do you think she was talking about Jeremy?"

"Maybe. I don't know."

Who was Jeremy? A vision of the dark-haired man being carried away by the police wavered with a dream-like quality.

Shuffling footsteps went into the hallway and faded down the corridor. The doctor lingered at the entrance for a moment, before she followed his distinct sound to the desk. The chair sighed when he sat. The whisper of pages flipping drifted over and lulled her to sleep.

14

The town of Deepwater looked just like the other five abandoned settlements Angela had searched. Weathered wood and brick buildings. Jagged shards of glass clung to window frames. The few remaining doors hung from rusted hinges.

Angela walked along the brittle red bricks that had once served as a sidewalk. She stepped carefully over the obstacle course of jagged edges and broken chunks. The last thing she needed was an injury.

"Detective Petersen," Dyllon yelled from behind her.

She turned as the captain jogged up to her. Of course, grinning.

"What can I do for you, Captain?"

"Dyllon."

"Fine." She sighed. "Dyllon."

The captain's smile widened, and Angela felt elated while her stomach cringed at the same time. "Good news. We have a lead."

"Where?"

"Over there. The dogs picked up her scent." He turned and pointed toward an old store.

To Angela's horror, members of the *team,* all just ill-prepared area police with their green uniforms, were entering the building, carrying equipment, stomping all over the evidence. "What are they doing?"

Dyllon's brow bunched, as if confused by her question. "Their jobs."

Finally, the break she'd been waiting for, and his people were in there contaminating the site. She couldn't believe the stupidity. "Why would you have them go in there before informing me?"

The captain opened his mouth to say something. Frustrated, Angela didn't give him a chance to respond. "Just never mind," she said, shoving past him.

Angela ignored his grunt of protest as she rushed down the street to intercept his people. But even with thoughts of the evidence being contaminated, the detective could barely suppress the grin tugging at her lips.

Stupid of the girl to seek cover during a storm. If she could've endured, the rain would have washed away her trail, washed away any chance of Angela finding her. Seems the vision of perfection was more flawed than Dr. Hirch believed.

She entered the rundown store with Dyllon on her heels. Thick dust coated everything from the ceiling to the floors. Small dunes formed against the back walls. Between the cracks of the floorboards, seeds had randomly taken root and grown into greenery. Empty shelves, which at one time had lined the walls, decorated the floors now, and an old counter with the glass broken out still held an antique cash register. Must and the underlying pungent scent of ammonia floated in the air and assaulted her senses.

Angela wrinkled her nose.

"Years of animal inhabitants and mold," Ranger Davis, area expert on what had been formerly known as Henry County, said. He stood against the wall next to the old counter; his long beak-like nose pointed into the air, resembling the snouts of the two German Shepherds sitting next to him. The dogs looked back and forth between the newcomers, their tails beating a tempo against the floor; their long black-spotted tongues lolled out, panting.

Two females and a male from the search party formed a half circle next to a mound of old rags. They looked up as the captain and detective approached.

"Careful where you step," said a woman, as if Angela was some rookie. Her hair curled like springs and bounced when she knelt down. "Look. There." Her finger swept across the area. "And there."

Angela's eyes followed from the large spot of coagulated dark crimson next to the rotting rags to an area where shoe prints littered the dust.

"And over there." Curly-head walked over to the crumpled shelves and knelt next to them. "This is recent." She handed one of the splintered shelves to Angela. Dust streaked across the long planks. Red dots were sprinkled along the grain.

"It seems there was some sort of scuffle."

"Plus, someone fired a shot," said the man. His voice was deep, like a trombone.

A large hole left jagged splinters in the wood above a mound of molded tarps. After Angela traced the edges with her fingers, she brought it to her nose. Gunpowder.

"Do you think she was shot?" the other woman asked. Her hair was straight as a pin, and thin. The pink of her scalp showed through the yellowish-blond.

The detective shook her head. "No, there isn't any splatter."

"She was taken," said Dyllon.

"Seems that way," Angela said while pushing the rags with the tip of her boot.

"Renegades?"

"Who else?"

Ranger Davis shook his head. "There hasn't been any activity here for years. Even before I took over."

Angela looked sideways at him. "That doesn't mean they aren't here."

"I'm very thorough at my job."

"I have no doubt." She turned to Dyllon. "I want an up-to-date map of this area. Satellite, if possible."

"No problem."

"I have all the information back at my office," Davis said, his voice carrying a hint of indignant annoyance.

"Great. That saves me time," said Dyllon.

"There has been no activity here. I conduct random patrols and investigate the area thoroughly."

Angela whipped around to face him, hands planted firmly on her hips. "There *is* activity here. Can you deny the proof?" She waved her hand. "It's everywhere."

Apparently, the expert had nothing more to say. He tightened his hold on the dogs' leashes and stormed out of the store. The way the floor groaned, Angela halfway expected the man to fall through in his tantrum. Once outside, Davis unleashed his companions. The dogs bounded happily out of view.

"I think you made him angry," Dyllon pointed out.

"Proof is proof. There is a nest of them, somewhere." She turned toward the woman with the springy hair. "Do a blood analysis against the sample on the shelves and the one on the floor. Also, find the shell casing."

She cast Dyllon a glance and nodded toward the door. He followed her onto the road. Out of earshot from the others and the disgruntled expert, she turned toward him. "Don't let the ranger out of your sight."

"I've known Davis for years. I completely trust him."

Angela's eyes narrowed. "I don't."

Dr. Hirch answered on the first ring. "*Hallo.*" The more he listened to Detective Petersen's report, the angrier he got. Retrieving his missing daughter was not going as he'd expected. Worse, the incompetent people he, himself, had put in charge were delaying his experiments. "Let me know of any further development."

He flipped the phone shut and tossed a pile of folders displaying the names of his *creations* on his desk.

Leland peeked over the monitor, his eyes glimmering with curiosity. "Well?"

Needing to calm himself, George waited a moment before he answered, "It seems Ellyssa has found friends."

"What does that mean?"

"It means someone has found her."

"Has she been harmed?"

A tic found residence in George's jaw. He fought to maintain control. "They do not know."

"What do they know?"

The doctor felt the last of his patience dwindling away. "There was some sort of altercation."

Leland leaned back in the computer chair, resting his arms behind his head. His fingers disappeared into his thick locks. "Renegades?"

The doctor nodded.

"Maybe she got away."

"Detective Petersen does not think so." Thoughtful, George's brow knitted together as he pulled Aalexis' file over to him.

He opened the folder to the blank-face stare of his youngest. What was going on with them? First, one escaped and another was growing defiant. He needed to finish his work before anything else went wrong.

"I have something to show you." Leland's voice broke into George's thoughts.

Still holding Aalexis' file, the doctor stalked to Leland's computer. "This had better be good."

"It's even better than good." The young man scrolled through the file menu of recent tapings until *Subject 67-Ahron* was highlighted. He double-clicked and hit the play button, then slowed the frames down.

Ahron stood at one end of a bulletproof chamber, his platinum hair glowing iridescent under the overhead lights. Thirteen meters away, an AR-15 rested on a tripod, bolted into the floor and targeted on his chest. The bolt slid back and ejected a shell casing when the rifle fired. While a small wisp of smoke dissipated in the air, the speaker boomed. The boy completely disappeared as the bullet passed through and drilled a hole in the target behind him. Ahron returned, solid, unharmed.

With his cursor, Leland moved a slide bar down, sectioning each second into tenths. "Count from the moment he disappears until he reappears."

As the frames ticked by, George counted. "Seventeen."

"Yes, three-tenths longer than before. Now, watch this." He went back to the previous screen and clicked on Xaver's file. Same setup as Ahron's, Xaver also stood at one end of the chamber, his young face appearing bored. Again, an echo of the rifle boomed from the speakers, right after smoke appeared. The bullet fell to the ground a meter away from Xaver.

Leland spun around and faced his mentor. "I've been measuring every test. The time increases, even if it is minutely. You were right."

Pride lifted George's spirits, a smile pulling the corners of his mouth. His cause was not lost; his prodigies' powers were growing. He would get Ellyssa back. He just needed to exert patience and not forget his self-control. His plans would come to fruition, a perfect creation born.

The smile on his face grew.

He could only imagine the manic expression his assistant must be witnessing. Blinking, he turned away and concentrated on his composure. If he was to be the bringer of greatness, he had to keep his sentiments in check.

"Their powers are growing," George said, managing to keep his voice level. "Tomorrow, I want you to start new instructions. I want Ahron to stay invisible longer. Xaver needs to extend his energy shield to protect others."

"What? Who would we use as guinea pigs?"

Emotions under control, George leveled his eyes on Leland's. "There are imperfects at your disposal."

"I-I can't do that."

"Of course you can." George clapped the assistant on the shoulder. "The outcome is worth the sacrifice." He paused for a moment as he tossed Aalexis' file on Leland's desk. "The test results show no indication of any type of breakdown in emotional responses."

"Maybe pubertal changes," Leland suggested, his voice distant.

"I tested for the possibility." George paced back to his desk. "Nothing, but there is one thing."

"What?"

"Aalexis is a very powerful, intelligent teenager. Superior to all others The Center has created thus far. And she knows it. I would say it was more of a God complex incomparable to all the others. She feels we are wasting her time and her talent on batteries of tests. She feels she has already proven herself." He shrugged. "The tests are useless on her."

Leland's eyebrows thrust upward. "Great. A thirteen-year-old narcissist."

A hint of a smile played across Dr. Hirch's lips. "Yes."

"It could lead to dangerous consequences."

The doctor shook his head. "Not at all. She is obedient to me. We just need to find something to challenge her. Something beyond her current capabilities."

"Like what?"

"So far, everything she has done has been in a controlled environment without extraneous variables. We need to see how well she manipulates matter while under pressure."

15

The monitor lit up, illuminating the small workspace at the desk. A blinking command told the user to enter a password. After checking over her shoulder, Ellyssa slipped her flash drive she used for lessons into the USB port and entered a sequence of symbols. In less than a minute, the command hardcoded into the system and opened a backdoor. A list of files popped onto the screen.

She scrolled through the list until she found Dr. Hirch's file. She clicked open and another list of subject numbers, from fifteen to seventy-six, came into view.

Seventy-six? There was a seventy-six?

Ellyssa clicked on a random file and a colored photo of a female baby downloaded onto the screen. The face of what should have been a cherub was completely deformed. One eye drooped below the other, and the mouth and nose slanted strangely to the side. Two stubs stuck out from the side of the ribcage, resembling unformed nubs on a fetus. Its tiny feet were twisted inward. The baby had been terminated a couple of weeks ago.

Ellyssa clicked back to the subject numbers and scrolled to number twenty. A black and white photo of a female dressed in a hospital gown appeared. Her eyes were widened in horror and a silent scream was forever plastered on the digital face.

Frowning, Ellyssa wondered what had happened to her. She double-clicked the file next to the picture and read about a young female known as Subject 20, Ida. The emotional breakdown after she had lit test subjects on fire with nothing more than a thought. Ordinary citizens had been used for testing. The subject couldn't handle the guilt.

Guilt...the word floated in Ellyssa's head as she followed the link offered at the side, and read Dr. Hirch's notes. According to the doctor, Ida was less than a savory soldier. She was weak and ineffective. Her IQ was average. Her ability to start fires was on a hit-and-miss basis. She'd been terminated.

Guilt?

"Hey?"

The doctor's voice hovered along the edges of Ellyssa's daydream. She flipped around to Doc's wide smile. Her lips twitched in response.

"I brought you some lunch." He held a red tray.

"Thank you, Doc. I am hungry." She crossed her legs and positioned the tray on the crook of her knees. A slice of bread, a blob of peanut butter, and a small glass of milk.

"Please, call me Mathew. It'd be nice to have someone refer to me by my real name." He looked apologetic at the food. "I know it's not much."

The scent of garlic clung to her caregiver's clothes. He smelled wonderful. She thought about talking to the doctor about his lunch so she could steal the image, but that would be intrusive. And, for some unforeseen reason, doing so seemed wrong. The images she'd already picked from him had been, overall, helpful, and goodness thrummed inside him.

Ellyssa liked the doctor, which was completely foreign in her limited experience with emotions. She hadn't ever liked anyone before. Including her father and her siblings. Even stranger, she also trusted the doctor after all he'd done for her.

The emotions she'd kept guarded her entire life were finally free to roam. No worries about being discovered, about being punished.

"It is fine, thank you."

Mouth watering like an open floodgate, she swabbed peanut butter onto the bread and took a bite, then washed the stickiness down with warm milk made from a powder mix.

"The others will come around. They're just a little shocked to learn you came from The Center."

She nodded while she took another bite.

"I was hoping we could talk."

Ellyssa stopped chewing and swallowed the bread in one lump.

Mathew sat on the edge of her cot, clamping his hands together. "I know it's hard to trust. But there are some things we need to know."

"Like what?"

He looked away. "I've been trying to understand." His gaze swept back to her. "Can you describe the man who called to you?"

She placed her bread on the plate. "I really did not see much of him. The *Gestapo* brought him to The Center. I was intrigued. I had never seen anyone with dark hair before. He looked fit, but dirty. He wore a dark short-sleeved shirt and camo pants, like you and Rein, and all the others I have seen, wear."

"What did you mean by him calling you?"

Ellyssa had known, eventually, someone was going to ask her. How could she explain without giving herself away? She might trust the doctor, but not enough to reveal her secret.

"He yelled in my head, *Kansas City*. I do not know how to explain it. I just came. I had to."

The expression filling Mathew's face was hard to read. Shocked surprise mixed with disbelief?

"It was Jeremy." He looked down at the floor. "It had to be." He pulled at the fingers of one hand.

"Jeremy?" The name rolled off Ellyssa's tongue.

The doctor nodded as his face fell. "He had the ability to speak to you without vocal words. Only a few of us knew about his ability."

Ellyssa's face slackened and her jaw dropped, mimicking the shocked surprise Mathew's face had held. Renegades had abilities? These skills were only supposed to be possible through genetic engineering. The Center would be very interested in these extra senses developing within inferior beings.

Ellyssa felt... She really couldn't identify the sensation. Not good? Shameful? These people who'd helped her were lots of things, but not inferior. Her father had been wrong, wrong on so many accounts. Inferior beings couldn't have developed a way of survival as these people had.

Averting his eyes, Mathew clamped his mouth closed as if he'd said too much. She could read the confusion on his face as he struggled between what he should and shouldn't tell her. After a few seconds of silence, he straightened his spine and pulled his shoulders back like he had come to a decision.

"What happened to him?" he asked.

"I think he was terminated," Ellyssa said. "His voice…stopped."

Sadness flowed into Mathew's eyes. "I see." He leaned close and touched her hand. "Thank you," he whispered. There was a hitch in his voice.

A rolling sound hummed down the rocky ground of the corridor. "Let's keep this between you and me for right now." Standing, he replaced his previous smile as if nothing had transpired, unlike before, it didn't reach his eyes. "It's your lucky day," he said as a female dressed in the same clothes as everyone else came in pushing a cart with a bowl on top. On the bottom shelf sat a pitcher with steam rising from it.

"We're washing your hair."

Ellyssa's heart thumped pleasantly at the thought of being clean. She'd never imagined little things such as washing hair could bring such joy. It was a little silly, but she couldn't stand the filth any longer. Her head felt like a thick, muddy tomb encased her scalp. She hurriedly gulped down the rest of her lunch while the doctor grabbed a bottle, towels, and a brush from the cabinets.

The female stared at Ellyssa, a small grin twitching at the corners of her full lips. She was tall, thin, and fit. Her eyes were crystal blue and her features were pleasing, with high cheekbones and a small chin. Waves of blond hair cascaded around her shoulders. An acceptable citizen, according to society's standards.

Her manners weren't up to par, though. "You look awful," she said, her nose curled in disgust.

"I'm sure she appreciates your evaluation," Mathew remarked as he placed the items on the cart.

"Hey, I call it as I see it." The female smiled and took hesitant steps toward Ellyssa with her hand extended, as if trying to tame a small animal. "I'm sure you don't remember me, you were pretty out of it, but I'm Trista. I helped you get settled onto your cot."

Ellyssa eyed her offer of friendship warily.

The smile faltered. "It's okay. I don't have cooties."

Ellyssa glanced at Mathew. He nodded encouragingly.

Trust.

She shook her hand once, quickly releasing afterward. The gesture pleased the newcomer.

Beaming, Trista said, "I have something else for you." She bounced to the cart and showed Ellyssa a pair of pants and a black shirt. Trista eyed the clothes, then Ellyssa. "I think they'll fit. Good guess on my part." She spun around. "You need any help?" she asked the doctor.

"I don't think so. We got it covered."

"Suit yourself. Bye, Ellyssa. It was nice to finally meet you." Trista's voice followed her out the door.

"Can you stand?" the doctor asked as he wheeled the chair over to the cart.

Afraid of getting sick like earlier, she eased onto her feet, faltered, and slowly stepped toward the chair. Her natural grace was gone. Her muscles felt strange and foreign to her, but at least they supported her.

Mathew smiled as she moved toward him. "I think it's time for you to get some exercise," he said, as if reading her thoughts. "It'll make you feel better. We'll start on that tomorrow. Would you like that?"

"Yes."

"Good. Have a seat," he said with a wave of his hand. "I'll help you get started."

Surprisingly without hesitation, Ellyssa sat and leaned her head back, dipping her hair into the water, completely vulnerable to attack. Mathew grabbed the pitcher and wet down the rest of her head. He handed her a bottle.

"It's homemade," he said, smiling.

She poured the shampoo into her hand, the scent of honeysuckles sweetening the air, and she began scrubbing her head. Almost immediately, her head felt lighter as the grime loosened away.

"One second." Mathew dumped the old water out into a basin and filled the pitcher from his supply. "This won't be as warm, but it'll do the job."

Cool water ran through her hair. As he rinsed away the soapy dirt, she took her trust a step further and closed her eyes. When he was done, he wrapped her hair in a towel and handed her the brush.

"Enjoy."

She vigorously dried her hair, then worked the brush through the tangled strands, happy she'd cut it. At the old length, the bristles would have snagged in the knots. She pulled the brush through, over and over, until her hair was almost dry. When she was done, she placed the brush on the table, hoping he would let her keep it.

Mathew pulled a cracked mirror from his desk. "Have a look."

The person who looked back at her was almost recognizable. Her cheeks were fuller, her skin naturally milky white, her eyes clear, and her hair glistened under the lights. She ran her fingers through the tresses.

The doctor shook his head. "You look a million times better than you did a few days ago. Your resilience never ceases to amaze me."

Aside from her father monotonously telling her she'd perform well—if you could call that praise—no one had ever complimented her before.

Unsure of the correct reaction she should display, she uttered, "Thank you." A smile touched the corner of her lips, but fell away when memories of her father hitting her for showing happiness followed.

Mathew studied her for a moment, a frown deepening his wrinkles. "I have something for you," he finally said. He went to his desk and pulled two books from the drawer. "I thought you might be interested in reading to help pass the time. These are my favorites."

Unable to speak, Ellyssa took the proffered books. The leather felt smooth and worn from years of use. She ran her finger over the indentations of the titles written in gold. Barely readable, one said *Of Mice and Men* by someone named John Steinbeck, the other was labeled Mary Shelley's *Frankenstein*. No one had ever given her anything before. Touched, her eyes felt strange as a tear formed. An unusual reaction to something that should've made her feel happy. She blinked it away.

"They are very old. And treasured. Please be *very* careful with them."

"Thank you," she finally responded.

Mathew beamed. "Have you read either of those?"

Ellyssa shook her head. "No. I was not allowed to read fiction."

"Never?"

"Novels are a waste of time, not lending any educational value," she recited her father's words.

The doctor's face scrunched. "They bring to life another world. Of events. Of people. They open the door to your imagination. They make you think."

"They do not teach you anything."

"They teach you everything. About love, life, people, the thrill of winning, the sadness of losing. They teach you about people's faults, and overcoming all odds. Read them first and then judge."

She couldn't help but smile at his exuberance. "I will."

Just when she thought his grin couldn't grow anymore, Mathew surprised her with a positively huge one, exposing his teeth. Ten years erased off his age. He patted her on the shoulder. "Plus, it'll give you something to do tonight while I'm away."

As if on cue, Ellyssa heard others coming down the hall. Their whispers entered the room before they did.

Rein, Jason, and a petite female walked in. All of them were dressed in the same gear, down to the firearms slung over their shoulders.

The female was not at all what Ellyssa considered attractive. Braided red hair swung around a very pale face, marked with huge red freckles. Thin lips were pressed together into a tight line. The longer she stared at Ellyssa with her hate-filled beady eyes, the whiter her knuckles turned where she clutched the rifle.

Without entering the female's mind, Ellyssa knew the redheaded female hated her. Her facial expression was easy to read.

Apparently feeling the tension in the air, the doctor squeezed Ellyssa's shoulder before addressing the others. "I'll be ready in a couple," he said as he walked to his desk to grab his backpack. "Candy, do you mind grabbing the first aid kit?"

"I owe you one," the woman snarled in a musical voice, unbefitting her appearance. Ellyssa recognized her from the night she had been captured.

Frowning, Mathew shot the woman a glower. "Candy, I hardly think she knew what she was doing."

"Doesn't matter." Candy tipped her head up, then marched over to the metal cabinets.

Ellyssa tore her gaze from Candy and placed it on Rein. He was looking at her, his jade eyes questioning. Ellyssa's heart picked up speed, and the small hairs on the back of her neck tingled. She didn't like it…she didn't think. Feeling strangely uncomfortable, she blinked and looked at Jason. He wasn't paying any attention to her at all.

Mathew handed Rein the bag. "I'd like a word with you."

Rein followed the doctor to his desk. Mathew gestured while he spoke in hushed words. Ellyssa thought she heard Jeremy but wasn't sure. Rein looked shocked, then sick.

Finally, the two parted, and Mathew returned to Ellyssa's side. "Who's staying?" he asked to no one in particular.

"I am," answered Jason.

His lips pulled down into a scowl. "I'm not—"

"It'll be fine," Rein interrupted.

The doctor stared at Rein for a moment, then placed his hand on Ellyssa's shoulder. "I won't be back until tomorrow. We have…things to do."

Ellyssa nodded.

"This is my corner here," Mathew said, pointing at Jason. "You will stay on the outside of the door. There isn't anything she will need."

"Yeah, yeah. Whatever." Jason pulled the strap of the gun and walked out the door.

As the others left, Mathew walking behind them, Ellyssa settled against her pillow. She let her mind drift away and slid into Jason's thoughts. He was examining his filthy fingernails as he thought about coming in and talking to her. Sitting in the chair next to her bed, her laughing at his wittiness. Then Jason's thoughts drifted to him holding her and pressing his mouth against hers…hard.

Disgusted, anger raised its head and she tensed.

Ellyssa yanked free of his thoughts and pulled the covers over her shoulders. If he decided to act on his thoughts, she'd tear him apart. Part of her wanted to just for him thinking his sick desires.

She sat and waited for what seemed like hours, occasionally poking inside his head. His thoughts shifted quickly from one thing to another. At one intrusion, he thought about being in bed with Candy. *Repulsive.* Another time, images of fried chicken and potatoes lingered. Her stomach growled. Eventually, his thoughts clouded over into fuzzy pictures of people and colors.

Positive he wouldn't wake, she picked up *Of Mice and Men.* She flipped through the well-loved pages; the scent of old leather was enjoyable. Relaxing against her pillow, she read the beginning of the classic.

16

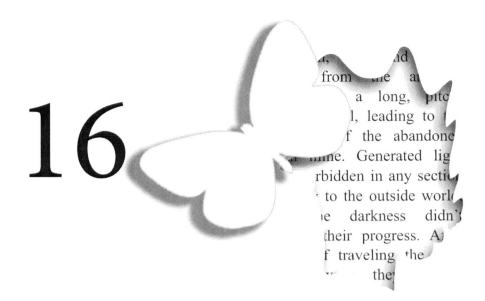

Rein, Doc, and Candy went from the artificial light into a long, pitch-black tunnel, leading to the entrance of the abandoned coal mine. Generated light was forbidden in any section leading to the outside world, but the darkness didn't hinder their progress. After years of traveling the unlit passageways, they stepped without worry about tripping or bumping into rocky overhangs or old beams.

Upon rounding the final corner, the doctor's and Candy's heads were silhouetted against dusky light, pouring through a rectangular slit leading outside. Originally, the opening had been larger, but with the fear of discovery, the first Renegades to establish the settlement had worked to cover the hole, arranging rocks and mounds of dirt to appear as if the manmade cave had collapsed.

The old mine had been overlooked for years until the searches for remaining people had finally ceased, except for the yearly patrols conducted by the ranger, Davis. The Renegades had been careful not to bring any suspicion to the area for decades. At least, until Rein had introduced Ellyssa to their hideout.

Rein didn't even know what to think of her. Her unusual demeanor was alien, like she'd survived with limited human contact or in a vacuum. Her facial expressions seemed forced and hesitant, as if the appropriate responses were unfamiliar to her. Plus, he held no doubt that, if she hadn't been on the verge of dying, she would've kicked all their asses. With or without their firearms.

And how had she recovered so fast?

It'd only been eight days.

Ellyssa should still be broken, bruised, feeling crappy, yet she looked wonderful. After being washed, her hair was lustrous and her eyes vibrant, piercing blue contrasting against her flawless, porcelain skin. He liked looking at them.

Then, the whole business with Jeremy. He couldn't think about that right now. It'd have to wait until they returned and talk to Jordan.

Rein crawled through the small opening after Doc and Candy. The first stars shimmered into view as the dark blanket of night worked to cover the heavens. The thick, balmy air held the hint of impending rain. Humidity clung to his skin. He pulled at the fabric stuck to his stomach.

"God, I hate this," said Candy. She reached up and swatted the back of her neck. "Damn mosquitoes."

"Shh," said Doc as he ducked behind a bush.

"Don't shh me."

Rolling his eyes, Rein followed behind as they silently glided through the vegetation. Fifteen minutes later, they moved out of the brush onto the dirt service road used by the ranger during his routine patrols.

"Stay on the edge where the dirt is packed. We have to be very careful now," said Rein.

"I told you this would happen," said Candy pointedly.

Rein didn't bother replying. What could he say?

Rein stepped quietly behind Candy, her braids bouncing in rhythm with her steps. He hoped she'd forget he was even there. Ever since he'd turned down her advances, he hadn't been in the best standing with her. Apparently, he'd really pissed her off. Not that he cared. The girl had a way of setting his teeth on edge.

As if Candy knew what he was thinking, she glanced over her shoulder with a smug look. "Don't think I didn't notice the way you were staring at the little spy."

Stunned, Rein's steps faltered. "What the hell are you talking about?"

"You know exactly what I'm talking about."

Was she insane? Check that—she was. "No, I don't."

"Whatever." Candy snickered.

As usual, she'd crawled under Rein's skin. Irritated, he contained the urge to whop her upside the head, sending her bouncing braids twirling. Barely.

Silence enveloped the group as they turned onto a short drive leading to a barn. Part of the roof had caved in years before Rein was born, and the south wall sagged dangerously. Seemingly unusable, it was the perfect hiding spot.

Doc and Candy stood watch on each side of the drive, while Rein made his way to the door. Grunting, he worked against gravity and bent wheels to slide the door back and out of the way.

Filtered moonlight streamed through the doorway and glinted off a 1934 Oshkosh Model F. Nothing more than a block of rusty metal sitting on bald tires. The old truck still ran, though, thanks to Woody, who had a knack with all things mechanical, and the members of the resistance who could supply the parts.

Rein hopped into the cab and slid the key into the ignition. A prayer later, the engine sputtered, coughed, wheezed, then sprang to life. A gunshot boom sounded, and a plume of smoke shot from the exhaust; the puttering smoothed to gentle grunting. The gears ground when he shifted the stick into first and released the clutch. The truck clattered to the end of the drive.

Much to Rein's dismay, Candy jumped into the cab first, followed by Doc. She gave Rein a big, toothy grin as she settled next to him. Annoyance working his jaw, he released the clutch, and the truck jerked onto the road.

Using what little light the cloudy sky provided, Rein drove slowly. The worn tires grated across the dirt. He tried to ease over the potholes and ruts, but the moon stayed hidden behind wispy clouds, making navigation hard. The truck bounced along, jostling the passengers and rattling their teeth.

Content to sit in silence for the next three hours of their journey, Rein stared straight ahead and tried to ignore Candy, who kept knocking into him every time the truck went over a hole. Doc had to ruin it.

"I think we're wrong."

Afraid of where the conversation was headed, Rein gripped the steering wheel tighter. "What are you talking about?"

"About Ellyssa. I don't think she's a spy."

Rein rolled his eyes. "She might not be, but she's something. She's from The Center."

Candy nodded her head.

"She also said she escaped," reminded Mathew.

"Yeah, spies never lie," Candy said, sarcastically.

Doc turned toward Rein. Although he couldn't see the older man's eyes, he definitely felt them.

"I don't think she's lying. Do you…really?"

Rein didn't reply. He had no answer as to whether or not he believed Ellyssa a spy, but she *was* hiding something. Part of him thought he should've heeded the others' advice the night they'd found her and left her for dead. But he couldn't.

"Are you guys serious?" Candy chimed. "I can't believe the two of you."

Doc shrugged. "I'm just saying."

Candy snapped her mouth closed and crossed her arms over her chest. She'd stopped bouncing into Rein, which suited him just fine. Her hatred for Ellyssa ran deep. He remembered how embarrassed she'd been when Ellyssa had bested her. It'd taken all three of them to hold the redhead back from attacking the unconscious blonde. Candy wasn't someone you wanted to piss off.

For the next two hours, the cab of the truck was filled with the sounds of wheels and the rattling of the engine. When they reached the outskirts of an abandoned town, he pulled off the road and behind an outcropping. Doc jumped out, and Candy scooted over to follow him.

Humidity rushed through the open door, along with the soft hum of insects. Uncomfortable beads of sweat formed on Rein's brow, and his clothes became a second skin. He grabbed the rifle and the flashlight from under the seat, and joined Doc and Candy on the other side of a ditch, next to a line of thick bushes.

Rein ducked under the vegetation and stepped onto a worn path next to an old tin silo. Compared to the other buildings they used for storage, the silo was in great condition. The roof wasn't bowed, and the walls were still solid. Even the door hung straight.

He silently walked along the path to the front of the structure. Maybe it was his nerves, but the night held an eerie quality with the leaves rustling in the breeze. Then, a crunching noise sent a shiver of alarm up Rein's back.

"Shh," Rein said, bringing up his rifle at the same time a raccoon jumped out, silver eyes glinting under the beam of the flashlight. The rodent sniffed the air before disappearing into the undergrowth. Relieved, he turned off the light.

"Jumpy much?" Candy said.

Since Ellyssa, yes, he was. Someone *would* be coming for her. It was only a matter of time. Letting the comment slide, Rein said, "Let's just hurry up and get this over with."

Rein stepped inside and clicked on the flashlight. Darkness scampered back as the light reflected off the tin. He swept the beam back and forth, revealing the dusty wooden floor as he advanced into the storage silo.

"Davis," he called.

No one answered.

"Davis," yelled Rein, his voice echoing in the other room.

"I thought he was supposed to meet us," said Doc.

"I thought so, too."

Doc shrugged. "Maybe he got tied up."

"Maybe." Rein agreed, but deep down he didn't believe it.

Davis usually showed as expected, except for a few rare occasions, and at those times, their contact had previously warned them. A sense of foreboding rooted in Rein's chest. He swept the beam across the floor to the right. As expected, crates had been stacked in the corner.

"Let's get the stuff and go. I want to be back before morning," Rein said, lifting one of the boxes.

17

Ellyssa remained in a low Chen-style stance, her slower phases accumulating energy before she let loose powerful moves, when Mathew entered with her tray. The aroma of eggs and ham lingered in the air, as he carefully passed by to avoid her flowing movements. The scent was tempting, and despite the fact she had not completed her *Tai Chi* routine, her mouth watered and she could no longer concentrate.

"Hope you're hungry," Mathew said. "I have a great menu planned for the day." Chuckling at his own joke, he placed the tray on the table. "Bon appetite."

Ellyssa smiled at Mathew's mispronunciation. Of course, she doubted the Renegades had the opportunity to study languages as she and her siblings had. All of them were fluent in French, Italian, Spanish, and others. "I think you mean *bon appétit*."

Chagrin blushing Mathew's cheeks a slight pink, he shrugged.

"Now I know where you went the other night," Ellyssa said, eyeing the food.

He smiled. "Mission accomplished."

Ellyssa hopped onto her bed and pulled the tray onto her lap. "What is the occasion? Why all this?" She shoved a spoonful of eggs into her mouth. After days of boring food, the scrambled eggs tasted wonderful. She followed them with a piece of smoked ham.

"Well, you're going to have a visitor today."

She stopped chewing and eyed him warily.

"I think it's time you meet Jordan."

Ellyssa swallowed. "Jordan?"

"Yes, especially if you're going to be staying with us for awhile."

Setting her spoon down, she looked at him. "Staying with you is not a good idea."

Mathew sat on the corner of the cot. "Where else are you going to go?"

She shrugged. "I do not know."

"What do you plan on doing?"

Ellyssa had no idea. "I do not have an answer for that either."

He leaned over and patted her on the thigh. "Eat."

As Mathew grabbed one of his beloved books and leaned against his desk, Ellyssa picked up her spoon and continued eating, but the enthusiasm was gone. What *was* she going to do? From a young age, she had been taught that Renegades were the enemy and needed to be terminated. But the people she'd met here treated her differently than she'd ever been treated before.

Like she was human, instead of an experiment.

What surprised Ellyssa the most was that part of her wanted to stay. To belong. The other part realized the danger, if she did stay. There was no doubt that her father would find her. A struggle raged inside and rolled around with the new sense of belonging. To have people who truly cared for her, like in the family homes she'd passed in Chicago when she'd wondered what that type of life would've been like.

Her appetite completely diminished, she pushed the now rubbery, congealed eggs around on the plate.

"Done?" a deep voice asked.

Ellyssa looked toward the opening. Rein stood inside, his dark hair framing a face set into a frown. At least his arms weren't crossed over his chest this time. As soon as he spoke, Mathew closed the book and stood up from his perch.

"Can I have a word with you?" Rein asked her.

She lifted a shoulder and set her unfinished breakfast on the table.

The doctor picked up her tray. "I'll be right back."

Mathew stopped at the door and whispered something to Rein before he left. Ellyssa thought about popping into either of their heads to find out what the secrecy was about, but, by the look on Rein's face, she figured she would find out soon enough.

"Do you mind if I have a seat?" Rein asked as he wheeled the chair over next to her cot.

"Please." She crossed her legs.

Inhaling, Rein plopped into the chair and leaned forward, resting his elbows on his thighs. For a long time, he didn't say anything. Just sat hunched over, looking down at the floor.

Ellyssa respected his time to gather his words, as she admired the spikes sticking from his head in no particular order. His muscular shoulders stretched the fabric of his black shirt, and his biceps rippled when he wrung his hands together.

Finally, Rein lifted his eyes and settled them on her, the dark green pulling her in. Her heart picked up speed and her stomach formed a ball. Unexpected, unexplainable, and pleasing, she wavered between liking the feeling and hating it.

"Jeremy." Rein paused and waited for a response. Ellyssa nodded, and he continued, "Was part of this community. He went to Chicago to meet with a member of the resistance. Doc and I think he is the one that you saw. Will you tell me all that happened?"

"I already told Mathew."

His face softened, changing the hard countenance to one of pleading. "I know. Will you tell me?"

Unable to speak while his two jade eyes bore a hole straight through her, Ellyssa glanced away and floated into his mind. Rein was concentrating on her. Her hair had started to grow out some. Not surprising, as it grew fast, almost as fast as her body healed. Her eyes flashed, livening her fair complexion. His mind drifted to her body, which led to images of the night in the old town. He wondered if she was dangerous. If she was a spy. He didn't want to believe such things; yet, he still wondered.

Ellyssa couldn't blame him. Under the current conditions, she would've thought the same things. Besides, in spite of his curiosity and confusion, nothing screamed betrayal. He was being sincere.

She looked back at him. "I was going to...training, when the *Gestapo* brought him in. He was struggling in their arms. I stopped and watched. I had never seen anyone with dark hair. He looked at me and his voice entered my mind. He told me *Kansas City*. Later that night, while I was in my room, he found me again, shouting the same thing. Then, his voice suddenly stopped."

Rein nodded, as if he understood why the communication had been broken. "Not many knew Jeremy was special. I was one of them. Jordan and Doc." He paused for a moment, as if gathering his thoughts, before he spoke again. "Then you just left?"

Ellyssa nodded.

Rein looked away. "He was supposed to meet some...people in Kansas City." After a long moment, he turned back toward her. "Did you work at The Center?"

Ellyssa hesitated, unsure how much she should say. The Center had been her home, after all. "No," she finally said.

Rein raised his eyebrows, encouraging her to continue.

"I was a student."

He blinked. "I don't understand. The Center's not a school."

"That is correct. It technically is not a school. But it was for me. It was my school and my home. I was born there."

"What?"

Ellyssa hesitated, wondering if she should tell him everything. She probed his mind again. No threat or danger populated his thoughts, just a cloud of confusion.

What was the saying? "What the hell"? Now, instead of being invited to stay, they'd truly understand the danger and force her to leave. The thought hurt. Her chest felt the weight.

Carefully, Ellyssa picked the words needed without exposing all her monstrous secrets. She masked her face in preparation for his expected response of anger and resentment. "I am genetically engineered."

Rein's expression fell, lips slightly parted. She noticed how full they were and the pinkish tint. Unlike his face, his body went rigid.

Dumbfounded, words stuck in Rein's throat. He couldn't move, as if all brain function had ceased, while his mind tried to wrap around what Ellyssa had just said.

"I thought The Center devised training for *Gestapo* and military operations."

"They do. My father's research is...not well known amongst the general population."

Pulling his hand through his hair, Rein leaned back in his chair. Genetic research was not a secret amongst the Renegades; they were kept well-informed. But they were actually engineering people at The Center?

He took in a deep breath, and the words rushed out when he exhaled. "What do you mean? You weren't born?"

"Of course I was born. I was not hatched." Ellyssa seemed a bit indignant. A second later, what little emotion she had expressed faded away, replaced with a void expression.

"That's not what I meant."

"A proper female was selected as my incubator. By definition, she would be considered my birthing mother, though I never met her," Ellyssa said in a robotic-like tone.

"They took you from her."

"Technically, she had no right to me. She was paid for her services."

"You never knew her?"

"No, nor any other female figure who would be considered like a mother. Only assistants and nurses."

A mixture of emotions twirled in Rein—horror, shock, pity. Worse of all, he couldn't believe how calm she was about the whole thing, with her blank face and unemotional eyes. Trying to hide the feelings that he knew were playing across his face like a collage, he stood up and walked to the desk. He picked up the book and pretended to examine the cover.

"That bothers you?"

What was he supposed to say? *Yes, that's weird.* He set the book down and turned toward her. She still held the same blank expression, as if nothing ever troubled her.

"If it makes you feel better, I know *mein Vater*."

Lines formed above the bridge of Rein's nose. "*Mein Vater?*"

"My father," she explained. "He is the one who created me and raised me. I guess you would consider him my family."

Rein felt his mouth fall open. "Created you?"

"The DNA of my father's sperm and a donated egg were modified, then fertilized outside of the womb. He then used In Vitro Fertilization to impregnate the female. So, for all intents and purposes, 'create' would be the correct terminology."

"Why?"

"You know the answer."

He did know the answer, and he was looking at the byproduct of it. Hitler's world improved upon. Her flawless, perfect face, lustrous hair so pale it resembled snow, and her eyes—the color of a perfectly clear sky. Beautiful beyond compare.

But that only described her physical appearance. Her intelligence was sure to be off the charts. And the night they had found her— her instinct to live, her prowess in fighting even in her weakened state. Her uncanny healing ability.

"A human being superior to all others?"

She nodded.

18

Dr. George Hirch stepped off the elevator into the control station buried three floors below ground level of The Center. Only Leland, of all imperfect assistants, was permitted in the Top Secret area.

Four rooms surrounded the booth, two in front and two in back. Each was numbered consecutively, from right to left. Ahron stood in Room One while Xaver occupied Room Two. Each of the boys had two citizens taken from the population, substandard humans and therefore disposable.

A female and a male occupied the room with Ahron. They were tied to chairs, one on each side of his son. Their eyes bulged in rounded sockets, and their faces were contorted into inhuman expressions of terror. Duct tape sealed their mouths shut.

The doctor looked down at his sixteen-year-old son. "Are you ready, Ahron?" he asked, through a microphone. George's voice bounced back at him, clipped and concise, void of emotion. He felt pride at his ability to interact without exposing his inner feelings.

"Yes, *der Vater*." The boy's voice sounded clearly through the speaker.

George ignored the muffled cries of the test subjects. He turned his head toward his other creation. Xaver stood in a room exactly like Ahron's, only he had two males with him. Their faces held similar expressions of terror.

"And you, Xaver?"

"Yes, *der Vater*."

George clicked off the switch, so his conversation couldn't be overheard. He maneuvered the control until the computer monitor showed the targets framed in red. He looked at Leland, who sat in front of the monitor connected to Xaver's setup.

"Are you ready?"

His assistant shook his head and rubbed a shaky hand through his locks. "I don't know about this. If something goes wrong, they could die. And what about the civilians?"

"The boys will not die. They will protect themselves first."

"The others?"

The doctor shrugged. "Part of the greater good."

Leland's face paled. "We can't let innocents die."

His assistant was starting to annoy him. "Are you ready?" George muttered, through clenched teeth.

Leland's lips parted, but he must have read George's face and deciphered it correctly. The protest died on his tongue and fear actually lit behind the assistant's eyes. The younger man nodded and turned his attention toward the monitor. He maneuvered the controls until all the targets in Xaver's room were highlighted, too.

"Remember what I said."

Without taking his eyes off the screen, Leland gave a curt nod.

Pressing the button on the microphone, he said, "On the count of three."

The boys reached out both hands, placing them on the shoulders of the civilians.

"One. Two." Three never came. As agreed, he and Leland pushed the buttons at two sending a command to the M-16s, and gunfire echoed in the rooms below, in short bursts of three, for a period of twenty seconds. When the time expired, the volley died away and left behind muffled screams. George turned on the exhaust fan and the scent of discharged gunpowder cleared from the rooms.

Even though the doctor had expected the outcome of the experiment, astonishment still fluttered in his chest. Unable to contain himself, he smiled. Both of the boys still stood, untouched and unharmed. Each room contained one dead subject and one live subject.

Ahron stared down at the female, her body tied to the chair, her eyes glazed over in terror. Blood bubbled from a wound on her chest, and more pooled below her across the white tiles, painting the floor crimson. The young boy's face held no concern for the woman. No sorrow. Nothing at all.

The subject in Xaver's room was beyond identification. Instead of a head, a bloody stump sat on the man's shoulders. The fourteen-year-old didn't even bother looking at the dead man. Nothing in his expression hinted at horror.

The two remaining subjects' faces contorted from trying to scream, their cries drowned behind the tape. They struggled against their bonds.

"Two are still alive," said George. "One in each cubical. Excellent."

Grinning like the Cheshire Cat, he looked at Leland, who stared at him like he was an abomination. Leland's horrified face was drained of all color and on the verge of turning green. His dilated pupils swallowed the blue of his eyes.

Apparently, his assistant didn't have the insight George's genius held. Of course, George was a successful Center Child, unlike the failed Leland, so his intelligence and perceptiveness exceeded, by far, his assistant's scope.

George didn't like the way the inferior man looked at him. His triumphant smile faltered. "Clean up the mess."

Stunned, the younger man's eyes didn't leave the doctor.

"Leland, come to your senses."

Leland blinked at the sound of George's voice. "What?"

"Take care of the survivors, too."

"Wh-what am I supposed to do with them?"

"Exterminate them."

Red flooded Leland's face as he flew to his feet. His hair flipped over his forehead and dangled in his eyes. He pushed it back.

"Kill them? Are you mad?"

Anger swirled inside George, threatening to dissolve his calm demeanor. His lids narrowing, he advanced on his assistant. "I am seriously starting to doubt your ability to stay on as my assistant."

Leland averted his gaze. "It's just—they're human beings."

"They are experimental subjects. Did you honestly think I would release them back into the population afterward? Even you are not that ignorant."

"I-I don't know if I can."

Dr. Hirch pointed a finger at his assistant. "You can and you will, or I will find your replacement," he said, the hidden meaning apparent in his tone.

Leland jerked his gaze from the floor and faced the doctor. The younger man's face paled, white as a sheet of clean paper. Without acknowledging the doctor's threat, he turned toward the monitors. His hands shook as he typed in new commands.

The doctor inhaled and composed himself. "When you are done, bring the videos to my office."

"Yes, Dr. Hirch," he said, his voice unsteady.

George opened the door and walked down the steps into the hall between the rooms.

"Open."

A click sounded, and the doors swung outward.

He surveyed the rooms. Bullets littered the floor around Xaver's feet where his shield had stopped them from penetrating. Behind Ahron, fragments of the wall had been blown away. Chunks of wood and plaster lay splintered on the ground. He motioned for the boys to join him. Obediently, they strolled into the hallway.

George glanced at the surviving subjects. Their eyes pleaded for mercy. George's face took on the expression of a compassionate father. "You will be fine. The Center is grateful for your cooperation." He stepped away from the door. "Close," he said, as he moved down the hall.

The doors swung shut, clicking as the bolts slid back into place. More muffled screams followed.

Ignoring the sounds of lost hope, George strolled down the hall toward the elevator. Xaver and Ahron followed.

Although he knew his children didn't care about approval, as their father, he felt praise was warranted. "I am proud of your work today."

He pushed a red button and stood back when the doors slid open. Ahron and Xaver stepped inside.

"Your progress is astounding."

"Thank you, *der Vater*," they said, in robotic monotones.

He followed and hit the ground floor button. As the elevator doors shut, more shots echoed down the corridor.

19

Rein sat next to Jordan in the elder's holey—so nicknamed by the original settlers. Resembling a long honeycomb, the name suited the line of holes on the west side of the cavern. Some were bigger, some smaller. Some had been naturally formed; most had been dug out over the years as more living quarters were needed. All of the holes were considered home by their occupants.

Although considered the leader, and the oldest descendant remaining from the original survivors, Jordan didn't have anything special. A sleeping bag, a few blankets, a pillow that had seen much better days twenty years ago, and a beautiful music box that had belonged to Jordan's mother. The box had a couple dressed in 1800's garb dancing to music composed by someone named Mozart. Jordan couldn't remember the name of the piece.

Rein carefully fingered the delicate box while the haunting music played. Ever since he was a little boy, Rein had loved watching the figurines. He still did, although now, he grieved over the loss of knowledge of classical music along with all the other knowledge lost due to their circumstances of hiding away.

Rein looked up from the twirling couple to Jordan, his dark skin even more pronounced under the low light, and shadowed by his dreadlocks. His black eyes, which usually held humor and hope, seemed gaunt and tired. Jordan hadn't been his regular self for days.

"I want to trust her. But, considering where she is from and what she is, it is hard."

The older man smiled, emphasizing his many wrinkles. "And why are we any more trustworthy?"

Shocked, Rein arched his brow. "What? We're the good guys."

"Good guys." Jordan chuckled. "From your point of view. But we must remember, hers is different. She was raised in a society where perfection is important, where the thought of individuality is considered—well, evil. They consider themselves working toward a common good. At least, that's what I think she was taught." He thrummed his fingers against the ragged pillow lying in his lap. "She was taught we're the enemy and must be stopped. But her being here, her hearing Jeremy..."

Rein twinged at the sound of Jeremy's name. He couldn't help it. Jeremy had been like a brother to him. After all, Jordan had raised Woody, Jeremy, and him.

When he and Doc had returned, they went to Jordan with the news. A small ceremony was held in his honor and bravery, but it was hard to accept he wouldn't be returning.

Jordan reached out and laid his hand on his wrist. "Her listening to Jeremy," he continued, "and seeking us out, tells us she's found a flaw within her society. Within her belief system."

"What if it's a trick?"

"A lot of wasted energy on their part. They can't learn any secrets from us. We are a small community with few people, a few weapons. If they knew about us, the would've just come and wiped us out."

Rein nodded. Their community had nothing to offer, nothing of any importance. All they did was survive.

"Now, take me to go meet our visitor."

Rein wanted to protest further. He still wasn't sure if Jordan meeting Ellyssa was such a great idea. His objections had landed on a deaf ear, though.

Resigned, Rein crawled from the holey into the passageway. His knee popped when he stood. He offered his hand to the older man and helped him to his feet. Jordan's bones, however, did more than pop; they creaked like rusty hinges.

"I still want her guarded."

Jordan patted him on the shoulder. "I trust your judgment. But, she ain't the first one from the outside world who has come to live here."

"I know, but she is different." Grabbing the elder under his elbow, Rein asked, "Are you ready?"

"Lead me to her."

Ellyssa had just finished the very last sentence of the novel, *Of Mice and Men,* when Mathew stopped outside of the room and spoke to her latest babysitter. She had no plans of doing anything, although an armed guard wouldn't be able to stop her if she did.

As the guard's footsteps faded down the corridor, the doctor strolled in, his expression lit in excitement. He eyed the book as she placed it on the table. "So, what did you think?"

"I have never read anything like it. I cannot thank you enough for sharing this with me." She fingered the leather binding.

"And?"

"And." Ellyssa thought for a moment.

Someone like the characters in the book could never have existed in her society, where the lack of understanding and compassion thrived. It made her ponder the realities of the world she'd lived in. Mentally incapacitated, undeniably flawed, yet Lennie still brought companionship to George. He served a purpose. The dreams and hopes the two shared… no wonder fiction wasn't allowed in The Center's sterile environment.

The characters had made her examine empathy and relationships, expanding her ability to feel. She let the emotions simmer within her, tasting each as it affected her.

"The loneliness, the foreshadowing of killing things one loves. The hopes and dreams living inside men, although it perishes at the end." Pausing, Ellyssa tried to place a name to the intense emotion. The very thing she lacked knowledge in. Finally, she settled for the simplest of words. "It was sad."

Mathew nodded. "Yes. It's part of being human. Of becoming complete. Of learning compassion and sympathy for others beyond yourself. Mostly, to never give up."

To never give up. The words repeated in Ellyssa's mind. She wondered if that was what kept the Renegades going and living in the dank, dirty tunnels. Hope of living freely.

"You'll love Mary Shelley. It's a classic."

"I am looking forward to reading it. Fiction engages."

Mathew's eyebrows bunched together. "Say, *I'm.*"

The corner of Ellyssa's mouth pulled back. "Why?"

"Seems, if you are going to be staying for awhile, you need to stop talking like a robot. Relax a little."

"I do not think..."

"Humor me."

She grinned. "All right. If it will make you happy." She thought about the word, how it would roll off her tongue. "I'm."

A hint of a smile shadowed his face as steps echoed into the makeshift hospital before the owners appeared. One set was stealthy and sure, the other shuffled.

"Keep practicing. It'll become second nature," Mathew said, patting her hand. "You up for some company?"

Ellyssa put the book down and rose from the bed, as Rein and a black man entered. Stopping short, she stared in disbelief. Besides history books, never in her life had she seen a black person. His skin was dark and wrinkled, his eyes black as night. His wiry grey hair bounced freely in tangled clumps. He wore the same dress as everyone else, only his clothes hung off his thin, frail body.

Everything she'd been taught about people of other races surged forward. They were untrustworthy, imperfect. Emotions swirled inside her, confusing her. Unsure what to think, what to do, Ellyssa slipped into her old skin, expressionless, her body poised to defend herself.

Responding to her defensive posture, the smile gracing the doctor's face fell, replaced by a curious scowl. Rein's eyes narrowed and his body visibly coiled. The black man stood there, just as relaxed as when he had first entered. He placed a wrinkled hand on Rein's forearm.

Ellyssa quickly sized up the competition, preparing for their first move. The black man and the doctor would be easily disposed of. Rein would prove a bit harder, but not beyond her capabilities.

Brushing off the old man's hand, Rein stepped forward, but Mathew popped in front of him with his hands held up, warding off expected hostility.

"Ellyssa, what's wrong?" Mathew said.

She tore her eyes from the black man and focused on the doctor. "I trusted you."

Unprepared for her response, Mathew blinked. "Yes. I promised no one was going to hurt you. And no one is." He turned his body halfway toward the black man. "This is Jordan," he said, sweeping his arm in introduction.

Still wary, Ellyssa stepped back, but her body remained tense. "Jordan? Your leader?"

Mathew looked from her to Jordan, then back to her. He raised his eyebrows. "Oh, I see," he said with a nod. "There are people of many heritages who live among us, Ellyssa. Quite different than what you are accustomed to, I'm sure."

With a quick step forward, Jordan brushed by Rein, who tried to hold him back, but the old man knocked his hand away. Although feeble-looking, the leader moved with vigor. He extended his hand to Ellyssa. "Pleased to meet you, Ellyssa. I've heard much about you."

The drawl of Jordan's dialect was even more pronounced and slower than Rein's or Mathew's. 'Pleased to meet you' sounded more like 'Pleaz ta mitcha.'

Ellyssa stared at his proffered hand for a moment, noting the tan skin of his palm. Her gaze floated to his face. Amusement glimmered in his eyes, but so did tiredness. His full lips twitched, as if on the verge of breaking into laughter.

With his hand still extended in the air, she jumped into his head. An onslaught of goodness thrummed inside the old man. He was very sick. He held absolutely no ill will toward her, only inquisitiveness about who she was and why she was here.

Against everything drilled into her from a very young age, Ellyssa took an instant liking to the older man, which surprised her.

Hesitant, like a wild animal taking food from a child, she stepped forward and placed her hand in Jordan's. His grip was surprisingly strong, considering his health, and…leathery.

"It is-" Ellyssa paused. "I mean, it's nice to meet you, too," she replied. She glanced at Mathew, who nodded encouragingly, a smile of triumph gracing his face. She grinned back at him.

"Do you mind if I stay and speak with you?"

Ellyssa's smile faltered. She didn't want to answer the old man's questions she'd seen floating in his head. She was still unsure what to reveal. Maybe everything. Maybe nothing. She chewed on her bottom lip as she debated, then stopped as soon as she noticed the common display of indecision. She erased all expression from her appearance. "Of course."

Ellyssa returned to her bed while Mathew rolled the chair over next to her cot. With an audible grunt, Jordan took the offered seat. Mathew settled on the empty cot next to hers, while Rein leaned against the edge of the doorway. Rein ran his fingers through his chestnut hair, rearranging the spikes into a new pattern, before he folded his arms. Unease etched his face as his eyes moved from her, to Jordan, to Mathew.

She didn't understand him at all.

"From what I was told, you were called here?"

Ellyssa tore her attention away from Rein and nodded.

"And, as I'm sure Rein or Doc told you, we have reason to believe Jeremy was the one who was captured and taken to The Center."

"Yes."

"He was special. Extraordinary, actually."

"That is my understanding."

"Do you know how he came to be here?"

"No. I was not informed."

Jordan looked at the doctor.

Mathew shrugged.

"About thirty years ago, when he was still a newborn, not more than a couple of months old, I took him in, like I did Rein and Woody, and raised him."

Ellyssa's gaze shot to Rein. She had no idea what he must be feeling losing someone he loved. No idea at all.

The brightness in Jordan's eyes faded a little and a slow tick worked in his jawline as he continue, "I loved him like he was my very own.

"We don't know much about his mother, only that she was unmarried. She had him secretly. I guess her original plan had been to raise him and slowly integrate him into society." He pulled his frail shoulders into a shrug.

"When he was born with the dark hair, she knew he would never be accepted. Somehow, she learned about one of our people. She left the baby with them, and they brought him to me.

"For years, he grew, he played, and he was intelligent, but he never spoke. No babbling or cooing, like other babies. Not until he was three, but even then, his words did not come the conventional way." Jordan leaned forward. "He spoke in my head."

Forgetting to maintain unresponsiveness, Ellyssa's eyes widened. Although, she knew of Jeremy's gift, had experienced it herself, the possibility of such an occurrence outside of The Center still seemed unfeasible.

"His words were as clear as those I am speaking to you now. But there was more to it. He could make you know things, understand things."

"That is what happened to me," she uttered in disbelief.

"I thought I was going insane, when he first did it to me." Chuckling, Jordan eased back.

The old man's laughter was deep and throaty, and fell from him easily. She liked it.

As the chuckle died, Jordan's dark eyes fixed on her, his expression turned serious. "Do you know why he could do that? Did it have anything to do with The Center?"

Ellyssa considered the chances of Jeremy's condition being a byproduct of The Center. It would definitely explain Jeremy's unique ability. And it wasn't like her father would ever admit such a weakness on his behalf or The Center's. After all, the only reason Ellyssa had found out about Subject 20, Ida, was because... She paused at the thought.

It was because of Jeremy.

Did the strange dark-haired male somehow know he'd come from The Center?

Ellyssa dismissed the idea. If he'd known, then Jordan would've known. But maybe, somehow, he had felt a connection. One strong enough that he'd reached out to her.

As their expectant stares stayed locked on her, Ellyssa wondered how they would react to her own unique ability. Would they accept her as easily as they had Jeremy?

She was torn.

Her complete treachery toward her father, her brothers and sister, of everyone in society. But wasn't what her father planned a betrayal, too? Genocide of all society, to be replaced by new and improved models.

Ellyssa's gaze flicked to Rein; his eyes scrutinized her, waiting for an answer.

Now was not the time to share. But, eventually, she had to tell them.

Ellyssa wet her lips. "I am not sure. He could have been born at The Center. If he was, though, I would not have been informed of such matters."

Jordan nodded, as if he'd expected as much.

"Why was he so far from home?" she asked.

The older man glanced at the doctor, who flipped his head in approval. "We have members in Chicago. They help us with supplies—food, medicine, other things. There are others in Kansas City, to help with delivery."

She assumed "other things" were weapons, but she didn't press the subject. No reason to. At this point, it really didn't matter.

He looked over his shoulder at Rein. "I think it's time."

Rein pushed off the wall and came to help Jordan up from the chair.

Jumping to his feet, Mathew rubbed his hands together. "Excellent."

Ellyssa's eyebrows knotted together. "What?"

Jordan held his wrinkled hand out to her. "We thought it was time for you to see something beside the inside of this room. How would you like to meet the other residents?"

She stared at his outstretched fingers for a moment. The touching these people participated in was unnerving, but not unpleasant. It was something she'd have to get used to if she planned on staying.

The thought startled her.

Was that her plan? To live in a cave with Renegades? She'd considered the idea before, but not with such definitiveness. Unexpectedly, the idea felt somewhat…comforting and thrilling. Returning to The Center was not an option. She was a failed experiment and expendable. One thing her lessons had taught her, above everything else, was self-preservation.

Ellyssa took Jordan's hand and curled her fingers around the meaty part of his palm.

Ellyssa walked beside Jordan, her fingers entwined within his, as they worked their way down the winding passages. She busied herself with memorizing the layout. *Never hurts to be prepared.* Long cables, like the ones running from the makeshift hospital, dangled from the ceiling and connected fluorescent tubes, spaced every four to six meters. Up ahead, the tunnel appeared to end.

"Is this it?"

Jordan chuckled. "No, there aren't any lights in the section ahead."

They rounded a corner into inky blackness. Blinded, she faltered.

Jordan tugged on her arm. "It's okay."

"What is this place?"

"This part is a coal mine, abandoned way before The War. We keep the hospital here, and some of our supplies, due to the drier air." Jordan stopped and placed Ellyssa's hand on the rocky surface. "We stay in a cavern. Follow the wall."

With slow, careful steps, she did as instructed, until the wall fell away and her hand slipped through a fissure. Surprised, she gasped and stumbled forward, almost falling inside. Her shoulder scraped the rocky exposure.

The old man laughed and rested his hand on the small of her back. "Sorry. I should've warned you. You'll get used to it. Like second nature," Jordan said. "The fissure is large enough for you to fit through, but not two, side-by-side." He slid his hand from her back to her wrist. "Rein, take her other hand to help guide her."

Not liking the disorientation, she popped into each of the men's heads to locate them. None of them had any ill intentions. She felt a large hand bump into her shoulder and slide down the side of her arm, making her skin tingle with a current like electricity. Shocked, she pulled away.

"It's just me." Rein's voice floated at her from the darkness.

"Did you not feel that?" Ellyssa asked, clenching and unclenching her hand.

"Feel what?"

How could he not feel the tingle when he touched her? Confused, she frowned. "I-I do not know. Nothing."

He found her again, his fingers grazing over the curve of her elbow to find her hand. The tingles followed. He interlaced his fingers with hers, and gave a squeeze. Warmth traveled up her arm and into her chest. Her heart responded. Unsettled, she clamped her mouth shut. The physiological responses his touch elicited frightened her.

"Rein'll go first."

As soon as Jordan spoke, Ellyssa was pulled inside, the same shoulder knocking into the edge again. She immediately felt the change. The previous openness disappeared, and the darkness pressed against her.

Was she insane? Trapped between a rocky enclosure and Renegades, and disoriented. They were at an advantage if she failed to pick from their brains a trap. Yet, here she was, trusting a group of outsiders she'd been conditioned to kill. Not in a million years would she have thought this possible.

The thin corridor snaked around bends and curves, growing cooler as they proceeded. The dryness of the air gave way to moisture. Like a computer, Ellyssa's brain absorbed every detail. The steps. The temperature changes. The ambiance of the enclosure. She filed the information away.

After the last curve, the fissure opened wider and into a lighted room where fluorescents hung from the ceiling. The air in the open room was wetter, cooler, and carried a pleasant, mineral scent. Strange buzzing echoed through an opening ahead.

"The first settlers found it while exploring," Jordan yelled over the din, between winded huffs. A greyish tint lingered under the older man's pallor. "It ended up being a great hiding place during the initial raids."

Impressed with the hard work completed over the years with limited resources, Ellyssa followed the three men into a smaller room, adjacent to the area with the fissure. The loud humming emitted from a large generator. Several secured cables snaked in from adjoining corridors and joined together at a center point, then spliced into the machine. She had often pondered how the electricity was supplied, but she had never expected such an elaborate setup.

The shock of seeing such technology stunned her. Although forced into caves, the people who rebelled were anything but barbaric. They were far from ignorant, and their ingenuity proved it. Once again, her father had been proven wrong.

Ellyssa circled the generator, studying it. "How do you keep such a machine running?"

"Battery packs charged by solar energy," Jordan answered, his words drawn out as if he were tired.

He took a step toward Ellyssa and stumbled. She caught him, but barely. He felt so light in her arms, so fragile, like a frayed string.

"Are you okay?" she asked.

"Fine, maybe a little tired." He chortled, as if embarrassed. "Doc, do you mind escorting me to my holey?"

Mathew moved his eyes between Ellyssa and Rein, then a grin she had trouble identifying appeared on his face. He winked at her. "No problem." He took the back of their leader's elbow and led him from the generator room.

Ellyssa waited for the echoes of their shoes against the rocky ground to disappear before she turned her attention to Rein. "Is he going to be all right?"

"He's getting up there in years."

She nodded, understanding that the settlers of this area didn't have the medical advancements, nor the superior genes, that helped prolong life.

"Solar energy batteries?" Ellyssa asked, indicating the machine.

Rein pointed at a power pack, roughly the size of a processor. "We have three of those. While one is working, the other two are being charged."

"But…maintenance?"

"We keep up-to-date."

"How?" she asked.

"The Resistance," Rein said quickly, as if he didn't want to elaborate.

Ellyssa could have easily picked it from his brain, but she didn't. If she were to stay in this type of society, she'd have to learn to trust them, along with earning trust *from* them.

Rein walked over to the machine and knelt next to the battery. "See this red line?" He pointed at an indicator stretching across the expanse of the machine. It was lit to a halfway mark. The red haze highlighted his cheekbones and tinted his dark hair.

"This shows us how much power we have left." Standing, he dusted off his knees. "We turn off lights at certain points during the day to conserve energy."

"How many people live here?"

His mouth pulled to the side, as if considering whether divulging such information would prove fatal. A few moments later, he responded, "A hundred forty-seven."

The number was higher than she'd expected. "All are descendants?"

"Some are. Most are from other camps we brought in. Others were kind of adopted, like Jeremy and me, from parents in society who didn't want to send their less-than-perfect children to the concentration camps, or have them killed." His tone sharpened as he spoke. "You know they do that, don't you? They use the imperfect children as slave labor or, if they are lucky, kill them." Anger flashed in his green eyes.

She averted her gaze and picked at a thread from the seam of her T-shirt. "I am aware."

"I figured as much." He huffed past her to another tunnel. "Come on."

She stood her ground. "I might have been aware. That does not mean I agree with how the people are treated. I ran across several things I have not agreed with. That is one of the reasons I left."

Spinning on his heels, Rein's face hardening into stone, he spat, "You should've done something."

Ellyssa felt a bubbling churn in her stomach as rage boiled up. An emotion she knew, and knew well. Muscles twitching, aching to release pent-up energy, she spat back, "Like what? What could I have done? Why do you not tell me what you would have done?" Her voice matched his venom.

Rein rocked on his feet as if she'd slapped him. Lids narrowing, his face pinched into a scowl. He stepped forward, his hands balled into tight fists. Ellyssa instinctively coiled, like a snake about to strike, waiting. The moment never came. As fast as the air sizzled with intensity, it dissipated. His features and stance loosened.

Skeptical, Ellyssa tossed away her previous reservations and plunged into his head. Rein's thoughts were jumbled, fleeting, shifting from one to the other faster than a deck of cards being shuffled. Brief doubts about why she was here, what she wanted, whether she should be trusted. Regret filtered through for blaming her for a situation she hadn't caused. He wanted to accept and trust her as easily as Jordan and Mathew had. She was just so damn confusing.

Rein focused on her appearance. The angry pink in her cheeks began to fade, and her hair glowed yellow under the light. He wondered if her hair felt as soft as it looked, like silken thread.

Ellyssa's midsection quivered and heat pulsed in her veins. She pulled out.

He squared his shoulders, but not in a confrontational way. "I don't know," he stated, pulling his fingers through his hair. "I'm sorry."

"Your apology is accepted." Her tone was still sharp, but only to mask the sensation of uncertainty.

After all, she was the outsider here. For the most part, everyone she'd met had accepted her, although she should be considered the enemy. What he—the whole community for that matter—knew had happened in the past was nothing compared to future plans. Society was to be exterminated to make way for a perfect human being. A perfect soldier. Ellyssa and her siblings' genes being the key.

Maybe she should leave. Her father would not give up until she was returned home. The longer she stayed, the greater the risk.

They deserved the truth. She'd have to reveal her secret eventually.

"Ellyssa?"

Snapped from her thoughts, she looked at Rein. He was smiling, not a happy one, more filled with chagrin.

"I really am sorry. That was unfair. It's just—" He shrugged.

"I understand."

"Are you hungry?"

Nodding, Ellyssa's head filled with questions about when she should tell them the whole truth. She turned back toward the direction of the hospital. He shuffled behind her, but instead of following, he put his hand on her shoulder. His grip was firm, and thrilling. She wheeled around, ready to defend; his hands flew up in surrender.

"Wait," Rein said, amused. "We're going to the dining hall. It's time to meet the others. Jordan insists."

His hand glided from her shoulder to her hand. His touch was different than when he'd held her hand through the enclosure. The soft stroke of his fingers traced along her skin like a feather. She looked at him.

Pulling his lips into an uncertain grin, Rein entwined his fingers within hers, and a pleasant shock ran through her veins, turning her blood into a mixture of ice and lava. Her pulse quickened.

"Come on," he said with a tug.

Ellyssa followed behind him, cherishing the heat radiating off him. She relished how his touch felt different from the doctor's or Jordan's, how her heart hammered in expectation. Unsure and elusive. New and tantalizing.

They entered a part of the tunnel where the lights had been turned off to save energy. Darkness closed around her, but instead of going on high alert, she relaxed. The inky black seemed to last forever, until they turned a sharp corner. Light stretched along the rocky ground and wall and, with it, came the sound of whispered conversations.

A bit further along, they stepped into a room where the ceiling towered overhead. Although the middle part leveled into a large floor, speleothem deposited mineral ornaments along the edges of room. Beautiful formations rose from the floor and dangled from above, and flowstone cascaded into layers of limestone steps. The lack of dripping water told Ellyssa the cave was dead. Ellyssa could only imagine its spectacular beauty in its heyday.

Shifting focus, her eyes flowed from the picturesque scenery to three rows of lights suspended from long wires. Then her gaze traveled toward the people sitting in the center of the room.

Ellyssa stood still, amazed at the variety of races she'd only seen in history books. Her eyes flitted from one person to the next, noting the subtle to extreme changes within skin tone, hair color, eyes, varying degrees of body and facial shapes, the little ornaments that hung from their ears or pierced parts of their faces. Children sat with parents, smiling and laughing. It was beautiful. So unlike the pale white, sterile world in which she had been raised. Here, everyone was an individual.

The Renegades sat at long, rugged wooden tables on log benches. A far cry from the formal dining room to which she was accustomed. Even without the amenities, though, the atmosphere welcomed her. Warm. Homey. All the things missing from her life.

Rein smiled encouragingly. "Let's get something to eat." He pointed to a line of people holding the same red trays the doctor had brought in to her.

She spotted Trista next to the row of hungry Renegades. The perfect blonde stacked dishes into a black bin. She smiled and waved at Ellyssa.

Ellyssa remained with her legs anchored to the ground. An air of wonder, like the day she'd escaped, bubbled in her.

She returned her attention to the people. The pale green eyes of a female she hadn't met stared at her. Another female, with reddish-brown skin and beautiful auburn hair, elbowed a male, with a large nose and huge brown eyes, next to her. Afterwards, heads swiveled around toward her.

Feeling awkward and out of place, a nervous smile popped unexpectedly onto Ellyssa's face as she continued to look at all the different Renegades. Then, she met Candy's glare. The redheaded female's eyes kept moving from her face to her hand intertwined with Rein's, and back. The fiery redhead's face pinched into a look of revulsion. The exact opposite of Jason's, whose gaze scrolled the length of her body, hungrily.

Ellyssa's smile fell away.

An urge to jump into both of their heads stirred, but to get a read with so many voices was impossible. She kept her shield firmly in place.

Ignoring the crew of onlookers, Rein pulled her toward the line, where others waited to be served. As they passed the tables, conversation resumed, but the words were clipped. She still felt their stares burning into the back of her head.

"Everyone pitches in here," Rein stated, giving her hand several little squeezes. She wasn't sure if it was for encouragement, or him gauging her response. "Some are assigned kitchen, cleaning, hunting, et cetera." He grabbed a tray and pushed it into her grasp. "Today's special is deer stew."

"What?" Ellyssa's stomach churned. She hoped she had masked the disgust. It would seem rude after all Mathew had done for her. But deer...? At The Center, protein came from animals raised in a sterile environment and fed an all-grain diet, free of bacteria and germs, not from wild animals. Then she started to wonder about the food Mathew had brought her. She'd never considered questioning its origins. Her stomach sloshed again.

"You'll love it."

The corner of her mouth pulled back as a male with pretty teeth and tight curly hair poured a ladleful into a bowl and handed it to her. Grudgingly, she peered into the bowl. Little chunks of meat, carrots, and potatoes swam in the watery broth.

"This way." Rein led her between tables until he stopped by a male with neatly-combed ash-blond hair, hunkered over his bowl and shoveling spoonfuls of soup into his mouth. He looked up when Rein set his tray down and sat across from him. He was nice-looking, about Rein's age—early twenties—with a straight nose and strong chin.

"Ellyssa, this is Woody." He patted the space next to him.

"Hello," she politely said as she took the offered seat.

Woody watched her, grey eyes sliding across her face, before he jerked his head in response. A piece of his hair flipped up and fell into his face. He brushed it away and resumed eating.

A slight frown formed between Rein's eyes. "Woody?"

Woody dropped his spoon on his tray. "I told you how I felt, Rein," he sniped, then stood.

The moment he spoke, Ellyssa remembered his voice, still irritable, like in the old store. Ill at ease, she wanted to know what he'd told Rein, but instead she poked at the pieces of deer meat.

"If you'll excuse me." He walked to a cart with large brown bins and tossed the remains of his dinner in. Then he disappeared into a tunnel on the far side of the room.

Red flushed over Rein's face. "I'm sorry."

"No need to apologize."

Determined to try the meal, she spooned some of the stew in her mouth. Surprisingly, it tasted better than she'd originally thought. Either that, or her taste buds weren't as picky as they used to be. Fine dining wasn't something someone indulged in when on the run. She finished the watery broth with her slice of bread.

"Did you like it?" Rein smiled. "By the look on your face, I wasn't sure."

She nodded. "Yes, it was good."

"Good." He got up and took both trays to the bins. "Would you like to see more?" he asked. His eyes shifted over Ellyssa's shoulder, and his smile fell.

"Hey," called a musical voice, sending a grinding displeasure down Ellyssa's spine.

Ellyssa spun around and watched as the braids on Candy's head bounced in sequence with her steps, beady eyes set in a glare. The redhead stopped right in front of Ellyssa, their noses almost touching.

She pointed her index finger at Ellyssa and jabbed it in the air. "Just because they're letting you take a tour, against my protests, don't think you can just parade around here whenever you want." Candy's hand moved forward to poke her in the chest. "I'm keeping—"

But before Candy made contact or could finish her sentence, Ellyssa's hand snapped out and grabbed her by the wrist. Candy's ugly face grimaced and her beady eyes widened. Silence spread as conversations stopped, and Ellyssa could feel hundreds of eyes on her. She held fast to Candy's gaze.

"Do not ever touch me," Ellyssa hissed, emphasizing each word. "Ever." She released her wrist.

Candy rubbed her wrist, still shocked. Ellyssa gave her one more warning look before turning away. She almost bumped into her escort, who looked as shocked as Candy. Ignoring Rein, Ellyssa brushed by.

"Hey, I'm not done with you."

"Stop it, Candy," Rein snapped.

"Don't tell me what—"

"Shut up," Rein warned.

Ellyssa heard him jogging behind her, his steps loud against the ground. "Wait up."

She slowed until he reached her side then resumed her pace.

"That was amazing," Rein said.

Without responding, her steps quick and short, Ellyssa followed the tunnel as if she knew where she was going. She didn't have a clue. This network of long corridors hadn't been included in the tour. She assumed, if she followed the cables, they would eventually lead her to the room with the generator. From there, she'd find her way back to the hospital room.

Rein reached down and grabbed her hand. "Ellyssa," he said, stopping.

She turned on a heel and faced him, her face composed and blank. "What?" she said calmly, even though a surge of anger enveloped her, and she fought a mounting desire to go back and finish what Candy had started.

"I knew you were fast from your response in the store. You took us completely by surprise." He blinked, shaking his head. "This time, though, I didn't see anything more than a blur. How do you move so fast?"

Ellyssa paused before answering. "Special training."

Rein's lids rose. "Special training. Like, for what? To be a soldier, or something?" He paused for a moment. "The Center. Of course."

Ellyssa wished she hadn't said a thing, not now, at least. She nodded.

The emotions on Rein's face changed visibly, one to the next, as he absorbed the realization of what she had just shared. The twisting features stopped, not into a look of anger or surprise or hate as she'd expected, but one of comprehension.

"I knew there was something about you, but I had no idea."

"I am afraid there are a lot of things you do not know about me."

20

Detective Angela Petersen still couldn't believe she'd agreed to go out to dinner with Dyllon. She knew better than to get too close to the locals. Yet, here she was, sitting across from him in a low-lit restaurant at a cozy table meant for two.

She tried to keep her gaze on the menu, but every once in awhile, she'd look up and catch him staring at her. The flame from the votive candle reflected in his sea-blue eyes and emphasized the definition of his cheekbones.

Angela set her menu down. "When I agreed to dinner, I assumed it was to discuss the case."

"It is," Dyllon replied indifferently.

A waiter appeared wearing a tux and carrying a bottle of expensive Merlot, which he presented to Dyllon before opening it and showing the captain the cork. Dyllon nodded and the attendant poured a small sample into the glass. After swirling the red liquid, Dyllon tasted it. He placed the glass back on the table, and the server topped his off, and filled hers as well.

"Then what's all this about?" Angela pointed her finger at his black suit, which made her feel completely underdressed, in a grey angora sweater and a pair of jeans. "And that?" she asked, swishing her hand to the side at the dining room, where all the tables only contained couples on dates, all in suits and dresses.

Dyllon shrugged. "The food here is great."

"This is a little above and beyond."

"Look. We've been working together for...what...close to three weeks. Every night you go back to the motel, alone. I thought it'd be a nice change for you."

"Why would you care?"

He blinked. "Because, whether you like it or not, we're working together. Don't you ever go out with people you work with at The Center?"

It was Angela's turn to blink. "No," she said, as if the fact should be obvious.

"How do you work efficiently without camaraderie?"

"Much like here. I'm head of security. When I give an order, it's followed."

Dyllon gave her an empty look as a different waiter came and took their orders. When they were alone again, Angela leaned forward and said, "I just don't want you to get the wrong idea."

"I'm not getting any ideas." He collapsed against the back of his chair. "I'm tired. You're tired. We both needed a break. So just enjoy. I was only taking you out as a friendly gesture."

The corner of her mouth drew back. Life away from The Center certainly was different. Time for socializing was limited back home. So, maybe..."Friends?" she said.

"That's it."

Angela relaxed. "I'm still Detective Petersen."

"You can still call me Dyllon."

She smiled. "Touché."

"Now, since we've ordered, and you're somewhat more...relaxed than usual. I have some news." Dyllon pulled out a brown file he had hidden in his lap and handed it to Angela.

Interest piqued, she leaned forward. "What's this?"

"Open it."

Angela flipped to the first page, titled SUPPLIES, with a list of dates in one column and items in another. She glanced over office supplies, personal effects, lists of groceries, and medical necessities. "What?"

"Keep reading."

Turning to the next page, she saw much of the same type of ordering with Davis' signature scrawled at the bottom. "The park ranger?"

Pleased with himself, Dyllon folded his arms over his chest. "Seems he's been doing some excessive ordering. Not much. You've got quite the nose, Detective. Seems Davis might be an appropriate suspect." Dyllon held out his hand. "May I?"

Angela returned the folder and he put it sideways on the table.

"A lot of effort went into how carefully these orders were placed. An order for extra blankets, a year ago. And look here," Dyllon said, pointing to a longer list, "an abundance of medical supplies just last month." He flipped through to another page. "Two years ago, too." He leaned back with a smug look.

Flabbergasted, she stared at him. "And he was never questioned?"

"Why would they? His ordering might've been more than needed, but not often enough to arouse suspicion. A few extra boxes of bandages, two extra bottles of aspirin. Rangers often overstock so they don't have to drive hours into town every week. Plus, the time between each order." He shrugged.

"I knew it," Angela said, anger in her voice. She placed her hands on the edge of the table and pushed her seat back.

"Where are you going?"

"He needs to be questioned."

Dyllon held up his hands. "Wait."

"What?" she snapped.

"What do you think will happen if you question him now?"

Sighing, Angela leaned back in her chair. "Enlighten me."

A brow rose. "He'll lie."

"I have ways of making people talk."

"Do they always work?"

She wanted to say "yes," she could be very persuasive, but the truth was that it seldom worked. It seemed the Renegades and members of the Resistance were extremely loyal. "Sometimes."

"It's your call, Detective, but I think we should watch him. Maybe he'll lead us to their camp."

Of course Dyllon was right; it'd be better to wait. Angela hoped the doctor would see things their way. She fished her cell from her bag, saying, "I have to report our progress."

"Of course."

Aalexis stood against the far wall in the rectangular, soundproof room, directly behind seven rifles. The long muzzles pointed toward the front of the room, but none were sighted on the black-silhouetted target hanging from a long cable. The alignments were off by a few degrees.

Dr. George Hirch held no doubt she'd be successful. Aalexis' deadly ability lay concealed by platinum-blond hair cascading over her shoulders in beautiful ringlets and a cherub face, even if her façade remained as devoid of expression as her eyes.

George pushed the intercom button. "When I give the signal."

"Yes, *der Vater*," Aalexis responded in a monotone.

He checked the monitors one more time, then flipped the switch. A red light inside the room flashed, right before all seven rifles fired in sequence. In a blinding flare and seven loud pops, it was over. Whiffs of smoke extended from the muzzles and dissipated, and the sound of gunfire echoed into nothingness. Clicking sounded as the target moved toward the doctor's booth.

As expected, every shot drilled right through the head. Seven distinct punctures in a perfect circle.

Aalexis was toying with him.

George glanced at the faux angel. His daughter remained statue-like, as if the experiment bored her. As if nothing challenged her anymore.

Still, she was a sight to behold. A beautiful sight. A memory Dr. Hirch would retain of how powerful his daughter was. His mighty creation, born from his genius. No other had accomplished such feats. *He* would lead humanity to perfection.

He was just beginning to test the limits of her powers. Of all of their powers.

She needed more of a challenge.

George picked up the handset and punched in a number.

"Engineering," a soft female voice said.

"This is Dr. Hirch. I need seven more rifles set up in room seventeen."

"Yes, Dr. Hirch. Right away."

He hung up and pressed the intercom. "Aalexis, I want to conduct another test. Please wait patiently."

For the first time since they'd entered the room, Aalexis acknowledged the doctor with more than words. She faced him. Fury flashed within the depths of her eyes, before the same glazed, monotonous guise returned.

"Yes, *der Vater*," she replied. Her attention returned to the front of the room. She placed her hands behind her back in an at-ease stance.

George watched her warily, but nothing in her demeanor changed. Still as a statue, even when he buzzed the workers in with his requested items. Three men, wearing Center orange jumpers, wheeled in a cart weighed down with rifle cases and mounts. Without a word, they began assembling the tripods.

"Be sure to sight them off the target," he said into the intercom.

One of the men waved his arm in acknowledgement.

As the final rifle was positioned, Leland strolled into the control booth. He glanced at Aalexis. "How'd she do?"

"As expected," George answered without looking up. "Is Micah prepared to go?"

"Yes, but once again I would like to voice my protest."

"Duly noted," said the doctor without even glancing up.

"Sending him to Detective Petersen could be dangerous. We're already missing one subject."

Dr. Hirch's spine stiffened. Leland was grating on his nerves. "We will bring her home."

"We haven't even finished the extraction of the genes. Not to mention the testing."

George faced Leland. His assistant peered at him indignantly, his arms crossed over his chest. "Once again, Leland, you overstep your bounds," he said, his tone sharp and unyielding.

The young man's arms fell to his sides as he glanced away. "You've been taking unnecessary risks lately."

"Micah is not in any danger. I am sending him to be a…special set of eyes. If there is a traitor, he can help. Now." George turned toward the window and pointed. "Watch this."

The red light flashed, reflecting off the young girl's porcelain skin. The room reverberated with gunfire and clouded with smoke.

When the air cleared, the target dangled from one clip, folding over as though waving. Dr. Hirch brought it inside. Heavy scents of gunpowder and burnt paper filled his nostrils. His nose wrinkled as he smoothed the shredded creases. Tattered and ripped, the target's head was unrecognizable.

George couldn't help himself. A grin spread across his face as he looked at his assistant. "Not even fourteen could stop her."

Leland's face held a perfect example of surprised shock, his eyes and mouth round disks.

21

Ellyssa set the borrowed copy of *Frankenstein* across her chest when Mathew, Rein, and Jordan stepped through the door. She'd heard them coming, and the whispers as Rein dismissed her current babysitter, but didn't think much of it until she saw their faces. She needn't read their minds to see their visit had to do with her confrontation with Candy a few days ago.

She crossed her legs and waited while Mathew grabbed the desk chair for Jordan. The older man took the offered seat. His smile didn't mask the worry in his eyes, and the greyish cast to his skin foretold trouble.

His illness concerned her. Over the last few days, she'd grown used to the dark man and come to cherish the stories he'd shared. His war tales his parents had passed down varied greatly from the history books and had given her a different side to ponder.

"What is going on?" she asked, as Rein and Mathew sat on the cot closest to hers. The question was meant for all of them, but she was looking at Rein. He ran nervous fingers through his messy locks while his eyes darted to Jordan. Hesitantly, she followed his gaze.

The old man patted her hand. "Ellyssa, tell us who you really are." His drawl was slower than usual, tired.

"I have told you."

"But there is more. Right?"

His unsettled gaze bore through her, and she felt...guilty, like *Subject 20*. So much to explain and no idea where to begin.

She inhaled deeply. "Everyone is going to die," she stated, matter-of-factly. Starting with Jordan, she looked from one male to the next, stopping at Rein. No glint of understanding surfaced. Rein, like the others, watched her, waiting for more.

"You do not understand. There will be complete genocide. Not like before, when only those of races lacking the required characteristics were murdered." She paused. Murder—it was the first time she'd described the extermination for what it truly was. The visionaries of her society had murdered millions of innocents. She swallowed the lump of realization. "But one where every human will be killed and replaced."

Jordan chuckled. "How can they possibly kill everyone? There will be survivors. Just like my folks survived."

She shook her head. "Not this time. They are perfecting the ultimate soldier."

The laugh died on the leader's full lips. "What does that mean?"

She glanced at Rein and Mathew. Both males looked skeptical.

"Yes, some of your ancestors survived because of their ability to hide; others did because of their genetic codes. But the type of soldier that is coming will be far beyond human understanding. Superior above *all*."

As usual, Rein responded by crossing his arms. She watched as his shirt stretched over his taut muscles, and a small flame ignited in her midsection. She felt the warmth reach her cheeks.

"I told you," she said directly to Rein, "I was created. Specific genes were joined together. Superior genes. I am not the only one. I have brothers and a sister."

She picked up the book the doctor had loaned her and showed it to Mathew. "It is funny that you chose this to be one of the fictional books you wanted me to read. It hits so close to home." Fingering the leather binding, she said, "Only, it is my siblings and I who are the monsters. It is not fiction at all."

A strong hand squeezed her shoulders. She looked up and met Rein's eyes. His expression was soft and empathetic. "You're not a monster."

A single tear squeezed from the corner of her eye, followed by another. She tried to command them to stop, but her body finally had a will of its own.

A wet trail coasted over the contour of her cheek, before disappearing with a swipe of Rein's thumb. Surprised, she blinked as Rein's palm cupped the side of her face. Never had anyone touched her face with gentleness and warmth. No impulse to pull away surged through her body. No urge to fight. Amazed by her own reaction, her desire, she reached up and grasped his hand. The tenderness of the gesture felt alien...and wonderful.

"That is true," she said as Rein leaned back. Instantly, she missed the heat of his skin. "What you need to know is that we were bred as prototypes. I have one sister and three brothers. Each of us was bred to be a perfect soldier. We are stronger, more intelligent, faster, emotionless, and have studied combat and weapons since we were toddlers."

"Emotionless?" Doc asked.

"Emotions are not allowed in the makeup of a soldier," she recited the well-known words. "Emotions show weakness, and with weakness comes hesitation, and with hesitation comes death. Our job is not to die, but to be the bringers of a new world.

"Something went wrong with my programming, though. Although most of the sensations I feel are...rudimentary, I have always been able to feel emotion, unlike the others."

"Like what?"

"Hatred and anger have been approved for survival and soldiering purposes. But, I also have felt the pleasure of doing a job well done, and sorrow or shock at things I have seen."

"What'd your father think?"

"Nothing, because I masked them."

"And he never suspected?"

"I would not be here if he had." Ignoring shock on their faces, she continued, "You witnessed my ability to heal. You have seen how fast I can move. I have other talents, as well."

Ellyssa stopped, unsure how to proceed. The time had come for her to reveal her deepest secret, and she feared their responses.

She looked down at her hands twisting in the folds of the blanket. "After years of research, my father found the genetic sequence for extrasensory skills. The oldest of us can know about people through the objects they have touched. One of my brothers is a phaser. He can blink in and out of existence. The other can form an energy shield. If you throw something at him, it will bounce off without harming him."

Stopping, she gauged the reactions of her audience. Mathew's face pulled into something she would consider horror. His rounded eyes and clenched jaw were hard to decipher. Jordan's face read disbelief. She fought a mounting urge to place her hand under his whiskered chin and close his mouth. Rein's expression she didn't understand. No mistaking his composed countenance. Arms folded, jowl set. His trademark stance. Closed to everything, and angry. Not quite the response she'd expected, after he had showed her kindness.

Ellyssa looked back to Jordan. She took in a deep breath and continued. "The youngest, my sister, can move things with her mind."

She stopped again and chewed on her lower lip. How could she tell them about her talent without alienating herself from her newfound family?

Family? A strange concept, but one she realized she didn't want to lose. Especially now, since she'd had a sample of true companionship.

Of course, not everyone considered her part of their community. But Jordan? Mathew? Rein?

"And you?" Rein probed.

She had to tell them. "I can read minds."

Silence blanketed the room. She studied the minute flits of twitching mouths and eyebrows, and muscles working along jaw lines. She wanted to jump into their heads, but she refused. Trust was a two-way street.

Rein broke the silence. "Are you doing it now?" he whispered.

"No," Ellyssa answered indignantly.

"What does it all mean?" asked Mathew.

"You're a prototype?" said Jordan.

Nodding, she said, "Yes. We all are. After my encounter with Jeremy, I ran across the records when I was erasing mine from the mainframe. With our genes locatable, he can isolate the coding sequence."

Realization dawned within the older man. The whites of his eyes grew more pronounced. "He can bring them together into one."

"Yes. A super-human able to seek you all out and destroy every pocket of resistance—hidden or not. My father's goal has always been to accomplish Hitler's dream."

Jordan slouched back in the chair. The rusted springs squeaked in protest. "Human genocide."

"Precisely."

Looking off, Mathew pulled at his chin, his eyebrows leveled in thought. After a moment, his gaze settled back on her. "If you could read minds, why didn't you know about this sooner?"

"It was strictly prohibited for any of us to use our gifts against Father or any of his assistants. To do so never even occurred to me." Ellyssa flicked her eyes at Rein's scowling face. "I am sorry I did not inform you sooner. But…" What could she say? She waved her hand in defeat. "I did not know how. I did not know who to trust."

Jordan stood with Mathew's help. His knees cracked. "We understand. We were as much an enemy to you as you were to us." He started to turn, but stopped. "What made you run?"

Staring off, Ellyssa chewed on her lip before replying, "As The Center's children, we went through rigorous programming to eradicate all emotions except anger and self-preservation. When I saw my father's plans, not only did my self-preservation kick in, but I experienced a feeling of…wrongness, if he were to succeed."

"How strange for you," said Mathew, his voice barely above a whisper. "I can't imagine how that must have felt like."

Jordan held up his hand. "Thank you for answering our questions."

"She hasn't answered an important one," Rein said, his tone clipped and seething with fury. "When, exactly, were you going to tell us?" Jordan placed a hand on his arm, but he jerked away. "No. Don't. You just don't get it. This confirms everything." His eyes narrowed and fell on her. "Who'd you lead here?" he demanded, reaching for her.

Ellyssa's quick response had her on her feet on the other side of the cot. "I did not bring others." Although her muscles tensed, ready to defend, her voice quivered in desperation. She was suddenly afraid to lose him. A feeling of impending loneliness surfaced. "I told you they would come for me."

"Liar," Rein roared. "You've endangered us all." Red colored his cheeks, and his fists clenched and unclenched, as if he wished his fingers were curled around her neck. He pushed past the doctor.

Unable to contain her curiosity, Ellyssa peeked inside Rein's head. Fury, betrayal, and confusion swirled in incomprehensible images.

Somehow, Rein knew. He flipped around, the tendons in his neck standing out. "Stay the hell out of my head." He stormed out.

Mathew and Jordan turned toward her, her hand caught in the proverbial cookie jar. Beaten, she collapsed onto her cot.

Jordan stroked Ellyssa's hair. It felt nice, and more tears formed in her eyes. An emotional betrayal. Her father was right; emotions weakened her. Ellyssa inhaled and closed down, her face becoming an empty canvas, a veneer to cover her true sentiments. Inside her chest, though, misery twisted and seethed and clawed.

Jordan wavered for a moment, then his hand fell to his side. He looked askance at the doctor, who cocked a brow. "Don't worry, hon. I'll talk to him."

Lowering her head, Ellyssa nodded. After all, she had deceived them. Even without looking into their heads, she knew they believed that. She wished she'd said something sooner.

"I am sorry," she muttered, her voice monotone, unfeeling.

"Tsk, tsk. We'll have none of that."

Ellyssa looked at Jordan, and surprisingly, a toothy grin, minus the top front teeth, flashed across his dark face, deepening his wrinkles. She couldn't understand him at all.

"Rein is right. Whether I intended to or not, I have endangered you all."

"We were never out of danger." Jordan's lids lowered, not in anger, but in slyness. "You know why he is so angry, don't you?"

"Yes. He feels betrayed."

Laughing, Jordan shook his head. His dreadlocks swung like pendulums. "For someone who is supposedly smarter than the rest of us, you really don't know much about this world at all."

Not really sure if he meant that as an insult, she stared at him. Her defenses fell and confusion tightened her mouth.

Humor glinted in the old man's eyes. He laughed even harder as he walked from the room, his thin shoulders shaking all the way.

When they were alone, Mathew hopped over and sat next to her. "Rein'll come around, don't worry."

"Worried? I do not feel worry."

The doctor, the first person who had ever showed her kindness, the first person she had ever considered a friend, placed a finger under her chin. Ellyssa met his light brown eyes, and her stoic barricade melted.

"I'm not blind. I can see how you feel," Mathew said.

"And how is that?"

The corners of his lips tugged into a small smile. "You like him."

"I do not deny that. I like you, too."

"I know, but your feelings for him are more than friendship."

What an alien notion. She'd never *liked* anyone before, but to like them as more than a friend was incomprehensible. To form bonds brought disadvantage, her father would say.

Ellyssa thought about what the doctor had said. Was that why she had felt electricity at Rein's touch? Why he had warmed her? Maybe she did like him as more than a friend, but he didn't hold the same feelings for her.

"I might not be very familiar with emotions, but I know hatred. I thrived on it for years. He holds hatred for me."

Mathew brushed a piece of her hair back behind her ear. The gesture was reassuring.

"He doesn't hate you, dear. Far from it."

"I disagree."

"If you must, but you're wrong. Anyway, Rein and I have some business to attend to for the next couple of days. Jordan will be in to check on you, and different guards will be posted at the door."

Ellyssa held no doubt Jason would be amongst them.

Mathew frowned. "I don't see why we still have to go through the formalities. I'm guessing if you intended to hurt people, you would have no problem doing so."

No problem, whatsoever. She nodded.

"As I thought." He picked up the book. "What do you think?"

"I am not so sure about this one. Like I said earlier, the story strikes close to home."

"You know, the thing about *Frankenstein* is that many people portrayed the creature as the monster. But the creature isn't the monster at all." He stood and handed the book back to her. "It is his creator."

Anger carried Rein all the way back to his holey. He climbed into the cramped space with the scratchy blankets, lantern, and one of Mathew's beloved books, and lay across the pallet. His home.

He was annoyed at how Ellyssa dominated his thoughts, no matter how hard he tried to push her out. He wondered if she could read his thoughts, right now. If she could, she'd see how much she'd hurt him by her betrayal. But why should he be hurt?

An aggravated sigh escaped his lips.

Against his judgment, he'd trusted her. And she'd withheld information.

What would the community do? Where would they go?

It was entirely his fault. He should've left her there to die, like Candy and Woody had wanted.

Rein couldn't, though. Ellyssa's body had lain among the decaying rags, her breath ragged and uneven, her skin a sickly color, and the dirt-covered, sweaty hair clumped around her face. She seemed so frail, even after she'd attacked them in her feverish state.

Even then she'd been the most beautiful woman he'd ever seen.

What bothered Rein the most was that, if he had to do it all over again, he still would've saved her. No matter the evidence stacked against her, a deep, nagging sensation pulled at his heart, an unnatural draw he couldn't shake.

It was irritating.

Better to think of her lying, conniving ways, squelching his attraction, or whatever it was.

Better not to think of her at all.

Rein flipped to his knees and grabbed the knapsack he used on short excursions. He rummaged around his little space, arranging things to take—an extra shirt, a box of ammunition, a flashlight, and a first aid kit.

He was shoving the items into his bag when he heard Jordan's soft, shuffling footsteps. He'd heard them for so long, there was no mistaking the brush of the worn leather of the leader's shoes against the rocky floor. Jordan stopped outside his drape and a wrinkled hand appeared at the edge of his tattered curtain.

"Rein," said Jordan, his voice staggering breathlessly.

The way the old man's age had seemed to sneak up on him within the last couple of months worried Rein. He'd tried to ask Jordan about it on several occasions, but the old man had always led the conversation away in different directions.

Rein pulled the curtain back and popped out, so his elder wouldn't have to exert the energy to crawl into the hole. Jordan sighed with gratitude, his full lips stretching apart in relief. The old man's face looked haggard and sunken.

"I'm just about ready to go."

"Good. I believe Doc is waiting for you."

Rein yanked his bag out and draped it over his shoulder. "We should be back in less than two days." He paused for a moment, leaning closer to Jordan's ear. "I'm really sorry for bringing her here. It was a mistake. I think it's best if we remove her from the cave as soon as I return. I'll blindfold her or something. Take her far away."

"You didn't make a mistake, son," the old man replied, patting Rein's upper arm. "I believe Jeremy sent her."

Rein blinked. "What?"

"He must have seen inside her, like she can see inside us. Maybe he saw good."

"You didn't see her that day in town. She's dangerous."

Jordan's gaze settled on Rein, life and amusement still dancing within the dark depths of his eyes, even as tiredness pulled the edges of his lids and sagged his cheeks. "I've seen her strength, her will. She's a great addition to the family."

Rein couldn't believe it. "Her...special abilities put us all at risk. Even if her intentions are harmless, she is too valuable to them."

Jordan cast a look over his shoulder before he whispered, "That might be true. And maybe they'll find her."

"Then we're done."

Jordan shrugged his frail shoulders. "With everything that had happened in the past. The war. Our struggle to survive. I never was sure if there was a higher power or not, delegating the randomness of life on delicate strings. But I believe—believe without a doubt—Jeremy sent her to us. Maybe, to let us know what was cooking in the labs of The Center, to give us a heads-up.

"There are very few things I know in this world, Rein. Very few. But I know a good person when I see them. And she is good. Jeremy saw it. And I think you see it, too."

The older man staggered and Rein clutched his upper arm, holding him steady.

"Are you okay?"

Jordan patted the hand grasping his shoulder. "Fine, son. Just fine. Nothing a nap won't take care of. Help me to my holey."

Rein stepped to Jordan's side and steadied him as they walked down the tunnel. Much to Rein's relief, they passed no one on the trek. The last thing they needed was gossip and panic. When they reached Jordan's holey, Rein helped him inside.

"You mind what I said, Rein," said Jordan as he lay down. "I know you're thinking she was dishonest. Take into consideration how her truth might have come out in bits and pieces, but she got around to it. How much have we shared with her? How can we expect something we haven't freely given?"

The corner of Rein's mouth drew back. "I'll talk to her when I get back," he said.

"That's a good boy. Now go. Doc is waiting." Jordan rolled to his side, ending any further conversation.

22

Detective Angela Petersen sneered at Micah through the filthy window of the drug store in Deepwater. He looked a little different since the last time she'd seen him, taller and broader. His perfectly cut platinum hair framed chiseled features that had sharpened into those of a man. Occasionally, his azure eyes would cut sideways at her, accusingly, as if her less-than-perfect intelligence was to blame for Ellyssa's disappearance.

She hated him. After a month of having no contact with the little creatures, she'd almost forgotten how much she hated them all.

The detective stepped back when Micah squared off to her, letting Angela know he was watching. She would have to be very careful of everything she did, every call she made.

Certainly, Dr. Hirch had sent him to spy on her and report back all her failures. The whole operation the doctor had entrusted to her had turned into nothing more than a fiasco. Captain Jones hadn't helped matters either with his constant distractions.

Micah cast Angela another look before shifting through the pile of rags with the toe of his shoe. If she didn't know better, she'd swear the look was smug.

All The Center's children felt they were so superior. Their egos towered over that of the doctor. For creatures supposedly lacking emotions, they had no problem showing arrogance.

Anglea lifted her foot. The handgun weighed against her ankle. What she wouldn't give to shoot the condescending look right off his face, mess up his flawless features. That'd knock him down a peg or two.

Although unlikely, maybe she'd have a chance. If only she could get him alone. The cartridge could never be traced back to her. Renegades would be blamed.

Angela sighed. That'd never happen. And with Micah there, she'd never get a chance to even the score with Ellyssa. He would return home safe, and so would his sister. And she would return a failure.

"What're you thinking about?"

Angela gave Dyllon a once-over. An anxious energy swirled around the young captain. His cream-colored hair was combed perfectly, except for a small piece that flipped out disobediently behind his ear. He wore civilian clothes, a green T-shirt which brought out his eyes, and faded jeans that formed nicely around his hips and legs.

He was standing too close.

Angela's gaze darted through the cloudy glass and, sure enough, the boy watched them. Her lip curled as she looked away. The absolute last thing she needed was Micah to report that she was being chummy with the local police. The doctor wouldn't understand how differently things worked here.

"Why are you dressed like that?" Angela asked.

Dyllon's perpetual grin faltered a bit. "It's my day off. What's wrong?"

"Nothing," Angela snarled while she stepped away from the window, her strides long and quick.

Dyllon jogged to catch up with her. "Something's wrong."

Stopping on the other side of the street, Angela glanced at the drug store to make certain prying eyes were not following them. The doorway was clear, but the glass was too filthy to see through. Although the hairs on her neck didn't tingle, she couldn't be sure. She started to walk again, her pace slower.

She paused at the end of the broken walkway. The only way the boy could see them now was if he stepped outside. "Have you found out anything about Davis?" she asked.

Dyllon touched her arm.

"Don't."

Small lines furrowed in the middle of his forehead. "What's wrong? Why are you acting like this?"

"May I remind you, Captain, I am not one of your officers, but your superior?"

Confusion clouded Dyllon's features while he studied her. He looked over his shoulder, and when he looked back at her, his bewilderment was replaced with a knowing look.

"I get it. No more friendly working together," he whispered.

Angela nodded.

Dyllon straightened his back and lifted his chin. "Yes, ma'am. I just brought you this," he said, officially. He shoved a clear plastic bag she hadn't even noticed into her hand. "The items you requested to be tested."

The bag contained a fragment of the blood-spotted shelf and the shotgun casing from the store. The analysis on both items had run into a dead-end. The blood was not in the computer system, the wounded individual obviously birthed in secret, and the shell was not from a registered gun.

Angela slid the evidence under her arm. "Thank you."

He glanced at the empty storefront, then turned toward her. "I understand."

Working with the captain and his team had been somewhat pleasant. A break from the stress of The Center. That time was over, Micah reminded her of who she was. "No. No, you don't."

"Who is that kid anyway?"

Angela glanced at the store Micah was in. She couldn't see him, but knew he was somehow watching her, filing away every move she made to report later.

She'd been made a mockery of. All this time, Angela thought she had known everything about the subjects, priding herself in her ability to observe. She hadn't known anything, except what the doctor wanted her to. It astounded her and made her question herself, that she had provided security for the doctor's creations without ever being aware, until the recent events had unfolded. And even with all that had transpired, the doctor still had refused to answer her other inquiries, stating *a need to know basis*, as if she was some lackey. Anger and jealousy curled in her and, for a moment, she thought about blowing the whole operation out of the water as she looked back at Dyllon's expectant face.

The confession stuck on the tip of Angela's tongue. If she did, she would be more worthless than how she already felt, and her purpose at the moment was to prove her superiority.

Of course, it was Dr. Hirch, and not her, who invited the captain to know about Micah. There was no way around it. She scoffed and shook her head.

Dyllon gave her a strange look.

"Come with me. You're about to find out." Angela pulled her shoulders back, her demeanor icy. She marched back toward the drug store and walked through the entrance. "Micah," she said.

"Yes," he replied. After being in the company of Dyllon and the other Missouri citizens, his accent sounded strange to her ears.

"This should interest you."

Micah took the bag, showing no interest. He emptied the shelf fragment into his hand. He fingered it with his eyes closed. After a moment, his lids opened, but his expression didn't tell her if he could make a reading. It remained as stoic as before.

"Well?" she hinted.

"Blood is rather personal. Gives a clear picture, even with the interference of others. It belongs to a woman with red hair and freckles."

"Red hair," Dyllon exclaimed, his eyes rounded into spheres of disbelief.

Angela wasn't sure if it was due to Micah's parlor trick or if it was because there was a girl with red hair. She shushed him.

Micah's impassive eyes shifted to the captain. "Not very pretty. Small. Very forthright. She is angry."

"How do you know all this?" asked Dyllon.

"I receive images from things I touch. They come to me, much like a movie."

Angela shot a *shut up* glare at Dyllon. Taking the hint, Dyllon's mouth snapped shut before he could question Micah's talent further, but she could see the amazement on his face like a neon sign.

"Can you tell us where she is?" she pressed.

Micah turned toward the detective. "Of course not. Parts of the physical body can only give physical details. I need a personal item from the subject. But even then, I doubt I will come up with an exact location."

"What about the casing?"

He dumped the casing into his palm and closed his fingers around it. "This was taken off the floor by one of your officers and analyzed by a researcher." He handed the shell and the bag back to the detective as he spoke to the captain. "The evidence has been tainted. Touched by too many people. I suggest that if you find anything else, you leave it alone."

"Of course, Micah." The captain's tone was polite, but brusque.

"I am finished in here," Micah told Angela. "If you do not mind, I will examine the other buildings."

He said it in such a way as to give her little choice in the matter.

"My officers have already examined every building in town, including the residences. There wasn't anything of any significance."

The young man settled his azure eyes on the captain. "If I am correct, Captain, there is suspicion of possible laundering of excessive supplies. I imagine that, if that is the case, then they would use a store on this main road as a drop-off point. Easily accessible." He started for the door. "And in the future, do not question me again."

Resentment worked at Dyllon's jaw. He opened his mouth to say something, but Angela bumped his arm. A deep scowl bunched his forehead, but he held his tongue.

Angela waited until the sound of Micah's footsteps faded. "Be careful what you say or do around him," she said in a low voice.

"What a pompous ass," said Dyllon, the words seething into long drawn-out syllables. "Who does he think he is?"

"Shh." She waved her hand in his face. She edged toward the door and poked her head out. Micah walked along the weathered planks. "You have to be careful." She waited a moment longer, just to ensure the boy wasn't going to return.

"So, we were never looking for a Renegade?"

"No," she said, turning back around toward him.

Dyllon hadn't moved, his face a mask of awe and anger. His gaze slid from the door to Angela. "I can't believe that. Are all of The Center's children so...?"

"Yes, I believe so. They are superior to us in every way," she said matter-of-factly. Superior to her, despite all of her hard work. Her gut twisted in rage at the unfairness of it all; jealousy tugged at her core. "They're stronger and faster, and the gifts they possess are beyond comprehension," she continued.

"Can they all read objects?"

"It seems the subjects of The Center possess many gifts."

"Like what?"

"My job is security," Angela stated, her tone terse so there wouldn't be any more questions from Dyllon. "You do realize that everything you've witnessed will be kept to yourself. I need not remind you what could happen without me threatening you."

"Yes, I do understand that," Dyllon said, moving toward the door. "I just don't understand why."

She lifted a shoulder in response. "I'm assuming they're the next wave of soldiers."

"Soldiers? The war is long over."

"The road to perfection is never-ending."

23

As afternoon sunlight filtered through the narrow gaps of the barn's roof, Rein woke, sweating. His shirt stuck to his skin and his pants felt heavy and constricting.

Judging by the bright light, there had to be at least another six or so hours until nightfall. He kicked his blanket off and flipped onto his side.

Sleep evaded him. The stifling heat made the task nearly impossible. He rolled over and watched Doc's chest rise and fall. Perspiration beaded along the older man's forehead. Soft snores pushed his lips apart.

Jealous, Rein concentrated on the soft, lulling sounds of the sleeping man. Eventually, despite the warm air, his eyes drooped, then closed. He became one with the worlds of in-between, teetering on the edge of reality and dreams, until snapping sounds and shouts roused him. His eyes popped open and Doc was staring straight at him, his eyes bugging.

"Is someone in the barn?" Rein mouthed.

Doc shrugged. "I think it came from outside," he whispered.

As quietly as possible, careful to avoid the old creaking floorboards, he shifted to his stomach and placed his ear against the loft floor. He stayed still and waited for any sounds at all.

Silence.

Convinced no one was sneaking around below them, he lifted onto all fours and shuffled over to one window. A broken shutter hung to the side, obstructing the view.

Hunkered down, he put his hand on the piece of wood and started to move it away when someone shouted. A male's voice, deep and young. He stiffened, unmoving. Another male answered. He wasn't exactly sure where they were, but he knew they were close. Gathering his courage, he pushed the board over and peeked.

At first, he couldn't see anything unusual, only the old road, where heat waves wafted from the broken asphalt and shimmered like a mirage. Beyond, the remnants of a town curved into view.

"Can you see anything?"

The suddenness of Doc's voice caught him off-guard. His breath hitched in his chest. "No," he exhaled.

He shuffled to the side to get a better view. Two figures, in dark clothing, appeared like ghosts.

"Wait." He motioned for the doctor to come closer. "Over there," he said.

Doc leaned over his shoulder. "What are they doing?" Barking answered his question, and the doctor pulled back, lengthening his spine. "Dogs. Ellyssa?"

"Yes," he said while another person leading two dogs joined the first group. The searchers stood next to the road, talking. "They're searching the town."

"What are we going to do?"

"For right now, we're going to stay here," Rein said, backing away. He picked up his blanket and shoved it in his backpack.

"We can't just stay here."

"We can't leave. Not yet."

Rein grabbed his rifle and moved toward the shadows in the back of the barn. Behind a pile of wood and rusted tools hid a crawl space. Rein peered inside. Mold scented the air. A hole in the roof let light sneak into the cramped space. Dust particles floated in the sun streams. Spider webs dangled across the opening.

"We can hide in here until night."

"I don't know about the floorboards," Doc said, pointing. The floor buckled across the small space.

"I guess we won't be moving around much." He waved his hand in a polite gesture. "After you."

"Oh sure, let me be the guinea pig."

Doc dropped his bag and, with Rein's help, hefted himself through the opening. Scooting on his belly, he turned around until his head faced the opening. "Okay, you're next."

"One second." Rein went back to where they had slept.

"Hey, where're you going?"

Lifting his finger to his mouth, he opened the trapdoor and kicked the rickety ladder. It cracked but held fast. On the second kick, it was less resistant and broke free, collapsing onto the floor. He retrieved the extra shirt from his bag and, with a back and forth motion, rearranged the decades of dust as he backtracked to the crawl space.

"How are we going to get down?" the doctor asked, his voice low.

"Shh."

He handed Doc both bags and the rifle, then pulled himself through the gap. The boards protested angrily. He gingerly turned around and laid across the planks, sliding the gun under him, muzzle pointing out into the loft.

Hours passed, and the sun slid across the sky. Shadows lengthened and danced across the loft. Except for the occasional voice carrying across an unknown distance, or the echo of barking, it stayed silent.

Tired from staying in the same position for so long, a kink biting at the back of his neck, Rein rested his head on his arms, fighting to stay awake. The doctor had dozed off a half-hour earlier. He felt the pull on his lids too, urging him to join Doc, when the squeak of rollers along a rusted track broke the monotony. He nudged the doctor.

"We have visitors."

From beneath, two distinct sets of footfalls stepped across planks. Rein put his finger to his mouth, but the doctor didn't need any warning, his body tighter than a taut wire.

Whoever roamed below didn't bother to be quiet. A crash sounded, and Rein knew the boxes next to the door had fallen over. He tracked the sound of the intruders to where the ladder lay useless on the ground. From the light scraping, it sounded like someone was pushing bits of wooden litter around with his foot, before he proceeded deeper into the barn toward the back, where Rein had parked the truck directly below the crawl space. His body became like Doc's, still, unmoving; even his breath was shallow.

For the first time ever, he was happy he'd followed the procedures dictated by Jordan. The rules were a big pain, but he performed them religiously without fail.

Then, a seed of doubt sprouted. Had he cleaned out the cab?

He thought back, trying to remember. The backpacks were with them, trash shoved inside. The gun wasn't in the cab. He remembered picking out everything. Yes, he'd cleaned it out, and he'd smudged dirt on the window to make the truck appear abandoned. The hard, dry ground didn't show tire tracks, and Doc had placed rubble around the rusted hunk of metal. All necessary precautions had been performed.

Hopefully, the searchers would wander around a bit, and then leave.

"Alex," said a disembodied voice. "Where are you?"

"Over here. Check this out," said Alex, apparently the one directly below them.

Heavier thumps echoed through the floorboards and stopped. "Wow. Is that an Oshkosh? I've only seen these in history books."

"I know. I can't believe it was left behind."

"Probably broken or something. Not worth bringing out during the evacuation."

"No. It must have been missed during the sweep."

One of the searchers smacked the truck with his hand. A metallic bang sounded.

"We can file a report on it later. If they want the metal, they can come get it."

The silence wavered for a moment, and was broken by a loud popping; the truck door opened. Rein closed his eyes. Although he had never believed in a higher power, he mouthed a prayer anyway.

The door slammed shut, and he heard some more scuttling around. Something scraped across the floor, accompanied by muttering, as if suddenly the intruders were afraid of being heard. Rein strained to hear, but their voices were too low. Then his fear was realized. The trapdoor leading to the loft swung open and two huge hands appeared, followed by blond hair. Rein and Doc ducked into the concealment the darkness offered.

"Just a little further," said a man as his head popped up like a jack-in-the-box. Sharp, angled jowls completed the squareness of his face.

"You weigh a ton," said the voice belonging to Alex.

"Muscles."

Rein realized the man wasn't kidding. He positioned his hands accordingly, and lifted his body on two arms befitting tree trunks. Muscles bulged and rippled under the dark clothing. He tilted to the side to bring his leg up, but a sharp snap stopped further movement. He readjusted.

Snap.

"Hold up," he screeched. "Stop."

"Can you see anything?" said Alex.

His partner scanned the area, craning his head to see behind him and around the door. "Just dust. No one would be crazy enough to come up here. It's not safe."

"Come on, it's getting dark."

"Okay."

But before he lowered himself, the man glanced toward the back of the barn. Rein's prayer died and was replaced by a thrumming heart. Doc's chest stopped moving, as if he'd lost the ability to breathe.

"Wait," the muscle-bound man said, narrowing his gaze and inclining his head forward.

"What?"

"Just..." He didn't finish, his stare unwavering.

Rein felt the man's eyes boring into him, the tension of the trigger familiar against his finger. If the man noticed them, he'd have to be quick. First Mr. Muscle, then Alex. Sweat dripped from his hairline and down his neck.

"Do you see something or not?" Alex asked, his voice strained.

His companion's voice seemed to break the scrutiny of the muscular man. He blinked. "I thought..." He squinted again before he relented. "No, nothing, just shadows. Lower me down."

A mountain of relief collapsed on Rein as the man disappeared, and he risked breathing again. Doc followed suit, as his chest expanded. He listened as incorporeal voices faded and the barn door closed. Emptiness, and the certainty the searchers had left, didn't matter; neither man spoke until complete darkness engulfed the barn.

"It's night, let's get out of here," said Doc, pulling himself forward. His feet hit the floor with a dull thud.

"Wait." Rein placed the shotgun to the side, before flipping himself onto the ground.

"What?"

"I'm guessing they're camped close by."

The doctor looked disheartened. "We can't just stay here, like sitting ducks."

"I don't think they'll come back. At least, not tonight." Rein went to the corner of the barn. He pulled out his blanket and spread it across the floor, then took a seat. "We have to leave the truck behind, now that they know it's here, and hoof it back to the caves."

"When?"

"Tomorrow night. Hopefully by then, they'll move along."

The doctor sighed while he settled next to Rein. "I'll take the first watch," he said, pulling the rifle on his lap.

Rein's lips pursed in uncertainty.

"What? Just because I never carry doesn't mean I don't know how to use one." He slid the bolt back and chambered a round. "Desperate times call for desperate measures."

24

Sweat dripped down Ellyssa's face. Her body remained in perfect balance while she strengthened her arms and legs. First, an extended knife strike to the throat of her invisible enemy, then she spun around into a roundhouse kick, taking out her enemy's knees. Much like a dancer, she moved fluidly, as she practiced the sequence of *katas* she'd been performing daily since she had turned three.

The discipline had developed her, mind, body, and spirit, into the warrior she was bred to be. It helped keep her muscles strong and flexible even without the ability to run or use weights. She felt them pull under her skin, tightening, flexing, and stretching. Even after her accident, her body was ready, if need called for action. And, eventually, the call would come. Right now though, the exercise kept her focus off Rein.

She swept her foot from *Hachi-dachi* to *Zenkutsu-dachi* and snapped her arms out into a series of *tsukis*, yelling *kias* to accompany the movements. Performed perfectly, as always. If she had on her *gi*, instead of the black shirt and camo pants, the material would snap with the strength and form of her attack.

The *kata* completed, she brought her hands up and around, ending with her feet together and her arms at her sides. She bowed. Clapping erupted behind her. Unsurprised, Ellyssa turned around and bowed to Trista, who'd been watching her for the last five minutes.

"That was wonderful. I've never seen anyone do anything like that." Trista bounded from the entrance toward Ellyssa, her blue eyes sparkling in excitement and her ponytail bouncing in blond waves. "Can you teach me sometime?"

"I'd be happy to," Ellyssa said, wiping the sweat from her brow. Her hand froze in mid-swipe. She'd spoken like a normal person without even thinking about it. Mathew was right, practicing brought it about like second nature.

Trista's face lit and exhilaration oozed from every pore of her being. "Great!"

Half-afraid the female was going to hug her, Ellyssa stepped back and began wiping down her arms. Even with Jordan and his daylong visits, she still didn't feel comfortable with everyone. Saddened over her inability to completely trust Trista, she turned from her visitor and washed her face in the basin.

Trista didn't seem to notice her discomfort. She went over to Ellyssa's cot and sat down. "I'd like that," she said, crossing her legs. "By the way, Jordan wants to see you."

Ellyssa's gaze flashed toward the door leading into the tunnel. "What about the guard?"

"Oh, don't worry. I sent him away. Your days of being guarded are over." She picked up the novel Ellyssa had been reading and wrinkled her nose. "You like this book?"

Her eyes fell to the book Trista was thumbing through. To have a family, people who loved her, wasn't that the true reason for existence? It definitely wasn't to live in loneliness.

"I do."

"I'm not much into reading. I know I should be, but…" She shrugged.

"All I have ever read were text books. Never any fiction. Just facts and more facts."

The arch in Trista's eyebrows and the pull of her mouth told Ellyssa how much she thought she'd missed. Even being raised in a cave with very few modern amenities, things Ellyssa took for granted, Trista was the one feeling sorry for her. Just like that, though, Trista was smiling again, all teeth and happiness.

Trista tossed the book back onto the cot. "Are you about ready?"

"Let me change shirts." Ellyssa went behind a screen and pulled on a different black T-shirt. She tucked the hem in around her waist and stepped toward the door.

"So, no more guards?" she asked as Trista joined her in the tunnel. Even though Ellyssa had only been escorted through the passageway once, she walked with confidence.

"I don't think so. I overheard Jordan telling Woody it was ridiculous to treat you like a prisoner."

"Are they changing where I sleep?"

Ellyssa sidled into the dark corridor that led into the generator room. The cool air settled on her skin.

"Not yet. Have you seen the holeys?"

Ellyssa shook her head.

"They suck. You should wish they let you stay here. At least you're off the ground."

"You sleep on the ground?"

Trista looked at her as if the answer was obvious. "Did you think all of us had our own rooms with cots and such?"

"I've not really thought about it at all," Ellyssa responded, proud how easily the words were rolling off her tongue. She rounded a bend. Humming emitted from ahead. She stepped into the generator room with Trista following behind and entered the tunnel leading into the dining area.

"We live in little holes, like little grey moles."

Ellyssa smiled at the dry humor.

"You think I'm kidding?" Trista asked.

"No."

"It's awful. You wait and see."

They stepped into the empty room. The long benches rested on top of the wooden tables. Two people with olive-colored skin washed the counter where the food was distributed. They looked up when Ellyssa and Trista entered, and nodded a greeting before continuing with their chore.

Trista pulled on Ellyssa's sleeve. "This way." She moved in front. "Jordan's not doing well," she continued in a whisper, her cheerful demeanor disappearing in a whiff. It amazed Ellyssa how Trista could cycle through emotions so quickly.

"When I went to wake him this morning, he was wheezing and coughing more than usual." She turned to face Ellyssa, her expression downcast and her eyes worried. "His lips were blue."

Ellyssa's forehead crinkled in concern. "Is he doing better now?"

"Once I got him standing, his lungs cleared and his color returned, but I wouldn't say he is actually doing better."

Trista started off again, heading down a different tunnel that opened into a magnificent room. Rows of long, thick columns jutted from floor to ceiling like in spiraling towers. Minerals sparkled under the yellow lights that swung between the pillars.

Trista stopped where the light faded into a tunnel. Voices carried from a room ahead. Some were loud, others were normal; all carried urgency.

"This is the main hall, where we have our meetings. Everyone is in attendance," she warned.

Ellyssa had expected the Renegades to have more of a problem with her than she would with them. She forced her lips into a fake smile, and shrugged. Shrugging said a lot.

Quietly, they entered the back of the room. People filled the benches, facing away from the newcomers. Jordan sat in the front on a natural platform. He was slumped over, and under the fluorescent lights, his skin appeared waxen.

Woody stood next to him, his arm around the older man's shoulders. His ash-blond hair fell loosely around his head. Worry lined his features, cutting deep around his eyes. He tilted his chin to Ellyssa, then leaned closer to Jordan's ear. As he whispered, the dark man's eyes shifted toward her, and a tired smile lifted his cheeks. Jordan motioned for her to come closer. A collage of Renegades pivoted their heads toward her, their faces holding a mix of distrust and confusion.

Mumbling lifted in the air, followed by laughter when a musical voice said, "Bitch."

Ellyssa saw Candy sitting in the first row next to Jason. She hadn't seen the fiery redhead since the day in the dining room, which was fine with her. Ellyssa ignored Candy's narrowed gaze and Jason's lustful eyes, which had swept up from her feet and stopped at her chest. She stepped onto the platform next to Woody.

Jordan tried to rise to his feet, but Ellyssa shook her head. Upon closer inspection, he looked worse than she had first realized. His brown skin was shaded grey, his dreads fell limp, and his lips were tinged blue. Even though tiredness clung to him, dragging him down, his chocolate eyes still held humor.

Ellyssa blinked away the sudden stinging in her eyes. This old man had touched her in such a short time. A true friend. She forced control over her emotions and smiled.

"As I'm sure you already know through the grapevine, this is Ellyssa, the newest member of our little family," Jordan announced, as his eyes shifted toward Candy. "I expect everyone to treat her accordingly."

Voices lifted. Some were pleasant, others held anger. Ellyssa glanced sideways at Candy and Jason; they were huddled together, whispering. She wished there weren't so many people, so she could get a read on them.

She decided to chance it, anyway.

Focusing on Candy, with her brilliant red hair, pinched face and glaring eyes, Ellyssa lowered her shield just a fraction, and, instantly, images and noise bombarded her. She stumbled back. If not for Woody, she would've fallen. He held her upper arm while she slammed her defenses up against the onslaught. With the voices quieted in her head, she looked out into the small audience. Everyone was staring at her.

"Are you okay?" Woody asked.

"Yes. Thank you." She turned toward Jordan. "I'm sorry. Please, continue."

Jordan peered at her for a moment, his shoulders drooping, as if the weight of his head tired him. In just the few seconds she had been on the platform, the leader had grown even paler.

His head bobbled forward as he continued addressing the crowd. "As I said, I expect her to be treated accordingly. There is a lot we can learn from her, as much as she can learn from us. I am putting her on the council."

Ellyssa blinked back. "What?"

Protests broke out among the people.

Woody stepped forward. "Shut up!"

As the mob quieted, a man with hair the color of pitch stood. "From what I understand, she's from The Center."

"She can't be trusted," a female in the back complained.

Candy bolted to her feet, her face as blazing red as her hair. "How can you even offer her a position on the committee without talking to us first?"

"The decision has been made, Candy," said Jordan.

Candy's face changed shades of red, lighting her freckles on fire. They brightened past the shade of her hair. "No one asked me."

"You're only an alternate."

"What about Jason? He holds a seat." She glanced at Jason. He turned away, his shoulders hunched defensively.

Candy's eyes narrowed dangerously. "How dare you?" she spat. "After everything we talked about?" She faced the crowd, sweeping her arm toward Ellyssa. "She's a spy. She's going to destroy us."

"Listen," Jordan croaked.

Words never followed. The leader bent over, coughing. His face turned the color of ash, and blue flooded his lips. He hacked again and blood seeped from the corner of his mouth.

"Take his other arm," Ellyssa ordered Woody, whose feet were apparently bolted to the platform. "We need to take him to the hospital."

Ellyssa's voice broke Woody from his shock, and he moved to take Jordan's arm.

Jordan waved them both away. The old man spat reddish-green mucus onto the stony ground. "I'm going to finish this," he said. "Then, I will go."

Jordan's face drew into a weathered scowl, and his eyes hardened as he looked out into the crowd. "I have led you, and our community has survived while others were captured." His voice was amazingly strong and unwavering. "Ours survived against all odds. But it wasn't just because of my leadership; it was because we accepted new members. We brought in new knowledge, new ideas, new ways of doing things from all walks of life. It was because of *all* of you."

The elder struggled to stand, and Ellyssa assisted him. He straightened his back and leveled his gaze onto his people. "It is no secret that I am sick...and old. And as a last word to you all...my last plea. Trust me on this. I wouldn't lead you astray."

"No," Candy roared. "She can't be trusted. None of you saw her that day in the store. The way she moves, how fast she is. It's not natural."

Jason grabbed her wrist and tried to make her sit, but she ripped away from his grasp and whirled around on him. "And you," she seethed accusingly. "You traitor." She stomped from the room, her footfalls slapping against the stone.

All eyes followed her until she disappeared down a tunnel. They returned their attention to the old man.

"Trust me," Jordan said.

Jason and Woody laid Jordan on the cot next to hers. His breaths came in short, wheezing gasps.

Looking lost, Jason rocked on his feet for a moment before retreating back into the tunnel; hands shoved in his pockets. He stayed at the edge of the entrance, his eyes downcast.

"What are we supposed to do?" Woody asked.

Ellyssa didn't have an answer for him. Her medical education went as far as first aid, not enough to cure what ailed an aging man. All she knew to do, Trista was already doing—applying a wet cloth to his forehead. "I don't know." Strangely, even now, she noticed how her speech flipped-flopped back and forth.

The old man started choking again.

Ellyssa's heart sputtered. Panic. She squashed the sensation before it incapacitated her. Slipping into her old skin, her comfort zone when chaos emerged, she became stoic; the turmoil inside her faded away.

"Grab that bowl," Ellyssa said to Woody.

Woody handed it to her, and she put it under the old man just in time for Jordan to empty the contents of his stomach. Phlegm and bile filled the bowl, sloshing over one side.

"I am so sorry," she said.

Jordan looked at her with dulled eyes. Beads of perspiration glimmered on his forehead. "No need for sorrow," he muttered.

"I do not know what to do."

He grinned. "Neither do I."

Trista wrung the cloth out in a basin of water and placed it back on his head.

"What will make you comfortable?" Ellyssa asked.

"I want you to listen," he said to Ellyssa, his voice low. She knelt closer to hear him. "My son, Jeremy, found you for a reason. I know it."

He inhaled. Ellyssa could hear the sickening rattle deep inside his chest. She glanced at Woody; sorrow fixed his features and his eyes filled with tears.

"I know there is conflict, but I believe in you. You'll do what is right."

Watching the old man fade away right before her eyes put a chink in her armor. "Jordan," she said, fighting to hang on to her impassiveness, "I do not know what you mean." Her voice shook.

"You will," Jordan said. His lips curled into a grin. Then, with his last breath, the leader's eyes glazed over, forever stilled.

"Jordan." She shook his arm. He didn't respond.

Misery and loss, profound and unending, completely enveloped her, the strength unlike any sensation she'd felt thus far. Powerless, not knowing how to respond, the emotion smothered the logic of her mind. Her apathetic cocoon shattered into tiny fragments, the pieces forever gone. Tears floated in her eyes before overflowing down her cheeks.

"What am I supposed to do?" Ellyssa looked helplessly at Trista.

"I'm going to let the others know," Trista said, her words almost undecipherable as she backed out of the hospital.

Jason left with her.

Ellyssa shook Jordan's arm again, tears streaming down her face. She tried to blink them back, but they just kept coming, like an incessant drip from a leaky faucet. No matter how hard she tried, she couldn't make them stop. She remembered the first time tears had reached her eyes when she divulged her secret to Jordan, Rein, and Mathew, but this was different. She had absolutely no control.

She moaned, then sobs racked her body.

A hand touched her shoulder. She turned. Woody stood over her, his grey eyes shadowed.

"There's nothing you can do," he said, his voice cracking.

Woody pulled her to him and wrapped his arms around her. Ellyssa had never thought about needing comfort, needing the touch of another human being, given by a man who didn't care for her. She needed it now. Returning his embrace, she buried her face in his chest and let the emotion take her into new territory.

25

After crying what seemed like a river of tears, Ellyssa sat on her cot. Her eyes were dry and raw. The memory of Jordan, his face peacefully at rest, was imprinted in her brain. His people had gathered to pay tribute as he was lowered into a grave, tossing in wildflowers.

Ellyssa had never witnessed a funeral. When someone died at The Center, the empty shells disappeared into the incinerator, burned like trash. But here, the death of a loved one was mourned. Their memory cherished.

She wished she had more to cherish. The loss she felt in her ches,t for a man she'd just met, was profound. The way he'd touched her life, in such a short time, amazed her. No wonder emotions and attachments were prohibited at The Center. She felt drained.

Ellyssa felt so alone.

Then, there was Rein. She wanted to talk to him and apologize for harboring her secret, risking his trust. He'd been gone longer than any of them had expected, but no one seemed worried. Woody had told her that sometimes there were unforeseen hang-ups, delaying travel. His words didn't comfort her.

The sadness, the loneliness, the worry ate at her. Ellyssa needed serenity, to block out everything.

She stood and started her *tai chi* exercises. The fluid movements and slow breathing were calming, much more so than *karate*. It was one thing she'd secretly relished for as long as she could remember.

Ellyssa's feet slid across the floor, lightly, as if she could defy gravity, her hands fluidly moving from side to side, lightening her sorrow. Finishing the second in the series, she pulled her feet together and bowed to the wall.

"Doc said you were a beautiful sight to behold, but I never imagined," Woody said.

She had heard Woody come in and hoped he would go away. She didn't feel like talking to anyone, even after the moment they had shared. Besides, she didn't know how to act now that he had seen her at her weakest. He'd witnessed a whole new Ellyssa. She ignored him and started on the next set of graceful movements.

"Ellyssa, may I have a moment?" Woody asked.

Ellyssa's hands flopped to her side. "Yes." She returned to her cot. "Please." She offered him a seat across from her.

"I won't be staying," he said, much to her relief. "I just wanted to say I'm sorry for my previous behavior."

"No apology is necessary."

"No, there is. Jordan was right." Woody's voice choked on the old leader's name. "You can teach our people a lot."

Placing his elbows on his knees, he looked at her, his tired grey eyes full of sadness, his hair in disarray. "I was part of society at one time. I ran away when I was eight."

Ellyssa was taken aback. "You ran away?"

Woody nodded. "My eyes aren't quite right, and my hair..." He waved his hand as if presenting the trouble crowning the top of his head. "My real mother couldn't stand to look at me anymore—because of my imperfections. I overheard my parents. They wanted to send me to the camps. I ran."

"How did you survive?"

"One evening, late at night, I was rooting around in some trash cans, in search of something to eat." He chuckled as a look of disgust registered on Ellyssa's face.

Partly aghast at his rummaging for food in garbage, and the other part angry over her lessening ability to pay attention to control, Ellyssa blanked her face.

"A woman heard me and came out to investigate," he continued. "I tried to hide behind the can, but she saw me and easily coaxed me out with a piece of bread." Shaking his head. "I was bought with a piece of bread. Can you believe it?"

Ellyssa didn't know whether to respond. The answer was *yes*, though, she could believe it. Regular society's children were not taught the art of survival.

"I was lucky. Very lucky. The woman who coaxed me out was part of the movement."

"Just how many are there?"

"More than you would think. More than we even know. The lady," Woody continued, "brought me here. Jordan took me as his own." He rubbed his hands together and stood. "Listen, I just wanted you to know I'm sorry."

"Accepted."

He left the room.

Feeling better, Ellyssa finished her exercises with a lighter heart. She liked Woody. Not only for holding her when she'd broken down, but for exposing a part of himself to her.

26

Ellyssa was amazed how close the storage room was to where she'd been staying the last few weeks. Not once had she heard scraping boxes, or people filing in and out for supplies.

She opened the closest box and pulled out an industrial can of peaches, like the ones the cafeteria at The Center served. She folded the lid down and placed it on top of another box with the same contents.

"You should see this place when it's full," Trista said, carrying a carton marked with a red cross. "This is nothing."

"How long will this last?"

Trista looked around. Beside the one box of medical supplies, the few remaining boxes held a dwindling stockpile of food. "Maybe a week, with hunting."

"I am amazed you have this much."

"We get a lot of help." Trista set the medical supplies next to the doorway. "So, what'd you think of the council members?"

Ellyssa pushed a large box against the wall as she thought about her newly assigned duties.

Yesterday, a council meeting had been held. Unfortunately, it had been Jason who escorted Ellyssa to an unfamiliar part of the cavern, where the meetings were held. Distrustful of him, she'd kept her mind open to his thoughts.

The images she'd received had been twisted, violent…and lustful.

Ellyssa had prevented herself from taking him down right then. Thoughts were thoughts. Actions were what counted and, so far, he hadn't done anything.

When they'd reached the meeting room, Jason had entered first, brushing against her as he passed. His brief touch had caused nausea to roll in her stomach. He was lucky she'd fought the impulse that had swelled inside her. Maintaining her composure, she'd pretended nothing had happened.

Woody had smiled encouragingly as Ellyssa had entered the tiny room, furnished with an old, rectangular table and metal folding chairs, like the researchers used during training at The Center. She'd made her way to sit next to him, then met the other council members.

Eric, who was fifty—his grandparents among the original survivors—had caramel skin, like he was from Eastern descent, and hair a shade lighter than his complexion. He was friendly, and shook her hand when he introduced himself, as if they were old friends.

Brenda, the only other female council member, was about forty, with premature greying hair and big eyes framed in blond lashes. By the way she spoke and presented herself, Ellyssa had determined that she was very intelligent. She had found out later after the meeting Brenda had defected from society about twenty years ago.

"They were very accommodating," Ellyssa finally replied to Trista's question.

"Rein?" Trista asked.

The mention of his name let loose butterflies in Ellyssa's chest. Was he back? Hopeful, she turned toward the bouncy blonde. "Has he returned?" she asked.

Trista frowned. "No."

"Oh." Ellyssa poked around in a box, trying to hide her disappointment. "What about him?"

"You know, what do you think?"

Taken aback, Ellyssa gawked at her. "About Rein?" She felt the heat creeping up her neck. Was this girl talk? She'd never participated in the social custom of talking about boys. Not that she'd ever participated in anything more than flat, emotionless speech.

A sly smile curled Trista's lips. "Well?"

Flustered, she felt heat rise in her cheeks. "I don't know. I don't know what I am supposed to think."

Scrunching up her face, Trista thought for a moment. "Do you like him?"

Ellyssa felt an urge to look away. She clicked her tongue, secretly relishing the feeling of embarrassment, while buying time to find an answer. Should she admit her feelings? Trista's eyebrows arched above her blue eyes while she waited.

"Yes, I like him," Ellyssa admitted.

"He likes you, too."

Ellyssa's lips curved into a smile. "How do you know?"

"The way he watches you."

"And how is that?"

"Like this." Trista peered intensely at Ellyssa and then wagged her eyebrows. "How's it going, baby?" she said in a deep, sultry voice that wasn't even close to mimicking Rein's. "How about a kiss?" She puckered her lips and made dog-calling sounds, swaying her shoulders seductively.

Shaking her head, laughter burst forth from Ellyssa as if it had been waiting for the chance to spring forward. It was absolutely marvelous to allow the experience without worrying about punishment. Almost everything about the community had been positive, opening her to intense experiences she'd never fathomed possible with her upbringing.

Still giggling, Trista shoved more cans into a box as Ellyssa's thoughts moved to Jeremy, the catalyst of her being here. She wondered why Trista never mentioned him or his ability. Maybe there was a reason Jeremy's skill had been kept secret, and an even bigger reason hers had never been mentioned.

Instead, she said, "Can I ask you a question?"

"Sure," Trista answered, grinning.

"What about Jason?"

Trista's smile faltering, she said, "What about him?"

"I don't know. It is just..." Ellyssa shrugged.

"He's creepy," Trista finished.

Ellyssa's mouth twisted to the side as she nodded.

"He's harmless enough. But I know what you mean. He's a little weird."

"Exactly. Where did he come from?"

"He was born here. His mother and father died in a cave-in, along with my parents. They were expanding this section of the cave so the supplies could be stored further away. You know, for safety reasons."

Uncomfortable at the direction the conversation turned, Ellyssa became impassive. "I am sorry. I did not know."

Trista didn't seem to notice the change in her demeanor, or her monotonous form of speech. "No need to apologize. It was a long time ago."

Ellyssa couldn't imagine what it would be like to lose people you loved and depended on. Her closest understanding of feeling sorrow had been for Jordan, and that still felt like her heart had been removed without painkillers. Not knowing whether she should attempt to offer comfort or stay silent, she watched Trista, hoping for a telltale clue.

"Seriously. It happened years ago. I still miss them, but I choose to remember my parents with happy thoughts. I don't want to dwell on the fact that they are gone."

"What type of thoughts?" Ellyssa asked, genuinely curious.

"Well," she replied, her face lighting up with pleasure, "things like my mother singing to me. She had a wonderful voice. And my father carrying me on his shoulders and pretending he was going to bang my head into the overhangs. Or, when we went outside and he'd toss me in the air. I thought he was the strongest person on the face of the earth. Invincible. Anyway," she continued, "back to Jason. He's harmless enough."

"He has never hurt anyone?"

Trista frowned. "No. Never. Why would you ask that?"

"Just the way he looks at people, once in a while." She folded the flaps of the box inward.

"That's just the way he is."

Ellyssa carried the box with the peaches from the storeroom and followed Trista through the passageway linking the old coal mine with the cavern. The bulky boxes made navigation difficult, but both managed by turning their loads sideways.

A woman with auburn hair piled high on her head waited in the dining room. She took the box, offering Ellyssa a polite smile, and placed it on the edge of the serving pans.

"Looks like fruit for lunch," she said. "Hunting was disappointing today."

"That will be changing soon, Bertha. Ellyssa knows all about roots and scavenging in the woods. She's going to show us how."

"Is that so?" Bertha asked, opening the box and removing a can.

Trista nodded. "And spices."

That seemed to pique Bertha's interest. "Spices?"

"Yes," Ellyssa said as she unpacked the goods. "There are many edible things most people don't know about. Cattail roots can be reduced to flour for baking breads. You can boil milkweed leaves with salt, and it tastes like spinach. All parts of the dandelion plant can be used. Very nutritious."

"Dandelions." Bertha wrinkled her nose.

"Dandelions are very good for you. Rich in vitamins and minerals."

"Really?"

"Really. There are many uses for them in medicines and such, too." Ellyssa stopped unpacking and glanced at her company. "I'm surprised none of you know this."

"No need to," said Bertha, taking a can and opening it. "We've always had supplies, and hunting and fishing."

"Surely, in the beginning, the founders had no contacts. They must have survived off the land."

Bertha shrugged. "I don't know when or how the contacts were established."

"Hey, will you show us some of the plants today?" asked Trista.

"And maybe afterward you can show me how to prepare them," Bertha added.

"My pleasure."

Ellyssa handed a can to Bertha. The woman gave her another smile, not just a polite one, but one of acceptance, possibly of friendship.

There wasn't much to do except pour the contents into tin bins for serving. Ellyssa found she enjoyed helping and being part of the community. This was unlike anything she'd ever had before.

Dr. Hirch sat in front of his computer monitor, playing and replaying segments of each of his children's training. He'd stop, rewind, and push play again, trying to catch the exact moment when each displayed their ability.

A sight to behold. The beauty as Xaver's rounded face was protected from debris, or Ahron's flickered in and out of existence. What really astounded him, though, was Aalexis. The beautiful girl sat, as innocent as an angel, blond hair haloing her cherubic face. The subtle twitch of facial muscles, and the bullets curved as they changed trajectory and centered on the bull's-eye.

George's pride and joy. The final step before true perfection. Without Aalexis' unexpected mutation, he wasn't sure the dream would even been realized during his lifetime. After all, he had never planned on the ability manifesting at this stage. It had been a complete fluke.

But now, they had her and the others, their DNA sequences almost isolated, and once Ellyssa was returned, plans would continue to progress.

George turned and looked into a monitor, his face mirrored in the black surface.

A perfect human. A soldier above and beyond the expectations even Hitler had envisioned. People created in his image. George would be the master builder. His children would honor his name forever.

The imperfect world annihilated and replaced with Utopia.

He replayed the image of Aalexis frame-by-frame, her demeanor unemotional, her face unreadable. The roar of gunfire, and then he caught what he'd been looking for. The air wavered, ever so slightly, as the molecules readjusted at her whim.

George stopped and pressed replay to make sure it hadn't been a glitch. When the moment popped up, he hit pause. A disturbance in the air was definitely noticeable.

He clicked the drop-down menu, and pulled up the file containing Aalexis stacking blocks. He watched it over and over, frame by frame clicking along for thirty minutes before he found the disruption. In order for her to manipulate objects, she had to manipulate space.

Astounding.

It would stand to reason that Ahron and Xaver had the same ability. Each was limited separately, but when combined together into one…

Could his soldier be able to blink someone from existence? Could he entrap people within force fields? The possibilities were limitless. Only testing would expose the still-uncreated creature's capabilities.

Technically, with just the three, he didn't even need Ellyssa or Micah for the fighting aspect. Aalexis and her two brothers would be indestructible. But the combination of Ellyssa's and Micah's talents would greatly enhance the ability to seek out remaining Renegades. The despicable insects could no longer infect the population with their inferior genes, or their thoughts of independence.

After another hour confirming the air disturbance with Xaver and Ahron, Dr. Hirch shutdown the computer and went to his apartment. He pressed his thumb against the biometric scanner. The door slid open and admitted him into an environment of grandiosity that matched his achievements. Many antiques furnished the rooms, as well as symbolic artwork, including Hitler's favorite painting, *Isle of the Dead* by Arnold Bocklin and its counterpart, *The Island of Life.* He had won them both in an auction after the Führer's death.

He paused at the *Isle of the Dead*, admiring the detail of the brush strokes, the cypress trees in a dense, dark grove, and the precipitous cliffs. It conveyed hopeless desperation, which was Earth before Hitler.

Next to it, *The Island of Life*, showed a depiction of joy, of a perfect life, with swans and green trees and happy people under a blue sky with puffy white clouds. This was what life was expected to be once all the imperfections were eradicated. Peace and beauty.

When George closed his eyes, he could almost taste the salt of the ocean on his lips and feel the gentle breeze embracing his skin and caressing his hair. Carefully, he touched the frame of the cherished picture, imagining the day when blond, blue-eyed people walked the earth with no threat of inferiors.

The future was within his grasp.

"Where did Davis say he was going tonight?" Angela asked.

Dyllon handed her the receipts from Davis' account. Several items and dates had been highlighted in yellow. "He requested to visit his family in Kansas City. I checked it out. His mother, father, and two sisters live on Cypress Street. Both parents are highly regarded and teach at the university. One sister is an elementary school teacher, and the other is a secretary." He placed the file on Davis' family on top of the receipts.

"What about his friends?" asked Micah, taking the file out from under Angela's hand. His eyes scanned the paper as he read. Before it was naturally possible, he flipped the page and started the next.

Heat flooded Angela's cheeks. She snatched the receipts and began tracing the dates and purchases with her finger.

"He doesn't seem to have a lot. Mostly keeps to himself. I took the liberty of contacting the Kansas City police; they are going to conduct a few interviews with his neighbors."

Dyllon placed down a green daybook. Before Angela even had a chance to glance at it, Micah was flipping through the pages. DAILY LOG was marked in bold, black print.

Angela hated him.

Returning her attention to the receipts, she found a truck rental dated a little over a year ago. "What's this?" She flipped the receipt over, with her finger underlining the cost of the rental.

Dyllon opened a small notebook he'd pulled from his pocket and thumbed through some pages. "Here," he said, turning the book around so Angela could read it. "Apparently, he was helping a friend move."

"I want you to find out which friend."

Micah tossed the daybook onto the table. "Do not bother."

Angela shot Dr. Hirch's child a look of warning as she stood to face him. "You seem to have forgotten—I am in charge."

His face blank, void of the expected anger or of any other type of emotion, Micah's azure eyes leveled on Angela's. Emotions or not, she knew he was coolly challenging her.

"If you wish, we can call *der Vater*."

"Maybe we should," Angela said, calling his bluff, although, deep down she knew she didn't stand a chance. She pulled out her phone and flipped it open.

"Go ahead, or you can listen to me, instead."

Narrowing her lids into a skeptical glare, she closed her phone. "What?"

"There is no point finding the friend he helped. We should follow him."

"Into town?"

"Yes."

"Do you think he has something planned?"

Micah didn't bother elaborating any further. He closed the logbook and set it back on the table.

Angela's eyes landed on the book, then back on him. "Could you see something from the daybook?"

Instead of answering her question, Micah simply repeated what he'd said previously. "We should follow him."

27

Exhaustion clung to Ellyssa's body like a needy toddler. The weight of it dragged on her feet as she made her way to the cot. Physical demands didn't contribute to her weariness, though. Heat and humidity were the culprits. She hadn't ventured outdoors for weeks, and her body had adjusted to the cool underground living.

Despite the exhaustion, today had been one of the best days Ellyssa had ever experienced. Full of sun, blue skies, tall trees, and fresh air, not to mention the people who were really interested in what she had to say. Even a couple of the mothers and their children had come for the unscheduled lesson.

A ten-year-old female child, with bright dark eyes and wavy hair, had a natural gift for finding roots quickly. Excitement shone in her smile every time she'd brought back a bag full of wild delicacies.

What surprised Ellyssa was that she'd enjoyed watching the children. She'd never given them any thought at all before, never even wondered about them. But interacting with the young Renegades today, as they discovered and learned and explored, holding their mothers' fingers with chubby little hands, made her appreciate the pleasure they'd brought to their parents.

After class, Ellyssa had returned to the kitchen with Trista and Bertha. She'd shown them how to prepare some menu items, and instructed them on others. If not for their yawns and haggard lids, Ellyssa might've kept on talking.

Now, as her body met the cot, she was happy she'd called it quits, too. Yawning, she yanked off her dirty shirt and pants and replaced them with fresh ones. Tomorrow, Trista had promised to show her where to do laundry.

No more guards. People depended on her knowledge now. Being accepted, true happiness lifted her heart.

Ellyssa rolled over and bunched the pillow under her head. For the first time ever, she drifted to sleep grinning.

Ellyssa woke to the sound of a click. In the haze of sleep, she thought she was back in the abandoned store in Deepwater. But the next thing she heard erased anything as hopeful.

"Ellyssa," said a whispery voice, a tinny note resonating within the syllables of her name. The same voice that grated down her spine, like fingernails on a chalkboard. Jason breathed heavily.

Completely awake, she didn't answer, trying to assess the situation. Sending out the tendrils of her mind, she entered Jason's.

Nervousness and anxiety elevated Jason's desire. Diseased pictures, red and lustful, spiked through. His mind spoke of revenge and strength, control, and her body receptive, wanting.

Ellyssa's stomach rolled, and bile rose within it.

Somehow, Jason had concealed his true nature. She'd never seen this side of his fantasies. Maybe his conscience had squashed them, until now. Maybe his memories were distorted by his own perception of right and wrong.

"I know you're awake. I want you to roll over, slowly."

Ellyssa heard the click again. It wasn't a gun, as she'd first suspected. It sounded like metal on metal. Slow and steady, she rolled onto her back. Jason leered over her, ropes draped from his left shoulder, a butcher knife poised in his right hand. He tapped the blade against a button on his pants.

Click.

Running his finger along the length of the blade, Jason watched her. "Let me explain to you how things are going to work. You're going to roll onto your stomach and place your hands behind your back."

Ellyssa, still in his mind, watched his objective play out to the finale. Excitement thrummed inside him.

Jason planned on taking her arms and tying them to the frame of the cot, spread-eagle-style. The next part involved him kneeling between her legs.

He was insane.

Instead of flipping over, Ellyssa stared at him, her eyes holding steady, her face an emotionless mask. Fear of him didn't exist. Not for her. She wanted him to be aware of the fact that intimidation wouldn't work.

As she held his gaze, Jason's tongue darted out, snakelike, licking his dry lips. Strings of spittle stretched on the edges of his mouth. Sweat trickled from his left temple and coasted down the side of his face. He ran his free hand through his dark hair, pushing back the strands hanging over his forehead. A tic developed over his right brow and jumped at regular intervals, beating with his pulse.

For a split second, Jason's confidence wavered under her scrutiny. Ellyssa wasn't cowering like he'd expected. He wasn't used to the defiance. Unease settled as Jason wandered if he'd be able to force her to keep quiet.

Blinking, Jason broke eye contact, but, as his gaze floated down to her breasts, he reclaimed his conviction. *Of course she would keep quiet. Women like it rough.*

He stepped back and poked the tip of the knife into her thigh, applying pressure. "Roll over," he ordered, his tinny voice steady and demanding.

When she didn't comply, he leaned into the knife.

Anger boiling, her natural instincts stampeded to the front, overcoming everything else. She didn't feel her skin slice from the pressure of the blade, or the trickle of wet sliding down her thigh.

Jason clicked his tongue, as if in reprimand. He pushed harder. This time she felt the stab of the smooth metal, but not enough to hinder her. He pulled the blade away. "Now."

Ellyssa did as he commanded. Not out of fear, but waiting for the mistake that would give her the upper hand, without her being harmed.

As she settled onto her stomach, Jason moved to the other side of the cot, slowly, quietly, barely a whisper from the soles of his shoes along the ground. No wonder she hadn't heard him come in, alerting her to the intrusion. When Jason wanted to be sneaky, he was better than she'd expected.

Jason placed his knee in the middle of her spine, grabbed her right wrist, and twisted, pulling it behind her. Ellyssa's breath hitched as his weight crushed her ribs. Her face pressing into the pillow, he rotated her hand, the palm facing inward, hitching her thumb, and brought it over her head.

"One little move," he said, leaning over her, his fetid breath brushing her ear. He jabbed her in the ribs with his weapon. "I'll break your wrist."

Ellyssa tried to nod.

After warning her again with a quick jab from the knife, he withdrew the sharpened point from her side as he yanked her hand down to the frame of the cot. He shifted his weight and leaned over to secure her hand to the metal leg.

It was a stupid move on his part.

His hands busy, the weapon no longer a threat, she bucked up onto her knees, and in one fluid motion, flipped him over the cot and landed on her feet.

Jason squeaked in surprise, as his back smacked the ground. The knife clattered next to him. His fingers found the hilt, and he popped up brandishing the blade.

Armed or not, Ellyssa moved toward him. Her body fluid, fast, she struck. Once, twice in his face, her backhand strike finding its mark. His head rocked back with each impact. Blood spewed from his nose and more flowed from a split lip.

Blindly, Jason swiped at her, the blade flashing. She blocked, but he retreated before she could disarm him. He stepped back, weapon between them. His eyes wild and fearful, he studied her, regret pouring from his mind.

"You made a mistake," Ellyssa said, circling him as a predator would prey.

Jason jabbed the knife in the air. "Stay back." He tried to move toward the only escape route.

As if he could outrun her.

Crouching, ready to spring, Ellyssa's instincts to survive surging within her, she slid to the side. His back stayed facing the metal cabinets. He swiped the blade through the air again. A sloppy swing, poorly aimed.

Fear poured from him, scenting the air with a musky odor.

On the verge of attack, taking him down like an animal, another sound—one she recognized—stopped her. A shell chambered into a shotgun. Even she couldn't outmaneuver a bullet.

"What's going on here?" Candy demanded, her musical voice wavering, unsure.

With her back toward the new threat, Ellyssa didn't respond, but the look on Jason's face said a lot. Relief, followed by a sneer. Indecision churned in Ellyssa as she tried to decipher what Candy's eyes had witnessed.

"Candy," he said, his voice nasal from his broken nose.

"You, over there," she said, indicating for Jason to move to the back.

The smile fell away. "She attacked me."

"I said, get over there. Ellyssa, put your hands where I can see them and turn around."

Ellyssa waited until Jason moved closer to the cots before she extended her arms. He still brandished the weapon, light reflected in the lustrous surface. She faced the fiery redhead. The double barrel pointed at her chest.

"I told you, she attacked me," Jason said.

While the shotgun stayed trained on Ellyssa, Candy's eyes darted toward Jason. "Why are you even here? I woke up and you were gone."

Ellyssa waited to hear which lie would actually spout from his mouth; his mind was cluttered with all sorts of excuses.

When he didn't answer, Ellyssa did. "He tried to rape me," she said.

The muzzle of the gun dropped. "No." Candy shook her head and her braids swung back and forth. "That's not true. Jason?"

"Babe, she's lying." His voice was steady and calm.

"I am not lying. He came in here with a knife, and threatened me."

"You lying bitch," Jason screamed. "You know me better than that, Candy. I've never hurt anyone."

In an instant, Ellyssa saw it all. What Ellyssa had glimpsed in Jason's mind weeks before played out differently in Candy's head. Jason had hurt her, and the shame of Jason's actions had kept Candy quiet.

"That is a lie. Is it not, Candy?"

Candy's lips pursed ever so slightly and her eyes widened. "Wh-what?" she stammered.

Ellyssa composed compassion on her face. "A few months ago, when you first started to…date, he hurt you. His touch was not gentle, as you had imagined, but rough as he took you in the storeroom. The bruises on your thigh took forever to fade."

Candy shook her head. "Wh-…How?"

"Shut up, you bitch," Jason screamed, stepping toward Ellyssa.

The gun pivoted from Ellyssa to him. "You stay put," said Candy.

"Don't listen to her," Jason said. "She's a freak." His tinny voice took on a pleading note.

Ellyssa glanced behind her. Jason was staring at her, jaw locked, body trembling. Deciding he wasn't going to attack, she faced Candy. The redhead had her targeted again.

"Candy, you do not have to do this." She took a step forward.

"One more step, and I'll blow your pretty face off," Candy stated.

Ellyssa hesitated. "I know what he did."

"Shut up!" Candy screamed, pulling the butt of the gun firmly into her shoulder. "Ever since you got here…" She slammed her mouth shut.

Ellyssa felt the jealousy in her mind. The anger. The hurtful embarrassment of someone knowing her secret.

Candy's finger twitched nervously against the trigger. "I want you to shut up. Shut up!" Her squeal tumbled through the room and out into the hall.

Ellyssa tensed, seeing the confusion, the hurt, in Candy's mind. She readied herself, but before Candy could pull the trigger, a dull *thunk* sounded, and the armed woman's fingers relaxed. The gun clattered to the floor as she crumpled. After kicking the dropped weapon into the passageway, Rein stepped over Candy. He swung the muzzle of his rifle up, targeting Jason.

"What's going on?" Rein demanded.

Heart skipping a beat before accelerating into overdrive, Ellyssa stared at Rein, his hair even more disheveled than usual. She lacked the ability to fully comprehend what he'd just done. Done for her. His gaze darted toward her, green eyes questioning, but the words caught in her throat.

"She attacked me," said Jason, the syllables of his words blunted by his wound. The blade of his knife pointed outward. He took a step.

"Is that true?" Rein directed the question at Ellyssa.

Ellyssa parted her lips, but before she said anything, she peered into his thoughts. He was unsure whom to believe; images flipped between her and Jason, as he tried to decipher the truth. What he had walked in on was two against one, but could it be that Ellyssa had initiated the confrontation?

Ellyssa read the uncertainty, the doubt, and how he felt for her. Then, he focused on the silvery surface of the knife, questioning why Jason had it. She pressed her lips together.

"Of course, it's true." Jason shuffled closer toward her; she felt him nearing, his mind working on contorting the facts. "The damn bitch almost killed me. If it wasn't for Candy, she would've done it."

Then, Ellyssa perceived his plan before he could launch it—Jason lunging at her, knife sinking into her chest, shutting her up, keeping his secret safe. She turned just as he pounced, ready for him, but the moment never came. A deafening shot rang out, and Jason tumbled off-course, screaming as he landed close to her, his leg stretched out before him. The knife skidded across the rocky floor, out of his reach.

Jason whimpered in pain, his eyes darting toward Rein, accusing him of betrayal. The thigh of his pants quickly turned from camo to dark crimson.

Adrenaline pumping, her body on high alert, Ellyssa turned, preparing for Rein as he moved forward, but he no longer carried the weapon. The rifle lay on the floor, a meter away from Candy.

She popped into his mind. He meant her no harm. He'd protected her.

"I did not need your help," Ellyssa stated, as he came toward her.

"I know." Rein hesitated for the briefest of seconds as he grabbed a cloth then crossed the remaining distance. "I just wounded him. Would you have stopped?"

Knowing she wouldn't have, she didn't bother answering. Ellyssa glanced at Jason. Blood pooled under his leg.

"You should help him," she stated as she turned around, looking straight into Rein's eyes.

Startled to find he stood so close, Ellyssa stepped back. Rein moved closer, erasing the distance she'd made and more, his face centimeters from hers. The nearness unnerved her. His scent intoxicating, she remained still and gazed into his eyes. Golden flakes swam in the green and burst around his pupil, like rays of the sun. She couldn't help but focus on them.

"Hold this to your wound," he said, tossing the towel he'd grabbed to Jason. His gaze never left hers.

Jason mumbled under his breath, then hissed as he pressed the cloth against his leg.

Still connected to Rein's mind, sensation overwhelmed her. Ellyssa didn't fully comprehend what Rein was doing when he first rested his hands on her shoulders; then it hit her. Stunned, unmoving, her heart responded with a new beat. The hardwired senses jammed as her arms dangled at her sides like useless, dead attachments. He pulled her in closer, his scent thick, tantalizing, inebriating.

She broke the link, but not before she saw that he had decided not to doubt her any longer. The feeling that followed was indescribable.

"Are you okay?" Rein whispered into her hair while his fingers traced circles on her back.

Words stuck in her throat; she nodded, relishing the tingles he left behind.

"I'm so sorry."

His touch melting away the last of her defenses, Ellyssa shrugged. She didn't know what else to do.

Rein released her and stepped back, his expression uncertain. Ellyssa could've kicked herself for not responding the correct way, by holding him back in return. The small gap between them left her cold, wanting.

"I'm sorry about before, too" he stated. Maybe he was thinking her unresponsiveness had to do with what had transpired before he'd left.

Biting her bottom lip, Ellyssa lifted her hand, hesitated for a moment, then pressed her palm against Rein's face. Stubble from a few days' growth scratched her skin. She loved it. The prickly hair, the warmth from his skin, the way he looked at her.

Rein took her hand in his and kissed the inside of her palm, sending a stream of lava through her. Her breath caught, as her body adjusted to the new surge of awareness she'd never experienced before. Blood pounded in her veins and her heart swelled.

Everything and everybody else disappeared for a few moments, but then reality whirled back as Mathew came barging in, panting. He stopped at Candy, who had started to stir.

"What happened?" he asked, kneeling next to her. "I thought I heard a gunshot." He pushed back a clump of red hair behind her ear and revealed a darkened red blotch.

Trista, and two others Ellyssa had only met once, ran in behind him. She glanced at Ellyssa, her face pale. Before they even had a chance to start asking questions, Rein began barking orders.

"Trista, go get Eric and have him bring his weapon. You two," he said, pointing at the newcomers, "go to the passageway, and don't let anyone else in."

The others retreated, but not before getting an eyeful. Ellyssa heard their whispers as their footsteps faded down the passageway.

Mathew pressed a tender area around Candy's wound and she moaned. Her eyes fluttered open. "Jason," she mumbled.

"Shh," Mathew said. "You're going to be okay." He examined the gash on the back of her head. "Who did this to her?" His gaze met Rein's, then dropped to the floor where Jason babied his leg and whimpered. "Oh, my God," he muttered, his eyes widening.

Candy turned her head, her face scrunching in pain. At first, she didn't seem to understand, but then emotions played across her features as realization ripped through her. Her eyes kept moving from Jason to Ellyssa, anxiously. Maybe embarrassed?

Strangely, Ellyssa's heart went out to her. Ellyssa knew Candy's secret, the one that she'd tried to keep from everyone. She wished she could transmit her thoughts, like Jeremy, to let the redhead know her secret was safe.

"No," Candy cried, tears squeezing from the corner of her eyes. She struggled against Mathew as she tried to get up. After a few more attempts, she crumpled in defeat, sobs breaking free.

"Get me a clean rag and the bandages from the locker," Mathew ordered to nobody in particular, "and the ointment."

Ellyssa went and retrieved the items and handed them to him. "How bad is she?"

"Just a gash," he answered as he cleaned the area. Blood pooled in the wound and leaked over the torn skin. "She'll have a headache."

Ellyssa knelt next to Candy and patted her hand, awkwardly. Candy didn't pull away with disgust, so she continued. "What else can I do?"

Mathew's eyes raked her, accusingly.

Why shouldn't it be she who appeared guilty? She was the enemy. But Mathew? Her delusion of acceptance had been nothing more than that—a delusion. Hurt, she stood and backed away, while the doctor's trained hands worked on the injured woman. Soft sobs escaped Candy's lips.

Rein grabbed Ellyssa's hand and pulled her protectively against him. "He attacked Ellyssa. And Candy," he said, pointing at her, "was helping."

"No. That was not what happened. Candy had nothing to do with it. She was as confused as you were," said Ellyssa.

Rein glanced at her.

"Candy came in after Jason attacked me."

"That's a lie," yelled Jason, his tinny voice high-pitched. "I was defending myself."

Rein whipped around and took a threatening step. "Why'd you have a knife?"

Jason sputtered, his mind flickering faster than she could perceive, reaching for some explanation. No conclusion decided upon, he refolded the bloody cloth and pressed it against his wound.

Hatred burned in Jason's mentality as he blamed Ellyssa for his crumbling world. Then a little light flicked on, and his psychological world reformed. Still, he didn't see himself at fault, his perception of right and wrong tilted in his favor. After all, Ellyssa had invited him to "visit". She wanted him; he'd seen it in her eyes. It wasn't his fault she'd changed her mind. Jason was the victim.

"We'll let the council decide," said Jason. "Are you going to help me or what?"

"Just hold the cloth to it until I'm done," Mathew answered, his fingers nimbly picking stray hairs from Candy's laceration. She hissed every time his fingers grazed the tender spot.

Shutting out Jason's sick sense of morals, Ellyssa continued, "Rein walked in and..." She trailed off. Rein knew the rest of the story.

"And?"

"Jason tried to attack her with a knife, and I shot him," Rein said.

"I see." Mathew's lids narrowed as he watched the writhing man on the ground. "Tomorrow, we'll figure everything out." He wrapped his arm around Candy and slowly helped her to her feet. "We need to get you into bed."

Candy's face screwed up like she was going to protest, but as soon as she stood upright, all color drained from her skin, leaving behind a waxy pale green. Her eyes rolled up under her lids, and she went limp.

"Whoa," Mathew said, struggling to support the deadweight. "Help me, Rein."

Rein cradled Candy in his arms and laid her on the cot next to Ellyssa's. Mathew covered her with a blanket.

Ellyssa approached Candy's while the doctor tended to Jason, and Rein busied himself with rearranging furniture, dragging one of the cots far away from where Ellyssa slept.

Candy's eyes opened, landing on her. "Please," she whispered.

"It is safe with me," Ellyssa mouthed.

The corner of the redhead's lips curved into a weak grin as her eyes closed. Soft, even breaths signaled she'd fallen asleep.

"It's a only a graze. Took a chunk of flesh, though," Mathew said from behind her. The doctor had torn away the leg of Jason's pants, and had the wound already cleaned. "Hold this here." He pushed a bandage against the injury and began ripping off strips of surgical tape.

The male Ellyssa had met in the council meeting, Eric, darted through the door, holding a shotgun. He skidded to a stop, his eyes settling on the pool of blood, then on Doc. "What the hell happened?" he said.

"Long story. I'll explain later," Doc replied, as he secured the dressing. "Help me." He assisted Jason onto his feet.

Eric grabbed Jason's elbow and helped the doctor walk the injured male to the other side of the room, where Rein waited next to the cot he'd moved.

"Is someone going to tell me what's going on?" Eric asked while helping Jason onto the cot.

"I didn't…" Jason started.

"If you utter another word," Rein interrupted, "I'll finish the job."

Jason snapped his mouth shut.

"I'll catch you up to speed," Rein said to Eric as he poured water from the basin Ellyssa had used into a bucket. Rein's low voice carried over as he mopped up the blood off the stony ground with Eric.

Mathew approached Ellyssa. "Let me have a look at your injury," he said.

Ellyssa blinked in surprise. She'd forgotten all about Jason sticking her.

"What? You didn't think I'd noticed?" He took her by the back of her arm and led her over to his chair. He pulled apart the ripped fabric, exposing a small gash.

"I had forgotten about it."

"It's not deep." Mathew swabbed ointment on it and applied a bandage. "I want to apologize," he said, patting her knee.

"No need."

"No, there is. You're my friend, and I doubted what happened. I'm sorry."

"I understand."

"That doesn't excuse my behavior," Mathew stated, moving toward Candy. He pulled a penlight from his pocket and shone the light into Candy's eye.

"Hey! What the hell," she said, her voice drawn and tired. "I was sleeping." She batted his hand away.

"I have to make sure you don't have a concussion." He repeated the process, against her objections. "Good," he said, smiling. "You're going to be fine, but in the morning, you'll have a headache."

Candy grumbled something and turned to her side.

"It's a mistake that won't happen again," Mathew said to Ellyssa, slipping the penlight back into his pocket. "Why don't you help Rein?"

On the way to where Rein and Eric knelt, sopping up blood, Ellyssa grabbed a small pail and filled it with fresh water. She squatted next to them. "Here."

"It'll be days before the stain wears away," Rein said, dipping the rag into the clean water.

Ellyssa glanced at the pool of red that Rein and Eric had managed to smear around. She didn't want to have to look at the stain for the remaining time she slept there; it would remind her of all that'd transpired, remind her how fragile friendships were. "Yes, I know."

Then, she thought about Jordan. Neither Rein nor Mathew knew about their beloved leader. Should she tell them?

After a quick debate, she leaned back onto her heels. "I have something to tell you and Mathew."

"Doc already knows," Eric stated.

Rein looked from him to Mathew. "Knows what?"

Mathew's face fell. "I was coming to tell you, when…" He swept his hand in an arc.

"Knows what?" Rein repeated.

"Jordan." He didn't elaborate. The look of sadness told the story.

Rein glanced at Ellyssa, his face questioning.

Ellyssa's stared back at him. What were the right words to tell someone when a loved one died? What was she supposed to do?

Comfort? She knew Woody had made her feel better, but her feelings for the dead leader were nothing compared to Rein's, who'd been raised by Jordan. Something told her she should try though, that the response was right, but instead, she sat there, stupidly. The words were all wrong. She swallowed the consolations down and nodded instead.

The towel Rein had been holding dropped to the floor. Unshed tears glistening in his eyes, he stood and left the room without a word.

As the padding of his shoes disappeared down the passageway, Mathew pulled her close, circling his arm around her shoulder. "Go, talk to him," he said.

"I don't know what to say."

"There are no right words. Just be there for him. That's all you can do. Woody told me that's what you did for him."

"Woody?" she asked, surprised. "He was the one who helped me."

"Did he?"

She thought he'd helped her with feeling her first true loss, the profound sadness, but maybe they had helped each other. A moment shared between two people who had needed comfort.

She went after Rein.

Holding the music box, Rein sat in silence inside Jordan's holey. He watched as the little dancers twirled to the harmony, forever caught in an eternal embrace. No threat of blond police coming to destroy the only home they'd ever known. No death.

He envied the figurines.

His chest felt hollow. He wanted to scream in anger, bash things, break stuff. He wanted to cry. Nothing came. Empty, he was drowning in a sea of loss.

The emptiness lessened when he thought of Ellyssa. Her soft skin, the scent of her hair. He filled with warmth and yearning...and with love. Then guilt followed for his mind wandering from Jordan.

A vicious cycle feeding itself.

"Can I come in?" Woody asked, pushing the tattered curtain aside.

Rein preferred to be alone, but he scooted over, affording the room. Woody crawled inside and sat with his back toward the entrance.

"I never had the chance to say goodbye," Rein said.

Woody patted his shoulder. "He knew how you felt."

"I know." Tears stung his eyes; he blinked. "It's just, without his guidance…" He glanced at Woody. "I guess Doc told you guys."

"About the search parties? Yes."

"We'll have to prepare the group." He sighed, looking down at the whirling figurines. He wished he knew the right steps to take. "What're we going to do?"

"Survive. Just like we've always done." Woody lowered his head to catch Rein's attention. "Hey. You know what to do; we both do."

"Did the others—you know—take it well?"

"They knew it was coming."

Rein nodded, understanding. Jordan's failing health hadn't been a secret. "What about you? How are you doing?"

"I said my goodbye."

"Our little family keeps getting smaller and smaller."

Woody reached over and folded Rein's fingers around the music box. "He would want you to have that."

"But..."

"You always appreciated it more than I did."

Finally, the tears stinging Rein's eyes slid down his cheeks. "Thank you."

"Rein?"

Ellyssa's soft voice surprised him. He hadn't heard the echo of footsteps down the rocky path. Her prowess as a soldier, he was sure.

Woody gave him a sad smile, before he flipped over. "Here, let me out."

Ellyssa stepped back and Woody crawled into the tunnel. Before he left, he ducked down, eye level with Rein. "We'll be fine."

"I know." Rein said the words, but didn't really believe them. All that lay before his little community—his family—was an undetermined future. It was up to him to make sure they were all safe. His responsibility, because he was the one who had led the enemy to their door. "Would you call together a council meeting for tomorrow, after lunch?"

"Of course." Woody squeezed Ellyssa's hand once before leaving. Apparently, she and his best friend had reached an understanding.

Ellyssa hovered outside of the holey, as Woody's shoes scraped across moist rock. The sight of her warmed his heart; her hair reflected yellow from the fluorescent bulbs, her sky-blue eyes wide with concern, her face saddened.

Rein wiped away the tears and offered her a sad smile. "Please, come in."

Ellyssa crawled into the cramped space and sat on her heels. For a few moments, neither of them said anything as the figures danced within their glass dome. Finally, the music slowed, then stopped.

"What's that?"

"Jordan's music box."

Her full lips shaped a small *O*. "It's beautiful."

Despite the sorrow weighing in his chest like an anchor, he grinned at the wonder on her face. "Yes, it is. It belonged to Jordan's mother. The only thing she brought that wasn't an essential. It's Mozart, but he can't remember the piece."

"*Fantasia No. 3.*"

Rein looked up in surprise. "You've heard this?"

"Yes. We learned all about classical music. Hitler believed in the arts, regardless of his shortcomings. Appreciation was not allowed, though; it was just a learning tool." She leaned closer to him. "I secretly enjoyed the music," she said, as if the declaration betrayed her.

"I really miss him."

"I do, too." She twisted around, crossing her legs and resting her forearms across her thighs. Unconsciously, she wrung her hands together. "I know I am in no position to even say something like that. I barely knew him," she said, raising her eyes to meet his, "but in a short time, I really grew to like Jordan, much like I did Mathew… and you." A flash of red colored her cheeks. She glanced down, her blond hair falling forward, obscuring her face, fingers kneading in nervous tension. "I have never given trust so freely."

Rein thought she'd never looked as beautiful as she did now. The nervousness, the tension, the shyness...the vulnerability. He placed a finger under her chin. "It's not a competition of who feels worse, or who has the right to feel the way they do."

"I know. I feel as if I have no right to be sharing your grief, though." She flipped her hands up. "I don't know how to explain. I don't know how to act." He smiled at the ease with which she dropped her robotic tone. This was the first time she had ever spoken so freely to him.

"For all I was trained in," she continued, "for all the knowledge I have, I'm childlike emotionally. How am I supposed to comfort you?" She held his gaze, her eyes trying to tell him what her words could not. She blinked and looked away.

"You being here is helping me." He twined his fingers around hers. Heat flowed from her touch and ignited in his heart, where only minutes ago sorrow had reigned. "I'm really glad you're here."

A hint of a grin tugged her lips. "Just let me know when you prefer to be alone."

"I don't think that's going to happen."

Silence wavered in the air. He enjoyed watching her, her tentative exploration of a foreign world. For a long while, there was no one else but the two of them. No missing family members, no problems. Almost like they weren't in a cave at all, but were sharing this moment in a place free of worries.

"Ellyssa," he muttered as he wound the music box, then handed it to her.

Her face lit up as she watched the two figurines. "It really is beautiful. We were never allowed possessions back at The Center. Possessions subtracted from training."

"I have to tell you something, but when I'm done, you have to promise me we'll talk about it tomorrow during the council meeting."

She nodded while running her finger along the delicate designs of the box.

"You have to say it."

Frowning, she glanced at him. "Say what?"

"That you promise."

"Oh," she chuckled lightly.

He'd never heard her do that before. The quality of her laughter was musical, like wind chimes. He couldn't imagine coming across an emotional barrage like she had had over the last few weeks, the breaking down of years of training.

"I promise," she said, bringing the music box closer to her face. The figures reflected in the blue of her eyes.

He interlocked her hand with his and pulled it close to his chest. Funny how she made him feel whole, just from being with him.

"They are looking for you."

Clouds obscured the brightness, and her face blanked. "I do not understand."

"While we were out to get the supplies, we slept in an old barn. They came in."

What little pink was in her face drained.

"It's fine. They looked around and left, none the wiser. We came back here safely. I promise no one tracked us."

She snatched her hand back. "Are you sure?"

"Positive."

"I have to go. I am endangering you all." She handed the box back and moved toward the curtain.

"You're breaking your promise."

Her head snapped around. "What?"

"You promised me we would talk about it tomorrow, during the meeting. Not now."

"That was before—"

He placed his finger on her mouth. "No." He pulled her back toward him and circled his arms around her. There was no way he was letting her go. "Just stay with me."

"If I turn myself in, they will be none the wiser. The community will be safe."

"Tomorrow, please."

Without another word, she settled into him, her head resting on his chest. He buried his nose in her hair, inhaling her scent. Her mind reeled; he didn't have to have psychic abilities to sense that. Her tense shoulders and the stiffness of her back told the story.

He kept hold of her, humming *Fantasia* in her ear. After a while, the stress released from her body, and she melted into him. Deep, relaxed breaths followed, and she played with his arm, running her fingers across his skin, leaving behind a trail of tingles.

As time ticked away, comfortable with her in his arms, he said his goodbyes to Jordan, promising to remember everything he'd taught him, all he had said, and promising that, no matter what, the community would survive.

28

Ellyssa rested against Rein's chest as it rose and fell rhythmically in sleep. Sounds of padding footsteps moved quietly down the tunnel. It amazed her how well the community worked together, showing respect through tiny acts of kindness like that.

Rein would have to wake soon, although she didn't want this time to end. She'd enjoyed spending the night in his arms. Also, he had obviously needed the extra sleep. He'd spent most of the night awake and, every once in awhile, his shoulders would shudder as he let loose his grief. She'd stayed silent and let him mourn the loss of his loved one.

When he finally did fall asleep, his shoulders slumped and his head tilted to the side. His nose nudged the back of her neck, and his soft breaths sent pleasant chills across her skin.

She should've left when his breaths deepened, signaling sleep. She could easily have unwound herself from his grasp and slipped away in the darkness. But she didn't want to. Her feelings for him ran too deep.

It was selfish of her to endanger the other inhabitants all because of her weakness in wanting family, of wanting Rein. Of wanting more than she'd had at The Center. She had no desire to lose all she had obtained in a few short weeks.

The conflict pushing and pulling inside Ellyssa kept her undecided. She fully understood why emotions were forbidden at The Center, how they left people weak, conflicted. She debated, overwhelmed by the sudden onslaught, as if a floodgate had been smashed, and the treacherous feelings gushed like water, rushing through her and washing away everything she had been trained to do, what she had been raised to be.

She'd have to be careful as she experienced this new life. She must tread lightly. Think clearly. Surely, it was possible. After all, these people didn't wander around emotional wrecks. All her life, she'd learned to suppress emotions, to mask them. If she was going to openly experience sensations, she was going to have to maintain her composure and do what was right.

She pulled herself forward and twisted around to look at Rein. His tired lids opened, exposing a magnificent green. He smiled, and her heart skipped a beat.

"Good morning," he whispered, pulling her back to him.

She didn't struggle, but let his warmth engulf her. She wanted desperately to stay like this, but they couldn't. She had to convince him to let her go, and lead those hunting her away from his community.

"The council will be meeting soon," she said.

"I know."

He nuzzled behind her ear and, for a moment, everything was forgotten. Desire flamed in her midsection, coursing to her nether regions. She bolted upright, hand flying to her mouth.

"What?" he said, concern lengthening his face.

She twisted around, her back toward the entrance. Eyes wide, her heart thrumming an ecstatic beat against her chest, she peered at him. She waited for a moment, gauging his reaction, while the alien craving dulled to a low flame, and the pounding in her chest quieted.

"Nothing," she said into her palm.

He reached over and pulled her hand away. Electricity coursed through her from his touch.

"Did I do something wrong?"

She shook her head. "No. We should…" She grabbed the music box and handed it to him, hoping to distract him. "Um…we should go to the meeting. I am sure it has started."

He set the box down and scooted closer to her. "Ellyssa?" he said, his voice pleading. "What's wrong?" He brushed a piece of hair back behind her ear. Warmth trailed behind his finger.

She inhaled, her heart pounding. Releasing the pent-up air, she stared at him, taking in the golden bursts around his pupils.

"You have to understand. This," she motioned between them, "is new to me. The feelings I am receiving from your touch are...beyond my ability."

Unable to form the correct words to describe the experience, she stopped and looked down. She felt his eyes on her, raking over her. Judging her? She wanted to leap into his head, to know what he was thinking.

He reached over and lifted her chin, and when her eyes met his, she realized she didn't need to read his mind. His expression said everything. None of it was judgmental. His eyes held caring, understanding, and something more...desire?...need?...love? It was all so foreign, especially having grown up with nothing but hatred and anger available to her.

"It's new to me, too," he said. "Although different, you aren't experiencing this alone."

She gazed at him for a long while, chewing on her bottom lip, wondering how his lips would feel upon hers. How he tasted. Never had she wanted to know what a kiss felt like, how to initiate such a thing.

What if he rejected her?

Rejection? Her heart skipped from light and fluttering to heavy and stone-like.

"We should be going," she said, averting her eyes.

She crawled from the space into the empty passageway. Rein popped out, holding the music box. He grasped her hand and led her down the corridor toward the back.

"I thought the meeting hall was the other way," she said, pulling free of his grip.

He stopped and turned toward her. "It is. I want to put this up." He held out the box. "Is that okay?"

She nodded as he reached for her hand again. Entwining her fingers around his, she cherished the feel of his skin against hers, not knowing how long such things would last.

They followed the set of holeys away from Jordan's and turned down another passageway. More quarters lay before her, all looking exactly the same, holes carved out of rock.

He walked to the very end and lifted a red sheet. Squatting, he yanked out a knapsack and a ragged square of an old blanket. He wrapped the box in the blanket and placed it inside the knapsack, then cinched the bag tight and draped it over his shoulder.

"Let's go," he said, capturing her hand again.

Eric and Brenda looked up from where they sat, at the ends of the rectangular table, when Ellyssa and Rein crossed the threshold. Worry lined each of their faces. A quick glance around confirmed that Mathew wasn't present, much to Ellyssa's dismay, and neither was Jason. Both absences, her fault.

Woody caught her attention with a flick of his head. He smiled when she met his eyes, but when his gaze dropped down to her and Rein's hands, a small line formed between his brows. His smile faltered for the briefest of seconds, then was replaced with an even wider, albeit forced, one. Crossing his arms across his chest, he looked away and pretended to pick a thread off the sleeve of his shirt.

Unsure what Woody's reaction meant, Ellyssa's eyes moved from him and traveled over the solemn faces. Rein pulled her to the empty chairs next to Woody. Councilmembers' stares followed. Rein squeezed her hand, but it didn't alleviate the uncomfortable pressure surrounding her.

Ellyssa wanted to know what they were thinking. What they believed had happened last night. Did they blame her? That had been Rein's and Mathew's first inclination. Why should they be any different? Unlike Rein, the doctor, or even Woody, they barely knew her. Why shouldn't they place fault on her?

Ellyssa's head lowered, unwilling to look at the others. She concentrated, hard, zeroing on Brenda. The older woman's mind opened to her like a blooming flower. Within the din of the other's thoughts, Ellyssa was able to glean that Brenda knew Jason was hurt, and speculations were floating around the community.

She shifted to Eric, who thought Jason had gottn off too easy, if what Mathew had said was true. Then the static and buzz broke her concentration and incapacitated her ability to read. She raised her wall.

"No one is blaming you for anything, hon," said Eric as if he knew she was snooping.

Steadying her emotions, she looked at Eric. "I am sorry for causing trouble, but I will protect myself," she stated.

Even Ellyssa could hear the monotone of her voice. It sounded heartless and cold. Robotic. She'd never really paid attention to the sound before. She shifted in her seat, trying to relax.

Eric and Brenda looked at each other, the sudden change in her demeanor surprising them. Eric lifted a shoulder and returned his attention to Ellyssa. "When Jason fully recovers, he will stand trial."

"You have trials?"

"Of course," said Rein. "That surprises you?"

"Yes. Society does not have lawbreakers. The gene for deviant behavior is tested in vitro, and if it is found, the baby is aborted."

Brenda leaned forward, obviously appalled. "The woman isn't even given a choice. It's one of the many reasons I left."

"Ha," Eric said, "that's laughable."

Narrowing her eyes, Brenda shot him a look. "What?"

"No not that. You misunderstand." Eric chuckled. "You're a criminal. And so is Woody for that matter."

"Hmm, you're right," Brenda said, settling back in the chair.

Eric turned his gaze on Ellyssa. "Doesn't seem their way really works."

A small smile formed on Ellyssa's lips. "There are many flaws in society."

"Here we have trials. And Jason will have his chance to plead his case," Rein continued.

"So," Eric said to Rein, "Doc filled me in on a few of the details last night. Why don't you finish?"

Rein launched into the story, starting with the old barn and ending with leaving the truck behind and sneaking away. As he spoke, Ellyssa's smooth countenance melted, and she shuddered with impending horror. Sooner or later, the police would find the Renegades.

"The barn is about fifty kilometers away," he concluded. "That's what took us so long to return, and empty-handed."

Eric placed his elbows on the table, clasping his hands. "They're close."

"We need to start evacuation procedures right away," piped in Woody.

Ellyssa shook her head. "No. They are after me. If I turn myself in, they will go."

"Uh-uh," Rein protested. He turned toward her, the sunburst around his pupils darkened a shade. He gathered her hands into his. "This is your home now."

For a moment, as the warmth of his touch singed her skin and traveled through her body, she drowned in his green pools and wanted to believe. To be part of a family, and accepted, and explore the sensations Rein evoked in her.

But she couldn't.

The danger was too great. If the Renegades were discovered, they would be murdered.

"Do not be ridiculous, Rein," Ellyssa said. "It is far too dangerous."

"I agree with Ellyssa," Brenda said.

Rein faced Brenda. "It's not going to happen. I don't care what you say. If it was anyone else in the community, we would protect them. Ellyssa is now part of the community, whether you," he pointed at Brenda, "accept it or not. Jordan trusted her and made her a councilmember. We will honor his request."

Ellyssa placed her hand on his forearm. "Rein, listen."

A grimace tightening the corners of his mouth, he pulled away. "No," he repeated.

Ready to argue, Ellyssa scooted her chair back, preparing to stand, but a light touch on her shoulder stopped her.

"He's right," Woody said.

"No, he is not," she said. "I will do what I have to do."

"Wait a minute," Woody said, cutting Rein off in the middle of an objection. "They know we're here."

"Why do you say that?"

"It has been weeks. They should have moved on. They haven't."

"That does not prove anything."

"But it does."

"Rein said they had dogs. They tracked your scent."

Which stopped at the store where the Renegades found me.

"Your scent was lost within ours," Woody said, finishing her thought. "They might not know exactly where, but they know there is a group of us somewhere within the vicinity."

"But, if I turn myself in…"

"Do you honestly think they will stop the search for us?"

Ellyssa didn't answer. She knew they wouldn't.

"Time to vote," Rein said, a smile of satisfaction spread across his face.

"No. It is my decision."

"Oh no, it's not. We do this the democratic way."

Her mouth parted in protest, but Rein held his hand up.

"You accepted the invitation to be part of the council. You follow the rules." Rein turned toward the others. "All in favor of protecting a member of the community?"

Rein, Woody, and Eric raised their hands.

"Brenda?"

The middle-aged female looked at Ellyssa, sorrow tugging her doe-like eyes. "I'm sorry, but no. I think it's better for you to leave."

"Rein, I agree. Maybe if I go to them, I can lead them from you."

"Majority rules."

A sliver of hope entered. "What about Mathew? And Jason? They have not voted."

"Doc's vote is for you to stay, and Jason is temporarily suspended from his duties," Woody said. "Ellyssa, you know as well as I do that nothing you say will stop them from looking."

"There might be—"

He patted her hand. "You're one of us now. Please."

Ellyssa closed her eyes, wishing for a moment that she'd never followed Jeremy's phantom voice.

"We need to hold a community meeting. Evacuation plans need to be implemented," said Eric.

As their voices droned on about a section of the cave that needed preparation, Ellyssa listened halfheartedly. She should just leave and lead the *Gestapo* away on a fake trail. It would buy the Renegades time to relocate before the police came back to exterminate them.

Ellyssa's eyes moved from one face to the other as the members discussed plans. None of them had any idea how relentless her father was. Dr. Hirch wouldn't stop until she was back in his hands; he wouldn't stop until their number had been annihilated.

She had inadvertently signed these people's death warrants.

29

Hunched over, Angela darted behind an overgrown bush. She had her assigned electroshock weapon drawn, as if that would do any good. Even with the knowledge of Renegades definitely hiding in the forest, Dr. Hirch still forbade the use of guns, fearing an accidental shooting of his precious children. At least she had a real gun strapped to her ankle just in case she ran into one of the lowlifes. To hell with the consequences, they were armed.

She looked over her shoulder to see if Dyllon was in position. With a lift of his head, Dyllon acknowledged he was ready, then ducked behind a pile of rumpled tin sheets and rusted nails, the remnants of an old shed. A large oak grew from within the rubble.

The house hadn't fared much better. The roof was nonexistent. As for the walls, only one still remained partially erect, crumbling bricks threatened to collapse at any moment. A variety of bushes and plants had taken root, slowly returning the man-made structure to nature.

She wished she'd thought better of listening to Micah. After all, he had been wrong about Davis. If she were to be truthful, her initial instincts had been wrong about the ranger, too.

The ranger had gone to Kansas City to visit his parents, just as he had said. The police who had conducted the interviews had found nothing suspicious, except that the ranger had loaded two small boxes into his truck before he'd left. Most likely supplies, and hardly enough to support a community of Renegades. Davis was nothing more than a quiet man who kept to himself. No wonder he was a park ranger. A perfect predetermined career for him.

Not only had The Center's child screwed-up her revenge toward Ellyssa, he'd screwed-up her whole investigation, making her second guess herself by listening to him. First he wanted to waste time tailing Davis, then he insisted they wasted more time driving around, sightseeing.

Squatting behind a bush, Angela faced the woods. Trees grew densely around the overgrown field. She could make out a couple of rusted metal rods, leftovers of an old fence, poking from the ground.

They were wasting time. If not for Micah, they could be doing something more productive, like looking for clues to where Ellyssa hid. Instead, they were on this wild goose chase that Micah refused to talk about.

Angela had to admit, though, at first she had been convinced Micah had found something. After he had ordered Captain Jones to stop, he'd popped out of the vehicle to touch a toppled tree. Then Micah's eyes leveled with hers, and he told her this was the place. After the drive had been cleared, there were signs of tire tracks and clumps of crushed grass. For the first time in days, Angela's interest had been piqued and her hopes had soared.

Now though, after seeing the ruins of the old farm, she began to doubt. There was no way this wreckage held a secret storage cache.

She glanced at Micah, who had ignored her orders to advance slowly. His blond hair reflected the light of the Indian summer sun as he kicked the wreckage. He glanced at her before bending over and coming up with what looked like the edge of a broken tin sheet in his hand. Smugness traveled across his face before it faded. On first glance, she thought it was debris, but then she noticed the arc in which it moved, as if attached to hinges. His head bobbed out of sight, she heard the thud of the door closing.

"Dyllon," she beckoned, while rounding the heap to where Micah had just stood.

Dyllon trotted after her, his forehead bunched together. She knelt on her haunches, poking through the ruins. Bricks, dead branches, and other trash littered the ground around the tin sheet. At first glance, the heap looked as if it was nothing more than rumble, but when Angela really looked at it, she saw the telltale signs. The bricks were arranged in staggering stacks, the branches aligned to hide the entrance. She shook her head and stood.

Once again, if it hadn't been for Micah, she would never have seen it, mistaking the debris for what it appeared like, a mound of scrap. Although she hated The Center's children, she had to admit their extraordinary abilities were useful.

"He went down there?" asked Dyllon as he pulled he grabbed the edge of the door. It opened smoothly and revealed wooden steps, leading into darkness.

Angela switched on her flashlight. Well-maintained steps led to a dirt floor. Sighing, she descended, sweeping her light back and forth, and stepped into a basement carved into the ground. Along the walls, vertical chinks marked where picks and shovels had been used to dig the hole. Rafters, covered in an oily substance, ran the length every two meters. Angela touched a post closest to the stairway. A preservative stained her fingertips. She wiped her hand on her pants.

"I can't believe this," she stated. "They must have been here for years."

"It definitely took some time to dig out," remarked Dyllon.

"It took more than that. It took a lot of help," Angela said, moving deeper into the man-made storage area toward Micah, whose own light revealed cardboard boxes stacked against the farthest wall. "How else could they acquire these materials?"

"The park ranger," Micah said, his palm touching a container. He sounded bored, but the look he gave her was one of self-satisfaction.

Angela's pride plunged, like it was tied to an anchor. Of course, an operation this sophisticated couldn't have happened without the ranger's knowledge. Her initial instinct had been right all along, without the aid of genetically-enhanced perceptions. If she hadn't let her hatred of The Center's children, and her determination to prove herself an equal, affect her judgment, she would be standing before Micah a success. Instead, the boy would get the credit, and she, once again, had proven herself an incompetent failure.

Hatred and fury percolated.

Somehow Angela would prove herself. And Dr. Hirch would see her as an equal. Until then, though, she'd work with Micah. She'd been making a bigger fool of herself fighting against him. Time wasted on small stuff when she could have everything, and show them all her superiority. It would be a lot easier if none of The Center's children had been born.

Angela cast her gaze downwards as a smile graced her lips. *Much easier.*

She would have her revenge.

"Detective Petersen," Dyllon said, a confused frown sat on his face, "are you okay."

"Yes, of course." She waved him off. "How did you know?" she asked Micah.

"The daybook," he said. "A lot of people had touched it, contaminating it. But I had caught a glimpse of a male sitting in the passenger seat of a delivery truck. He was bouncing, like the truck was going down a rough road. When he looked up, I could see the layout of the land. Afterwards, he looked over at the driver's seat where the ranger sat.

Even now," Micah continued, a faraway glimmer in his eyes as his hand still touched the box, "I can see the ranger. There are others, but their images are blurry. All are from society: blond hair and blue eyes. Their faces are unclear. They are loading the shipment into a truck." He paused for a moment, his lids scrunched. "The next image is of him unloading the truck and bringing the items in here. He is alone. He sets the box down, and the connection is broken." He opened his eyes, azure burning a hole into her.

"But how did you know this was the place from the daybook?" Angela asked.

"I did not know," Micah replied. "That is why after we followed Davis and found nothing, I wanted to go down side roads. With the evidence of the Renegades, and what I had gathered from the daybook, I knew the place had to be close."

Somehow, even with the help of the area police, Davis had still been able to duck beneath their radar and deliver the supplies. Well, at least her radar, Micah's radar had a much wider range. His abilities put her at a disadvantage, made her a joke. Soon, though, the playing field would be level.

Her mouth drawn back tightly in disgust, she opened a box. Bandages, surgical tape, aspirin, scissors, and other medical supplies filled the container.

Dyllon yanked open the top of another box and pulled out a can of green beans and one of sardines. "They eat better than I do." He dropped the contents back into the box. "What now?" he said to Angela.

Micah cut her off, "We find the ranger."

30

Soft grey clouds rolled along the blue sky, joining together, obscuring the sun. Thick humidity clung to the Missouri forest, and the scent of ozone was heavy in the warm air. The heavy rain that had swept through the area left puddles of standing water and muddy trails in its wake.

Rein followed the group surrounding Ellyssa, as she pointed out different plants and described their uses. Every time she turned around, she smiled at Rein, clearly enjoying teaching the Renegades how to survive. In fact, he was enjoying the lessons as much as the others and even played guinea pig when his family hesitated to try something new. He had tasted the inner bark of the white pine, which was amazingly sweet, and chewed on pine needles, which weren't as good but were still edible.

Ellyssa dropped to her knees and unearthed a wild carrot. From her pocket she produced hemlock. She positioned them together in her hands. "As you can see, both taproots are white, so it is imperative to know the difference between them." She set both plants down and moved back, so that everyone could examine the similarities. "Look at the leaves. They are both triangular in outline, and both produce flowers that can be white or pinkish in color."

"How are we supposed to tell them apart?" asked Summer, a beautiful teen with chocolate eyes.

Summer was the first birth Rein had experienced. Her father had passed out, and her mother's screams had echoed throughout the passages. It'd scared the hell out of him.

"Is it fatal if we gather the wrong plant?" asked Summer's mother, her eyes the same color as her daughter's. Her fingers were intertwined with her husband's.

"Yes."

"Well? How do we tell, then?"

Ellyssa smiled. "Very easily, actually." She pulled some leaves from the hemlock and handed them to Summer. "Roll these between your finger and thumb." She waited as the teenager did as instructed. "Now smell."

Summer sniffed her finger and wrinkled her nose. "That stinks."

Ellyssa laughed. "Yes, it does. Now, try this one." She handed over the leaves from the carrot. "What does that smell like?"

"Carrots."

"A simple test." She dusted her hands on the legs of her pants. "Another way to tell the difference is by examining the stem. The wild carrot's stem is hairy while the hemlock's is smooth. Now, I would like all of you to try and find some wild carrots."

The group dispersed into smaller crews of two or three, leaving Rein and Ellyssa alone. She turned toward him, her eyes shining.

"You're a natural with kids," said Rein.

She appeared shocked at his observation. "No. I'm not."

Confused, he went to her and took her hand in his. "Why do you say that? Look how much you're enjoying the children and their families."

"I was never a child. Never had the opportunity to play or go to a normal school. How could I relate?" she said, her voice soft, thoughtful.

"But, you're doing a great job."

"It's not the same." She pulled away from him. "You forget, I was bred to survive. And to kill."

"And not to feel emotion either," he added pointedly. "And to talk like a robot. And. And." He went to her side. "And you're not any of those things."

She didn't reply, her stance stiff as she watched one of the groups reappear. Green leaves poked from their small canvas bags. They waved before disappearing down an old deer trail.

"Ellyssa," he said, touching her arm. "I want to show you something." He pulled her into an open area where the rain was not hindered by overhanging branches.

A corner of her mouth pulled back, questioning. "What?"

"Run."

Ellyssa stared at him, as if a third eye had opened in the center of his forehead. "I don't understand."

Grinning, Rein said, "Just run, would you?"

She crossed her arms. "I would feel silly."

He stepped close to her, his face centimeters away. She smelled of the outdoors, flowers and sun; her eyes were clear and blue as a summer's day. Ellyssa swallowed, hard, and met his gaze.

Rein cupped her cheek. "Trust me."

She nodded.

He smiled and stepped back. "Go!" he said, pointing across the field.

Ellyssa took off running through the meadow, the long blades of grass bouncing back behind her. Rein followed, not wanting to miss her expression. When she reached the middle where wildflowers clustered in a pastel burst of color, it happened. Hundreds of white butterflies erupted from the tangle of leaves and stalks, fluttering in the light breeze and soft shower. They danced wildly around her, swirling in a frenzied state.

Ellyssa stopped, her eyes wide in wonder. "Oh." She reached her hand out, and a small butterfly landed on her finger. She brought it close to her face, examining it. "Beautiful," she said.

"Not as beautiful as you."

She froze; her face blanked. Not the response he was expecting.

Then, suddenly, laughter erupted from Ellyssa, loud and uninhibited. She took off running in a circle, her hair fanning behind; her hands brushed across the flowering plants, scaring more butterflies from their hiding places. Their wings beat white against the overcast grey. She stopped in front of him, a smile on her lips.

"This is the most perfect day I have ever experienced."

Rein stepped closer to her; the back of his hand brushed her cheek.

"Thank you," she said, shyly, her eyes focusing over his shoulder.

He placed his finger under her chin. "Look at me."

She did, her gaze timid. She chewed on her bottom lip.

He rested his hand on the small of her back and pulled her close. With his free hand, he pushed a damp piece of hair behind her ear. Droplets of rain glistened in her lashes and reflected the blue of her eyes. Her soft breath brushed against his cheek.

Rein's heart picked up speed. "It's never too late to enjoy the small things in life," he said, breathless.

Unexpectedly, Ellyssa wrapped her arms around him, encircling his neck, her fingers buried in his hair. At her touch, chills ran down his spine.

Rein's lips, wanting, anticipating, quivered. He dipped down and found her mouth. At first, she didn't respond, her muscles tense, and he feared he'd overstepped his bounds. Then, she relaxed. Her lips parted and formed around his, soft and inviting.

Heat radiated from her. Fire ignited, sending currents of pleasure through his veins. He moved his hand to the back of her neck and held her tighter, cherishing every contact their skin made.

New pulses tingled and traveled.

Rein's tongue teased the edges of Ellyssa's lips, coaxing her. She relented, exploring his mouth, tasting him, her deepest desire exposed. Never in her life had she experienced an explosion of such intensity.

Heart fluttering, like the wings of the butterflies in the meadow, Ellyssa's midsection quaked. She didn't know what to make of these physical reactions. Was this love? Desire? Infatuation? She had no idea.

When they parted, Ellyssa was breathless, her chest heaving. Rein tipped his head back as he watched her, his green eyes shimmering pools.

Was he sad? Regretful? Happy?

Before Ellyssa had a chance to analyze his expression any further, Rein pulled her in and hugged her, his lips grazing the top of her head as she buried her face against his chest. She felt bared, something she'd never allowed before. It showed weakness. Ellyssa no longer cared. She craved his touch, his embrace, his kiss. Her mind wouldn't stop working, though.

What was he feeling? Thinking?

Her insecurities amazed her.

She could easily peek, answer her questions, but resisted.

Rein pulled back, cupping her chin in his hand, then he bent over to brush his lips against hers again. Her blood turned to lava and traveled from her lips to her chest. Her knees weakened.

He wouldn't have kissed her again if he hadn't felt something, would he? Once again, she stopped herself from reading his mind.

"Ellyssa," he said, his eyes meeting hers, "I've wanted to do that for so long. I just didn't know how." He paused while he nuzzled her ear, inhaling deeply. "Did you mind? Was it wrong?"

Unable to speak, her thoughts put partially at ease, Ellyssa shook her head.

He sighed. "I have something to tell you. Something I knew from the first day, though I didn't recognize it. I was blinded by our differences."

Terrified of what he was going to say, Ellyssa chewed on her lip. After a moment of hesitation, she whispered, "What?"

"I love you."

Panicking, Ellyssa stepped back. Rein's hand slipped down her arm and swung to his side. Just a moment ago, she'd wanted to know if he felt like she did. The problem was, she had no idea what her feelings meant. Most of her life, the hatred and anger she was allowed to feel had fueled her as a soldier. The limited feelings—a tiny bit of pleasure, and maybe fear—she'd masked. For the first time ever, she felt like fleeing.

Rein must've seen the fear in her eyes, because his face fell. "I understand if you don't feel the same way."

Ellyssa's breath stuck in her throat like a rock that wouldn't dislodge. She closed her eyes and worked on calming herself. It was harder than it should've been. When she could breathe again, her eyes opened on a face filled with sadness, maybe agony, all because of her.

"It is not that. I do not understand what these feelings are," she tried to explain. "I am not sure I know how to love."

"That's not true." Rein gathered her hands in his and kissed her fingers. "Why did you leave The Center? Why did you come here? Look at all you have experienced—how much you've grown. Sorrow, compassion, friendship, betrayal, loneliness, loss, acceptance, and happiness." He paused and cupped her cheek. "I've seen you truly happy. Smiling. Laughing."

Wanting so much to see things his way, she inhaled. Confusion churned in her body as she tried to sort out the sensations.

Rein held her hand against his chest. His heart beat rapidly beneath her fingers. "Does your heart feel like this?" he asked.

There was no denying it. She nodded.

His finger traced down to her midsection. Her muscles jerked at his feathery touch.

"And does your stomach quiver when I touch you?"

"Yes," she whispered.

"Blaze?" He moved closer and nuzzled her ear. "Do you feel it now?"

Ellyssa paused for a moment, enjoying the reactions he stirred in her. She'd felt them before, when she'd peeked into other people's thoughts. Their wants and desires. She'd always pulled out, afraid of discovering what she had been missing. She had lied to herself for years. She'd been lied to. There was nothing better than the way she felt now.

At that moment, she knew.

"I love you, too," Ellyssa breathed.

Rein nibbled her earlobe and ran his nose along her jaw, reaching her mouth, while her fingers outlined the muscles of his back. He kissed her, hard. Fire licked through her veins, consuming her. She pressed into him.

The sound of laughter and rustling foliage doused her flame. Summer and her parents appeared. Their hair and clothes were damp, shoes muddy, but their faces held grins. Shortly afterward, a cherubic-faced toddler ran into view, her mother close behind. Grasped in her chubby hand, the child held a variety of wildflowers.

Ellyssa's cheeks warming, she pulled away.

"It's time for us to go anyway," Rein muttered in her ear. His breath caressed her skin. "We have council business to attend to."

Their fingers interlaced, Ellyssa led the way to Summer. The teen showed Ellyssa all the wild carrots she'd found. "I checked every one of them," she exclaimed, her voice excited.

Ellyssa looked them over. "Very good." Summer beamed. "Tomorrow, if we have time, I will show anyone interested how to prepare these different plants for consumption."

"I'd like to go," Summer said. "Can we, Dad?"

A tall, lanky male, with light green eyes, smiled down at his daughter. "If everything's done, sure."

Ellyssa walked to the mouth of the cave with her students behind. She checked the plants as they filed in, while Rein stayed at her side. He seemed unable to keep his hands off her, touching her hand, brushing his fingers along her cheek, pushing strands of stray hair behind her ear. She relished every bit of contact.

The sun dipped behind the trees, and yellows and reds burst through the waning clouds. Ellyssa reveled in happiness and drowned in fear, both emotions in a constant struggle for dominance. How could she leave now? How much pain would that inflict?

As Ellyssa worried about the future, Rein leaned over and kissed her. "It'll be okay. Everything will work out," he said, as if reading her thoughts.

Was this a special power people shared when they had connected in a loving relationship? The ability to read each other without invading?

Ellyssa let Rein lead her into the old mine.

31

Woody entered the hospital, carrying a box of supplies. His usually smooth hair hung limp in his face, and dirt smeared his cheeks and nose. He set the box down and dropped on his haunches, eye level with Ellyssa.

Ellyssa ignored him, just as the council had ignored her protests. No matter what she'd said, she couldn't get the members to see things her way. She'd be staying behind, while Rein and Woody risked their lives.

Frustrated, Ellyssa shoved a package of bandages into the metal trunk and slammed the lid. She pushed the container to the doorway, where it would be taken to the evacuation cavern.

"Candy is doing much better today," Woody said, apparently not wanting to talk about the meeting either. "She's helping with kitchen chores."

"I am glad," said Ellyssa, shoving a six-pack of ointment into the last container.

"She wants to talk to you, but…it's hard on her."

"I understand."

Woody nodded. "Jason's trial will be tomorrow."

At the mention of his name, fury blazed. Ellyssa glanced over her shoulder at the bloodstained ground, a constant reminder of what he had almost cost her. She shoved down an urge to finish him off, a lingering instinct from an old life. She wasn't that person anymore.

Her eyes moved to the cot that Jason had occupied. A couple of days ago, before he had been relocated down the hall to a smaller room with a low ceiling, Jason had developed a low-grade fever. So far with the aid of cool baths and lots of liquids, Mathew had been able to control it, but the wound was not healing, and remained red and irritated.

Shaking her head, Ellyssa faced Woody. "Why hold the trial now? You and Rein will be gone," she said, her tone harsh.

Woody's grey eyes locked with hers, swirling clouds before the storm. He lifted his hand as if to touch her, but at the last second, he shifted and picked up a tube of ointment that had fallen to the ground.

"I know you're angry, but I promise, he will be fine." He handed her the medicine.

"I just do not understand why I cannot go. I am much better trained for such encounters."

"There aren't going to be any encounters. We're going to grab the truck and fetch the supplies. We won't make it without provisions."

"I still should go." Ellyssa slammed the lid of the remaining chest and flipped the latch.

"They need you here."

She stood, dusting off her hands. "That is not true. You got along fine until I came."

Woody followed suit. "No, we didn't. We've already learned so much from you."

"If not for me, you would all still be safe."

"You don't know that. With the resistance, our supply trips, every day is a risk. We had to evacuate once before, not long after I had come here."

Ellyssa stared at him pointedly. Was that supposed to make her feel better? If she had known being part of the community meant she would have to do what the council decided, she would've thought better of it.

They'd all voted against her, despite her concerns. Majority rules.

"Listen." Woody closed in on her, taking her wrist in his hand. "We can't risk you being caught."

"I could help."

"You know that's not the point." He paused. "I promise to bring him back safe."

"I want you safe, too," Ellyssa remarked, realizing as she made the statement, how true it was. Woody had helped her through a very difficult time after Jordan had passed.

Woody let go of her wrist and brushed her cheek with the back of his hand. His touch was light and caring; and much to her surprise, she found it pleasant. He offered her a small smile before looking away, red flushing his face.

Confused by his actions, Ellyssa searched his expression. Unsure what he was thinking, she wanted to reach inside his head and pull out the answers. She didn't. If she was going to live with these people, flourish in the community, she'd have to refrain from such behavior. She'd have to learn to read reactions on the surface. To trust. Still, she didn't understand his blush or his touch.

Was it friendship? Did he want more? And most of all, why did she like it? Maybe it was just the closeness. After all, his touch didn't send the sparks down her spine or accelerate the beat of her usual steady heart.

After a moment, when his face returned to its natural color, Woody looked back at her, his eyes still burning. "The other day, after Jordan…" His throat moved up and down as if a rock was lodged there. "You helped me realize."

When he didn't elaborate, Ellyssa said, "Realize what?"

Woody's mouth opened but no words followed, and his face displayed an unreadable collage. Finally, he just placed his hand on her arm. "Rein's lucky to have found you."

"I am lucky to have found him." She smiled, but Woody didn't return the gesture.

Was he angry? He didn't exhibit the usual signs of anger.

Sighing, Woody picked up a box and started for the door.

"Woody," she said, stopping him. "I appreciate you being there that day. I was overwhelmed, and if not for you, I am not sure it would have gone as smoothly as it did. You helped with my…transformation, I guess you might say. Thank you."

"My pleasure."

Woody left Ellyssa standing alone, slightly bewildered. The simple sensations she'd masked for years were nothing compared to the complexity of living with normal people. Emotions were ever-more complex than she'd first thought. Her lessons about the Renegades being nothing more than simple animals, controlled by their feelings, kept breaking down and reshaping. They were complicated entities. Shaking her head, she resumed packing the supplies.

A set of footsteps she recognized caused her heart to slam against her chest. Still angry, she pushed down her initial reaction to run into Rein's arms. After all, he had voted against her, too. Probably some male thing, thinking he was protecting her. *They* needed the protection *she* could offer.

Rein walked through the door, his backpack dangling from one shoulder and a rifle slung over the other. She acknowledged him with a simple nod as she latched the box. She stood and placed the last footlocker next to the door.

"These are ready to go," she said.

He dropped his bag and balanced his gun on top. "Ellyssa, I know you're angry with me."

"I'm not angry," she denied. Anger wasn't the correct description. Hurt and afraid. Afraid for him.

Refusing to look at him, Ellyssa went to the locker and grabbed the last two boxes of dressings and a roll of tape. She shoved them into the deep pockets of her camo pants.

Rein approached from behind and wrapped his arms around her waist. "I'll be leaving soon. I don't want to leave things like this." He kissed her earlobe softly.

She relaxed into him; she couldn't help it. It was like his touch evaporated all of her self-control. She cherished the feel of him, afraid this would be the last time. A premonition almost, a deep foreboding.

"I should be going with you."

"Why?"

She wheeled around. "You have no idea what you are up against."

"Our whole existence is avoiding society. We've survived this long."

"You haven't had any of the police sniffing this close before."

Rein's lips pursed. "Maybe not, but I did have the benefit of learning from Jordan. We know what to do."

"You don't understand. The people closing in have had the benefit of The Center's training programs."

"Are they like you?"

"No, but..."

Rein pulled her against him, stroking her hair. "We really need you here. If something happens, you can protect the community. You can keep it going."

Ellyssa started to protest, but he stopped the words with a kiss. Like the times before, at his touch a fire consumed her. She hungrily parted her lips, inviting him to explore, while she tasted him. Her hands ran across his back, examining the contours of his muscles. She moved up to his hair and tangled her fingers in the strands, trying to pull him closer, desperate to never let him go.

Rein's mouth parted from hers, and soft traces of his kisses and tongue traveled down her jawline to the hollow of her neck. Her breath hitched, a strong current flowing through her body. Adrenaline and hormones flooded. Everything forgotten, lost to the moment.

As desire engulfed her, Ellyssa lost control. She pushed herself against Rein, wanting him closer, finding his mouth. She released his hair and dropped her hand to his chest. She could feel his heart slam like hers. Her fingers trailed down over the hardness of his stomach to his beltline. She froze, as reality slapped her in the face.

Ellyssa knew all about the mating process, but the books she'd read had all been technical and cold, nothing like Rein's warmth and inviting touch. The texts had never described the fire, or the shivers, or the intensity of the emotional sensations blooming in her heart. Frustrated at her ignorance, she looped her arm around the small of his back.

"Ellyssa," he whispered into her ear, his soft breath sending chills through her body, fanning the flames. "I love you."

"I love you," she replied, her breath short.

Rein took her hand in his and led her to a cot. Not knowing what to do, she let him ease her onto the canvas and settled above her, his dark hair messed into a new arrangement, his body hard against hers. In an instant, her misgivings evaporated. New instincts charged forward.

Ellyssa pulled him down where she could nibble at his throat and the curve of his collarbone. Soft moans escaping, Rein lowered his head and met her lips. Eagerly, her mouth moved with his, her tongue exploring, her hips pressing into his.

Rein ran his fingers between the contours of her breasts, down her stomach, stroking the inside of her thigh. Heart thudding uncontrollably, heat rose in her midsection and traveled down. Warmth blossomed. She reveled in the sensation, and feared it at the same time.

Suddenly aware of the primal need coursing through her body, Ellyssa faltered. She wanted him, but the thought both excited and terrified her. Confusion mounted, but before she could overanalyze everything, he settled off her, his breaths ragged.

"Do you want to be with me?" he asked, kissing the tip of her nose.

Her chest heaving, she nodded. "Yes."

"Forever?"

She reached up and ran her fingers behind his ear. "Yes."

"Are you sure?"

Ellyssa frowned. "Of course."

Rein smoothed away the lines with the tip of his finger, then leaned over to kiss her again, his tongue darting playfully. He pulled back. "I want to be with you, too. What I feel for you is as foreign to me as it is to you." He gazed at her, his green eyes boring into her blue. "I love you, Ellyssa. I will always love you. I just want you to be sure it is me that you love. I know you've never…" He hesitated, picking his words. "You've never loved."

Bewildered, Ellyssa studied Rein. Then she understood. Like her, he had misgivings, fear of putting himself out there. Trust was hard.

"It's true, I have never loved," she said. "With what limited emotions I have felt, I have nothing to compare the feeling to. But in the emotionless prison I grew up in, how did I know joy when I felt it, or pride? How did I know the feeling I had at Jordan's death was loss?

"My sheltered life allowed complete oblivion against the wonderful things life has to offer: family and friends, a sense of truly belonging. I felt these reactions, and my body naturally responded. I've laughed. I've cried." She brushed her lips against his. "Because of you, I love."

Rein smiled, a beautiful smile that lit his face and reached his eyes.

The adrenaline, the hormones, the raging emotions slapping together like waves during a hurricane—she'd never felt so vulnerable. It was beyond petrifying, but she wanted to be with him.

Rein dropped his head and kissed her, his tongue teasing her lips, before darting into her mouth, rekindling the embers that responded in an instant blaze. Ellyssa dug her hands into his hair, pulling him closer.

Gasping, Rein pulled back. Shifting to his side, he lay next to her, their foreheads touching. "I want to stay," he said, while playing with a strand of her hair. "Woody will come looking for me soon."

"I know."

"Are you still angry? You know…with the council and everything?"

Ellyssa caressed the side of his face, memorizing every detail. "I was never angry. I think I felt hurt. I'm also very worried."

Rein kissed the tip of her nose. "Please don't. Next time we'll stay together. No matter what. I promise."

"I'm going to hold you to that," Ellyssa said.

Rein pushed off the cot and grabbed her by the wrist, pulling her up with him. He hugged her and kissed the top of her head, the bottom of her earlobe, and each corner of her mouth before lingering on her lips.

Holding him tight as he kissed her, enjoying the feel of his body against hers, Ellyssa didn't want to let him go, but the soft sound of footsteps—always the echo of footsteps—caused her to drop her arms and step away.

Mathew paused for a moment, his eyes darting between the two of them, a knowing smile playing across his face. "No longer angry?"

Ellyssa shook her head.

"Good." Mathew looked lost for a moment, as if struggling to decide what to do. Finally, he said, "Um…Woody."

"Yeah, I know. It's getting late."

Rein leaned over and gave her a quick peck on the mouth. She wished his lips would linger.

"Take care of her for me, Doc."

"Of course. Plenty to keep us busy."

"I'll be back as soon as possible." Rein said, as he gave her hand a gentle squeeze.

Mathew draped his arm over Ellyssa's shoulders as she watched Rein disappear out the entryway. Her heart fluttered as love swept through her, taking the place of everything essential for life, like air or food. She held on to the feeling, ignoring the foreboding that nibbled at her.

Mathew patted her shoulder. "It's going to be okay."

Ellyssa wanted so much to believe him.

32

Dr. George Hirch stooped over the computer screen where he spliced the DNA extracted from Ahron's, Xaver's, and Aalexis' somatic cells. After several hours of working in the lab, surrounded by bright lights reflecting off white walls, his neck and back throbbed, but the pain was worth the output.

He straightened and stretched. The process would take a couple of hours, as the DNA and the egg cell essentially adjusted to each other.

When Micah and Ellyssa returned, he'd splice all their genes together in the same fashion, only next time he'd stimulate cell division, then transplant the egg into a surrogate mother.

Clones would follow.

A whole army of them. Rows of perfect soldiers, blond and blue-eyed. Stepping together as they eradicated the imperfections.

And he would be worshiped as their creator.

Leland entered the lab, interrupting his daydream. "Here is another sample from Aalexis," he said, brushing his powder-blue eyes over the doctor. They were drawn and rimmed in red, much like George expected his own appeared. It had been a long day.

George stood, stretching again. "How did the simulation go?"

"Their powers are developing beyond our predictions." Leland handed George a chart. "As you can see, Xaver held his shield up for ten seconds longer. Ahron kept the same time on phasing, but he moved while he phased."

George's brow arched. "Moved?"

"Only a few centimeters, but still incredible. He was in one spot, and in the blink of an eye was in another."

"And Aalexis?"

"Aalexis cooperated, but the assistants had to work with her. She's becoming quite defiant."

The angelic face of the young beauty was dangerous, her innocent look deceiving. Aalexis was the perfect predator.

If Ellyssa hadn't escaped, his vision could already be underway.

Of course, growing his army without the mind reader could be done, but to know what your enemy was planning before execution was beneficial. Plus, his soldiers would need to be able to seek out hidden lairs. He needed all of his children's gifts added into the final sequence.

George wished he'd sent Micah earlier. The oldest of his children had proved invaluable in the search for Ellyssa. Without him, Detective Petersen would never have located the storage facility. His child could have saved precious days better used by splicing the genetic makeup.

"She knows how powerful she is," George said, eyes gleaming.

"Dr. Hirch, you don't understand how difficult she's becoming. Her sudden changes in attitude are unpredictable. The staff is growing wary of her." Leland pulled his hand over his face. "They're afraid."

The news caused George's smile to intensify.

"What if she hurts someone?"

George brushed off the notion with his hand. "Impossible. She has been educated on proper protocol. She will obey me."

"Like Ellyssa?"

A tic worked at George's jaw as anger responded. "The two are unrelated. Aalexis is just finding herself."

"None of the other children have proven to be so difficult. Even without emotions, they knew what was expected. They all obeyed, like good soldiers, without question." Leland pulled a stool over and sat down in front of the microscope. "What if she…becomes uncontrollable?"

"What are you suggesting?"

Glancing down at the Petri dish, Leland said, "It's just—you have what you need from her. Maybe she should be…"

Leland didn't finish the statement; he didn't need to. Without giving control a thought, George advanced on the younger man, grabbing him by the lapels. He yanked the assistant to his feet. Nose to nose, he glared into the startled man's eyes. He'd had enough of him.

"She is indispensible," he seethed, "unlike you."

Fear froze Leland's face in a partial shout. Panicky breaths wheezed between his parted lips.

Finding his restraint, the doctor released his grip and smoothed out the crumpled fabric of the collar. "Your services are no longer needed."

"Wh-what?"

His demeanor calmed, he stepped away. "Your judgment has become clouded. I will talk to career services. You will be placed in a more… appropriate job."

The fear melted away as the tendons in Leland's jerked. "You're playing with something very dangerous."

"I know what I am doing."

"You have no idea." Leland spun around and stalked toward the door.

George felt heat rush into his face at the young man's gibe. He inhaled once and maintained control.

"Leland," the young assistant stopped, his shoulders clenched, "your badge."

Leland yanked the identification off his coat and tossed it on the table.

"Security will meet you at the doors. I would not keep them waiting."

As Leland walked out the door, George hit the intercom and alerted the guards. Afterwards, he contacted the *Kripo* unit and spoke with the man Angela had left in charge.

"I want you to keep close tabs on Leland."

33

Under the soft glow of his flashlight and the moon, Rein examined the debris covering the drive leading to the weather-beaten farmhouse. Something was wrong. The decaying trunk looked out of place as did the bushes.

As a matter-of-fact, nothing had seemed right since he and Woody had left the cavern. Right from the beginning, Rein's radar had been tripped.

Davis' absence nagged him. The ranger had failed to leave a message. He had to have known about the search. They'd checked all the designated points for communication—nothing.

The rusty Oshkosh was still parked in the barn where he and Doc had left it. They were hoping it'd still be there, because it'd be easier to move the supplies, but neither had really expected to find it. Then it'd seemed as if the search teams had completely disappeared, which spooked Rein more than the thought of running into them.

"I don't like this," he admitted while helping Woody pull the rotting tree trunk out of the way.

Woody rolled his eyes. "What'd you expect?" Grunting, he lifted his side of the tree over a protruding rock. "Listen, we're going to load the stuff and get our asses out of here."

Rein hoped he was right.

They finished the job and climbed back inside the cab, him with his doubts and Woody with a reassuring smile.

"We should consider ourselves lucky we haven't run into anybody," said Woody as the truck jolted forward. "You worry too much."

Rein looked forward, concentrating on keeping the wheels aligned with the grooved tracks, once in awhile bouncing over a rut. Not an easy feat, but the full moon helped with navigation. "Seriously? After you being a jerk about Ellyssa, and your paranoia of about being discovered, now you're all calm when your fears are justified. They're searching for her."

"I was wrong about her," Woody said, his voice soft.

Although Rein knew Woody had had a change of heart about Ellyssa, he'd never expected him to admit his misjudgment. Surprised, Rein looked askance at his friend. "Really?"

"Yeah. The concern she showed for Jordan was something I'd never witnessed before," Woody said, as he faced Rein. "She'd only known him for a couple weeks, and supposedly she's an emotionless soldier, but she really cared about him." He glanced down, lips pursed before he continued. "She cried. And I mean cried. Not just a few tears, but an ocean of them." Sighing, he turned away. "Plus, she was there for me."

Rein's grip tightened on the steering wheel as jealousy reared its ugly head. He should've been there, not Woody, to hold her and make her feel safe during the emotional barrage. It was a part of her transformation that he'd never be a part of. A part of her she'd always share with Woody.

"Jordan was right. She's special, Rein," continued Woody, oblivious to Rein's reaction.

"I know," he replied in a low voice.

The dirt path roughened, and the two men bounced over the rain-washed potholes. The old truck rattled and creaked. Rein eased his foot off the gas and glided, trying to cut the jostling to a minimum. The last thing he needed right now was to leave a trail of parts.

From behind a thick fir tree, the rubble of the farmhouse glided into view. The mound of debris was silhouetted against the light of the night sky. Nothing appeared out of the ordinary. But with every meter the tires rolled, Rein's apprehension radar pegged.

"Something's definitely not right," he said, bringing the truck to a stop.

Sweeping his gaze across the field, Woody said, "There's nobody here."

"There's no one that you can see."

"Do you honestly think we'd have gotten this far if they knew about this place? They would've stopped us on the road. Hell, probably back at the barn."

"I don't know, Woody."

"You were all for this back home."

"I know, but..." His words trailed off.

"Rein, you're spooking yourself. Look, we at least have to get a few of the supplies, or we won't make it. Let's just grab a couple of boxes of food and get out of here." He paused. "Okay?"

Inhaling deeply, the word *no* dangled on Rein's lips. An urge to run twitched in his gut. Instead, he released the brake, and the truck jerked forward.

"Four boxes of food."

Pulling the truck next to the sagging wall, Rein pushed the gear into neutral. He left the engine idling. "Four boxes."

Woody glanced at him and wagged his brow. "This is it. Keep your eyes open."

"Stop it."

Woody scrambled out with his gun, and Rein reluctantly stepped from the driver's side. A low wind rustled through the grass, carrying the scent of fall blooms and pine. He peered into the line of trees, seeing nothing more than a rugged black outline that circled the overgrown field. There were no sounds of insects or curious wildlife.

Everything was eerily quiet.

He grabbed his rifle off the seat and moved to the other side of the truck where Woody waited.

Everything appeared normal, but the tiny hairs on the back of his neck said otherwise. He moved the branches aside and grabbed the edge of the old tin door. The door swung open easily, without a squeak. He gazed into the gaping hole. Darkness swirled.

"I hate to say it, but I told you so," Woody said with a smug grin.

Rein ignored him.

Switching on his flashlight, Woody said, "You ready?" He directed the beam into the mouth of the basement.

"Not really," Rein replied. He descended the steps anyway.

A chill met Rein at the bottom of the stairs, sending a shiver down his spine. He didn't remember the cold being so biting before. He swept his flashlight to the right. The beam revealed boxes and cartons of supplies piled along the walls. *Everything as it should be.* Relieved, he stepped toward the bounty, but as he moved, the light flashed deeper into the hand-dug basement. From his peripheral vision, a reflective glimmer caught his eye.

Rein stopped dead, as did Woody. His heart leapt into his throat and raced in his ears. His first impulse was to flee, to run up the steps, hop into the truck, and tear out of there. But voices, and the soft clicks of shoes on the scrap above them, told him escape wasn't a possibility. For a split second, ice ran through Rein's veins and his muscles seized. Then, everything fast-forwarded.

"Move," he shouted, shoving Woody toward the stairwell. His friend's flashlight clattered to the ground; the light winked out.

Woody stumbled under the steps and slipped behind a wooden beam as Rein rolled behind the stack of supplies. He flicked off his flashlight and gripped the gun, pulling it into his chest. The coolness from the metal penetrated through the thin material of his T-shirt.

Swallowed in blackness, as if time itself had disappeared, everything else seemed magnified. The clicks and voices from above, his breathing, his heart rate. Rein stared over where Woody was, but he couldn't make out anything other than a dark silhouette.

"Put your weapons out where we can see them," said a feminine voice, filled with authority. Deep satisfaction saturated her tone.

A familiar hum Rein had lived with all his life resonated, afterward a blinding light flooded the enclosed space. Ducking behind the boxes, Rein glanced at Woody. Terror drained all color from his friend's face as he pressed his back against the beam like he was trying to melt into the wood. His grey eyes were wide and scared, hair slicked to his head. Rein knew his expression mirrored Woody's.

"Don't move," Rein mouthed.

Woody gave him a *duh* look.

Rein worked to loosen his death grip on the rifle. As the blood ran back into his fingers, he slid the bolt back and chambered a round. The click echoed in his ears, drowning out the thumping of his heart.

"If you value your friend's life, drop your weapons and show yourselves. I want to see your hands first." The same feminine voice, only this time, anger pulled at each word. "Now!"

Friend?

Taking his eyes off Woody, Rein peeked through a small gap between two of the boxes. Beaten and bleeding, Davis sat slumped in a chair, a strap around his chest and two leather bindings around his wrist holding him in place. His head cocked strangely to one side, one eye blackened and swollen like his lips. Blood ran from the edge of his hairline down the side of his face. The ranger opened his one good eye and desperately stared toward the stairs as if looking for rescue.

The torture their contact had suffered was incomprehensible, but gauging from the lean woman in off-duty, civilian clothing, flared jeans and a black blouse, Rein began to understand. The woman's blond hair was cut short and cropped at her neck, and her face was pinched in hardness, sharpening the angle of her cheeks and thinning her lips into nonexistence. She aimed an electroshock weapon at Davis' head.

Her mouth pulled into a smirk as she thumbed a button on the weapon. Davis' muscles locked, his hands gripping the armrests and his head rocking from side to side. She released the button and Davis stilled, his head flopping back over to the side. Spittle streamed from the corner of his mouth to the collar of his shirt. His good eye rolled under his lid.

Horrified, Rein couldn't look away.

"Do you understand me, now? First, your weapons."

Hands shaking, Rein carefully placed his rifle on the ground where she could see it. Woody copied his actions.

"Put your hands where I can see them, and step out."

A grin stretched across the woman's face as Rein stepped out, palms up. Woody stopped next to him.

"That's better," she said. "Let me introduce myself. My name is Detective Petersen. And you are...?"

When neither Rein or Woody responded, the detective's eyebrows pinched together. "I see. Introductions can wait. You gave us quite the run, didn't you?" she said as she walked around Davis, her weapon still trained on him. "Captain Jones, would you remove their weapons?"

Two men stood next to the generator, both tall, muscular, and blond. The one dressed in a green police uniform was older with sea blue eyes and defined cheekbones. He shifted from one foot to the other, like he was nervous, and he kept glancing over at Davis with a mixture of regret and hate. The other was dressed in regular jeans and a T-shirt, young with alabaster skin, his hair platinum, his features familiar. He looked bored, unaffected.

The older one stepped forward, his electroshock weapon trained on them. He warily walked toward the men. "Step over there." He motioned toward the front of the staircase with the electroshock weapon.

Rein nudged Woody, and they both moved.

Captain Jones gave them a wide berth as he picked up both shotguns and swung them over his shoulder with one hand.

"Come down," he called as he backed to his previous position. He leaned both weapons against a beam far from Rein's reach.

Two policemen descended the steps, moving to opposite sides of Rein and Woody. Rein felt the cold touch of the electric gun against his neck. Buzzing surged within the weapon, and it vibrated gently against his skin.

"Now, the backpack," the detective ordered. "Toss it over."

Before Rein complied, the officer next to him jabbed him with the metal prongs. "Careful."

Slowly, Rein removed the bag from his shoulder and slid it across the ground.

"Micah."

The younger man grabbed Rein's pack. He looked up and stared at Rein with Ellyssa's eyes—only cold and completely emotionless. The color of his hair, the alabaster skin, the flawless features—too perfect.

Everything connected.

Numbness washed over Rein. He took a step forward, then he was on the floor with a electroshock weapon inches from his face.

"Get up," commanded the policeman, shoving Rein with the toe of his boot.

Pulling himself onto shaky legs, Rein looked at Woody. His friend tipped his head; he'd made the connection, too.

Gripping the bag, Micah closed his eyes.

"Your contact is very loyal," Detective Petersen said, strolling in front of Davis' chair, her gait confident, in charge. "Couldn't get names or the location of where you stay. Nothing."

Rein pursed his lips. She wouldn't be getting anything from him, either.

"I wonder if you'll be a little more cooperative." She slipped behind Davis' chair as he began to stir. "Of course, it can be done the easy way or the hard way." Grabbing a handful of hair, she wrenched his head back. Davis' eye popped opened as he screamed.

"You'll get nothing from us," Woody said, through gritted teeth.

"That's too bad," the woman said, not looking like she felt that way at all.

Without warning, she gripped her baton and whacked Davis across his jaw. Blood splayed from his mouth as he went lax against the strap. Rein flinched. The detective didn't.

"Captain," she instructed.

The captain, looking a little peaked, grabbed a bucket, sitting on the floor next to him and tossed water on the unconscious ranger.

Davis sputtered as more blood poured from his mouth. "Please," he begged, the word barely decipherable. A pleading eye rolled and locked on Rein.

Rein wanted to look away. He couldn't bear to watch. But the horror kept his gaze glued to Davis.

Detective Petersen slowly blinked, cat-like, with a smirk on her face. She enjoyed this. Patting Davis' head much like a dog, she said, "Shh. If you and your friends cooperate, you won't have to feel any more pain."

Davis whimpered in defeat that tore a canyon through Rein's soul. He wished there was something he could do besides helplessly watching Davis be tormented.

"Would you like to tell me where the camp is?"

An anguished cry pulled from Davis. He knew as well as Rein that the community couldn't be sacrificed. Tears ran down his face, mixing with the blood.

Straightening, the detective returned her attention to Rein and Woody. "Are you really willing to watch such a loyal friend be punished? No wonder you are all beneath us. How selfish."

Tsking, she smacked Davis close to his temple. A crack sounded with the impact. His head swiveled to the side and back. Passed out or dead, Davis drooped forward, blood streaming from his head. The woman went behind the chair and unbuckled the strap. Like a ragdoll, Davis slid from the chair and crumpled to the ground.

As strong as a magnetic draw, Rein's gaze stayed trained on the crimson pooling under Davis' head. Rein had known the consequences of being captured, the danger, but to have it play out in front of him was beyond surreal. The woman's viciousness, the way she enjoyed torturing her helpless captive. Even now, Rein saw the amusement flitting across the detective's face.

She flicked her head up, indicating Rein. The policeman next to him grabbed his upper arm. "You're next," he sneered.

"No," the picture of perfection said. His accent sounded just like Ellyssa's when she'd first spoken to Rein.

Within the nightmare, Rein had forgotten about him. Xaver held Rein's music box. His thumb stroked over the glass dome.

The detective whipped her head toward the young man, and she nailed him with a lazer-like glare. Apparently, she didn't like having her fun interrupted. "What is it, Micah?"

Ignoring her, Micah stepped toward Rein, and stopped.

"Your name is Rein," he stated.

Rein tried to hide the surprise at the mention of his name; he lacked the training of The Center's children. His eyes widened as they moved from the music box, Ellyssa had held a few days ago, to the azure-colored eyes of the boy. Hadn't Ellyssa mentioned a brother who could read things from touching them? His heart skipped a beat.

Micah watched him, his expression giving away nothing. After a moment, when Rein didn't respond, he nodded, and the guard next to him gave a small zap. Against his control, every muscle clenched as the short burst of electricity traveled through his body and tunneled through to his feet. He fell to his knees.

Micah wound the key. Music floated in the air as he held it up. The little figures glided in a circle.

"Interesting," he said, although his voice and face showed nothing of the sort. He looked from the box to Rein. "Very interesting."

"What?" demanded the detective, moving to Micah's side. "What do you see?"

"Platinum hair, sky-blue eyes, a flawless face. Beautiful." Micah's eyebrow arched. Finally, a subtle expression. "You know my sister?" he asked Rein.

Detective Petersen turned toward Rein. "You've met Ellyssa," she accused, "and you still live?" Her voice lost all of its superiority, and she sounded baffled.

His face smooth again, Micah closed his eyes, his palm cupping the dome. "Ellyssa is different, though. Her eyes and face show emotions. And…" he said, landing his gaze on Rein, "it seems she has a…liking for our Renegade here. She let you touch her."

"Where is she?" the detective asked, stepping closer.

Rein shook his head. "I don't know what you're talking about."

"Do not bother denying it," Micah said. "I can see everything. The conversation. The looks you share. You are in a cave."

"Which cave?" Angela extended her arm, holding the electroshock weapon firmly. "Talk."

Before Rein could answer, a loud *oomph* sounded from Woody's guard. The blond man leaned over, holding his stomach. Woody grabbed him by the scruff of the neck and pulled him in front of himself, like a shield, as two electrodes connected to long wires extended from Detective Petersen's weapon and attached to the guard's clothing. An instant later, the man flopped to the ground as tremors rocked his body. By the time Rein could comprehend what was happening, Woody had disappeared up the steps.

"After him," yelled Detective Petersen.

Rein watched as his treasured music box fell to the ground and shattered; the broken figurines skidded across the earthen floor.

"No!" Rein threw himself at Micah as he charged toward the stairs after Woody. It was like hitting a brick wall.

Micah barely stumbled. He grabbed Rein by the back of the neck and hurled him across the room, sending him into the boxes of supplies.

Cans fell on Rein. He covered his head with his arms.

"Hurry," Detective Petersen ordered the guards. She turned her attention to Rein.

Rein rolled over to his knees and attempted to stand, but a boot to the ribs knocked him back down. A current ripped through his muscles, leaving him helpless.

The last thing he saw was Detective Petersen's grin.

34

Ellyssa squatted on her haunches and slid the last box through the hole leading to the well-hidden evacuation cave. If someone searched the passageway, it would appear to dead-end, but further inspection would reveal two walls overlapping, and another tunnel leading to a drop-off into a natural cavern, a level below, hidden by an optical illusion.

"This is the last of it," Ellyssa said as two hands appeared and grabbed hold. The box disappeared.

"Don't forget Tyler's group," said Melody, the owner of the hands. The thirty-year-old woman had beautiful hazel eyes, offset by mocha-colored skin.

"After we move Jason, I will check on them." Ellyssa rose, dusting off her hands.

Thanks to the council, who ordered drills on a regular basis, organizing the community had been easier than Ellyssa had thought possible. Within two days, all of the Renegades had their personal items moved and most of the supplies stored away, excluding the generator, which had been disassembled earlier in the morning and was ready to move out.

Ellyssa adjusted the 12-gauge on her shoulder and picked up the flashlight. White light poured into the tunnel as she emerged from between the two walls. She moved further down and turned around. The light reflected off the mineral deposits, creating the perception of a solid wall. The illusion should easily mislead any investigators.

The cavern where they'd be hiding was far from paradise. Dampness pervaded the cool air, and water dripped incessantly. The accommodations were cramped. Worse than the dankness and overcrowding was that there was no way to gather or prepare food. All they had left were a few cans of peaches and some bread Bertha had made from dandelion flour.

Hopefully, Rein and Woody would be back soon with more provisions.

Still, even with the supplies, they couldn't stay there for long.

Ellyssa pushed the thought from her head as she entered the makeshift hospital. "Are you ready to move Jason?" she asked Mathew.

Grabbing his bag, the doctor circled, giving the room one more glance. His freshly cut hair revealed more grey than black. "Seems everything's in order."

"How's he doing?"

"The infection is getting worse. If I can't get the fever under control…" He shrugged. "He needs penicillin, not aspirin, and fresh bandages. I hope Rein gets back soon."

Ellyssa's sentiments exactly. She dropped her gaze.

"Hey. It'll be okay."

"I hope so."

Standing in front of Ellyssa, Mathew placed both of his hands on her shoulders. He hunkered down where he could look into her eyes. "Rein and Woody will be fine."

Forcing a grin that felt wrong on her face, Ellyssa nodded.

"We have things to do here."

"I know."

Mathew shoved an old, ripped sheet into the back of his belt. "Let's go," he said, the sheet sashaying behind him.

Ellyssa led them down the main hall. The swishing sheet whispered as it erased their footprints.

"Is everyone in the cavern?" asked Mathew.

"Most everyone. Except Tyler, Marissa, Peter, Ashley, and Caleb," she recited the names. "They're erasing signs that we here, too. I doubt they look as humorous, though."

"Ha, ha. Thanks."

"Looks like you are wearing a misplaced cape."
"Would you prefer to do the honors?"
"No, thank you."
"Then, I'd be quiet, if I were you."

Ellyssa enjoyed the exchange of banter with Mathew. To speak about mundane happenings, to joke and laugh, to communicate without training or sparring. At one time, the thought of doing such things had never crossed her mind. Ellyssa really loved her new home. She just wished Rein was with her.

On their way to Jason, the sound of shoes smacking hard against the ground bounced down along the walls. Ellyssa stilled, as did Mathew. No one was assigned to outdoor duty. No one should be coming from that direction. The frantic steps slapped louder as they drew closer.

Spinning on her heel, Ellyssa stepped in front of Mathew, pinning him against the wall. She chambered a round and aimed into the darkness. Before the possible intruder reached them, she lowered her mental wall, reaching with psychic tendrils. Mathew's adrenaline-induced thoughts interfered with her probing.

"Clear your mind," she whispered.

Panicky images flickered wildly. Ellyssa doubled her effort to filter him out. Her eyes squeezed together as she drifted forward, searching for the unknown.

The steps drew nearer, images and emotions bombarding her, quickly overshadowing any interference from the doctor.

Fear. Desperation. Supplies. A strange place. Blurry faces. A long stream of thoughts, running together, overpowered by hysterical terror.

She recognized Woody right away; afraid someone might be following, she kept her weapon aimed into the dark passageway. She left his screaming mind and reached for Rein's.

A void.

She pointed her flashlight into the inky blackness. Woody burst out of the shadows as if materializing out of nowhere.

His hand brushed against the wall while he ran. His usually kempt hair shone with sweat and was plastered against his head. His clothes were ragged, torn, and dirty. His eyes drew her attention. Their grey was clouded with alarm, wild and frantic. He ran toward them, but showed no signs of stopping, as if he didn't realize they were there. As if his only concern was escape.

"Woody," she said hesitantly. She held her hand toward him. "Woody."

His eyes raked over her and, impossibly, widened even more. Recognition flitted through him as he skidded to a stop. His breath ragged and his chest heaving, he placed his hands on his knees.

"Ellyssa," he panted, head down. "Rein. The community."

Dread filled her. Her worst fear, borne from the depths of her nightmares, took life. "What about Rein?"

Still leaning over, he nodded.

"Do they have him?"

"Yes," Woody panted.

"No." Gasping, Ellyssa stumbled back. In one single moment, her future turned bleak. Dizziness and nausea swept through her, like a windstorm, churning in her head and midsection. Holding a hand over her stomach, she forced the overwhelming reactions to retreat.

No time for panic.

Ellyssa thought the words, obeyed them, and replaced the sensation with the one emotion she had never been denied—mounting anger. She snatched Woody by the collar and yanked him close, until their noses almost touched.

"Where is he?"

"Ellyssa!" Mathew exclaimed, snatching her wrist. "What are you doing?"

She jerked her arm free.

The doctor stepped back, hands in front of him. "It's not his fault."

In an instant, a wave of misery washed away the anger, as Ellyssa looked into Woody's eyes. Emotional upheaval. Her inability to cope was incapacitating her logical thought process. She released him. "I'm sorry," she said, her voice breaking. "I just…" She covered her face and fought back the tears.

The next thing she knew, familiar arms wrapped around her and pulled her close. "I'm so sorry, Ellyssa," Woody said.

Ellyssa wanted to tell him that it wasn't his fault, but she couldn't. If she opened her mouth, sobs would burst forth. She buried her face in his chest.

"Is he dead?" she muttered, afraid of the answer.

"I don't know."

A flame of hope lit in Ellyssa's heart. Fueled by determination, she stepped back and looked at Woody. His look of pain and suffering shamed her.

"I'm sorry, Woody. I should have never treated you that way."

His breath still jagged and irregular, his grey eyes lingered on hers. "I understand. Believe me, I do."

She took his hand. "I need you to tell me everything."

Shaking his head, Woody straightened his shirt, the simple act appearing to calm him. "We don't have time. They're coming," he said. "They're coming. I ran… Following…" He flapped his hands around.

Ellyssa tried to grasp his fleeing thoughts, but his emotions and the flood of adrenaline rendered her gift useless. "Woody, I've never asked this before, but may I read you?"

Confusion mounted and added to the panic. "What?"

"Your thoughts are too frantic for me to understand."

He looked from her to Mathew.

The doctor gave him a nod. "I'll explain later. Let her do it."

Bewildered, Woody glanced back at Ellyssa.

"Please."

"I don't understand."

"I know. You will, though. I need you to calm down and focus."

Placing her hands on the sides of his head, Ellyssa exhaled, releasing every bit of her own emotions and tension. Woody's thoughts flipped wildly for a moment; but as he relaxed, the images cleared and became readable.

Woody running, dodging branches, bracken, and bushes. In his flight, he got tangled in thistle. Stairs leading towards light. An old farmhouse, leveled by years of neglect. Rein, still alive, with a nameless guard holding an electroshock weapon. A man, beaten and bloodied, slumped in a chair. Broken figurines. Unwelcome company.

She gasped, dropping her hands. "Micah."

"Who?" asked Mathew.

Woody's brow knitted. "Yes. That's the name of the blond boy. He said he was your brother?"

"Yes, I have a brothers...and a sister," Ellyssa said. "I'm sorry. There's a lot you don't know about me. The female who...tortured that male in the chair, is Detective Angela Petersen, the head of the *Kripo* unit from The Center. She is dangerous. I saw her mind."

"You. Saw. Her. Mind?" asked Woody, emphasizing each word.

"Yes. Like I did yours, just now. "I'll explain everything to you, but not now." Ellyssa paced in a small circle, hands behind her back. She stopped in front of Mathew. "Go get Tyler's group and hide. I will join you soon."

Woody grabbed her elbow. "Where're you going?"

She pulled his hand away, holding it tight within hers. Her fear for the community, for her friends, had wakened her soldiering instincts, but keeping her emotions in check was hard.

"To the entrance," she replied.

"Why?"

"Reconnaissance."

"Are you crazy? If you read my mind, you saw what she is capable of," Woody said, his voice fluctuating between disbelief and determination. "It's not safe."

"I have to go," she said. "I will meet you at the evacuation point."

"But..."

"I promise nothing will happen to me. I will be fine." Ellyssa leveled her eyes with his. "This is what I am trained to do."

"What about Jason?" Mathew asked.

She squeezed Woody's fingers. "Meet me in his room, instead."

"When?"

"I do not know. Wait for me. I will be there." Ellyssa faced Mathew. "Get the others to safety."

Reluctantly, Woody released her hand as the doctor pulled him away. "Come on. We need to hurry."

"Be careful," Woody said, his gaze lingering on her before he turned and walked toward Jason's room.

Those two simple words touched Ellyssa. She blinked, keeping a tear at bay. "I promise."

"I expect you to keep it." Mathew's voice floated from the darkness.

Ellyssa stood still for a moment, listening to their padding feet before she took off toward the hospital, the beam of her flashlight bouncing across the blackened walls. As she passed the room that had held the beginnings of her new life, her old life came to the forefront. Emotions squelched, shoes barely touching the floor, she moved silently, like a predator, to the entrance.

The access remained well-hidden. Sunlight oozed between the rocks that had been meticulously placed years ago. Light burned her eyes as she peeked through a gap. All seemed calm. Trees and long grass swayed in the wind, birds chirped, and the soft hum of insects punctuated the day. But off in the distance, right where the grass met the rocks leading to their hideout, vegetation and grass lay flattened, where Woody had trampled through the clearing.

There was no doubt in her mind that they would find their camp.

35

Perched for hours, unmoving, her breath controlled, Ellyssa watched the tree line listening for any indication of the detective. The cool snap of a twig. The soft whisper of clothing brushing branches. The rustling of leaves.

Deep down, she wanted to run into the forest and find Rein. Ellyssa knew such an impulsive act would put everyone at risk. Her soldier's instincts told her to wait, for her own protection, for the community's, and for Rein's. She needed an indication of how many, and who, before she acted.

Detective Petersen would definitely be leading the search party, but Ellyssa wondered if Micah was with her. Would Father allow the possibility of his being injured? It wasn't a secret that the Renegades were armed; Rein and Woody had had weapons when the detective captured them, but the detective would be blind to the number of people and the number of arms they would face.

Neither Rein nor Woody would ever conceive betraying their family. No, the risk proved too great. Micah would not be included.

Relieved, Ellyssa sighed. If her brother had accompanied the search party, she would have had to fight, which would've exposed her newfound family. For survival purposes, it was best for the community to stay under the radar and remain hidden.

A soft hum carried on the wind; disembodied words joined together into a long, hushed murmur. Ellyssa calmed herself, bringing forth everything she'd learned. Her muscles twitched in preparation.

Forty-five meters away, five people filed out of the trees, one after another. Three women, with hair tied back into buns, and two men, with hair cropped short. All sported dark green camouflage with tan boots. Not the traditional uniform of the area police, but one necessary for blending within the woods.

The five walked as if trying to be quiet, their postures slightly hunched, but their clothes scraped along plants and their boots padded on the ground. One female leaned over and whispered to a comrade. Ellyssa couldn't hear what she said, but once again, the hum reached her.

Their lack of training had to be driving the detective mad.

As if her ears burned at that thought, Detective Petersen materialized from a bush. She walked with a detectable, but quieter, tread than her comrades. Her short hair was slicked back and held in place with an elastic band. Her face held a scowl as she glared at the first five.

After her, a male appeared. He was tall and lean, his features angular. Ellyssa recognized him from Woody's memories. The detective had addressed him as Captain Jones.

Seven?

Their search party had to consist of more, maybe at a camp, or searching elsewhere.

The detective motioned for the others to circle around her. Hushed voices carried on the breeze. Angela pointed to the crushed grass, then toward the tree line on the opposite side. Afterward, in one team of two and one of three, the party split to cover the expanse, leaving Detective Petersen and the captain alone.

Slightly confused at these actions, Ellyssa watched as the detective spoke to the captain. She bent down and touched a blade of grass, then lifted her head and looked straight at the rocky overhang where the mineshaft lay hidden.

Ellyssa stilled, her breath nonexistent, as Angela's cold stare pinned her in place. Even though it was impossible, Ellyssa couldn't help but wonder if the detective could see her.

In a matter of minutes, their haven would be found.

Time to go.

Her heart smooth and steady, her pulse light and unhurried, Ellyssa backed away down the tunnel. No padding, no sounds of movement as her pace quickened. When she rounded the second corner, she flipped on her flashlight and hurried to Jason's room, where Woody waited. He leaned against the stone frame of the entrance with his eyes closed.

"Woody." Ellyssa touched his shoulder, then quickly covered his mouth, cutting off his squeal of surprise. "It is me," she whispered in his ear. "Understand?"

Wide-eyed, he nodded. She let go of him.

"I didn't even hear you."

"Yes, I know." She nodded. "We need to move. They're in the field."

Together, they walked into the room where Jason lay on a pad. His cot had already been moved to the evacuation cavern.

Under the yellow beam of the flashlight, Jason looked worse than the last time Ellyssa had seen him. His body was thin, skeletal-like, underneath the flimsy green blanket that was pulled up to his chin. His pasty face emphasized the dark circles around his sunken eyes, and his skin stretched tight over his skull. The blanket rose and fell as he gasped and his breath rattled in his lungs.

"We need to hurry," Ellyssa said, moving to Jason's side and grabbing the corners of the pad. "On the count of three," she said. "One, two…"

"Wait."

She looked at Woody, but he just shook his head and glanced down at Jason. The sickly male looked at Ellyssa, his eyes clouded and unfocused.

"Wait," Jason repeated, the word barely above a whisper. His tongue flicked out and licked his cracked lips.

"Jason, we have to go."

"No." Jason paused for a long time. His unfocused eyes jerked from side to side, and his tongue tried desperately to ease his dry lips. "Sorry," he mumbled.

Jason's apology meant nothing to Ellyssa. She looked away. "We do not have time for this."

Grasping Ellyssa's hand, Jason squeezed, his fingers barely applying any pressure. He was burning up, his fever out of control, and his touch made her skin crawl. She still despised him. He was very lucky her thought processes had changed. "I want you to know how sorry I am."

Ellyssa fought a shiver. "We will talk about it later."

"There will be no later."

"They are coming. We do not have time."

Jason dragged in a noisy breath and released it. "I'm dying."

"You will be fine." She tightened her hold on the pad and prepared to heft him up.

"Don't."

Her patience wearing thin, Ellyssa snapped, "Do you not understand? They are coming."

"Ellyssa," Woody said, his face sad, "let him finish."

The corner of Jason's dried lips curled into his a grimace, and his bottom lip split into a fresh sore. "I know I'm dying. We don't have medicine. Leave me."

Ellyssa shook her head. "We cannot do that."

"You have to. I can detain them."

She glanced at Woody and saw the debate raging behind his eyes.

"I'm dying," Jason said, as if those two words gave all the reason in the world. And, perhaps, they did.

Jason squeezed her hand again. This time with surprising strength. He paused, swallowing. She watched his Adam's apple struggle under his skin.

"Let me do this one last thing. Please," Jason whispered. "Dying wish." His lids fluttered closed, and his hand loosened its grip and slid to his side.

After all the times Ellyssa had read his mind, with his selfish, sick nature shining through, she'd never thought him capable of such an act.

Ordinary humans never ceased to amaze her with their raging emotions and turmoil. Compassion? Forgiveness? Such things went against every fiber of her upbringing, but that had been before she'd joined this family.

Ellyssa reached out and, tentatively, touched his cheek. There was no doubt Jason was dying. His mind was slowing down, the electric pulses firing weakly. Would leaving him be the most humane thing to do? In his current condition, neither the detective nor the police would bother capturing him. Wasted effort. As a matter-of-fact, they might think him contagious, and end his suffering more quickly.

"What do you think?" asked Woody.

Indecisive, Ellyssa nibbled on her bottom lip. "I do not know," she responded, as she lifted her gaze to Woody. "He is dying."

Woody smoothed out Jason's blanket and tucked it tight under his body. "I think we should do as he requests."

"But…"

Woody reached over and brushed her cheek. "He wants the opportunity to right his wrong."

Ellyssa closed her eyes and nodded. "I forgive you," she whispered. Without another word, she stood and left the room. She waited as Woody said his goodbyes.

"It was the right thing to do," assured Woody as he entered the main tunnel. He rested his hand on her shoulder. "It was nice of you to forgive him."

"I had to."

His fingers trailed down her arm and found her hand. "I know—"

Ellyssa stifled his words by covering his mouth and cocked her head to the side. A soft scrape flowed through the tunnel and reached her ears. Woody stilled when she did, a hint of fear masking his features.

She placed her finger to her lips. With a flip of her hand, she motioned him to follow, and led them toward their refuge. Surprised at the ease with which Woody moved, she glided beside him, silently. If she couldn't hear him, neither could they.

They escaped down the tunnel to the faux dead end, where Ellyssa paused to listen for footfalls. No sounds followed them, but the rustling of people echoed below her, voices, shuffling, and scraping.

"We have to get them quiet," she whispered.

Quickly, Ellyssa slipped to the back of the passage behind the overlapping wall. Within the confines of the enclosed space, the commotion clamored. She glanced over her shoulder at Woody and motioned for him to go first. He disappeared into the hole.

By the time she emerged into the cavern, Woody was already gone, hopefully spreading the word. Soft steps whispered from the crossing passage ahead.

Trista appeared around the corner of the intersection, holding a small plastic container. Dirt smudged every bit of her skin and clothing, and her cheeks were pink from exertion. Ellyssa motioned Trista closer.

"Hi," Trista said, oblivious to the danger. "Guess what? I'm a contender for the council."

Ellyssa held her finger up. "Do not say anything else. Do not talk. Do not work. They are in the cave," she said, her voice low.

The rosy color drained from Trista's face.

"Tell the others, and tell them to stay put. Do so quietly."

"Okay," Trista mouthed. She turned right at the T-section, rushing toward the living quarters.

Ellyssa stayed still, listening to Trista's footfalls. They seemed to thunder down the rocky corridor, every step sounding louder than the last. She was glad the detective's ears weren't as sensitive as hers.

A few moments later, the cavern quieted, until the only sound was the soft dripping of water. Ellyssa turned her attention to what lay outside the Renegades' asylum, listening for any movement or voice from above. So far, nothing. She didn't know whether or not that was good.

Woody rounded the corner and came to her side; his weapon was locked and loaded. "Anything?" he whispered in her ear.

Ellyssa shook her head.

Woody flipped his chin in understanding and remained still as a statue as they waited. His stealthy ability impressed her. He was a natural, and she wondered what he could've accomplished if he had received the same rigorous schooling she had.

Silent milliseconds stretched into the past. The waiting grated on Ellyssa's nerves. She was unused to standing around delaying the inevitable. She wanted to act, to attack, to render the danger harmless. Doing so put the her whole family in danger.

Antsy, Ellyssa closed her eyes and lowered her shield. Community voices immediately bombarded her, shouting in her brain. Voices filled with panic and fear. Too much. Her stomach rolled, and she raised her protection, blocking the onslaught.

She opened her eyes to Woody, who was frowning, his mouth drawn quizzically to the side. She leaned closer to him.

"I am trying to get a read on her."

He nodded.

"I will try again."

"Try concentrating just on her. Like you did with me," he suggested in her ear.

"That was different. There is too many voices down here."

"You can do it," Woody whispered. His warm breath brushed against her hair, and his whiskers rubbed against her cheek, sending a pleasant shiver reminiscent of Rein.

At the thought of Rein, Ellyssa's heart squeezed, painfully. She missed him, his eyes, his lips, his gentle touch. Since Woody had returned, she had barely given Rein a thought. Everything had whirled into action so fast. She felt guilty, as if she'd betrayed him, by putting him aside, even though he would've understood. Under the same set of circumstances, he'd have done the same.

Saddened by the image of Rein and worried beyond belief, Ellyssa pulled away from Woody, her eyes on the floor. She had to do this for Rein. She had to succeed.

Pulling in a deep breath and releasing it through her nose, Ellyssa prepared herself for the assault of thoughts. Lowering her shield, she was immediately bombarded, images and words and feelings slamming into her. Her head thumped, but she didn't care.

Rein strengthened her.

Gritting her teeth, Ellyssa's face scrunched in concentration. Voices echoed in her mind, panicky and scared. She pictured her stone shield, and the voices faded. Stone by stone, she reconstructed her defenses, reinforcing each section. In the middle of the barrier, she placed a metal door that swiveled on hinges. The voices were immediately silenced.

In her mind's eye, she approached the gateway and rested her palm against the cool metal. She pushed it open an inch. Thoughts rushed through, like water over a broken dam. She stepped back, letting the door swing shut.

She'd have to try another way.

Ellyssa directed her focus on the female *Kripo*. Bit by bit Ellyssa reconstructed the detective's face: the thin lips, the angle of the cheeks, the too-sharp nose, the hair, and the eyes, which lacked the blue of the sky. Detective Petersen's face wavered in her psyche as the mental picture strengthened, becoming more defined, details sharpening, until it seemed as if the detective stood right in front of her.

With the image of Detective Petersen strongly in her mind, Ellyssa reached out and opened the door again. Much to her relief, the voices of the inhabitants were muffled, indistinct, and easily ignored. She slipped through the crack, directing her flow through the tunnels of the mine, down one corridor after another, searching and feeling for the distinct electrical pulse.

Her limits thinning, Ellyssa reached further, until suddenly she felt the detective. It was like hitting a wall, one second flowing, the next, an instant stop. Ellyssa clenched her jaw and fortified her connection with the detective as if joined by a wire, mind to mind. When she felt certain the link was sturdy, she opened the gate wider, and let the images flow.

Pictures poured into her quickly as if the detective's mind was working in overdrive. One image shifted to another, as Detective Petersen's eyes soaked in the surroundings with a high-powered flashlight. She was skittish, and every noise tweaked her senses.

Stronger emotions swirled within The Center's employee. Deadly ones. Criminals harbored such feelings. As a new and improved citizen, the detective shouldn't be experiencing such useless sensations; the genes responsible should have been detected.

Jealousy, shame, and resentment rolled through the detective, as if the blood in her body carried them like a disease, and the effect increased when her thoughts shifted to any of The Center's children, especially Ellyssa. Her hatred for Ellyssa ran deep and wide, cutting a canyon through her mind.

Angela also kept thinking about the gun strapped to her ankle. Time and time again, her thoughts drifted to standing over Ellyssa, watching a pool of blood spread beneath her, turning her hair crimson.

"What was that?" a male asked, his voice clear in the detective's head, along with his image as she turned to look at him.

The captain from Woody's memory stood before Detective Petersen, only she now beheld a clearer picture of the man's physique, the curvature of his lean body and the chiseled features of his face.

The detective wondered if the captain—Dyllon was apparently his name—would still have her back if the operation finished in bloodshed. She questioned his loyalty, especially after they had captured the ranger.

The image of the male Ellyssa didn't know wavered in the detective's thoughts, beaten, bloody and dead. Dyllon had fought against the male's torture. He just didn't understand, his stomach too weak. Resentment for the captain bloomed within the detective.

"Shh," she hissed.

A groan resonated in the darkness, that of a suffering animal...or a human. Something was hurt. Sweeping her flashlight in broad arcs, the detective followed the sound down one passageway into another.

Ellyssa watched as they approached the entrance to Jason's room. She'd hoped Jason would've passed out from the pain and been overlooked. His groans echoed in the small enclosure.

Realizing she was powerless to stop them or help Jason, regret pulled on Ellyssa's attention, and the barricade weakened. The voices of her newfound family banged against the imaginary wall, growing in volume as Detective Petersen's mind began to fade.

Ellyssa couldn't fail. Regardless of what she'd become since she'd fled, she was a soldier. Only instead of destroying lives, she was going to protect them. Steadying herself, Ellyssa reinforced the barrier. The connection with the detective strengthened.

Detective Petersen maneuvered to one side of the entrance as the captain swung to the other. Without a word, she barged in, her light arcing along the blackened walls.

Nothing.

She was about to back out when the moan, clear and loud and definitely human, sounded. Slowly, she lowered the beam onto the floor, and the wide cone of light revealed a rumpled blanket.

"Cover me," she ordered.

Dyllon stayed in the background while she advanced, stopping whenever the lump moved. Her electroshock weapon leveled, the detective reached down and yanked the cover away.

The image of Jason filtered through, and Ellyssa immediately wished it hadn't. Guilt consumed her, tasting sour in her mouth. Whether or not he was dying, how could she have left him?

Ellyssa wanted to pull back, to leave the toxicity of the detective's pleasure at finding the rag of the male lying crumpled at her feet, and to erase the image of his skull-like face and the sickly hollows underlining his eyes.

Jason blinked and brought a bony hand up, trying to shield himself from the light.

"Who are you?" the detective demanded.

Jason opened and closed his mouth like a fish, as if the words he sought were just within his reach. Then, he started hacking. Pain registered on his face, while his body violently convulsed with each forceful expulsion of air.

Detective Petersen didn't think he was ever going to stop, and wondered whether she should put an end to the wretched person. Blood trickled from the corner of his mouth, and the wheezing sounded like liquid had filled his lungs.

Sickened, the detective pushed him with the toe of her boot. "Where are they?" she asked.

"They left me," Jason answered, his lips barely moving.

"Where did they go?"

He said no more, but looked at her, eyes glazed, his impurity boring into her. The detective didn't like it.

Detective Petersen pointed the electroshock weapon at him. "I'm going to ask you one more time. Where did they go?"

Jason lifted his shoulder before another coughing fit attacked. He curled over on his side.

"Have it your way." She pressed the trigger and electrodes shot out.

Horrified, Ellyssa watched all this play out in Detective Petersen's mind. Violent tremors rocked Jason's body, and he squeezed into a tighter ball while his muscles seized and convulsed. Deep satisfaction filled Angela while her anger traveled down the thin wires along with the electrical current.

Even in her old life, Ellyssa had never experienced such sick pleasure. Of course, it wasn't allowed. Just do your job and be done with it. Cold and impersonal. Detective Petersen was a different sort of creature.

The captain touched Detective Petersen's hand. "I think he's dead," he said, his voice distant.

She released the button. The body stopped convulsing.

"He's dead," he repeated.

Jason's stilled eyes were locked on the detective. Long strings of bloody saliva stretched from his mouth. His body still twitched, as if his nerve endings hadn't received the message yet.

"Of course," she said, backing away.

Dyllon knelt and pulled the blanket over the dead man's face. "Do you think he was telling the truth?"

"We'll send a team in with the right equipment."

Dyllon stood and walked toward her, the light circling him as if he was a saint. "What now?"

"Doctor Hirch wants to meet our prisoner. Maybe then he will talk." Detective Petersen closed her eyes, blanking out any further images. She spoke, but not with her mouth. *Come and get him, bitch.*

Rein, thought Ellyssa.

Ellyssa broke the connection and opened her eyes. "Jason is dead," she said, leaning close to Woody's ear.

He nodded, expecting as much.

"A search team is going to be dispatched. They will do a more thorough job of checking the caves."

"I understand."

"Everyone needs to be moved to the very back. Armed watches must be kept at all times. Make sure everyone stays quiet. No talking at all."

Woody looked skeptical. "You can tell them this yourself."

Ellyssa shook her head. "Rein is still alive, and they are taking him to The Center. I am going after him."

"That will be for the council to decide."

"I am going," she said, her tone determined.

Woody grasped her arm. "Wait. Let's talk to the council first, prepare them for what's coming."

"And?"

"I'm going with you."

"You will serve better here."

"You're wrong. There are contacts in Chicago. I can help."

"I cannot let you do that, Woody."

Woody stepped toward her. "Rein is like a brother to me. He's the last of my family. I'm going with you."

Ellyssa didn't want Woody's death on her conscience, and it was very possible he would die, most likely with her at his side. Then again, the Resistance might provide an easier way into the city.

"Fine," she reluctantly agreed.

36

Angela Petersen watched the sleeping prisoner. Rein was a mess. His clothes were torn and tattered and hung from him like rags. His dark hair was matted, and dried trails of crimson left winding paths from his hairline to his jaw and down his neck. Both eyes were bruised purple and black.

His chin rested on his chest, and his head rocked gently back and forth with the motion of the train. He looked uncomfortable, with his arms cuffed to a bar above his head and his ankles chained to one beneath the seat, yet he slept.

Angela admired the man, though. He had grit. Even after her brutality, Rein had peered at her through swollen lids, their piercing green filled with defiant animosity. If not for Dyllon, she would've knocked him hard enough to shut his eyes permanently. The captain's heart was too soft, and lacked the fortitude necessary to perform the tasks needed to extract information. Such relentlessness took a special type of person. A person like her.

And to think, Dyllon had almost tainted her thinking with his style of policing—forming bonds and such. What a sucker she'd been.

Angela supposed she should be somewhat thankful Dyllon had held her in check. Dr. Hirch certainly wouldn't have been pleased if she'd brought back a dead prisoner who had ties to Ellyssa. She just wanted to gather what information she could before returning to The Center.

When the beating had failed to elicit anything, Angela had tried psychology, tossing the remains of the dead Renegade she'd found in the cavern at Rein's feet, telling him how his so-called *friends* had left him to die. She had hoped such an act of cruelty would've had some effect on Rein, much like the tactics Vlad Tepes or Hitler had used, but it didn't produce the desired effect. His loyalty to the Renegades was commendable...and infuriating. He'd mumbled a goodbye to the dead man, which had earned him her baton against the side of his head.

Her dreams of destroying the camp of Renegades and capturing the doctor's prized possession had dissipated into a wisp of smoke.

Now, Angela sat across from the sleeping prisoner, defeated—not only by Ellyssa, but by ignorant Renegades, who were too loyal for their own good. With all that had gone wrong, she would never prove herself an equal to The Center's children. Anger twisted and coiled in her gut, wanting to strike.

Angela pulled her gun free of its hidden holster and slid the cold metal down Rein's cheek. He didn't wake. He didn't even move. He slept, oblivious to the death staring at him with one lethal eye.

Pulling the trigger would be such sweet bliss, but if she acted on her desires now, she'd be the one on the run. For the time being, she'd wait. One way or another, she'd have her victory.

She slipped the gun back into its concealed holster and looked out the window. They were close to Chicago. Farmlands on the outskirts of the city stretched for kilometers and kilometers. Yellowed stalks, left over from harvesting, stuck out from the rich soil. Soon, they would pass the dairy farms where Holstein cattle grazed lazily in the pastures, then buildings would dominate the landscape, architectural monuments of brick, steel, and glass.

She checked her watch. Twenty more minutes. A car would be ready at the station, and she and the prisoner would be picked up and taken straight to The Center.

She'd be home.

37

A white farmhouse materialized in the wavering distance on the other side of the plowed field. The two days of travel had been fast and nonstop, and Ellyssa was beyond exhausted. Hunger knotted her stomach and her muscles ached. Not the good type of ache born from physical activity, but the sort that came just before collapse.

If she felt this way, she could only imagine how Woody must be feeling. He should be faring far worse than she, but she'd never know it by looking at him. Through the whole journey, he'd kept pace with her. Even now, as she crept behind him in the ditch where tall grass tickled her skin and the scent of earth reached her nose, his steps were sure and strong, and his movements were lithe, like a cat.

Maybe she gave herself too much credit for being physically superior.

Woody stopped and pointed. "There it is," he said, his words drawn out from lack of sleep.

The corner of her mouth pulled back skeptically.

"I promise they can be trusted."

"I understand." Ellyssa said the words, but she had trouble believing them. Every fiber of her being was apprehensive of contacting people living in society, even though Woody had assured her they were old friends, and very dependable. It'd been hard enough to trust her adoptive family, but to give that trust to complete strangers who lived within society was on a whole different scale.

She looked up at the sky, where the sun loomed lazily in the eastern sky. "It's almost mid-morning."

"They'll get us to the train on time. This isn't their first rodeo."

Ellyssa wasn't sure what that was supposed to mean.

Keeping within the overgrowth, they scurried around the harvested field to the end of the wooden fence and down into a ditch. Down the way and across the street stood the farmhouse. Several small mounds of orange and red leaves dotted the front yard.

Hunkered down in the ditch where long blades of brown grass hid his head, Woody faced Ellyssa. Sweat and grime glued leaves and grass to his hair, and dirt smudged his cheek and chin.

"Sarah and Tim are old, but they've been part of our extended family for years. As a matter-of-fact, Tim's parents had helped some of the first Renegades."

"Are you sure they can get us to the train by one?"

Woody smiled. "No problem. After all, he manages the only delivery service in Warrensburg. He's our main source of supplies." He reached out and squeezed her hand before spinning around and walking duck-like toward the drainage sluice.

Ellyssa wished her confidence matched Woody's, but it didn't. Nothing had felt right since Rein's capture, as if her whole world hung by a frayed string. If it broke, so would she. Blowing out pent-up air, she mimicked Woody's waddling steps.

At the end of the ditch, Woody paused, looked left and right, and then, without one word of warning, shot out of the trench, like a rabbit, and sprinted across the street, behind some bushes, and to the side of the house. Ellyssa moved on his heels.

Woody stopped at a flat piece of metal that served as a cellar door. He opened it and gestured for Ellyssa to go first. She hesitated, as every instinct told her not to descend. Not to trust.

Once again, her old self squirmed to break free. For Rein, for her new life, she ignored that old voice's warning. She descended seven rickety steps onto a stone floor landing. Cool musty air greeted her. Woody came down behind her, shutting the door with a muffled thud.

"I promise, it's fine," he stated, apparently sensing her mood.

He brushed by her; a second later, an overhead light cast a soft white glow. Despite the odor, the cellar was neat and well-maintained, free of cobwebs and dust.

Woody grabbed her hand and herded her up another set of stairs. He opened the door into a spotless kitchen. Bright yellow, like sunshine, trimmed the walls and cabinets, and a tablecloth with pictures of sunflowers and yellow lace covered a dinette. Pictures of fruit and vegetables hung from hooks, and knickknacks covered every available shelf. French doors opened into another living space where muffled voices, probably from a television, whispered softly.

"Who's there?" called a female from the adjoining room, followed by a grunt as if she was struggling to stand.

The voice was old, but smooth and cheerful, and surprisingly without fear. Ellyssa couldn't image anyone being so calm on hearing someone in their house. She, herself, would've attacked immediately and asked questions later.

Ellyssa edged into the shadows of the stairwell with thoughts of leaving, but Woody pulled her into the kitchen. He tossed her a reassuring smile.

A frail, thin female, barely taller than a teen-ager, shuffled into the kitchen, wearing a floral-print dress. Ellyssa thought a good stiff wind would toss her into the air. Her hair was the color of rain clouds, and wrinkles folded her skin. Her eyes widened when she recognized Woody, revealing a blue that defied her age, and a huge smile spread across her face.

"Woody!" the older female exclaimed. She shuffled over to him, her arms held out expectantly.

"Sarah, it's so nice to see you," Woody said as he hugged her. When he pulled away, he extended his hand toward Ellyssa. "This is my friend, Ellyssa."

"Aren't you a pretty little thing?"

Ellyssa felt her cheeks warm. "Thank you."

"And shy, too." Sarah held her arms open. "Any friend of Woody's is a friend of ours," she said as she pulled Ellyssa into a hug.

Surprised at the reception, and unsure how to respond to Sarah's unquestioning acceptance, Ellyssa's arms hung limp at her sides. She glanced at Woody, who slyly smiled and shook his head.

"Now," Sarah said, stepping back, "what can I do for you two?"

"We need to get on the train," answered Woody.

"Which one?"

"This afternoon."

"Oh." She glanced at a clock hanging above a buffet. "That's cutting it close."

"But you can do it?"

"Have we failed any of you yet? I just need to get Tim." Sarah opened the refrigerator and pulled out a bowl of chicken and some potatoes. "I bet you're hungry."

At the sight of the food, Ellyssa's stomach quivered in anticipation, but they didn't have time for personal comfort. She placed her hand over her midsection to suppress the rumbling. "Not to be rude, but shouldn't we be making preparations?"

"There is always time to eat." Sarah placed the containers on the table and eyed Ellyssa. "You need to clean up a little, though." She pointed to Woody. "You, too. There are fresh clothes in the linen closet. Change."

He held his hands up in defeat. "Yes, ma'am."

"But…" Ellyssa started to protest.

Woody cut her off. "No use in arguing. We won't win."

"He's right. So both of you…scoot. I'll get Tim."

Ellyssa followed Woody through the living room, where she stopped in amazement. She always wondered what a real home looked like, but she never expected this. Soft colors added warmth to the homey living room. A small television sat on a shelf across from a tan couch. A grandfather clock ticked in the corner. The walls were painted eggshell, and family portraits hung from thin wires. It was completely different from either the sterile environment she'd grown up in, or the cavern where she now resided. No experiments or training; no hiding underground.

"What?" Woody asked.

"I have never been in a home."

He frowned. "Really?"

"This room invites you in." She ran her fingers across a mahogany table littered with glass figurines.

Woody smiled. "Come on."

Ellyssa followed him down a short hall and into the bathroom. A soft blue set the tone in the clean and orderly washroom. A light, floral perfume scented the air and fuzzy rugs lay across the tiled floor. Lotions and soaps lined the shelf above the sink.

Woody handed her a towel and a washcloth. "Clean up," he said, as he squirted soap onto his cloth.

Ellyssa scrubbed her face and arms, then dried them. As she ran a soft-bristled brush through her tangled hair, Woody left and returned a moment later with a clean pair of camo pants and a black T-shirt.

"I'll go across the hall," he said, handing her the clothes. He shut the door behind him.

As soon as she exchanged her filthy, stiff clothes with the fresh ones, Ellyssa felt better, more calm and relaxed. There was still much to be done, but the task didn't seem as hopeless. Woody was right. His contacts would prove to be useful.

A knock sounded on the door. "Are you ready?"

"Yes."

Woody opened the door, and the scent of food followed. Ellyssa's stomach voiced its outrage.

Laughing, Woody grabbed her hand and pulled her into the hallway. "Let's eat."

They entered the kitchen just as Sarah opened the back door.

"Have all you want," the old female said, indicating the bowls on the table. "I'm going to fetch Tim."

Ellyssa sat down at the table and glanced at Woody.

He plopped a spoonful of potatoes on his plate. "Make yourself at home," he said, grabbing a chicken thigh.

She helped herself to the creamy potatoes and selected a piece of chicken. She took a bite and flavor exploded in her mouth. The seasoned bird was juicy and delicious, and the potatoes were buttery. She devoured everything on her plate, leaving only a few crumbs.

The back door opened and Sarah entered, followed by her husband in service industry attire. Tim was a burly man with a rounded stomach, huge jowls, and a friendly face. Except for the beard he sported, he was hairless, including his eyebrows. His head was as shiny as a polished doorknob. He lit up when he saw Woody.

"Son, how've you been?" he asked, gripping Woody's hand and shaking vigorously. "And who is this pretty girl?"

Ellyssa, once again, found herself blushing. Woody wrapped his arm around her shoulders and pulled her close.

"This is Ellyssa. She's new to the community."

Tim eyed her for a moment, sizing her up. "I see." He paused before holding out his hand. "Nice to meet you, Ellyssa."

Although he gripped her hand firmly, Tim didn't shake it as vigorously as he had Woody's. Maybe because she was a female, or maybe the man didn't quite trust her.

"Nice to meet you, too, sir."

"No need for formalities. We're all friends. Just call me Tim." He glanced at Woody. "What brings you here? I hope things are alright in the community?"

Woody's face fell. "We just need to make the train."

"Why the rush?" Tim asked, pulling on his beard.

"Listen, I don't want to involve you any more than we have to."

"I understand. One o'clock is cutting it close. You're lucky Sarah came out when she did, I was just about to head out. I have a delivery to make. You can be part of it."

Based on her upbringing, and her father's betrayal, trust was something easier said than given, even after staying within the little community. Ellyssa couldn't chance the possible consequences, not with Rein's life at stake. With ease, she slipped into Sarah's mind, then Tim's. Guilt immediately followed. How she hated that emotion. Neither of them had ulterior motives. They were willing to help just as they'd done for years and years.

Without another word, Tim opened the back door and led them onto a wooden porch. A beautiful backyard stretched behind the house. Large apple and peach trees, still bearing harvestable fruit, reached toward the sky, and fall blossoms fragranced the air. A rock path led from the porch to the garage.

Tim led them into the garage where a cargo van waited. Shipping crates were stacked against one wall, while the other had a long table covered with labels and documents.

Rubbing his hands together, Tim looked around at the different containers. "Yes, that will do nicely." He placed his hands on his hips in satisfaction.

"Will they not get suspicious?" asked Ellyssa, her tone monotonous. She hated the sound of her voice, but she couldn't help it. Apprehension kept sneaking around in her and she needed to focus, not worry.

Pursing his lips, Tim gave her a hard stare. "You're not from around here, are you?"

Wary, Ellyssa hesitated a brief moment before answering, "No. Why?"

"The way you speak and your accent, both are dead giveaways. From The Center?"

She saw no reason to lie. "Yes. How did you know?"

"Sarah and I have been helping Renegades for more years than I can remember. You're not the first I've met from The Center."

Although, Ellyssa had suspected the possibility of others escaping, Jeremy's mother for instance, the thought of them crossing Tim and Sarah's path surprised her. "You have met others?"

"Of course. Guess you haven't heard about anyone running away though, have you?"

"No."

"And you never will," Tim stated with conviction as he crossed the room to a rectangle-shaped crate. He lifted the lid. "Your chariot."

Ellyssa peeked inside the crate. The inside was lined with packing material. A comfortable ride, maybe, but one she wasn't going to take. One thing she'd been taught was never to let herself be trapped. Always have an escape route. Shaking her head, she stepped back. "There must be another way."

"Not unless you plan to walk. Take a look inside here," he continued. "There is a latch that will let you out if the need arises."

Tim fingered the release mechanism. A simple set up, one pull of the lever, and the lock popped open. That made her feel a little better, but her flesh still crawled when she thought about being locked up for the few hours. What if they piled stuff on top of her box? She suppressed a shudder and pushed the thought out of her mind.

"It's very important for you to stay still. No moving. No talking. You understand?"

"Yes," she said. She sounded more confident than she felt.

He moved to another crate and lifted the lid. "This is how it works. I'll take you to the warehouse, get the rest of my load, then take you to the station. You'll get loaded on the train, and a member of the Resistance will retrieve you at the other end. If all goes well, the next set of eyes you see will be on a friendly face."

"And if things go wrong?"

"Then the whole operation will be a bust." He tapped the wooden crate. "Hop in."

Ellyssa glanced from the coffin-like box to Woody. He didn't look to please with their travel accommodations either.

"Don't worry, dear," Sarah said, patting her shoulder reassuringly. "We've kept our work under the radar for decades. We know what we're doing."

Woody sidled next to Ellyssa and gave her a one-arm hug. "Remember, this is for Rein," he whispered in her ear. "I promise, nothing will happen."

Keeping her eyes on Woody, Ellyssa stepped into the crate. His encouraging half-smile did nothing to make her feel better. Without any other recourse, she lay down. Tim closed the lid and she was instantly submerged in darkness.

Despite her calm demeanor, panic bloomed throughout her body. Her heart stuttered for a second before it picked up speed and pounded against her breastbone. Her breathing increased dramatically. An incredible desire to get the hell of that crate overwhelmed her.

It took every bit of self-control Ellyssa had not to flip the latch. *The latch.* Closing her eyes, she focused on the small contraption to freedom. Knowing it was there helped to ease her frantic mind. She inhaled deeply, and exhaled slowly, over and over, until the beat of her heart slowed.

Times like these, Ellyssa understood and appreciated the need for suppression. She had to maintain control.

She felt the box lift and skid across the van bed as Tim positioned the container. A short while later, the engine fired up and they were moving.

The rocking of the van was lulling. On more than one occasion during the drive into town, the soft lure of sleep tempted her, but she couldn't afford the luxury. She had to concentrate on the next leg of their journey.

To find Rein.

38

Rein wasn't exactly sure where he was, but he assumed it was The Center. Detective Petersen had mentioned the place when she'd thought him asleep. She'd had also scared the hell out of him when she'd been tracing the outlines of his face with the gun. Definitely bat-shit crazy.

The Center felt like what Rein had heard about hospitals. Disinfectant lingered in the air, and everything was white. Shiny white walls and floors, no pictures, no inviting furniture, nothing with color. Even the man who sat at the desk had whitish-silver hair, cut short and neat, and wore a white coat over a white shirt.

The man busied himself with files. He appeared much younger than his actual age, if Rein was to judge by his silvery hair. The tendons of his neck stood out when he moved his arms, suggesting powerful muscles, and the sculpted features of his face were as smooth and flawless as that of someone in his early thirties.

For the most part, the man in the lab coat ignored him, occasionally glancing up as if to ensure Rein hadn't moved. The only words he'd spoken to the detective had been in German, Rein assumed, after she had Rein seated and secured to the chair, one ankle tied to each leg and hands wrenched painfully behind his back.

Whatever the man said hadn't made the detective happy. She'd stormed out of the room like a petulant child. Rein imagined she was upset about having the privilege of knocking him around revoked.

Perhaps she was afraid the man in the lab coat would take his turn, impinging on her fun.

Rein snickered and the man looked up. His face showed no emotion at all, blank and unreadable. It was a look Rein recognized. The chortle died on his lips. The man resumed his previous job of ignoring the prisoner.

As an undetermined number of minutes ticked away, the muscles in Rein's neck and shoulders began to cramp from staying in the same position for so long. He moved his head from side-to-side. His tendons pulsed under a spasm. Hissing, he stretched his neck by placing his chin on his chest, but that proved to be a mistake. The muscle seized, and he groaned as he attempted to raise his head.

Damn, it hurt.

The man stood and approached him. He was larger than he'd appeared behind the desk, and his face still held the same absence of expression. His eyes said something, though. They were the same color as Ellyssa's, and hardness sizzled within their depths. Afraid the man in the lab coat had one of the secret talents Ellyssa had told them about, Rein sucked in a breath and held it.

"Nice to meet you, Rein. Please accept my apologies for the extreme treatment you had to endure. Detective Petersen can be quite…uncouth, at times. I hope your injuries are not too unbearable."

The man spoke politely, his speech clear and sharp, and with a slight accent like Ellyssa's. He reached in the pocket of his lab coat and extracted a bottle of pills.

"I am sure you can understand the need for precautions, though," he said, offering three round tablets and a glass of water.

Eyeing the medication, Rein shook his head. "No, thank you."

The man closed his fist and the pills disappeared. "Suit yourself."

"Who are you?" he muttered, through gritted teeth, pain stabbing his neck.

"You do not know? I assumed, with my daughter's mental breakdown, you would know." The man smiled, but it wasn't one that extended friendship. This smile was cold and calculating.

"Dr. Hirch?"

He nodded. "Now, of course, Rein, I am going to need some information from you."

"I have none to give you."

"I am ever so sorry to hear that." The doctor returned to his desk and pushed a red button. "It is regrettable that Ellyssa is not here. If she were, we really would not have to go through all this unpleasantness. She would read your mind and tell me what I needed to know."

"Maybe at one time."

Anger flickered across Dr. Hirch's face, shadowing the sharp contours of his cheekbones, but as soon as the emotion appeared it was gone. His features blanked as he regarded Rein.

"Yes. I understand from Micah that something has transpired between you two. Rather unfortunate. She is amongst my prized creations."

"She's a person."

"By all accounts, she does fit the criteria. But she is so much more. You, brought up in your closed-minded environment, would be too blind to appreciate her talents. With her, the possibilities are endless."

"What possibilities would that be? Murdering innocents?"

For a moment, Dr. Hirch looked as if Rein had slapped him. "Ahh, Ellyssa has informed you of things better left secret." The doctor tsked disapprovingly. "But murder is incorrect. 'Cleansing' would be a more appropriate word. There is a difference."

"You can call it what you want. But in my eyes, there is no difference."

"You have no vision of perfection."

"Perfection? People, in themselves, *are* perfect. Creativity, emotions, the innate quest to find the truth—these are things which evolved humans. All of them. Not just what you choose. Natural selection is what made our species unique and successful in nature."

"The innate quest for truth is what brings us visionaries, like Hitler," the doctor replied, his voice no longer matching his demeanor. "Crime is almost nonexistent, as are humans with physical or mental handicaps."

He strolled back to his desk and picked up the file he had been previously studying, then waved it at Rein. "The transference of imperfect genetic code is what caused the maladies of humanity. People were too stupid to realize their mistakes. They kept reproducing genetic failures. Hospitals were full, causing financial hardships; prisons and asylums were filled with undesirables, and mortality rates were skyrocketing. Heart disease, cancer, deformities of the body and mind. They all took their toll.

"You speak of natural selection as if you understand the concept. Natural selection is how we gained the intelligence to select the appropriate DNA sequences. Because of our visionaries, of our intelligence..." Dr. Hirch paused for a moment. "Because of *my* intelligence. We were able to accelerate the process to the point human beings would eventually attain. We are smarter and physically stronger, and our life spans are longer.

"Look at me," he continued, patting his chest. "I am an old man by yesterday's standards. Most men of seventy would be past the age when they could contribute to society. But I...I function as a thirty-year-old. I am one of the first successes. Everyone will soon be like me." A wild glimmer sparked in his eyes, and he paused to recompose himself. "Actually, better than me."

Rein sneered, "And what you've done to me, to other Renegades, is what you call progress. You are no better than a common murderer. Life chose diversity for a reason. All of this will fail."

"You are wrong. Society is flourishing, and will continue long after this 'diversity' of yours is a thing of the past," Dr. Hirch said as he strolled behind Rein. His voice took on a compassionate tone. "The pain must be intense. Your arms have been in an unnatural position for some time. Maybe, after you answer some questions, we can make you a bit more comfortable."

"Is lying part of your perfect society?"

The doctor chuckled. "You are a bit more insightful than others I have captured, Rein. If only..."

"I'm sure my level of comfort is tearing you apart."

"Nevertheless, you *will* give me the information I seek."

The door behind Rein opened and soft steps approached the doctor. From the corner of Rein's eye, a small girl, no more than thirteen, stepped into view. She walked like a robot, back straight, steps sure. Long platinum hair was pulled into a braid that hung between her shoulder blades, and her porcelain face held a void, flat emptiness that even surpassed Ellyssa's when Rein had first found her.

As she passed, she regarded him with lifeless azure eyes. A chill crept down his spine.

"*Der Vater*," she stated, without inflection.

"Aalexis, I am sorry for interupting your training, but I have use for you here."

The young girl didn't respond. She stood there as if bored.

"The reason I have summoned you is for an experiment. One that I think will test your unique capabilities." Dr. Hirch held his arm toward Rein. "I would like to introduce you to Rein. Rein, this is Aalexis." He placed his arm around her and gave her thin shoulder a squeeze. "He knows your sister."

She glanced at Rein. "Is that so?"

"Yes. It seems Ellyssa has been staying in his hidden camp. Do not worry, though; he has treated your sister well."

"I see."

"We have a problem, though."

"What is that, *der Vater*?"

"As you know, it is imperative Ellyssa be returned to us. Rein knows where she is, but he is refusing to cooperate. I was hoping you might persuade him."

"What would you have me do?"

"Why not use your recent discovery. He would make an ideal test subject."

Aalexis leveled her gaze on Rein, and right then he read what lay beneath her calm demeanor. The propensity to kill. With a calculated movement, like a predator stalking its prey, she took a step toward Rein.

Rein prepared himself. He shut his eyes, tucked his head to the side, and clenched his jaw, waiting for the beating. Nothing happened.

He peeked out from under his lids. Dr. Hirch and the young girl watched him. Humor gleamed within the doctor's eyes; Aalexis still looked the same as she just had.

Confused, Rein's eyebrow arched. "What?"

Dr. Hirch chuckled. "Aalexis is not going to touch you," he said, as if Rein should have already realized this. "Unlike the detective, we are not barbaric."

Aalexis' smooth forehead crinkled.

A sharp pain shot through Rein's stomach, as if he'd been stabbed with a hot poker, and his insides had been stirred. Fire seeped in and coursed upward into his chest. The intensity of the pain was like nothing he had ever experienced, like a boiler exploding within his skin.

Scream after scream ripped from his mouth and echoed in the room, reverberating in his ears, but nothing drowned out the acute burning that consumed his every nerve.

"Enough, Aalexis."

The pain instantly stopped, disappearing like nothing had ever happened. The aftereffects still remained, though. Gasping, Rein slumped forward in the chair, the ropes holding his limp body in place. Sweat poured from his forehead and dripped into his eyes.

"I hope this little demonstration has changed your mind about helping us."

Wearily, Rein lifted his head as high as he could. Through the pain-induced blur, he could barely make out the forms of the doctor and the girl. He tried to form words, but his mouth refused to work. He barely managed to shake his head before it fell forward.

"You leave me little choice. Aalexis, if you would."

Pain flowed again. At first it was a slow, a faint burn, like someone had touched his insides with a match, one after another. But as the intensity grew, it clouded his mind, until it dominated the core of his being. In retrospect, he wished he'd accepted the medication the doctor had offered earlier.

In the moment, Rein's screams filled the air.

39

Ellyssa heard muffled voices as the crate was lifted from the train and loaded into a vehicle. She stayed perfectly still, her breaths shallow.

Whoever had moved her crate, slid her into place onto another vehicle. The wood of her enclosure grated along metal. Silence followed, except for the hum of motors or the occasional mumblings from some passerby.

Ellyssa wondered to whom she and Woody were entrusting their lives. Was it a friend? A foe? Fingering the release, her brain screamed for her to lift the lid and peek, if for no other reason than to be prepared. The risk of exposure was too great. Pressing her lips together, Ellyssa forced her hand to let go of the lock. She had other means to seek information.

She blanked her mind, opened her gated barrier, and drifted into the closest person. A male, his thoughts teemed with anxiety, incoherent and hard to read. She slipped into another male, next to him. Jumbled images flickered through him, including a deep concern for their packages. He was looking at a female, who seemed calm. The female had blond hair and blue eyes, easily recognizable as a citizen.

Ellyssa concentrated on the female. She felt rushed to get their *special* cargo loaded. She directed the two males, both also citizens, to load the other crate. Ellyssa recognized the rectangle box as the one containing Woody. Relieved, she pulled away from the stranger's mind.

After a few minutes, the vehicle tipped down slightly as Woody's container slid into place next to hers. She floated into Woody's head, just to be sure. No anxiety or fear plagued her friend. He was calm and relaxed. Darkness pooled around him.

The anonymous persons opened the truck's doors and, once again, the truck dipped as three distinct people clambered inside the cab. The engine turned over, and the sensation of movement followed.

Ellyssa hadn't the slightest idea where they were headed. The Renegades' nameless cohorts' minds said nothing of a location. She tried using the sounds of her surroundings to gather her bearings, but all she heard were engines of other cars as they stopped and accelerated along the street.

She wanted to call out to Woody, but the soldier side of her obeyed the Tim's instructions to stay silent. She hoped the contacts would stop soon and release her. Every fiber of her being rallied to be freed.

The vehicle dipped and swayed to the left and right as the driver maneuvered around curves and corners. Then, there was a long straightaway that seemed to last forever. The truck gently rocked back and forth, and the soft hum of tread on the blacktop was hypnotic. Sleep pulled on Ellyssa's lids and she caved. The next thing she knew, the truck skidded to a stop and its doors open.

Wide-awake now, Ellyssa waited. People shouted and doors creaked. Her box was slid toward the back of the truck, and then lifted out. One of her carriers grunted as he adjusted to her weight, and then she bounced with each step they took. From what she could determine from the ruckus, Woody followed close behind.

"Tilt it to the right," said a female.

Ellyssa was shifted to the side, moved forward, and righted again. A moment later, she was jostled as the contacts placed her on a hard surface. A thump sounded close by assumedly from Woody's box.

No one spoke, but there was plenty of noise as people—she counted fifteen—shuffled around. She also heard clicking, like ammunition being loaded.

Anxious, she touched the latch, the metal cool under her fingertips. No one had moved to let either of them out. With freedom no more than a flick away, the temptation grew. What if her sudden move surprised them? What if a jumpy citizen had a twitchy finger? What if the *Gestapo* stood waiting? She decided to be patient.

Footsteps approached. Metal scraped along metal and the lid swung open. White light flooded in. She flinched at the sudden brilliance and closed her eyes. False light flashed behind her lids as her pupils adjusted. She blinked a couple of times before opening her eyes on a face that mirrored her shock.

"Ellyssa?" Leland asked.

A trap!

Why else would he be here?

Ellyssa's instincts kicked in automatically. Before she could think, she reacted. Her fist snapped out and connected with Leland's chin. His head whipped back, and he stumbled out of view. She pushed herself out onto her feet into a small audience of surprised faces, her back toward the table holding the crates.

"*Easily disposed of*," Ellyssa thought, as she evaluated the five carrying guns.

Next would be Leland. He posed the most danger, after the armed people.

The doctor's assistant leaned against the wall. His hand covered the lower part of his face, and he stared at her with wide, disbelieving eyes. She noted the blood on his shirt.

Surprisingly, no one had made a move toward her, and all the muzzles were pointed down, but Ellyssa had no intention of waiting for them to react. She kicked the gun out of the hands of the male directly in front of her. Before the weapon even hit the floor, she stepped forward, palm out, with the intent of striking his nose. The male flinched, face scrunched, waiting for impact.

"Ellyssa! No!"

Woody's voice stopped Ellyssa from following through, her hand a fraction of a centimeter from her target. She glanced sideways.

Woody was stumbling toward her with a piece of packing foam twisted around his legs. He waved his arms frantically. "It's okay. You're safe."

Confused, she looked at the armed guards. The muzzles remained pointed toward the floor. She looked at Leland. He hadn't moved at all, his hand still covering his mouth and chin, eyes still wide with shock.

Woody kicked off the foam and rushed to her side. He grabbed the hand threatening the stranger, pulling it to his chest. His warmth radiated within her, reminding her of Rein. Ellyssa paused.

"You're safe," he repeated.

As Woody slid his arm around her shoulder, Ellyssa glanced around at all the surprised faces. The male she'd almost struck bent over and picked up his weapon off the floor.

"What happened?"

She pointed at Leland. "Do you know who he is?"

Woody's eyebrow cocked. "You do?"

"Yes."

Leland lowered his hand. Blood splattered his face, and his bottom lip was split wide open. He took a tentative step forward. "I can't believe it," he said.

"You know each other?" asked Woody.

Leland nodded. "I used to work at The Center." Directing his attention to Ellyssa, he brought his fingers to his mouth, touching his injury. "I've never seen any of you move like that. You were a blur."

"What are you talking about? You ran experiments on all of us, like we were rats," she sneered.

"Yes, but during tests, none of you ever performed with such efficiency. It seems, when you feel truly threatened, your instincts go into hyperdrive." He shook his head. "You were amazing."

Woody looked between the two of them. "Will someone explain what the hell is going on?"

"You do not know?" she asked Woody. She turned toward the crowd. "Do any of you know?"

A pretty female, no older than thirty with curly, golden-blond hair, stepped forward. "You're one of The Center's children."

Stunned, Ellyssa faced the curly-haired female. "You know about us?"

"We're well informed of the atrocities happening within The Center."

"Did you know Leland is Dr. Hirch's assistant? He helped raise us, train us, and perform experiments on us. He is an active part of the atrocities."

"Was," Leland corrected. "I no longer work for the doctor."

Ellyssa faltered. "What?"

"He reassigned me." Keeping his distance from Ellyssa, he walked over to the table. "It was a hard blow to our cause."

Her eyebrows knitted. "What cause?"

Leland studied her for a moment, a slight tick working at the corner of his mouth, then he waved his hand in an arc. "All of this. What do you think we've been working toward all this time?" Before Ellyssa could respond, he continued, "Freedom. I've been gathering information."

The possibility of Leland performing such an operation was unbelievable. Her father's intelligence far surpassed the young assistant's. Ellyssa scrutinized him from behind narrow lids.

"You don't believe me? You can easily know," he challenged.

The others stood silently, perhaps shocked by his request. Ellyssa didn't have to read their minds to know they had been informed of the gifts bestowed on her and her siblings. They watched, seeming to expect her to perform some miracle, like she was some sideshow attraction. Anger percolated through her veins.

"You know I cannot," Ellyssa whispered, casting a sidelong glance at Woody. She hoped he wouldn't say anything about her own recent discovery of learning to block out the white noise.

"Why don't we go outside?" Woody suggested as he squeezed her upper arm.

"Good idea," said Leland. He turned for the door. "The rest of you, stay here, please."

Curly-haired, who had spoken earlier, stepped forward, her gaze raking across Ellyssa, like she was a dangerous animal. "Do you think that's wise?"

After her initial reaction upon seeing Leland, Ellyssa didn't blame the female. Her fear was valid.

"It's perfectly safe," the former assistant assured.

Leland held the door open for Ellyssa and Woody. Ellyssa's muscles tensed as she walked past the male who had been a huge part of her earlier life. As soon as they were outside and away from the house, she wheeled around. Fear registered on Leland's face, and he stepped back, but she had no intention of hurting him. Right now, she wanted answers.

"You have been part of this the whole time?"

He nodded. "Yes."

"How could you do that to us? To fellow human beings?"

He sighed. "I'm sorry, Ellyssa. Sorry for everything Dr. Hirch subjected you to, and I'm sorry I helped him. But what would you have had me do to stop it? What could I do?"

Ellyssa opened her mouth to say something. Anything. Words tumbled around her head, but truthfully, the situation had always been out of Leland's hands. He was blameless. Just like she had been when Rein had confronted her. If not him, someone else, and maybe they wouldn't have been as kind. She shrugged.

"Unbelievable," Leland stated, shaking his head.

"What?"

"The change in you. Your facial expressions." Leland's hand twitched, as if he wanted to touch Ellyssa's face to verify his observations. "How long have you been experiencing emotions?" he asked.

"It doesn't matter. Please continue with your story."

"I suppose it doesn't matter." he said, still looking at her with amazement. "Anyway, being part of the whole process gave us more information than we could have hoped for. I was able to share the technology involved as well as Dr. Hirch's plans. I had to stay."

"Why were you reassigned?"

"He started to murder citizens for the sake of experimentation. I began to protest." He straightened his back. "The others' abilities have grown."

"What do you mean?"

"Wouldn't you rather see for yourself?"

It felt strange for him to invite her into his mind; she, like her siblings, had been forbidden to use her abilities on her father or his assistant. After the files she'd found on the computer, she understood why.

Secrets not meant for any of the children's eyes.

She easily blocked out Woody as she focused on Leland and delved into his thoughts. Everything opened before her, like pages in a book. A story unfolded, from the time he had come to assist her father, when she was about five, to when the doctor had released him.

Finished, she blinked and looked at Leland. "Aalexis?"

"Her power has grown beyond all expectations."

"What do you mean?" asked Woody.

Ellyssa touched his arm to silence him. "I will explain later." She faced Leland. "What now?"

"Tell me what brings you here, first."

Ellyssa exhanged a look with Woody. "We are going to The Center. One of our friends is a captive."

Shock flitted across Leland's face. "You're risking your life?"

"Yes."

"You've grown, Ellyssa." He paused, thoughtful, and raked his fingers through his hair. "Dr. Hirch's coding has failed. If it happened to you, then what of your siblings? Aalexis is already showing signs."

Ellyssa thought about Leland's experience with Aalexis. She'd wondered how her younger sister was developing. "I don't know."

"And you just used a contraction," he said, with a slight shake of his head. "So much has changed. To answer your question…we were just discussing what to do when you showed up. Of course, I had no idea the visitors would include you." He paused for a moment, smiling. "I think you both had better come with me."

As soon as Ellyssa walked inside behind Leland, everyone quieted, all of them watching her. Some looked concerned, but most were uncertain.

Without a word, Leland walked through the throng, into a back room and kicked aside a rug to reveal a door in the floor. He pulled it open and moved down a set of lighted steps.

"You'll like this," Leland said.

Grasping Woody's hand, Ellyssa followed Leland into the basement. The room was small, with brick walls and a cement floor. The air was cool, but amazingly dry. A dehumidifier hummed in the corner.

"Weapons?" she asked, indicating the unmarked boxes.

"Some of it, yes," he answered, looking at hers and Woody's interlaced hands. "But that is not what I wanted to show you."

He approached a table set against the wall closest to the stairwell. A white tarp covered the contents.

"This is right up your alley," he said, pulling off the cover.

Sticks of dynamite coiled together in sets of five, held by black tape. Wires ran from a digital timer to a thin golden bridge wire, inserted into an electric blasting cap.

"We were discussing the possibility of destroying the entire Center," Leland said.

40

Rein woke on his back, with no memory of how he'd gotten to where he was. Absolute darkness spun before his eyes. Not even a sliver of light spilled from under a door or through a crack.

His mouth felt like a desert, tongue swollen, lips dried and cracked. The cool of the tiled floor felt great against the side of his face. Despite his fevered state, chills swept through him. With every shiver, his muscles shrieked.

The only parts of him that didn't hurt were his arms. The deadened limbs were still tied behind his back, and he was lying on them. He carefully rolled over to one side. Blood rushed into his numb arms, sending needles that stabbed from within.

Unimaginably unbearable.

Rein mewed pitifully, as tears welled in his eyes.

Ellyssa had told him what her sister could do, but she'd said nothing about the actual power the little girl wielded. He'd never felt anything as intense as the sense of being disemboweled and coals burning in his stomach.

Not once had she touched him.

Not once.

Aalexis had crawled inside his head, pulling and tugging, making him experience pain that wasn't really there.

Even worse, Rein had almost betrayed his family. The treachery had formed on his lips more than once during his torture.

He hadn't divulged their location, though.

He'd been too busy screaming.

Light stormed into the room, its shards stabbing Rein's eyes. He slammed his lids shut. When he finally peeked from beneath his lashes, two figures stood silhouetted against the brightness, distorted by the shine curving around the edges of his vision. One was tall and broad, the other small and thin. Foreign words were exchanged between them as they stepped toward him.

Rein screamed.

41

Ellyssa felt better than she had for the last few days. She was clean, she was fed, and she was going to get Rein.

Hopefully, he was still alive. Hope—just like the characters had in *Of Mice and Men*, and that story ended with death. Despair reared its ugly head. She shoved it back down.

Ellyssa glanced at Woody, who kept turning the bomb over in his hand while he studied the mechanics. As Woody's nervous fingers fumbled with the wiring, the strain of worry crumpled his face. Ellyssa wondered if his unease was because of Rein, or because he held enough explosives to blast the house off the map.

"Once we are inside, we report to Maintenance. They will assign us floors, and we go to work. That simple." Ellyssa patted his shoulder. "Everything will be fine."

Woody's eyes met Ellyssa's, his grey mixing with her sky-blue, like the heavens were brewing up a storm.

"Ellyssa, I want to tell you something." Woody hesitated, and he looked away.

"Go ahead," she urged.

Woody leaned over, face intense. "Before we do this, I want you to know how much I care for you." He gazed at her pointedly, brows arched, as if this sudden revelation was supposed to enlighten her. Nothing extraordinary happened.

Confused, Ellyssa scrutinized him. He kept staring at her, encouraging her to find the answer. Denying herself the easiest route to explanation, she said, "I care for you, too."

Sighing, the corner of his mouth drawn back in frustration. Those signs were easy for her to read.

"That's not what I'm talking about," Woody said, sharp and irritated. The same tone he had used when she'd first met him.

She placed her hands on her hips. "Then, tell me what you do mean"

Woody opened his mouth, but before he could say anything, Leland bounded down the steps. Looking back down at the explosives, Woody started to fumble with the wiring again.

Leland stopped at the foot of the stairs, his head turning from Woody to Ellyssa. "Did I interrupt something?"

Ellyssa gave Woody a hard look. "No. I was explaining how to set the timer."

"Oh." He sounded relieved. "It's rather easy. Just like a kitchen timer."

"Haven't really used one of those," Woody said. He set the bomb down with the others on the table. "But it seems relatively simple."

Leland smiled. "Of course," he said, setting the bag on the ground. "I have some stuff for you." He pulled out a yellow wig, the color of sunflowers, and a small white container. He held the container out to Ellyssa. "You should find this interesting."

"What is it?" she asked, taking it.

"Open it."

Ellyssa unscrewed the lid. A flimsy lens floated in liquid. Although she'd never seen a contact lens before, poor eyesight being a thing of the past, she knew what they were. "Where did you get these?"

"Actually, I don't even know. I requested the item, and a day later, I have it. The Resistance is a lot bigger than you think. Bigger than what I even know." Apparently pleased with himself, he smiled. "These don't improve your eyesight. They change your eye color. Once we are done, no one will recognize you."

"What about me?" asked Woody.

"I have a pair for you," Leland answered, pulling out another container. "Your hair will be fine, especially for a job like the maintenance crew."

Woody's face reddened. "What's that supposed to mean?"

"It means your hair color makes you acceptable for that type of work," Leland said matter-of-factly, blind to how the words affected Woody.

Ellyssa squeezed Woody's hand. "It's how society runs," she reminded him.

Leland reached back into his bag of tricks, like the mythical Santa Claus Ellyssa had read about, and withdrew two orange jumpsuits. He handed one to Ellyssa and one to Woody. "And you'll need these." From his pocket, he produced two badges, each with a barcode on one side and a magstripe on the other.

Ellyssa was taken aback. "How did you get these?" she asked, reading the name Amanda Keller.

"I made them," he answered, as if creating fake identifications was something he did every day. "I learned more than one thing in all my years of service." He wagged his eyebrows and handed Woody his.

"Impressive."

"Very," agreed Woody. He showed Ellyssa his badge. Carl Mueller was printed above the bar code.

"We're all set, then. Shift change," Leland checked his watch, "in seven hours. You'll be working nights. Easier to avoid personnel."

"What about pictures?"

"As soon as you don your new looks, I'll take care of them." Leland touched Ellyssa's upper arm lightly. It was the first time he'd ever tried such a gesture of friendship. "I promise, by the time you get to work, you'll be in the system."

The fall evening was much cooler than when she'd left The Center weeks ago. Crisp air blew from Lake Michigan, and Ellyssa pulled the collar of the long jacket tighter around her neck.

She blended in easily with the sea of blonds wearing orange jumpsuits under coats. Smiles plastered on their faces, they strolled to their respective jobs. Just another night of fulfilling their duty.

With Woody a few paces behind, she passed the white sign with bold, black letters—*Center of Genetic Research & Eugenics*—and through the gate.

The Center loomed ahead, reminding her of Frankenstein's castle. She'd never thought she'd see her old home again, much less go inside and, yet, here she was. Her heart thumped, like a rising crescendo.

Anxiety. She'd left The Center fully feeling that sensation, and now, she returned with it.

Before the emotion could fully grip her, causing beads of sweat on her forehead—a sure sign in the cool temperatures that something was amiss—she concentrated on blocking the unproductive emotion. She had to keep calm.

For Woody's sake.

For Rein's.

At the thought of Woody, she peered over her shoulder. He walked behind her, head held high, gait strong and sure. The nervousness and uncertainty he'd displayed earlier in the day were gone.

Before they'd left, she'd worried that he wouldn't be able to blend into society, but after the briefing with Leland, as he explained procedures to them, Woody was raring to go. His relaxed demeanor amazed her, especially since the backpack hanging from his back carried four bundles of explosives.

The dangerous job of arming the homemade bombs in engineering, two levels beneath the main floor of The Center, fell on Woody. Boilers, propane tanks, and gas heaters were jammed together on the lower level. It made sense to place the explosives there, but the problem was getting out in time.

Ellyssa didn't like the idea of Woody endangering his life, but what choice did she have? She had to find Rein, and she knew the layout of the building. She had a pretty good idea of where Rein would be held; it was the getting there that would prove difficult. One hour from the time she and Woody parted was all she would have.

Following the line of workers, she entered her old home through a set of double doors. Immediately, all the color of the outside world washed away in brilliant white. A disinfectant smell wafted through the air, giving rise to a hospital-like atmosphere. The ceiling rose high above her to where three red banners with black swastikas hung; their colors contrasted sharply against the blinding white surrounding her. Toward the back, the day-workers exited the building. Neat and orderly, one set in, the other set out.

To the left, two guards in drab grey uniforms manned the check-in station. One perched on a stool in front of a computer, the other scrutinized the workers with a smile. He greeted a few of the people as they passed.

Ellyssa approached the security guard at the computer. He was an older male, about fifty, with grey streaks at his temples. He smiled at her, just as he smiled at everyone else.

"How are you today?" she asked, swiping her card.

"Fine. Thank you."

He paused while he matched her face with the picture on the monitor. "You're new?"

"Yes. Today is my first day."

"You'll love working here. I've been here for twenty years."

"Really?"

Funny. Ellyssa had lived within these very walls for almost as long as he'd worked here, yet she'd never met him. Of course, she'd never met anyone other than the doctor and his assistants. Aside from a few field exercises, she'd never left the few approved floors, which were connected to the entrance by private elevators that could only be accessed with a special card.

Security was tight at The Center.

The guard nodded. "You'll need to report to the maintenance office first, one level below, to fill out your paperwork. Go to the first set of elevators, push L1, and the office will be to your left when you exit. Just walk down the hall," he said, dismissing her.

"Thank you."

Ellyssa went to the elevator as directed and pushed the down button. While she waited, she turned toward the throng of people, searching for Woody. He'd just passed the guard station with the bag nonchalantly slung over his shoulder. He fixed his eye on her and made his way to the elevator.

"You're new, too?" he asked.

She couldn't help but smile at his role-playing. "Yes."

"I hope you don't mind if I accompany you to the office, then?"

"Not at all."

The elevator doors slid open, and Ellyssa stepped inside. Woody trailed behind her. Alone in the little compartment, she pushed the button marked L1 before anyone else could join them. When the doors slid shut, his demeanor melted. Panic emanated off Woody so thick she could almost taste it.

Ellyssa understood how he felt, her own heart pattered against her ribcage. Not from nerves, though, but from worrying that she wouldn't find Rein in time.

She wished they didn't have to go through the formalities of reporting, but if they didn't, an alarm would sound. Any deviation from routine would end badly.

"Everything is fine," Ellyssa mumbled from the side of her mouth to calm him.

Closing his eyelids, Woody inhaled deeply, and transformed right before her eyes. Calm Woody placed his hands behind his back and rocked on his heels. His ability to hide his emotions almost matched hers. She shook her head in amazement.

The doors opened to an empty hallway with bare walls. Ellyssa stepped out and turned left. Woody followed. The hallway was long and narrow, with a big red door at the end and an *EXIT* sign posted above it. They passed door after door with tempered glass windows, all marked with their departments: *Accounting, Finance, Resources*.

A few doors from the exit was Maintenance.

She knocked.

"Come in," said a female, her tone pleasant.

Ellyssa opened the door to find a woman in her early thirties, standing behind a dented metal desk, her hand extended in greeting. The plaque on her desk said, "*Mary Hahn.*"

"Miss Keller and," she looked at a paper on her desk, "Mr. Mueller. I've been expecting you."

Ellyssa shook her hand and stepped aside so Woody could do the same.

"Please, have a seat." Mary indicated to the only two chairs. "There are only a couple of transfer papers to fill out, then I'll send you to your shift managers to report for duty."

Ellyssa smiled. "Thank you." She took the seat next to Woody.

Mary eyed Woody's backpack. "After you report to the crew leader, you can diposit your bag in the staff break room. He'll show you where it is."

Woody's hand tightened on the strap, but he offered a genuine smile. "Thank you."

"I'm afraid there won't be time for introductions or a tour today. Inspections are being conducted in the morning, and it rests upon us evening workers to make sure everything is spic and span and running tightly."

"That is fine. I prefer just to get started," Ellyssa said.

"An eager beaver. I like that."

Ellyssa and Woody wrote down the memorized information Leland had provided them without faltering. When they were done, Mary handed them their assignments. Ellyssa was to report to Mr. Baker on the second floor, Woody to Mr. Smith on L2, one level below them.

Leland was a genius.

"I do apologize that I'm unable to accompany you. But, as I stated, busy, busy, busy."

"Maybe tomorrow, then," said Woody, his tone suggestive.

The supervisor's smile widened. "Of course. It would be my pleasure."

Less than five minutes later, they walked back toward the elevators.

"Nice touch," whispered Ellyssa. "You ready?"

"As ready as I'll ever be."

Ellyssa pushed the up arrow and the doors slid open. She moved to enter the compartment, but Woody grabbed her wrist. When she faced him, he moved his hand to cup her cheek, his thumb smoothing away the worry. She closed her eyes, enjoying his touch. Soothing.

"Please, be careful," Woody said.

Lifting on her toes, Ellyssa placed a quick kiss on his cheek. "You be careful."

"One hour."

"One hour," she promised, stepping into the elevator.

The doors snicked shut.

42

Ellyssa picked up a cleaning cart and strolled down the walkway, between partitions that separated six offices. It was an easy one-person task, but her assigned supervisor, Mr. Baker, kept following her, with his arms crossed over his chest.

"I understand your directions," Ellyssa said, hoping her voice didn't carry the irritated tension she felt. She pushed the cart over to a desk. "My previous employment was also cleaning." She picked up a wastebasket and dumped the contents into the larger bin fastened to the end of her cart.

Mr. Baker smiled, flashing white teeth. "I have no doubt of your abilities," he stated, but made no move to leave. His eyes followed her as she moved from desk to desk. He grinned, and his tongue kept darting out, wetting his lips.

What was he doing?

Without further hesitation, she read his intentions as clearly as if he'd said them. He found her attractive and was trying to get up the nerve for small talk.

Great!

The supervisor's choices were limited. He'd have to pick up on her hint, or she'd have to dispose of him.

Ellyssa hoped he'd make the right decision. She straightened and faced him. "I have a boyfriend," she announced.

The smile disappeared. "Oh?"

It wasn't really a question, and she didn't bother answering.

Glancing at his watch, Mr. Baker said, "Well...I need to go upstairs. I'll be back down in a few, and I'll check on your progress then."

"As you wish."

Much to her relief, he left.

Ellyssa checked her watch. Ten minutes wasted. Time was ticking away. She left the cart next to the restroom and headed for the stairwell.

Stairs would only get her so far. The research labs and experiment rooms where she needed to go were below her and completely self-contained, like a separate entity from the main building, accessible by only one elevator, and that connected to Dr. Hirch's office and to her old living quarters on the top floors. No ordinary personnel were ever allowed, Top Secret security clearance only.

She descended, slowly at first; but as she took step after step, her pace increased. The tap, tap, tap of her rubber soles meeting linoleum echoed through the enclosed well. The sound wasn't loud, but it was loud enough to make her uneasy and create a desire to look over her shoulder.

She stepped onto the platform of the main floor and rounded the corner to the basement.

"Excuse me," said a deep voice.

Her heart leapt. *No time.*

Breathing in, she turned to face a tall, muscular man wearing a grey uniform. Static from the handheld radio secured to his utility belt squawked. Relief swept through her as she realized he was just a security guard, and not a trained *Kripo*.

"May I help you?" she asked, her voice higher than usual.

"I've never seen you before."

"I am new."

"May I see your identification?"

"Of course." She handed him her fake credentials.

"The stairwell is off-limits during evening hours," he stated, eyes flicking from her to the card, "Miss Keller."

"Sorry. I wasn't informed."

"May I ask what you're doing?"

"I was...going to the main floor. I left my bag there."

"Why didn't you take the elevator?"

Ellyssa felt the seconds slipping away. Anger bubbled. Sliding into her soldier state, she dissolved all of her emotions and met the guard's eyes with a steady gaze. Fear registered on his face, and he blinked.

"I decided to take the stairs," she said, deadpan.

He frowned at her sudden change. "Who is your crew leader?" he asked.

"Mr. Baker."

The guard hesitated, as if he was unsure of his next action. "I think you should come with me," he said, his hand moving toward the radio.

"I am sorry, but I do not think so."

Ellyssa took a step, whirled around, and side-kicked him in the stomach. The guard folded at the waist as a rush of air expelled from his lungs. While he was bent over, she brought her knee up; his whole body lifted with the force of impact, then he went down. Blood spurted from his nose. His eyes and mouth grew wide with disbelief.

Grabbing him by the lapels, Ellyssa pulled him up and threw him against the wall. A sickening thump sounded when his head bounced.

Ellyssa's new self yelled at her to stop, but she couldn't. The danger he posed was too great. One life to save many. To save Rein and Woody. She walked toward him, her movements cold, calculating. She took his head in her hands and twisted, efficiently. His neck snapped as easily as a twig, and made the same sound. She released him, and he crumpled to the floor. No longer breathing, he was only a lifeless, grey-clad lump.

She stepped over him, grabbed her card off the floor, and then flew down the remaining flights of stairs.

43

Ellyssa bolted out of the stairwell onto L2, directly into an empty room. She edged to the doorway. A short way down the hall were closed metal double doors marked, *Engineering-No Unauthorized Personnel*. Clicking gears and whooshing of hydraulics emitted from behind the closed door.

Woody's assigned area.

She glanced at the moving hands ticking away on her wrist. She retreated to the far corner. Her mind cleared and she searched for Woody. The whispering thoughts of strangers dulled to a mild hum.

Woody was easy to find, his signature familiar and loud. Ellyssa felt his anxiety, his fear. From what she could determine, he stood just on the other side of the door. His eyes darted around, focusing on the other workers. He fumbled with a wrench. His gaze moved down. At the foot of a beam, his bag lay jammed beneath a plate of metal. A strap poked out. He shoved it under the plate with the toe of his boot.

Ellyssa pulled back. He was safe...for now.

Twenty-five minutes from now, he'd arm the explosives. Afterward, they'd have fifteen minutes to clear the building.

Silently, Ellyssa moved to the middle of the hall, to a wall grate. Six screws held the plate in place. Withdrawing a small toolset from her pocket, she set to work, dislodging the grate.

She removed her shoes and socks, and stripped out of the jumpsuit, down to a soft cotton shirt and a pair of sweatpants. She put the uniform inside the duct and crawled in feet first.

Warm air brushed Ellyssa's face and caressed the skin of her arms. Metallic odors, and the scent of oil, hung heavy in the recycled air.

Hoping no one would notice the missing screws, she positioned the grid back in place. Her arms extended out in front of her, she pulled herself forward. The process was painstakingly slow. The duct left little room for movement, and jagged metal edges scratched her skin and snagged her clothes.

For the most part, darkness kept her company except for slivers of light from other grates. Occasionally, she'd see machinery or the occasional pair of legs through the crisscrossing bars. She crawled as quickly as she could.

Ten meters in, she reached the vertical framework where airflow traveled to the labs below. The whirling fwomp, fwomp, fwomp of the large fan blades sucked warm air from the higher levels.

Poking her head over the edge, Ellyssa peered down the chute. Dim, filtered light illuminated the next section three meters below. Dust particles danced in the greyish glow.

She wiggled her body over the gaping hole until her toes dangled down. Then she backed down, legs swinging through the vertical duct, followed by her chest. Pressing her knees against one side of the airway and her back against the other, Ellyssa wedged herself in. Then she started the painstaking process of wriggling down.

One little slip, and Ellyssa knew she'd shoot down the shaft, like a bullet through a gun barrel. Only she wouldn't be projected over a long distance, but would instead end up broken and bleeding at the bottom of the duct.

Two meters down, her muscles started to quiver under the exertion of holding her body weight over the aluminum precipice. Using her legs, she pressed herself tighter against the side and relaxed her arms, gently shaking them. She'd done many similar exercises that called for intense exertion, but none had proved as taxing as duct-climbing.

Her endurance in question, Ellyssa wondered how much further she had to go, how much time had passed, and vaguely, if anyone found the guard yet.

Ellyssa repositioned her hands and shifted down another half meter, her back and knees sliding along the framework. She paused, scooted, paused, and scooted until her feet and butt found open space. Carefully, she locked her arms, holding herself in place, and lowered one of her legs, her toes searching for the edge.

As she slowly stretched her leg, the muscles in her arms spasmed, and before she could correct her grasp, her back slid. Suddenly, air was rushing past her, and her knees banged against the edge. A tinging echoed through the ductwork. Suppressing a startled cry, her fingers latched onto the side and gained purchase before she plummeted downward.

Ellyssa dangled in the long chute, arms tense against the pull of gravity, breath locked in her chest. She listened for any activity. Nothing, so far. No shouts of surprise, no blaring alarms.

With a low grunt, Ellyssa hefted herself up and over into the cross-section. Using her shaky arms, she slithered forward, snakelike, through the L3 duct, until she reached light filtering through a grate in little jagged rectangles. She twisted onto her side.

Ellyssa closed her eyes and reached out with her mind. Like fingers searching for a hold, her gift stretched, looking for Rein. Emptiness extended beyond, behind, and to the sides. Further and further she searched, until his energy, his signature, pulsed, like a flash of light in a dark corner of a room.

Ellyssa exhaled. Her heart reacted with relief, and the link sizzled and weakened.

She redoubled her efforts and latched onto him. Except for a spark of life, there were no images, no thoughts, no feelings. His eyes were closed, and she swam in black ink with him. Something was wrong.

An unpleasant physical sensation suddenly hit her, like a wave battering against rocks. Pain. The feeling was strong and intense, unlike anything she'd felt before. It enveloped her, twisting within her veins.

Horrified, Ellyssa yanked herself away, and Rein's tormented scream traveled back with her, piercing the empty hall, reverberating in her ears, in her bones. Then it was gone. An eerie quiet settled.

He was somewhere on the north side, where vacant rooms were used for storage...and for torturing the one man who meant more to her than life itself. His scream still echoed in her head.

All fear of being caught vanished as she bludgeoned the grate, striking again and again with her fist until it gave way. The grille dropped to the floor with a clang that shattered the silence.

If they had not known of her presence before, they did now.

Ellyssa twisted her body and struggled out until her legs spilled onto the cold linoleum floor. She popped up, ready for someone to spring out at her. No one did, but every hair on her body tingled.

Two doors, both leading to classrooms, stood directly in front of her. To the right, the hall dead-ended at a closet marked *Utilities*. To the left was the main hall, connecting the south, where she stood now, to the north. Closest to her was the one and only elevator that led to her father's office and her old apartment floor, their only source of escape... if they were given the opportunity.

Ellyssa checked her watch. Eight minutes had passed. It seemed as if an eternity had crept by since she'd crawled through the opening of the grating in the floor above.

That gave her seventeen minutes until Woody's job was completed, then fifteen to leave the building.

Not enough time.

Panic popping, her heart pounded uncontrollably, thudding against her ribcage. Logical thought scampered away. Indecision plagued her.

She couldn't work like this.

Control.

She breathed in and slowly blew out the air. In and out. In and out. Rein. She had to find him.

She shut her eyes, quieting her whirling mind, her rapid pulse.

Calm.

With her back pressed against the wall, Ellyssa crept to the corner, bare feet padding noiselessly. She peered down the uninviting main hall. Long fluorescent lights hung from the ceiling, just like in the cavern, and reflected off the white tile floors and walls. Every few meters, doors opened into rooms.

She slunk around the corner and into the hall, her steps sure and silent. She opened her mind for Rein. For any signature at all. Rein flickered in the distance, softly pulsing, alone. That didn't make sense. If no one was on the floor, who had caused him to scream?

Ellyssa checked her watch again. Fifteen minutes until Woody armed the bombs. Two minutes gone, disappeared, never to be reclaimed, as if time had finally sped up to make up for its lag within the confines of the ventilation system.

Quickening her pace, she slipped through the shadows of the hall. The corridor seemed to lengthen before her as she hurried, every intersection posing new threats. Still listening, still watching, keeping her mind open, Ellyssa continued without hesitation.

Time moved forward; she lengthened her stride, her bare feet slapping against the tile. The sound echoed along the walls, but she no longer cared.

At the next-to-last intersection, Rein's signature flashed like a beacon. His presence filled her with longing for his smile, his touch, his kiss.

She stopped in the middle of the intersecting passageways, vulnerable to enemies. Surprisingly, the halls remained empty; only shadows moved in the corners.

Unease twisted her gut. This was too easy.

Three doors occupied the small hall, two to the right and one to the left, all leading to rooms she'd never frequented.

She stepped. His signal grew stronger. She stepped again, reaching for him with the wisps of her mind.

The last door on the right.

Pain flared, resonating within his being, his every fiber, and filled her as well. Fear terrorized his mind. Darkness swirled.

"Rein!" she yelled.

His name?

The sound rang in Rein's ears, but the pain overshadowed it. By the time the fire subsided, he wasn't sure if he'd ever heard his name at all.

"Rein!"

Ellyssa?

Panic twisted his stomach. She couldn't come in here.

His eyes snapped open to blackness, thick and mucky like an oil slick. He drew in a breath to warn her, to tell her to run, but when his lips parted, all he could manage was a desperate whimper. He swallowed and tried again. His voice refused to cooperate.

Ellyssa.

He hoped she could read him.

Don't come in here.

It was the best he could do.

Trap!

Rein's voice echoed in Ellyssa's mind. His thoughts were disoriented, his fear and pain immense.

She glanced over her shoulder. No pounding footsteps. No minds to read.

She turned the knob and pushed the door open. Light spilled across the floor in an arc.

The room stood empty, except for a few old wooden chairs and a rickety metal desk that was missing a leg. On the far wall, a chalk board hung under an old round clock, its hands frozen long ago.

Rein?

For a moment, Ellyssa thought she'd made a mistake. That the confusion in his thoughts had misled her. She hesitated, about to turn around and check the adjoining room, but a shadowy movement in the far corner caught her eye.

"Rein," she breathed. She took a tentative step inside.

Rein's head bobbed at the sound of her voice, like he was trying to raise it. Instead, it lolled to the side and came to rest on his shoulder.

The sight of him brought relief…and fear…and anger. What had they done to him?

Forgetting caution, Ellyssa ran to him and dropped to her knees. She placed her hands on the sides of his face. "Rein, it is okay. I am going to get you out of here."

His lips parted and one corner rose as if he was trying to smile. His face was bruised and dried blood caked the sides of his head and matted his hair. His jade eyes shone with relief, with happiness…with love. The shine flashed, then was gone. The green hid behind darkened clouds of pain.

Face twisting, Rein's teeth gritted together. "Trap." His voice barely rose above a whisper.

"We have to go."

She wrapped her arm around his waist and pulled him to his feet. As soon as his legs locked under him, bright light swept the room. Ellyssa's pupils contracted painfully.

"Ellyssa, my daughter," her father said in German, "I have waited long for your return."

Ellyssa should've felt surprise since she'd felt no other presence, but she didn't. She turned and blinked several times in rapid succession. Three silhouettes wavered in the corner behind the door. She squinted, trying to focus. Details emerged from the blond hair to the porcelain-like faces.

Her father had aged. His skin was not as smooth as before; worry lines etched his forehead, and his hair looked more grey. He smiled, as he had throughout her childhood. The smile that never reached his eyes.

Next to Dr. Hirch, standing with their hands behind their backs like good little soldiers, were Aalexis and Xaver. Both as she remembered, beautiful and expressionless and deadly, just like her.

Ellyssa helped Rein back to the ground. He looked up at her, his eyes apologetic. The black and purple marring his face shadowed his cheeks making his injuries look much worse under the light than she'd first thought. Fury enveloped her.

"I will get you out of here," she mouthed. Ellyssa brushed her lips quickly against his before she straightened. Squaring her shoulders, she faced her creator.

Dr. Hirch's eyes rounded at her display of affection.

"*Der Vater*," Ellyssa stated, her voice as deadpan as her face.

The blue of his eyes sparked with anger. "I am glad you have returned."

"Not by choice."

"Yes, I know. Your adventure has clouded your judgment. Something we will have to remedy."

"I am fine as I am now."

Dr. Hirch strolled closer, the hated smile plastered onto his face. "You disappoint me. You showed the most promise of them all. Your gift is exceptional. Of all my creations, none could read minds. To be able to seek people out before opening a door. To know how many were present. Truly a worthwhile addition."

"Apparently, I am flawed."

He shook his head. "Not flawed. Confused is all. Nothing that cannot be fixed. As you are aware, your brothers' and sister's gifts have evolved, as I am sure yours has. Xaver simply pulled his shield around us, blocking our thoughts from you."

Although shocked at the news, Ellyssa's expression showed nothing. "I see."

"It is time for you to return home."

"I think not."

Displeasure narrowed his lids into thin slits. For a moment, she thought he was going to lose control. Although they were infrequent, bursts of emotion sometimes plagued the doctor, like when he'd slapped her when she was a child. After a moment of indiscretion, he pulled himself together.

"After all I have done for you. I created you, made you a superior being," he said calmly.

"You made me into an unfeeling killing machine. A monster." Ellyssa looked at her sister and brother. "He never told any of us his true plans. The extermination of humanity. Not just impurities, but all humans." Her eyes moved to her brother. "Then the extermination of us—his so-called children. To be replaced with soldiers far superior even to us."

She faced her father. "There is no room for us in your perfect world." Despite Ellyssa's outward demeanor, her voice seethed with loathing.

"Enough," her father said, calmly. "You will come with us now."

"I do not think so."

"Xaver is not the only one who has honed his talent." He indicated Aalexis with a nod. "Aalexis."

Aalexis stepped forward. *"Der Vater."*

"Would you care to demonstrate?

"Of course."

Aalexis' smooth forehead bunched and, an instant later, Rein squealed. He fell to his side and writhed on the ground.

Ellyssa's feet remained anchored to the ground as she watched him, his face contorted in misery, and his arms wrapped around his midsection.

Scared for Rein, angry at her helplessness, Ellyssa bolted toward her little sister with every intention of ripping her apart. Aalexis was no match for her. But before she reached her, she slammed into Xaver's barrier. She placed her hands on the invisible surface and pushed.

Rein screamed again, a tormenting cry. She couldn't bear to watch him suffer. Ellyssa turned away. "How?" she asked her father.

"One's body and brain are nothing more than matter. Just a little manipulation of the thermal nociceptors," replied the doctor.

Rein whimpered, and her heart tore from her chest. All Ellyssa wanted was to run to his side and ease his pain. She couldn't. She had to keep her emotions in check; she had to stay focused.

Straightening her back, she faced her father. "Stop it," she said coolly.

The doctor nodded toward Aalexis, and her sister's forehead smoothed. Rein stopped writhing, but soft sobs shook his shoulders. He stayed curled in a tight ball, hugging himself.

Ellyssa stared at her creator. The hatred he had always allowed flowered into a seething revulsion toward him. The strength of the sensation became a separate entity, taking its own shape within her.

She had to get Rein out even if that meant she couldn't go with him. It almost seemed justifiable—the creature being destroyed with the creator in a fiery hell. "Let him go, and I will stay."

"How touching, but I am afraid that is impossible. You know as well as I do the dangers Renegades pose. Tainting the genetic pool. Devastating."

"If you let him go, I will inform you where the camps are," she said, her voice monotone. Her revealing the location of the Renegades was inconsequential, since none of them would be going anywhere.

Dr. Hirch's grin widened. "Are you lying? How interesting. I hope I can erase the damage they have done to you." Rubbing his hands together, he faced the door. "Besides, I do not need you. I had another source."

Micah appeared, dragging Leland behind him. Her older brother gave Ellyssa an impassive glance before dropping the Renegades' inside man at Dr. Hirch's feet. Leland's skull thudded against the linoleum, then rolled to the side, his dead eyes looking up at Ellyssa. Bits of bone showed through his smashed eye socket.

"Did you really think I would just let Leland leave, knowing all he knew?" he gloated. "Apparently he did." He shook his head, as if disappointed in his former assistant. "It is almost a shame. He was one of the best at his job. Unfortunately, he couldn't be trusted. Not by me, nor by the Renegades. His devotion was not as strong as that of the others. Maybe due to the fact, he had seen firsthand what Aalexis is capable of."

The doctor stared at the dead man for a moment before returning his attention to Ellyssa. "Your Renegade friends here in Chicago are all dead."

Ellyssa carefully hid her horror. Did Leland betray Woody, too?

"Soon in Missouri, too," Ellyssa's creator finished.

Ellyssa studied him, trying to read his actions, but to no avail. The doctor was a great liar. He'd been dishonest with them all for years and years. With her gift rendered useless because of Xaver, she had no way of telling what was the truth and what was a lie.

Her father moved away from Xaver and stepped closer to Rein, who remained a crumpled in a ball. The doctor gazed at him, confidence rolling off him. She raised her hand and pushed, but nothing blocked her. Xaver's shield was down.

Her father was opening them all up to her, apparently not seeing her as a threat with Aalexis, Micah, and Xaver at his side. Or maybe he assumed she'd not use her gift on him.

He had thought wrong.

While the doctor busied himself with his prideful thoughts, Ellyssa slipped into his mind. The action almost felt wrong, after the years of training she'd endured. She expected him to know, as if he could feel her crawl around inside his head. She plucked from him the information she sought.

The explosives remained a secret—Leland had been honorable in that aspect. But troops moved toward her newfound family in Missouri.

Ellyssa's heart fell, but she remained stoic. Rein still had a chance. She opened herself up to all of them, plucking thoughts from their robotic minds. Just down the hall, she noticed a surprise for her father approaching.

Dr. Hirch held his hand out toward Ellyssa. "Now, if you will come with me, we can put this unpleasantness behind us."

A smile played across Ellyssa's face. "I think the unpleasantness is just about to begin, *der Vater*."

A loud shot ricocheted through the room and Micah crumpled to the floor, his azure eyes glazed in death. Detective Angela Petersen edged around the door jamb, a P229 in her hands. That type of gun was assigned only to *Gestapo*, but the detective seemed to be very astute when it came to acquiring illegal firearms. She had a duffle bag full of them hidden away in her closet.

"Too bad you didn't create one with the gift of precognition, isn't Dr. Hirch?" Detective Petersen said as she stepped over Micah. She skirted along the wall, the barrel pointed at the doctor. She made a slight waving gesture at the doctor with her weapon. "Join your children."

Dr. Hirch stared at his head of security, his mouth slack. Stun shock shut any logical thought processes on the doctor's behalf. It took him a few seconds to regain his composure and his thoughts to settle into coherent images. He had to get back within the safety of Xaver's shield before he unleashed Aalexis on the detective. With Detective Petersen's firearm pointed at him, the sudden pain might cause her finger to twitch and his life to end.

Without giving his fallen son a second glance, he stepped closer to Xaver and Aalexis. "Xaver," he said. The doctor's thoughts were cut off from Ellyssa as Xaver's shield rose in place.

Safely inside Xaver's bubble, Dr. Hirch said, "You realize you will not make it out alive." He had his hand held out in a silent command as he spoke.

"You give me too little credit," she sneered, jabbing her gun into the air. "You and your precious 'superior' children. All of you think I'm so inferior. But it was I who found where your daughter ran to. It was I who uncovered an operation that'd been going on for decades."

The detective glanced down at Micah. "I bet you never imagined, Doctor, how fragile your children are. They succumb to bullets, just like everyone else," she said, cocking her head to the side. "You too, Ellyssa. Join your family."

Ellyssa shook her head and stepped between Detective Petersen and Rein.

"Fine. You can be first. Ever since that day in the park, I've imagined this moment. Watching the life seeping from your 'superior' flesh."

The detective took aim at Ellyssa as her father gave the signal. Xaver's shield lowered. It seemed Aalexis gift couldn't work within the protective safeguard. Thoughts rushed toward Ellyssa, but the one she was concerned was the command to squeeze the trigger given by the detective's brain. Ellyssa ducked. The air displacement lifted her hair as the bullet whizzed by. Her ears rang with the crack of the gunfire.

By the time Ellyssa righted herself, the detective was writhing on the floor as Rein had before. Detective Petersen screamed and screamed.

Within all the activity, red lights started to flash, and a bell rang loudly throughout the corridors. Fire alarms. Woody's signal to Ellyssa that also served to save uninvolved workers. The countdown had begun.

Everything happened at once. The screams stopped, but the detective remained on the floor. Dr. Hirch appeared confused and unsure, human emotions shining through his usually-calm façade. Her sister glared at the detective, her forehead smooth. Xaver stood to the side, watching the doctor as if awaiting orders. The red lights continued to flash, and the piercing alarm reverberated through Ellyssa's bones.

Reacting, Ellyssa grabbed the forgotten P229. She spun around and squeezed the trigger. The sound was lost within the racket, but a red teardrop spread down the white of her father's lab coat. He looked down, then gazed at Ellyssa in surprise before he toppled to the ground.

A shrieking *"NO"* soared over the alarm; the next thing Ellyssa knew, heat exploded in her stomach, consuming her. Her jaw locked and she fell to the floor, completely incapacitated. Bringing her knees to her chin, she rolled to her side.

The intense agony, the loud whooping alarm, and through it all, Ellyssa heard Rein.

I love you.

She focused on him. Her memories drifted to his smile, his touch, his warm embrace. All of her concentration centered on him, and his mind.

Through Rein's eyes, she saw herself wrapped up like a ball, her face pinched. His hand reached for her. Slowly, everything except Rein faded as Ellyssa's mental barricade slid into place. The pain subsided, and her muscles unclenched. The aftereffects of the assault, though, still warmed her insides, like embers that were just starting to cool.

Shielded from her sister's gift, Ellyssa rose to her feet just as the last fire alarms faded away.

Flashing red tinted Aalexis' porcelain face as she bunched her forehead tighter.

Unaffected, Ellyssa advanced on her. "It is no use," she said. "Your gift can not affect me anymore."

Aalexis' eyes narrowed as her mental focus shifted. Ellyssa saw what she had planned. Chairs scratched across the floor as an invisible force pushed them.

Ellyssa jumped out of the way before two of the chairs crashed into the wall behind the spot where she'd just stood. The desk lurched forward, and its legs screeched as they were dragged across the linoleum. Ellyssa sidestepped the assault and bolted toward her sister, knocking Aalexis into the wall. Air gushed from Aalexis' lungs and, for the first time ever, surprise crossed her sister's face before her pale lids closed.

Ellyssa spun around, intent on grabbing Rein and escaping. Before she knew what was happening, she was on the ground, pressure crushing her chest, large fingers stretched around her neck.

Xaver looked down at her, lips pulled into a snarl.

Ellyssa tried to break his hold with a swipe of her arm, but his fingers dug into her flesh, squeezing off her air. Clutching his hand, she tried to pry his fingers loose. He squeezed harder while smacking her head against the ground.

Thump, thump, thump rang through her skull as stars spun before her eyes.

The flashing red light, so bright against the white walls, hurt Rein's eyes. Warmth still flowed inside him, but the fire was extinguished. His face hurt, as did every inch of his body.

He glanced around.

There were still people in the room. The clashing and thumping of furniture. Struggling. Someone was wheezing, gasping. Foreign, guttural words were being said.

A blurry, shadowy figure undulated strangely next to the door. The body was distorted and bent in a way no human could bend. Limbs whipped around under the red flashing. He blinked, and the blur of the edges came together into two distinct people. The one on top he recognized as the boy who'd been with the witch and the madman. He held down a blond girl. She kicked frantically, trying to dislodge him.

Like pieces of a puzzle, everything clicked.

Ellyssa.

Never taking his eyes off the struggle, he rolled over to his hands and knees. His muscles quaked under the strain and threatened to hurl him back to the ground. He crawled to a chair, and used it for support while he staggered to his feet. Bile rose in his throat. He worked it back down.

Even if this was the very last thing he did, he would save her. He grasped the chair in one hand, and his foot slid forward.

Ellyssa's arms flailed wildly, trying to gain purchase on Xaver, scratching at his face, his eyes, but he eluded her attempts, his fingers forever digging deeper. Dots of light swam at the corners of her vision.

On the verge of passing out, blackness closed around her vision, her struggle weakening, her oxygen gone. Dimly, she heard a loud crack, and chunks of debris rained down on her. Xaver's fingers relaxed, and he collapsed on his side.

Sweet air rushed into Ellyssa's lungs. Wheezing, she readied herself for another attack.

Rein stood over her, two pieces of a chair back clutched in his hands. He wavered then stumbled, dropping the remains of the chair. Red light flickered across his face, darkening his bruises.

She scrambled to her feet and caught Rein within her arms, supporting him. He leaned against her.

"Can you make it?"

Rein nodded.

"One second," Ellyssa said as she pulled Rein over to where her father laid. Careful to avoid the blood that had spread across the doctor's chest, Ellyssa reached into his side pocket and pulled out the access card to the elevators.

"Let's go."

"Okay," Rein mumbled, his voice drawn and weak.

Ellyssa pulled Rein along, half-jogging, half-walking, out the door and toward where the elevator loomed at the south end, an unreachable goal. She glanced at her watch. The face was broken, the LED display black. She wondered how much time they had left.

She quickened her pace, dragging Rein beside her. She knew pain slowed his movements, and when they reached safety she'd kiss every inch of him. Right now, though, she had to keep him going. Gripping his hand tighter, Ellyssa jerked him along behind her and took off in a light sprint, hoping the elevator car waited on this floor.

The signature from a familiar mind touched hers.

Ellyssa slipped into the hall closest to the exit as the elevator doors slid open. Ahron sprinted out. As he passed her, she swung out her arm and clotheslined him. His head whipped back and he landed on his backside.

Shoving Rein into the main hall, she yelled, "Go!"

Without looking, Rein stumbled toward the elevator. Ahron recovered quickly and flipped over onto his hands and knees. Before he could rise to his feet, Ellyssa kicked him in the side. His ribs crunched, and he went down again.

She took off and slipped inside just as the elevator doors snicked shut. Her heart thumping against her chest, she slid the card through the reader then jabbed the fourth floor button, over and over, until the elevator began its ascent.

Breathing out relieved air, Ellyssa turned toward Rein. He pulled her into his arms.

44

As Rein held her, stroking her hair, time crawled along. Ellyssa could feel the seconds ticking away, galloping into minutes. As soon as the elevator bumped to a stop, Ellyssa pulled away from Rein.

"How are we getting out?" he asked.

"Answers later," she answered, yanking him through the parting doors into her father's office.

Ellyssa zigzagged around the doctor's desk and toward a large room that normally held her father's secretarial support staff. Desks and chairs sat neatly lined along together to the back of the room, where Lake Michigan could be viewed beyond the grounds behind The Center. She sprinted past the row of desks and down the length of the large glass panes, peering toward the ground until she found what she was looking for.

"Wait here," she said, dropping Rein's hand.

She picked up a desk chair and swung it like a battering ram. The window cracked. She swung again and again, screaming in frustration each time the window failed to break.

"Move," Rein said from behind.

He picked up another chair and launched it at the window. Shards of glass flew into the darkness as a cool breeze from the lake pricked Ellyssa's skin. Sirens from emergency vehicles pierced the night. Edging forward, Ellyssa looked down. No one stirred below. As expected, all the workers were at the front of the building lined in rows for easy accountability.

"This is it," she said.

"We're jumping?" he asked.

"Dynamite," she answered, grabbing his hand. Without a word of warning, she flung herself out into the air.

With all the boxes and bundles of paper that occupied the dumpster, Ellyssa had expected the landing to be softer. Instead, the impact had jarred her teeth and rattled her bones. She lay stunned for a moment, breathless. Then, she realized Rein's hand wasn't in hers. She panicked and fought to get upright. The cardboard worked against her, like quicksand pulling her down.

"Rein."

He groaned.

"Are you all right?"

His head poked out from the debris. A piece of paper stuck in his dark hair. "Compared to what?"

She released a sigh of relief as she struggled against the debris and went to him. "Can you move?"

"I think so."

Those were the only words she needed to hear. Ellyssa grabbed him by the shirt. "Come on," she said, her words labored. Staggering through the trash, they clambered over the boxes to the side of the trash bin.

Rein flipped over the edge onto the grounds behind The Center and she followed. As soon as her feet touched the ground, Ellyssa grasped Rein's hand and they were on the run.

A deafening explosion rocked the ground, followed by another. Warm air rushed past them and lifted Ellyssa off her feet. Rein's hand was ripped from her grip.

Landing in the dumpster had been like falling into cotton balls compared to the hard ground Ellyssa found herself tumbling across an instant later. Flashes of greens and browns whirled by at dizzying speed. After one last spin, Ellyssa stopped on her back.

The breath was knocked out of her, and for a few agonizing seconds her lungs refused to expand. Every inch of her skin burned. Gasping, she lay still until the last of the explosions died away. Dust billowed above her and little pieces of debris had started to land around her. Gingerly, she assessed the damage, moving toes and fingers, then legs and arms. Every muscle shrieked protests, but nothing seemed broken.

She turned her head, looking for Rein. He lay a meter beyond her. He was also on his back, and he was moving and groaning. She felt elated.

He turned his head toward her, his eyes searching for her too. He smiled when his gaze met hers.

She rolled to her stomach and crawled over to him.

"Can you get up?"

"If I lived through that, surely I can stand."

She brushed his cheek with the back of her hand. He winced, and she pulled back.

"Don't," he said, capturing her hand. "Never stop touching me." He kissed the tips of her fingers.

At the touch of his lips, a pleasant current traveled through her. Grinning—it even hurt to *grin*—she closed her eyes. "I promise."

Rein gave her fingers a gentle squeeze. "Good." He exhaled and made a face. "Do I look as bad as I feel?"

Ellyssa chewed on her bottom lip and nodded.

"My hair hurts. I never knew someone's hair could hurt."

She laughed. It felt good. Painful, but good. To think, in her previous life, something like that would've been locked away inside her, never to be fully experienced.

The corners of Rein's mouth curled upward. His lips looked delicious. Ellyssa leaned over and kissed him. His mouth opened to hers, and she tasted him as electricity found home in her veins. She wanted to stay with her lips locked on his, but she pulled away.

"We have to go," she said turning toward the building.

Woody had done an awesome job placing the explosives as directed. The Center had collapsed inward. There was nothing left but a pile of twisted metal and charred bricks. Her father's work had been destroyed.

"I know," he said, stroking her cheek.

Reluctant to find what lay ahead for them, Ellyssa pulled herself onto her feet. Without her aid, Rein stood up; the aftereffects of Aalexis' torture must've diminished under the flood of adrenaline.

"Let's go home," Rein said.

Ellyssa inwardly cringed at the mention of home. At the time, Rein must not have comprehended what her father had said about their home in Missouri. She didn't have the heart to tell him yet. He'd been through so much.

Without saying anything, she took his hand, and together, they limped farther away from the burning building toward the chain-link fence that surrounded the property. From there, they sidled along the fence until they reached the front. Rows and rows of workers stared straight ahead at the blaze. Flashing lights from the emergency vehicles doused them in red and blue.

Staying close to the fence, away from the lights and people, they made their way to the sign at the entrance. Ellyssa turned around and watched the reddish-orange glow. Hungry flames flicked through the debris, trying to consume all that was left.

"Do you think this is why Jeremy reached out to me?"

"Yes."

"It's not over," she said.

"I know. But together, we can make it though whatever awaits us."

With Rein's hand in hers, she turned and walked away from the burning remnants of her old life in search of Woody.

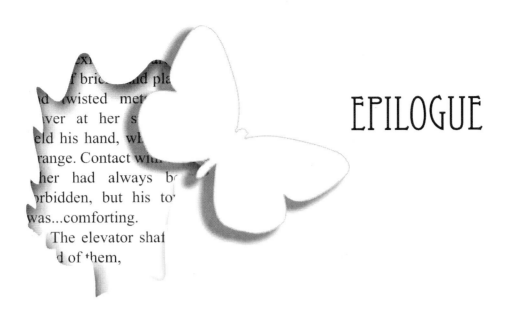

EPILOGUE

Aalexis walked around piles of bricks and plaster and twisted metal with Xaver at her side. She held his hand, which was strange. Contact with each other had always been forbidden, but his touch was... comforting.

The elevator shaft lay ahead of them, their only escape route. She hoped the cables would support their weight so they could climb to safety.

Extraordinary. The unfolding of events that had brought them into the hallway with loosely hanging lights and crumpled walls.

Before, when she had first opened her eyes after Ellyssa had knocked her out, she'd had no idea where she was. Bright red light reflected off a white ceiling, and an ache throbbed in the back of her skull. She'd turned her head and seen someone else stir. It'd taken her a moment to recognize her brother.

"Xaver," she'd called. "I need you."

He had responded right away and was at her side.

Then, the first explosion shattered from above. The sound had been deafening. The room had quaked and pieces of ceiling had rained down on them.

Xaver's eyes had widened, an unfamiliar expression to the both of them, then he'd covered Aalexis with his body. Even after their father's death, he had obeyed his orders to protect her at all costs.

After all, she was the superior one.

She was the most powerful.

Safe inside Xaver's shield, she had watched as everything her father had worked for crash down around them as explosion after explosion rocked the building. Then, Ahron had burst through the debris and into the room, flickering in and out of existence. Unfortunately, Ahron couldn't maintain the strength of his gift. The last explosion had ripped his body apart as shrapnel tore through him.

Aalexis and Xaver had remained protected inside his impenetrable shield.

When the last explosion had faded away, she'd tried to leave, but he'd held her in place.

"Wait," he'd warned.

Even after things had quieted down, bits of plaster and ceiling fell randomly and without warning. The building had to settle before they could safely venture out.

Her brother had saved her life again.

They finally reached the mangled shaft. The elevator lay crumpled below, in a pile of junk. Chunks of wood and metal dangled dangerously from above, but so did the cables. She could hear the crackle of fire.

Xaver grabbed one and yanked hard. The cable held fast.

She looked at the thick bundle, and then at her brother. "Will we survive?"

"I will protect you." He handed her the cable. "You ready?" he asked.

"Yes," she replied.

With vengeance on her mind, she crawled out from the tomb her sister had tried to bury them in.

ACKNOWLEDGEMENTS

There are so many people who I would like to thank for helping me as I plucked away on *Perfection*. If I could only express my appreciation to each of you for all you have done to see me through.

I'd like to start with my awesome beta readers: J.A. Souders, Willow Cross, LM Preston, Bethany Ray-Goodman, Roza Marie, Kristie Cook, and Charlie, and a special acknowledgement to Gina Panettieri. Thank you all for pointing out stupidity and helping me shape *Perfection* into what it is today.

A truckload of gratitude and virtual cupcakes to my agent, Lauren Hammond. If you didn't take a chance on me, then *Perfection* would probably still be a file on my memory stick, taunting me. I owe you so much.

Thank you to the wonderful, not to mention awe-inspiring, people at Spencer Hill Press. None of this would have happened without you. To Kate Kaynak, for seeing in *Perfection* what I could see. You are wonderful, and I can't even begin to thank you enough. And to Vikki Ciaffone, for not only holding my hand, but turning on a flood light so that I could avoid bumping into walls. You just rock. I owe everyone at SHP, including Rich Storrs and Alex Bennett, a standing ovation and a jet-full of thanks.

And a huge thanks to my extremely creative daughter who played the brainstorming game with me, my two super-intelligent sons for believing in me, and to my granddaughter who is just so awesome words can't even describe. None of you thought I was just wasting my time, which is just cool. You four are my pillars.

Journey through time & space

A cruise ship.
A beautiful island.
Two sexy guys.

What could possibly go wrong?

In the Bermuda Triangle—a lot.

~~~~~~~~~~~~~~~~~~~~

While training for a mountain bike race, high-school senior Mark Lewis spots a mysterious girl dressed in odd clothing, standing behind a waterfall in the woods near his North Carolina home. When Susanna claims to be an indentured servant from 1796, he wonders if she's crazy. Yet he feels compelled to find out more.

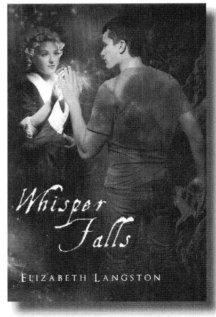

Also available as an ebook • **SPENCER HILL PRESS** • spencerhillpress.com

Middle Grade Books

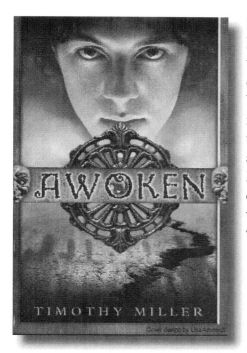

Fourteen-year-old Michael Stevens has never been ordinary; no orphan who hears music coming from rocks considers himself a typical teenager. When two-foot-tall, albino, doll-like men sneak into his room one night, transforming the harmless music into a frightening ability he cannot control. Michael finds himself in the middle of a war that could forever change the world he knows - reconstructing the very definition of humanity.

AUGUST 2013

Finn (not bleedin' Finnegan) MacCullen is eager to begin his apprenticeship. He soon discovers the ups and downs of hunting monsters in a suburban neighborhood. Armed with a bronze dagger, some ancient Celtic magic, and a hair-trigger temper, Finn is about to show his enemies the true meaning of "fighting Irish."

MARCH 2013

Also available as an ebook • **SPENCER HILL PRESS** • spencerhillpress.com

ABOUT THE AUTHOR

Photo by Trista Semmel

Judy lives in Texas, where she wanders out in the middle of the night to look at the big and bright stars. Besides knocking imaginary bad guys in the head with a keyboard, she enjoys being swept away between the pages of a book, running amuck inside in her own head, pretending she is into running, and hanging out with her kids, who are way too cool for her.